Sell Out

Fight for Truth, Book One

Tammy L. Gray

ISBN-13: 978-1517283575
ISBN-10: 1517283574

Print Edition

Cover Design by Sarah Hensen, Okay Creations
Cover Image by Dejan Ristovski, Stocksy.com

Dedication

For Abby

When friends become our chosen family

CODY

(January, Sophomore Year)

MY BREATH, HOT and rapid, drowned out the noises in the boys' locker room: the drip of the showers, the buzz of the air conditioner, the ticking of the clock that hung above my hiding place.

I wedged myself further between the lockers, pulled my heels as close as the bend in my knees would allow. The space was only a couple of feet wide, and my oversized stomach struggled to fit.

A creak ripped through the silence and my sanity. I squeezed my eyes shut, willing my slamming heart to quiet. *Just once, Lord. Make it stop.*

"Fatty James! We know you came in here."

I knew that voice. My nemesis. My tormentor. My reason for contemplating an end to this miserable life.

More whispers. More voices.

Sneakers screeched against the concrete floor. Closer and closer.

Fear coursed through my veins like icy crystals slicing each artery. The darkness held no protection. They were mere seconds from finding me.

A face appeared, staring at mine in the shadows. Tom Baker, senior class president, all star wrestler, prom king, and bully to fat losers… like me.

"Now, now, what do we have here? A whale stuck in a hole." His condescending "tsk-tsk" held a vicious promise. "Boys, we need to help Fatty James."

The world spun in a panicked haze.

Multiple hands grabbed and pulled while I thrashed and kicked. But I was no match for the six boys who pushed me on my back, their knees pinning down my arms and legs. My elbows slammed against the rough, dirty floor, and fire tore up my forearms. I continued to fight, calling on non-existent muscles to work miracles.

A thunderous boom exploded in my ear, knuckles hard against my cheek. Then came pain. A pain that stretched beyond the throb of my jaw and into the pit of my stomach.

They didn't need the blindfold they put over my eyes. Tom's face was already a blur, much like the others in the room I had yet to identify. My mind retreated to a cave inside my soul, that place where they couldn't hurt me.

Cold air wrenched me back. Back to their laughter, back to their jeers, back to the echoes of hate. My shirt was gone, tugged high above my head to expose the folds of body mass that defined my life.

"Wow, Fatty, you're a whole lot of man, aren't you? Let's see what else you're hiding under there."

Insistent hands grabbed at my sweat pants.

I twisted, bucked, jerked, and flopped around until a foot slammed into my rib cage. Stabbing pain ricocheted through my chest and spread through my now paralyzed legs.

The pants came off with one agonizing yank.

Blood rushed to my ears, drowning out the screaming in my head.

"Jiggle him around a little," one yelled. "We'll call him White Jell-O Whale to match those tighty-whities."

"Dude, check out his hooters!"

"No worries. I got his training bra right here."

I didn't see the line the Sharpie made, didn't see the flashes of the camera when they took the pictures, didn't see them dunking my pants into the toilet, didn't see the scars that promised never to heal.

Tom kneeled and placed his mouth to my ear. "When I say no one talks to that two-timing slut, I mean it. Next time, Fatty, I won't be so generous."

His words lingered long after their laughter had faded beyond the gym doors. They ignited a rage that burned worse than the sharp cut on my lip. My hands clenched, the fury growing and morphing into desperation that rivaled the depths of hell.

If I had to sell my soul to the devil in a letterman jacket, then so be it.

There wouldn't be a next time.

CODY

(September, Senior Year)

MUSCLES PULLED AND strained as I held him down, my weight pinning him to the floor of the wrestling ring. I shifted my leg, pushed hard against the rock solid back of my trainer.

I won't give in, not this time.

I'd been working out with my personal trainer, Matt Holloway, for over a year and had never taken control so fast. Sweat dripped off my forehead and onto his shirt with each push. The stench of hard work and stale rubber pounded my nose, but it fueled me to fight harder. Those two smells were ones I'd come to relish. They meant victory.

Matt slapped the ground. The noise as welcomed as iced tea on a hot North Carolina day. I'd actually pinned him. A first using the three-fourths ankle lace technique, and a compliment considering Matt's strength and skill.

I released my hold and stood, pain shooting through my quads and hamstrings. My arms were numb, the muscles spent from holding down a two hundred and twenty pound fighter. I rolled and flexed my forearms, trying to release the tension.

"You got it! Finally!" Matt jumped up, let out a whoop and clapped. Sweat blanketed him from head to toe, dripped down the layers of ripped muscles and black-inked tattoos. He was walking intimidation. The kind of guy you didn't want to tick off or meet in a dark alley.

He tossed me a towel and a water bottle, still shaking his head. "Cody James, defending state champion and captain of the mighty Trojan wrestling team." He paused, guzzling water between sentences. "Man, I'm proud of you!"

The guy rarely showed any emotion, so his excitement had me grinning through the fatigue. "Thanks."

"How are the other boys taking to you being the head honcho? Any issues?"

I distracted myself by watching a pair of guys jumping rope in the corner and the others slamming gloved fists into speed bags.

"No. It's all good." I had no intention of telling him I was captain in name only. Blake Mason had been groomed since his freshman year to be the leader, while I was just a walk-on last year. A walk-on who'd won state as a junior and shocked the entire school.

"Did you know there hasn't been a repeat champion in almost ten years? I've never seen anything like you, Cody. You're gonna make history when you win again." He slapped my back, and we headed to the treadmills for our cool downs.

I followed him, passing the small glass case that displayed three amateur trophies. There'd be more in there soon. Two of Matt's guys had gone pro, and I heard he turned down new clients every day. Why he chose me, I'd never know. I'd come to him a month after Tom attacked me, and I begged to learn to fight. Promised him I'd give everything I had. He agreed, then helped me lose the weight and pack on muscle.

In truth, he had done so much more than just transform my body.

He saved my life.

My spine shivered, and a familiar ache flashed inside my chest. The memory of "Fatty James" was always near the surface, ready to torment me.

Never again.

Matt set our treadmills to a fast, steady jog. He talked about the different moves he wanted to show me as we approached the season, animating widely with his hands. A grin cut through his usual kill-them-all expression. "This is your year, Cody. I can feel it."

I wished I could package his confidence. "Maybe."

"Maybe?" His eyes shot to mine. "Maybe isn't going to win you one match. What's going on?"

"Nothing." I suddenly needed to run faster. I hadn't expected the pressure that came with captain. I only wanted to make the team. Prove to everyone "Fatty James" was gone forever. "It's just a lot, ya know? The pressure to win, not just for me this time, but for the whole team."

"It is a lot. But that is what's expected from a leader."

"I know." I ducked my head and focused on the digital numbers ticking down on the treadmill. Fifteen minutes to go. My life had become a series of countdowns. Seven weeks until the Super 32 tournament, nine weeks until our first division match, five months until the state championship, and nine months until high school was over and freedom was finally mine.

"So, what's the plan of action? Coach have y'all in the gym yet?"

"We've gone through some drills. Most of the boys showed up ten pounds higher than their weight class. Blake and I seem to be the only ones who trained over the summer."

A muscle in his jaw twitched. "Kids can be so dumb."

"Coach Taylor screamed and ranted the same thing just yesterday." My heavy breathing didn't hide the humor in my voice.

"Don't you laugh that off, Captain. It's just as much your responsibility as it is the coaches' to get your team ready. You need to step up. Use the influence you have now to make a difference."

Matt's displeased growl brought a new round of guilt.

I didn't want to be a leader, didn't want to worry about whether or not the other guys took things seriously. I needed to win State, impress college scouts and stay out of trouble.

High school was prison. Do your time and get out. I wasn't there to offer inspiration. I could hardly find my own.

I PULLED INTO the senior parking lot still winded and sticky, despite having showered. After Matt's leadership lecture, he ran me until my breakfast came dangerously close to making a second appearance.

I brushed a towel over my face and neck, hoping it would dry my anger as well. Matt expected too much. I made the team; I won state. I wasn't Fatty James anymore. For me, that was enough.

Car doors slammed around me, and students flooded toward the building. Students I didn't know waved and yelled, "Hey, Cody." Not because they cared. I'd barely said two words to most of these guys. But because it was cool to be my friend now. Cool to talk to me in the halls. I'd penetrated the inner circle. Crossed the impossible barrier from outcast to superstar. And they all wanted my secret. It wasn't a complicated one—win matches and do whatever the king of Madison High tells you to do.

I was halfway down the hall when I heard my name again.

"Hey, Cody." The purr was from Jill Spencer as she leaned against my locker.

She was every teenage boy's fantasy—long legs, big chest, and brown, shiny hair she liked to flip around as if starring in a Pantene commercial. Every morning the skirts seemed shorter, the blouses lower. And I'd look, which is why she kept coming back day after day.

But no amount of cleavage was going to erase the memory of her calling out "Jell-O Whale" when she passed me in the halls my sophomore year. She was one of many seniors with selective amnesia when it came to the boy I used to be.

I stopped a foot from my locker and waited. We'd done this song and dance since school started. Her hinting for more, me politely declining.

She sidestepped, giving me access to my locker, but barely. She smelled like peaches and honey, and part of me wished I had selective amnesia, too.

"How was your workout?" Her hand slithered down my exposed bicep. "I've been known to give amazing massages if you need loosening up."

The image popped in my mind, making me feel like a traitor to my own convictions. I edged away from her. "No, thanks. I'm good."

"You know my dad has this charity event his company hosts every fall. The dinner is dull, but the after party is wild."

Her tone dripped with sugar and promises. It reminded me why I stayed far away from this fire-breathing dragon covered in perfume and soft skin. She batted her eyelashes and pushed her chest against me, the silk material of her blouse barely hiding the black lace underneath.

"I'll need someone to escort me..."

Her voice trailed off leaving an open door I had no intention of walking through. Black lace or not.

"I'm sure you'll have no problem finding a date." I slammed my locker shut and stepped back. Two years ago she wouldn't have shared a table with me, let alone her body. But Fatty James was dead, and I now held keys to the kingdom.

And that was what girls like Jill and what Madison High thrived on—power, status, and reputation.

The bell rang right as I slid into my chair for first period, earning me a scowl from Ms. Yarnell and a snicker from my other group members, Blake and Chugger.

"Cutting it a little close, aren't you?" Blake sat with his legs spread, arm perched on the empty chair back next to him. His relaxed posture matched the lazy smile on his face. He was famous for that smile. It was a look that did everything but melt off women's clothing. I could practically hear the swooning.

Every year, the departing "king" picked a new senior to run the school. It was a tradition dating back sixty years when the school was an all boys' academy.

This year's royalty—Blake Mason.

"Mr. James, can you remind me what time school starts?" Ms. Yarnell sipped her coffee and waited for my reply. She was an easy-going, hippie type but a stickler on certain rules. Don't be late to class, and Lord help you if she ever caught a cell phone in your hand.

"Eight thirty, ma'am."

"Good. Remember that tomorrow."

The rest of the class watched our group of three, but I was used to that. Being on the wrestling team meant instant popularity. Being friends with Blake meant superstar status. Chugger and I had both.

"Someone's on the naughty list." Chugger kicked back in his chair and folded his hands behind his head.

I pulled my history book from my backpack and set it on the table. "Matt tried to kill me this morning, and then Jill cornered me at my locker." I ran a hand through my hair. "Can't that girl take a hint?"

"I still don't get why you just don't go out with her. She's hot, man. I mean like, cheerleader hot," Chugger said.

"He would know. He's dated half of them." Blake's grin earned him a fist bump from his smug friend.

Every muscle on the back of my neck tensed. I'd heard more than I'd cared to about Chugger's girls. They'd come to him hoping for a status boost and walked away with a trashed reputation. "She's not my type."

"Do you even have a type? I've never seen you with anyone."

Blake snickered. "Oh, he has a type. Remember Vicky."

Chugger licked his lips and sighed. "Vicky Donner. Yum. Whatever happened to her?"

"She graduated." I wanted our trip down memory lane to stop. I'd gone too far with Vicky. Allowed things that went against every value system I had. Worse, I never called her after because I didn't know what to say.

No one seemed to care that she cried at school for weeks. Or that I behaved like a jerk. They only cared that I'd been invited to Blake's table at lunch and that I'd won two matches for the team. I even got a few high fives for the conquest. At the time, fitting in, being a part of the in crowd, and ending the bullying mattered more than my conscience. Now, I just wanted all the memories to disappear.

The room quieted when Ms. Yarnell began talking. Every day was the same. Twenty minutes of lecture. Thirty-five minutes of classwork. Ms. Yarnell said working together helped our social and communication skills. In reality, it was her way of forcing us all to participate. Luckily, we'd devised a system the first day of class that kept only one of us on the hook.

I slid the worksheet and book over to Chugger. "Your turn today."

Despite the fact that he slept with everything in a skirt, my teammate was a smart guy. Most of us were, though, since Madison High was an elite private school with rigid acceptance standards. Of course, the fifteen thousand dollar tuition meant those brains had to come with money.

Chugger flipped the pages and wrote furiously. "Tell him about tomorrow."

From a normal person, those words would be harmless, but from Chugger, they were loaded and bound to include some kind of trouble. I cringed. "What's going on tomorrow?"

Blake flipped the pages of his textbook, pretending to search for answers. "Senior skip day. We're heading to the lake. Jimmy's folks have a house out there and two ski boats."

Chugger looked up with a toothy grin. "Babes, bikinis and booze."

I winced internally at their words. It'd been the scene all summer, and I was long past fascinated with it. "Coach will have a fit."

"It's senior skip day; he'll get over it." Blake shrugged and popped a mint into his mouth.

Blake had been popular since freshman year. Mostly for his looks, but also because his brother had been a football god and the king of the school the year before we started at Madison. Blake was the only freshman to ever sit at the head table, and the student body had worshiped him ever since. Even though he wasn't technically the "king" our junior year, we all saw him that way.

Since getting the official title, he'd been pushing the limits with the faculty, too. Showing up late, leaving early. Anything to solidify his power. His charm typically earned him a smile and a pass from most of the administration, but Coach Taylor was a whole other animal—a rabid one.

"Senior skip day is supposed to happen at the end of the year." When grades and teacher recommendations no longer mattered.

Blake pulled the sheet from Chugger and pretended to write. "Last year's seniors had three of them. And, you know, I have to leave a legacy that exceeds Chuck Winston's. He was seriously the lamest king this school has ever had."

I grabbed the sheet next knowing it took Ms. Yarnell ten minutes before she was completely absorbed in whatever she did on her computer. "Principal Rayburn will suspend us." He'd already pulled the seniors together and warned this year would be different. But then again, he'd made the same threat the year I was relentlessly tormented. It didn't mean much. "And if he doesn't, Coach will make our lives a living nightmare."

"He won't suspend the entire senior class. The man's already on probation with the school's board of directors. A board my father's the president of, if you recall. Besides, we'll be back in time for practice. No harm. No foul." Blake's tone carried the same edge that surfaced when he got agitated.

Invisible shackles locked my wrists. The same shackles I felt every time Blake laid out some crazy scheme I didn't want to do. I popped my neck to each side. At some point, I had to start saying no. "I can't do it. Sorry."

Chugger's face dropped into a frown. "Then it won't work. Word's already out, Cody. If you don't come, the entire senior class will be busted. Besides, you owe us."

A chill inched up my neck. "I owe you?"

Chugger leaned closer. "We've put you in this position. Now it's time to take one for the team."

"What's that supposed to mean?" My hands curled into a ball. I'd earned everything I'd been given.

"He *means* we have to stay united, all participate or it's pointless." Blake scowled at Chugger, who begrudgingly returned to his task. "You're the captain. The team's not going to go without you."

"Yes, they will. I may be the captain in name, but you're the leader of this team, and we all know it." Because Blake "reminded" anyone who forgot, and the memory jog was rarely pleasant.

"Then do this for me. In a few weeks the weather will change, and wrestling will be all we eat, sleep and breathe for the next four months. With everything going on with Lindsay and my parents, I need an escape."

Recognition clicked, calming the flame that Chugger had stirred. I'd barely seen Lindsay and Blake together since school started. "Everything okay with you two?"

He hung his head, his shoulders rolling down into an uncommon slump. "We're taking a break. Things were getting too serious, and we just needed to step back for a little while."

Suddenly senior skip day didn't seem so shocking. Blake and Lindsay were an establishment at school. The class sweethearts since freshman year. Our very own Ken and Barbie. They obviously hadn't confirmed the split because news like that would have spread through the school like a virus.

Chugger's shocked expression said it all. "Lindsay's back on the market?"

Blake lunged and would have gotten the collar of Chugger's shirt if I hadn't intercepted the move. Although part of me wanted to see Chugger laid out, I held down Blake's arms and squeezed.

Our classmates whispered and watched because it was Blake. And they noticed everything he did. Thankfully, Ms. Yarnell tapped wordlessly on her computer.

His stare was murderous. "I said we're taking a break, you moron, not that she's available." As he attempted to struggle out of my rigid hold, Blake's ears turned bright red against his blond hair.

Blake stopped thrashing, but his nostrils still flared. He pointed his finger. "I better not see you look in her direction. You got it?"

Chugger threw his hands up. "Got it. Sorry man, I just assumed you broke up with her."

"Nobody broke up. Just drop it."

Blake settled in his chair, but his muscles were tight and his breathing shaky. He turned to me, his blue eyes hard and flinty. "You coming or not?"

Though his words offered a choice, his stare told me there was no option but his. The gauntlet was thrown, and we both knew I wouldn't pick it up. No one challenged Blake without consequences.

I forced the nagging voice in my head to still. Nine months until this nightmare would be over. I could do it. I could play the game for just a little while longer.

"Yeah, fine, I'll go."

SKYLAR

LIVER CANCER.

It'd been two years and ninety-five days since my father's doctor had uttered the words. Sixty days since it had returned, inoperable this time. Fifty days since my father canceled his sold-out European tour. And twenty-eight days since we packed up our villa in Germany and moved to Asheville, North Carolina.

And now, we had one day before our new normal began. Mine at Madison High, while my father's would be at Mission Hospital, undergoing an experimental chemo that would hopefully save his life.

Descending the stairs in our new home, I glanced at the dozens of framed albums that signified my father's music career. Gold. Platinum. Multi-Platinum. Pictures with presidents and foreign heads of state, A-list actors and directors, and my personal favorite, the one he took with eight-year-old Brent Williams for the Starlight Children's Foundation.

Meeting my father was Brent's wish. A day with Donnie Wyld—international rock legend and lead singer for the band that shared my name, Skylar Wyld. Brent sang on stage, signed autographs, rode in the limo and had the time of his life.

I touched the glass, my gaze lingering on the man who could captivate millions. We'd both need my father's determination if we were going to get through these next few months.

I found my dad in the kitchen. He sat at the bar, elbows propped with his head resting in his hands.

"You're awake." I kissed his cheek, his late afternoon shadow scratching my lips. The deep purple under his eyes reflected his exhaustion. The pain was getting worse.

"Yeah. Can't sleep all day."

But he was sleeping all day. Going to bed early, getting up late, taking three to four hour naps. I knew the tiredness was due to his medicine, and I prayed every night this new medical trial would work.

I grabbed three plates from the cupboard and started setting our kitchen table. "When is the wicked witch getting here?"

"Skylar." My dad rarely scolded me, but he'd made it clear I needed to watch my attitude with my aunt.

"Sorry. When is Josephine getting here?" My tone was anything but remorseful. The woman had invaded our lives. Not only was she here several times a day, taking up the little time my father was awake, but also she was pushy and pessimistic, and rearranged our kitchen after I'd spent two hours unpacking it.

I'd barely known Josephine as a child. We only saw her twice a year and, every time, she pushed me aside, interested in spending time with only my dad. Plus, I distinctly remembered my mom and dad fighting after one of her visits. Something they almost never did. Now, I understood my mother's irritation. The woman was impossible to like.

Daddy sighed, fatigue etched in the lines of his too-thin face. "Any minute now. We need to discuss our plan for tomorrow."

My entire body flinched. "Let me go with you. I'd be much

better company than your sister."

"No, Skylar. We've been through this. I won't let you be my caretaker. It's bad enough your life is getting turned upside down at seventeen. You don't need to take my illness on as well. That's why we moved here. So I could have Josie."

I wanted to yell how unfair he was being. That I was old enough to be of help to him. How moving us back to the States was a mistake. But I settled for saying, "This sucks."

I missed everything about Germany. My old house, the lack of paparazzi, Ricky and the rest of my dad's band. We were like family. I'd grown up with their kids. And now they were half a world away, replaced by a woman who grated every one of my nerves.

"I'm sorry, Skylar. I wish this wasn't happening either. But your life shouldn't stop just because I'm sick. I want you to reconsider Paris. You already took your SATs, and Ms. Stapler says you are well ahead of any other senior."

I eyed my father. His publicist had recently updated his style, chopping off his signature shoulder length hair for a more trendy style. He still wore the earrings and multiple leather bracelets, but I missed his old look. I didn't miss this old argument, though.

"I need to graduate. Officially."

"Ms. Stapler is a certified teacher and has been your tutor since you were ten. She'd write your diploma without a second thought. You could start applying to ESMOD fashion school now, and be in the seat by January."

I loved that he supported my passion to study in Paris, but my mind was made up. "I can't design clothes for teenage girls when I've hardly met any of them. High school sounds so, I don't know, different, romantic. *Normal.* I want the experience." And I wanted to be near my dad, even if he was pushing me away.

My father did a weird grunt-huff thing. "I've done high school. Nothing romantic about it. Just a bunch of kids with too much money and not enough to do. Been there, Skylar, and it's not something I want you anywhere near."

I resisted an eye roll. Daddy was a bad boy turned good. A rock star who spent his weekends with his only daughter and never drank anything stronger than black coffee. His constant traveling forced the homeschool thing, but sometimes I wondered if Daddy would have insisted on it anyway.

"Madison has the highest academic ratings in the county," I reminded him.

"It also has the highest median household income. I know these kind of kids."

We stared at each other, hoping we could change one another's mind. "I'm not leaving until you're better. If you won't let me stay home and help, then I'm going to Madison. It was our compromise. Remember?"

His long sigh told me I'd won. "You're so much like your mother. Stubborn." A shadow passed over his face, and his eyes stared off into an old memory. "Sometimes I look at you and think she's standing right there." Sadness coated his voice.

I slipped into his arms, squeezing him as tightly as his pain threshold would allow.

My mom died in a car accident when I was ten. She'd been the love of his life, the reason he gave up partying and became the father I knew. It took a year after her death before he smiled again. But we survived that tragedy, and we'd survive this one. We were fighters. And we had each other. Nothing else mattered.

CODY

EVERYONE DEALS WITH chaos differently. My way was music. So, pulling up to the radio station Monday night was the only thing that salvaged my foul mood. Every senior in our class was skipping tomorrow, along with half the juniors on our wrestling team. I wouldn't let myself think about the retribution that would come at practice.

The station halls were quiet, the offices empty—a reminder that my nine o'clock gig was not the prime spot whatsoever. I didn't care. The anonymity I had behind the microphone gave me a small taste of freedom every week.

I waved at Joe in the booth next to mine. He had the eight to nine hour and represented the metal heads. I was more classic rock, with only a few current artists. I preferred the obscure songs. The ones that never made it onto billboard charts. But, then again, I knew all about existing in someone else's shadow.

Twenty minutes flew by as I put together my digital playlist. That was the other thing I loved about working at a small station. The producers let us pick our songs.

A knock on our shared window told me I was up next. Joe took off his headphones and my "on air" light flashed.

I pulled the microphone forward and let my troubles melt away. "It's CJ your Monday night rock wizard, playing all those songs you won't hear anywhere else. Tonight's theme is one that rock legends have used to change the world. Resistance. From protesting wars to social injustice, these men and women have made their mark on American culture. First up is a band you all know I love, Skylar Wyld with their 1983 hit, "Going Nuclear." Don't forget, phone lines are always open. Tell me your best story of resistance, and I might just put you on the air."

I hit play and sat back while Donnie Wyld's electric guitar blazed out one of the best song openings I'd ever heard.

The phone line popped red and I smiled. My audience was growing every week, with more and more people calling in with their stories.

"This is CJ. Who am I speaking to?"

A male voice filled the line, and I could tell in the first sentence he was flying high. "Hey, Dude! That was a killer set you played last week. I downloaded every song."

"Nice. Glad you enjoyed it. Are you calling me with a story?"

"Nah. But since we're talking about resistance, I wanted to see if you'd play that song 'Fight for your Right' to p-a-r-t-y." He sang the title and burst out laughing.

I rolled my eyes as he continued to crack himself up. Stoners were stupid. I'd never get the appeal. "Sorry, man, that song spent way too much time in the top 20 to be on my radio show. But I'll do you one better. Here's 'Dying Inside' by Saint Vitus."

The guy was likely too jacked up to get the message behind the song. But maybe someone out in my air space would hear the pain in lead singer Scott Weinrich's words even if he or she couldn't always hear it in mine.

The phone light popped red again, and this time it was a

seventh grader who staged a running of the pigs down her school's hallway in protest of bacon in the lunchroom. I laughed so hard I had to run a commercial and gave the girl two tickets to Six Flags.

What could I say? I was a sucker for those who stood up for their beliefs.

Maybe one day I would too.

SKYLAR

I FINGERED THE small silver locket I never took off. I wore it for courage, maybe. But mostly because it reminded me of my mom—Brianna Da Lange. Inside, her picture was next to mine. Two redheads with big green eyes. Only hers were fearless. A supermodel at fifteen, she blazed down every runway from America to Paris, and here I trembled as I stared at Madison High.

My heart fluttered with a mixture of anxiety and adrenaline. A real school. Filled with teenagers and drama and the unknown. But it was also the first genuinely normal thing I'd ever done. And for some reason, normal brought peace. The idea that life could exist away from the flash and glamour of the band. Where maybe I could have two living parents, and a dog named Spot. Where no one was sick and pushing me away.

I flipped the locket, turning it over to read the inscription for the hundredth time.

Soar like wings of eagles

I could still hear her voice in my head. *Make every day count. Make every moment matter.*

If my mom had the courage to move to America alone with a three-year-old until my dad wised up and quit drinking, then I could face a building full of strangers.

Forcing my feet to move, I left my car and pushed through the metal doors. They creaked and closed behind me with a loud click. A click that echoed through eerily empty halls. There were no crowds mingling or running to class. No gaggle of girls huddled in a circle telling the latest gossip. Just rows and rows of untouched maroon lockers, and a linoleum floor so shiny the fluorescent lights seemed to bounce off its surface and into my eyes.

With shaky hands, I pulled my wrinkled schedule out of my bag and walked over to the locker I'd been assigned. My dad and I had come two weeks ago on a Saturday to meet with Principal Rayburn. We'd asked for complete anonymity with the faculty and students, and he assured us no one would know. It was a promise I desperately hoped he could keep.

It took two attempts with my combination, but the door finally budged. My school supplies consisted of one massive five-subject notebook, a handful of pens, and three folders. I almost bought one designed with a picture of my dad's guitar and Skylar Wyld etched in script across the bottom but decided I was tempting fate.

Metal slammed against metal, and my gaze shifted toward the sound. He was far away, almost to the end of the hall, but I could tell he was struggling. He juggled three books while attempting to shove his giant backpack into the locker.

Nerves prickled my skin, but I walked toward him anyway. This was it. My first interaction. "I can hold those for you."

His chin jerked upward, and the books went sprawling. Wiry glasses nearly followed, but he quickly pushed them back in place.

I'd always wondered if stereotypes existed in schools the way they were portrayed in books and movies, and now I was staring right at one. His button up, short-sleeved shirt had two pens sticking out of the top pocket and was tucked into jeans that didn't quite reach his ankles, which was odd, because he was shorter than I was and almost as skinny.

My internal makeover fairy begged to intervene.

Reaching down, I picked up the scattered books one by one, and held them out to him with a nice-to-meet-you smile. He stared like I was carrying razor blades and not textbooks. I pointed to the backpack jammed halfway in his locker. "You can finish that now."

"Huh?" The guy turned back to his locker. "Oh, yeah." He shoved and pushed until the backpack disappeared.

"I'm Skylar, by the way. This is my first day here." I looked down the hall, hoping he was the first of many to suddenly appear, but no one else walked up. "Where is everyone?"

"Like you don't know," he said without turning.

"What?"

"Nothing." Mr. Friendly reached for the books in my hands.

When I pulled them away, he scowled. "Just get on with it. I'd like to actually make it to class on time today." Under his breath I heard him murmur something about senior skip day.

"Did you say senior skip day?" I handed him the textbooks, and he put two in his locker before slamming it shut.

"Who did you say you were again?"

"Skylar." I pulled out my new schedule and handed it to him. "See, first day."

He skimmed the information and passed it back to me. "You have Yarnell for first period. She's a stickler on tardiness, but I doubt it will matter today. Come on, I'll show you."

I sensed he still didn't believe I was new, but I followed

him anyway. "What's your name?"

"Henry Watkins III." He came to a dead stop. "Did Blake put you up to this?"

"Blake?"

"Senior class president? Teenage heartthrob? King of the school?" He asked each question as if I'd crawled out from under a rock.

"I don't know who Blake is."

Henry's yeah-right snort had me pushing down a spark of irritation.

I grabbed his thin arm, careful not to squeeze too hard. "I really am new here. I moved to North Carolina a month ago." His eyes locked on my hand. I released the grip and held my hand up. "Girl Scout's honor." I'd never been in Girl Scouts, but it sounded good.

He tilted his head, his lips making a tight line across his face. "Where are you transferring from?"

"Nowhere. I've been homeschooled my whole life." He didn't seem surprised by my admission. Instead he seemed to get more agitated.

"So, tell me, Skylar from nowhere, why are you talking to me?" His sarcastic tone could have frozen fire.

"Why wouldn't I talk to you?"

He clutched the massive calculus book to his chest like he needed protection from me. "I've been banished." He looked in both directions. "If anyone sees you talking to me, you're finished at this school. Even if you do look like, well…" Henry's hand gestured the length of my body, "that."

If he'd meant "that" as a compliment, his social skills needed serious improvement. My feet itched to walk away and forget this small, strange guy, but my stubborn will trumped.

Plus, my gut said he needed a friend. "I don't see how talking to you will do anything but help me get to class. Please? If nobody is here, what does it matter?"

"People are here, just not on this hall. Principal Rayburn likes to keep the grades separated." He stopped like there was more to that explanation but didn't want to say so.

"Is that a bad thing?"

"It's a safe thing." Henry lifted his chin toward an empty classroom. "This is you."

Me. A classroom. Empty or not, it was still the first one I'd ever sat in. I touched my locket. "I'm nervous."

Henry's guarded scowl loosened. "Don't be. Ms. Yarnell is the coolest teacher here." I didn't miss that his voice had softened, too. "If you want, I can meet you after and show you where to go next."

My gut was right. "Yes. Thank you."

"Yeah, sure." He scurried off, leaving me to enter alone.

I stepped in and surveyed the room. Spicy incense hung in the air tickling my nose. The walls were a stark white, but greenery lined every shelf and windowsill. Six empty round tables filled the small room. I picked one near the back and sat, fidgeting, while my new teacher ruffled papers on her desk.

"Give me one second," she said without turning. Even from the back, I could tell she had a weird affection for vintage wear. Her long skirt stopped above leather sandals and swayed while she searched.

She found the paper she was looking for, grabbed a textbook, and slid into the chair next to me. "You must be Skylar."

"Yes, ma'am."

"It's very nice to meet you. I'm Ms. Yarnell."

She stuck out her hand, and the tension began to drift from

my shoulders. *You can do this.*

"I apologize for the lack of students. Seems our senior class decided to skip today." She looked my dad's age, but dressed like she'd grown up in the sixties. Her long brown hair was parted in the middle and hung straight as a board. She spent a few minutes explaining her policies and assignments and then sat back as if she'd finished a ten-course meal. "Now that the business is taken care of, tell me a little about yourself. I imagine you've had quite a unique life up to this point."

My face must have paled because she quickly laid her hand over mine.

"Don't worry, your secret is safe with me. I've listened to your dad's music for over twenty years now." She sighed and looked off as if watching a movie I couldn't see. "Skylar Wyld in Times Square was my first concert and ruined me for any other rock band. I had just graduated from high school. My girlfriends and I loaded up a SUV and drove 500 miles to see them play. Best weekend of my life."

She must have realized she was still holding my hand and quickly removed hers. "Anyway, I've been a fan ever since. Been to seven of his concerts."

Her words pulled the plug on my bucket of hope. There were only a handful of pictures of me online, most from after my mom died and the paparazzi hounded us. But die-hard fans knew her face, which meant they knew mine.

CODY

MY PARENTS WERE seated at the table sipping their morning coffee when I walked in the kitchen. Classical music played lightly in the background, and the serenity almost made me forget I was about to lie to them.

"Hey, Bud. You're up early." My dad was usually gone when I came downstairs, my mom close behind, but she liked to at least see me before she left. Our five-minute catch up session in front of the refrigerator had become a tradition.

I focused on that fridge, not wanting to meet his eyes. "Yeah. Blake needs a ride, so I'm gonna head out."

My parents exchanged a smile. They loved Blake. Gave him credit for the change I'd made over the past year and a half. If they only knew the truth. But truth wasn't what parents wanted. They wanted to believe their kids were happy and adjusted. Or a least that's what my parents wanted. They wanted reassurance that my days of listening to music for hours and hours, without friends or a social life were in the past.

My dad stood, dumped his cup in the sink, and walked over to the couch. "It'll be a late night for me. We're still waiting for those contracts to drop." My dad did something with the government. Something boring. Something that kept him from attending most of my wrestling matches.

"That's probably good. I've got a stack of invoices to sort through, anyway." My mom sounded partly disappointed and partly relieved. "What do you say, Cody? Chinese take-out for dinner?" She stood and turned off the coffee pot. "You can tackle calculus, and I'll tackle my four page spreadsheet."

My mom was a CPA. Another boring job, but one she secretly loved. They were simple, my parents. Drama-free routine was their idea of a perfect day.

"You okay?" She asked when I said nothing.

I thought about it—telling both of them that I was struggling. That I'd worked the last year and half to be a part of something I was starting to hate. I opened my mouth to answer, but stopped. They were the types to dig until they had the entire story. I'd never told them about that horrible day in the boys' locker room and never wanted to.

"I'm fine. Chinese sounds perfect." I grabbed my keys and gave her a quick hug. "See you tonight."

"Bye, Bud," my dad called from the living room. "Work hard."

I resisted a snort. I'd be working all right. Working to keep Chugger and the rest of the team from drowning in Lake Lure.

I LEANED AGAINST the wooden post on Jimmy's pier and assessed the group lounging on the sand beach that ran the length of his property. Blake had said the group would be selective, but I didn't realize he meant the junior and senior wrestlers and every hot girl they knew, including a few from other schools. Senior skip day had turned into a meat market, and Blake was sampling every piece of the goods.

Lindsay's glaring absence made it clear Blake had chosen today to announce his bachelor status.

Bass from Chugger's stereo was loud enough to rattle windows, and I wished for the fiftieth time that my friends had better taste in music. I knew they'd never appreciate the classics like Pink Floyd, Def Leppard or Skylar Wyld. But at this point, I'd even take Fall Out Boy or Maroon 5.

"You look lonely." Jill said as she brushed against my arm. Her presence bugged me almost as much as the music.

"Hey."

She'd gone all out today on the lack of clothing. Two triangles covered her ample chest and her swimsuit bottoms weren't much more than a string. I glanced at the ground wishing I had as much control over my body as I did my eyes.

"I brought you a drink."

A cold bottle of beer appeared in my line of sight. I took it and set it at my feet. "Thanks." I wanted to move, but I was trapped between the boat and Jill's very appealing body. She must have known this because soon it was pressed against mine.

"Jimmy said the rooms are open. We could go...talk."

Talk? Yeah, right. Jill wanted to talk as much as Chugger wanted to remain celibate through high school. I inched away, tying to focus above her neck. "Nah. I'm good out here."

"Jill, baby! Leave Saint James alone and come play with me!" Chugger yelled across the water. He'd passed drunk and into sloppy over an hour ago. Their theory to get wasted before lunch and sober up by practice was asinine.

Jill stiffened and gave a very unladylike gesture. "Chugger's such a pig. So, did you hear about Blake and Lindsay?"

"Yeah." I'd managed to put a foot between us and could finally take a deep breath of air. Jill was a lethal mix of cobra and siren. "You know, Blake's always up for talking." I cringed. My hope to reiterate my non-interest came out sounding like a first rate pimp.

She crossed her arms, pushing even more skin out of her top. "Blake's been in love with Lindsay since freshman year. No way those two are over, and I'm not about to end up a casualty in that triangle." She glared off in the distance, looking almost vulnerable. "Did you ever think that I might actually have feelings for you?"

"Why? Seriously, Jill. We have nothing in common." And we both knew what she did two years ago even if we weren't saying so. She saw me run into the boys' locker room. She could have helped. She didn't.

Jill bit her lip and her eyes sparkled with tears. For the first time I didn't know if they were genuine or just another ploy. "Tom Baker hurt me, too."

My stomach twisted into a familiar knot. *That name. That stupid name should not still affect me like it does.* I turned around, focused on the lake water and on pushing air in and out. Her hand touched my shoulder. It was hot. Hotter than the sun scorching the back of my neck. I shrugged Jill's hand away, but I still felt its lingering burn.

"You think you're the only one playing the game here? You're not. Everybody at Madison wants the same thing."

I spun back around. "And what's that?"

She blinked. "To get out."

"Yeah, but I don't hurt people in the process." I'd never be one of them. Surviving wasn't the same. Wanting to coast my senior year didn't make me a bad guy. It made me smart. It ensured I'd never be the guy on that locker room floor ever again.

She backed away. "Sure, Cody. Keep telling yourself that."

SKYLAR

HENRY DISAPPEARED AT lunch, but I found him outside huddled under a tree with his books and a sack lunch. A few others sat on picnic tables or threw around a football.

I took a seat next to him, ignoring the odd looks and whispers from those close enough to see.

"What are you doing?" he hissed.

I pulled out an orange from my brown lunch sack and began peeling. "Joining you for lunch."

"Listen, Skylar. You seem like a nice person, so I'm going to say it again. I'm branded. I get that you're new to all of this. But, if you had any sense at all, you would pretend we never met."

Movement and chatter returned around us, confirming this wasn't nearly as big a deal as Henry thought. "It's just lunch."

His thumb and middle finger furiously rubbed at his temples. "You don't understand. Madison isn't like other schools. There are certain rules. Traditions."

I swallowed a grin and dropped my voice to a whisper. "Like what?"

Henry's eyes flicked from the surrounding tables back to me. "Madison has a king."

"Like a prom king?"

Henry focused on his lunch, his mouth tight while he opened a Ziploc bag. "Never mind."

"I'm sorry. I wasn't making fun. Honest." Okay, maybe I was a little.

He ate his whole sandwich before continuing. "When an old king graduates, he selects his successor. Right now, that's Blake Mason. Before him, Chuck Winston. And before him, Tom Baker. And the list goes on...for decades." His shoulders fell. "I didn't take it seriously either." His pause was pained. "I made a mistake. And now it's too late."

"It's never too late." The words came out more forcefully than I intended. Having hope. Believing in the impossible. It was the only way I could get through the day anymore. "What I mean is, you take one day at a time."

Henry met my eyes. His soft brown irises were barely visible through the thick glasses. "Thank you. It's been a long time since anyone cared."

BY THE TIME the last bell rang, I was way past my fascination with public school. It didn't help either that my sixth period teacher, Ms. Bakerfield, was a grouch.

My now full locker was jammed with a myriad of books ranging from slightly thick to ridiculous. I sighed. Maybe I was ready for college. High school certainly wasn't what I expected.

Loud heckling and laughter echoed through the hall, and a flood of male bodies meandered past leaving a wake of sweat, suntan lotion and hard, thick muscles. Heat shot to my cheeks and down my arms. I shouldn't have looked, but I watched every step they took.

The tall, blond in front seemed to be the ringleader. He was pretty enough to be a model and moved with the confidence of a celebrity. I'd known a hundred of those types: smug smile, lazy stride, his eyes catching his reflection in the glass trophy case. He may have captured the attention of most girls, but he wasn't the one who spawned tiny fairies in my stomach.

Head lowered as he walked, hands shoved into his pockets, the object of my fascination trailed just a foot behind the others. He was taller than the blond, his body solid and strong with the muscle and strength of a seasoned athlete. His sun-kissed brown hair fell softly on his forehead, which still held a line from a now missing baseball cap.

All his friends were talking and cutting up. He wasn't. His back pulsed with tension and his steps seemed hesitant like he dreaded each one. I wanted to know why.

"Cody, pick it up. We're gonna be late," the blond one called out, stopping to wait.

Cody raised his head and, for two heartbeats, his eyes were all I could see.

My breath stilled. We weren't close enough to speak, but his gaze sliced through every layer of pretense until I felt completely exposed.

The other guy slapped his shoulders and pushed him forward, laughing while they walked. Cody's focus returned to his group, breaking the connection. A strange feeling of loss replaced it.

Henry joined me at my locker, but I was transfixed.

"Who is that?"

His sad sigh broke my trance. He pointed to the back of the blond who was the last to disappear around the corner. "That—is the king of Madison. Don't ever forget."

CODY

"AGAIN!" COACH SCREAMED as we ran our twentieth suicide sprint. His fierce demeanor went way beyond his gigantic frame and bushy white hair. The man's voice could scare wild dogs into submission.

Fatigued and dehydrated from all day on the lake, I barely made it to the side of the track before vomit spewed from my throat. I'd been the tenth one to puke and the last senior. Chugger blew chunks after just two sprints. Served him right for downing a six-pack.

"Look at that, boys. Your captain finally went down. Do you have anything to say for yourself, Captain?"

What I wanted to say would get me kicked off the team. I just shook my head.

"I sure hope you had a lot of fun today, Mr. Cody James, because I plan to recoup every one of those seven hours you spent goofing off. You hear me?"

"Yes, Coach."

"Good. Get back in line!"

Five sprints later, he released the underclassmen to the lockers and let us rest.

My knees buckled. Blake was also on all fours.

"I'm going to kill you," I whispered.

His smile showed as much remorse as a bratty two year old who'd just stolen the last cookie. "It was worth it."

A grunt of disgust left my mouth. Maybe for him. Not a moment went by that Blake didn't have some half-drunk girl in his lap. Why he wanted me there so badly, I'd never understand. He barely noticed.

Blake crawled to the edge of the track and tossed me a sports bottle. I squeezed it tightly, more of the water hitting my face than my mouth. Sprints sucked. Getting yelled at sucked. And we were only an hour into practice.

Coach's shout rumbled across our broken bodies. "That's enough resting. Pushups. Ready position."

My arms and chest ached. My legs burned. My mind kept drifting to the fire goddess I passed in the hall. I knew her somehow. Or maybe she knew me. Her stare was too deep for a stranger. I wobbled, reminding myself I needed to focus on practice and not some redheaded apparition.

"Down," Coach screamed.

We lowered, holding our elbows at ninety-degree angles for what felt like an eternity. I squeezed my eyes shut, pushed aside the pain ripping through my triceps.

"Up."

A relieved sigh echoed from the team. It didn't last long.

Thirty reps later, my hands went numb.

"Down."

Once again lowered, I sensed the minute Coach crouched down to talk to me. "Has your team had enough, *Captain*?"

"Yes, sir." My labored reply was quick and desperate.

He stood. "Up. Everyone but Cody head into the locker room."

I didn't dare look at my retreating teammates. My arms were rubber, shaking uncontrollably.

The others walked to the building, their footsteps crunching the dry grass.

"Down." Coach crouched next to me again.

He watched in silence. Judgment and displeasure radiated off him like heat from a Carolina blacktop. "I've been doing this a long time, Cody, and I've never seen a team abandon their captain like that without so much as a word. If you think your apathy doesn't reflect in those boys, you're wrong."

My pulse shot up like a bullet released from its chamber. *It's survival, not apathy!*

"You got something to say to me, Cody?"

"I never wanted to be captain." I was too tired to consider that statement's consequences.

"That may be true, but you are. I don't care if it takes all year and a million suicide sprints. You're gonna learn to lead this team. You got me?"

Angry tears burned my eyes. "Yes, Coach."

"You disappointed me today. You're better than this." He stood. "Now get up and get out of my sight."

I fell to the ground, every inch of my body throbbing and watched my self-respect disappear along with the coach. I grabbed some stray rocks and threw them hard across the track. Sweat dripped down my face and into my mouth. Heavy breaths sent the droplets flying. Fatigue and guilt mixed like bitter drugs I couldn't stop swallowing. I pulled myself up and made the slow trek toward the building.

Blake, freshly showered, waited for me in the locker room. I stepped past him to my gear and grabbed a towel and soap.

"Don't take things so seriously. He's all bark."

I slammed the door and walked away without a word. I was beginning to wonder if Blake ever wanted captain to begin with. Today felt suspiciously like a set-up.

SKYLAR

I CAME HOME to an empty house. I didn't like it. Every room felt like it had an echo, as if trying to prepare me for loneliness. I stuffed down the thought. Daddy was probably still at the hospital getting the treatment he needed to live.

I opened the fridge and raided the shelves for something with sugar. Plain yogurt, soymilk and vegetables. Yuck. Aunt Josephine must have shopped again. I slammed the door, grabbed a granola bar and started on my homework at our small kitchen table.

An hour later, the front lock turned and two different voices filled the house. One of them sent the hairs on the back of my neck to attention.

"It's a long shot at best. You heard the odds. The effect this chemo is going to have on your body—"

"Josie, let it go. Hope is hope, and right now that's what I'm clinging to."

They rounded the corner, and I shut my history book.

"Hey, Princess!" My dad broke into a huge smile.

I rushed in and hugged him. "What did the doctor say?"

"Nothing new. How was school? I want to hear all about it."

I let go, but he kept his arm around me while we walked to the kitchen.

"Hi, Skylar." Even my aunt's hello felt like a reprimand.

No surprise. Our dislike was mutual.

"Hey." That's the best she was going to get. Daddy needed faith right now, not odds.

She turned her attention to my father. "Donnie, I'm going home. I put dinner in the fridge. Just warm it up for forty minutes at three fifty."

Dad let go of me and hugged his sister. "You're the best. You know that, right?"

She patted his back and quickly let go like showing that much affection was beneath her. "Let me know if you start to feel…" She sent me a quick glance.

I scowled.

"…uncomfortable. See you tomorrow. Bye, Skylar," she said on her way out.

My aunt's patronizing smile made me want to stick my tongue out. I didn't. Instead I snarled, "Bye," with all the attitude I could get away with in front of my dad. I knew I was being a brat, but I couldn't help it. Like a lingering cough, every negative feeling I had about this move accumulated in one place. Her.

Dad's arm wrapped around me again, and I forgot all about his haughty older sister. "So, school. I need all the details."

We sat at the table across from each other. "It was all very bizarre. First, it was senior skip day, so none of the seniors were there except this one guy, Henry. My history teacher is nice but a total groupie. She recognized me immediately, but said she wouldn't tell. No one else seemed to. Principal Rayburn keeps all the grades separated except for combined electives, which is weird, right? Oh, and not one girl talked to me today." I blew out a breath, so he knew I was finished.

His brow furrowed. "Senior skip day? In September? What

kind of school is this?"

"That's all you got from my summary? Ms. Yarnell recognized me." My heart fluttered. If any of the seniors did, my dream would disappear before it ever started.

"Sweetheart, you knew that was a possibility." He reached out and pulled on a lock of my long, red hair. "You don't exactly blend in."

"I know. But I thought using Mom's maiden name would work." I studied the wood on our table, wishing for the first time my parents weren't famous. I just wanted one thing to feel stable. One thing that didn't feel as if I were two seconds from losing it.

My dad lifted my chin. His suck-it-up smirk made me smile. "That's better. Now, who's this Henry?"

I laughed at his overprotective dad vibe and told him all about my strange friend at Madison High.

CODY

SMACK. MY BACK hit the mat with an electrifying pain that resonated all the way to my fingertips. I knew from the sting of the shower I'd gained more than a tan at the lake, but never expected the blistering red that covered my back and shoulders.

"What's your deal today?" Matt's irritation came out in a low hiss. "You're completely off."

I gingerly pushed to my feet. Even the soft, Dri-Fit material of my shirt scratched like sandpaper. I swallowed and waited for the ache to subside.

Concern replaced the anger on Matt's face. "Are you hurt? Did something get tweaked in practice?"

"No, I'm fine. Let's just go again."

Matt eyed me skeptically and then crossed his massive arms. "Lift your sleeve."

He was too perceptive, too watchful. Begrudgingly, I pushed up the edge of my shirt to reveal the angry crimson already starting to blister.

"Geez, Cody! Why didn't you say something?" He unstrapped his headpiece, the signal we were finished grappling for the day.

I wanted to argue. I needed this workout. Needed to let out the growing fury in my gut. But contradicting Matt was suicidal.

He guzzled some water while I slowly lifted my arms to take off my own head protection.

"Where'd the burn come from?"

I looked down, kept my eyes locked on the tips of my sneakers. "At the lake yesterday." I would never lie to Matt; even knowing the truth was going to set him off like a torpedo.

"You didn't have school yesterday?"

"We skipped."

There was a heartbeat of silence, enough to send adrenaline pumping through my blood. "We?" His tone was on the edge, like a sharp razor one brush away from slicing a deep trench in my skin.

I summoned the courage to look him in the eye. It wasn't like I killed someone. Every single senior in the history of time skipped school once or twice. "All the seniors. It's no big deal, okay?"

A myriad of emotions passed over his face, surprise turned to frustration, which gave way to the anger that I'd seen far too often. "Did you plan this little adventure?"

"No, of course not."

"So, you just went along with it? Who cares what the fall-out means for you and your team?"

I moved in closer. I didn't know where the fight came from, but I was shaking, ready to go another round that was real this time. "What fallout? We didn't even miss practice."

His glare reminded me of a pit bull in full attack mode. "Were you drinking?"

Blood pounded in my ears. He wasn't my father. Wasn't even my coach, technically.

"That's what I thought." His disappointed tone was worse than the sunburn. "What is wrong with you? You're special,

Cody. Don't throw all of that away because some punk kids make breaking the law look cool."

Fury released the last of my control, and all the pent up resentment and anger I'd felt toward Blake and Coach, erupted with a volume that could pierce an eardrum. "What more do you want from me? I'm an eighteen-year-old kid in high school, not someone training for the Olympics. I'm here every morning, busting my butt for you, and then in the gym all afternoon getting screamed at by Coach. What's it going to take to be good enough for all of you, huh?"

Matt stepped away from me. "So, you're doing this for me, then? For your coach?"

"Yeah, I am. I'm trying to be the golden boy everyone expects me to be. Trying to live up to this ridiculous expectation you have, when all I want is to get this year over with." It was the most honest thing I'd said to him all day, and I instantly regretted it. I didn't have to look into his fiery eyes to know I'd pushed too far. My voice had never been raised against him. Ever.

Matt jumped out of the ring and threw his headgear across the room. It bounced off the wall with a bang that turned every eye our way. "Get out of my gym. And don't come back until that attitude of yours is fixed. I didn't spend the last year and a half helping you just so you could turn out like every other stupid kid!"

He stomped down the hallway and shoved open the door to Apocalypse—the room that held a punching bag and ear-splitting rock music where Matt unloaded all his frustration.

I hung my head, the adrenaline draining from my body. I'd forgotten the first rule of survival. Keep your mouth shut.

I PULLED MY truck into the senior lot and parked behind Chugger's souped-up jeep. He leaned against the bumper while Jackie, his newest girl, snapped a selfie next to him. The muscles in the back of my neck knotted, and I rolled my head to each side trying to work them out.

Chugger pushed off his jeep when I opened the truck door and said, "Dude, I'm soooo sore."

"That's what happens when you slack off all summer."

He wrapped his arm around Jackie and flashed an indecent grin. "Oh, I was very dedicated this summer…to extracurricular activities."

I ignored his innuendo. Locker talk I was used to, but not in front of his current girl. "Blake here yet?"

Chugger tilted his chin toward the entry steps. "I'd leave it alone. He's pissy this morning."

I readjusted the bag on my shoulder. Crap. "You know why?"

"If his legs feel anything like mine do, all it took was walking."

Jackie tugged on Chugger's arm. "You promised you'd give me your opinion on my dress for next weekend, and the magazine is in my locker."

I seriously doubted she'd even be around next weekend.

Chugger smacked her bottom and hobbled forward. "Duty calls." He shot one more glance toward Blake's tense back. "I hope he chills before first period."

I nodded with trepidation but started toward Blake anyway. No need to put off the grand apology he'd expect for snubbing him in the locker room. Matt dismissed my life as some afterschool special, but he didn't understand the core of what it took to fit in at Madison.

Lindsay's blond hair appeared over Blake's shoulder and then the two of them shifted, allowing me a glimpse of their interaction. Maybe it was instinct, but everything inside said, wrong, wrong, wrong. Her stance was too defensive, his too hostile. My gaze followed the line of his arm. He gripped her bicep, fingers digging deep into her sleeve.

My teeth snapped together, my skin too tight against my aching muscles. I should retreat, stay out of whatever argument they were having. Hadn't my earlier outburst gotten me into enough trouble? But the fear in her expression pulled me forward.

Lindsay saw me coming first, and her lips moved for the first time. Blake quickly glanced my way and dropped his hand. His shoulders were rigid, irritation plain on his face. My interruption was unwelcome.

I shoved my hands in my pockets and relaxed my stance. "S'up Blake, Lindsay."

"Hey, Cody." Lindsay's shaky voice was barely audible. I studied her face. If angels could be seen, Lindsay would definitely rival them in beauty. Pale blond hair. Big blue eyes. But her typical glow was darkened by sadness, and tears pooled near her lashes.

I cleared my throat and tried to ignore the glare of disapproval coming from Blake. "You goin' to class? Ms. Yarnell said our group will have extra work if you're tardy again."

He shot Lindsay a scowl that could kill on sight. "Yeah, let's go." A second later, he was off toward the building.

Lindsay mouthed, "Thank you," and walked back to her car, ducking her head like she was trying to curl into a small, invisible ball.

"Cody!"

Blake's harsh yell was like a slap to the head. I wanted to tell him to screw off. That he didn't get to dictate everyone's life. But that was fantasy. Reality waited with impatience. Sighing, I slowly made my way to where he stood hating every step I took in his direction.

"Your timing sucks." His cold stare was a warning.

I inhaled to pull back the millions of other things I wanted to say. "Sorry about that. I didn't realize you were fighting."

Anger blazed from his blue eyes. "She wasn't at school yesterday."

"Nobody was at school yesterday."

"Yeah, well, her friends were all with us, so where was she? I called her twice and checked in with her mom. I know she wasn't home." He walked fast, forcing a stride that was almost a jog.

"Considering what went down with you and Stacey Morgan, don't you think it's a good thing Lindsay opted to be alone?"

"She'd better have been alone."

Heaviness settled in my chest. I knew Blake was possessive and territorial when it came to Lindsay, but his clenched fists and pinched face went beyond a rational reaction. Jill was right. Anyone who stepped between those two would get singed in the crossfire.

Blake's feet halted, his dark expression morphing into an innocent one. "And I don't know what you're talking about. I barely said two words to Stacey at the lake."

That was probably true. They'd disappeared for thirty minutes and, when they returned, Blake had a grin that didn't need explanation. I didn't contradict him, though. No point in it.

By the time we reached our lockers, Blake carried on as if he'd never argued with Lindsay. His mood set the tone, and people circled around him, high-fiving the success of senior skip day. Not one parent was called yesterday.

Blake snapped his fingers in front of my face. "I thought you were all twisted about being late. Let's go."

Chugger made it to class minutes behind us but looked ready to explode into a firecracker of smiles. "Dude, did you see the new girl this morning?"

Blake perked up. "What new girl?"

"Oh, you'd remember. Nicest stems I've ever seen and a face like Aphrodite." Chugger sat back, his hand draped across his heart. "I think I'm in love."

I rolled my eyes. Chugger fell in "love" at least three times a month.

A hush fell over the room, followed by a low whistle from two tables over. The object of our conversation stood in the doorway glancing around for a place to sit.

My mouth went dry. The goddess from yesterday. The one I was beginning to think I imagined. Hair the color of fire encircled her like a halo of light. Her eyes met mine, and the strange connection from before hit me again. She was familiar, like an old toy from childhood that brought a rush of memory, but I couldn't place why.

Her shiny hair fell over her shoulder, messy in a way that looked intentional. She reached up and grabbed a strand. Twirled it with her finger.

Blake pushed out a chair, scraping it across the floor and motioned for her to join our group. I, along with the rest of the class, watched in stunned silence. He had kicked many a student out of that same chair the first day of school.

She shyly looked around for another invite, but no one else would dare after Blake had made such an obvious gesture. Her eyes locked with mine, and again they surveyed me as if she'd caught on to my secret that I was an imposter. My lungs burned with the need for air. I wanted to scream, "Run away, now, before it's too late."

But she didn't run. She moved with the grace of a dancer and slid into the empty seat. Her light perfume floated across the table—powdery and sweet. "Hi, I'm Skylar."

Blake's gaze trailed down her body, and his smile widened. I wanted to punch something. She wasn't a goddess anymore, but a sacrifice to the king of Madison.

Blake owned everyone at this school, his word akin to gospel, and I had never once gone against his rule. Yet, when I stared at Skylar's innocent face, one forbidden thought penetrated...*You won't own her, too.*

SKYLAR

I SHIFTED IN my seat. They were staring, all three, like I'd just walked the runway in nothing more than a strip of fabric. I adjusted my top, even though I knew my cleavage was fully covered. A roller coaster of nerves came swooping up, taking my stomach along for the ride. Today was already so much different from yesterday that it felt like a dream.

When I first walked in the classroom, I spotted a table with three girls and smiled, hopeful for an invite. But none of them would look my way. Now, they glared at me like I'd killed their favorite pet.

Why was it so impossible to make a girlfriend?

I sighed, accepting my fate to be forever surrounded by men. It was the curse of the band. Four guys and every one had sons, except my dad.

"First day?" The question broke though my disappointment. It had come from the blond. The future male model who had pulled out my seat. He scooted closer. "I'm Blake."

Oh, yeah, the king himself. My thoughts went to Henry. He didn't even look at me this morning. "Yes, I know. Your subjects have kept me well informed." Ugh. That was probably a dumb thing to say. The last thing Henry needed was my making his life harder.

Blake's slow smile didn't look offended. It didn't look overly friendly, either. It was a smile that spelled trouble. With a promise. "I'm glad to hear it. Keeps the introductions easy." His eyes shifted to the other two at the table. "That's Chugger and Cody."

Cody. The hallway guy who seemed so different from his friends. I knew his name before the introduction, but used the introduction as an excuse to fully check him out. Up close. Cody's wide jaw and strong chin made him look years older than a high school senior and borderline intimidating. He was tan like the others with a hint of red on his nose and cheeks. But those eyes. The brown color wasn't unusual, but the intensity, the laser focus that came at me had my insides quivering. Just like yesterday.

I looked away, studied the one referred to as Chugger. The name implied an overweight, brain-deficient frat boy, not the freshly shaven heartthrob in an Oxford button down. Hair the color of sandy beaches and eyes to match, his fair skin glistened almost as much as the humor in his eyes.

Did this table have a hotties-only policy?

"Chugger? There has to be a good story behind that name." I peeked at Cody in my peripheral. He was still studying me like an impossible math problem.

Chugger leaned in. "It's from junior high." His lids lowered, and a small dimple appeared. "I'm free tonight. We can swap stories…and other things."

Cody snapped to attention like a knight ready to defend my honor. Electricity streaked down my arms, and I felt a strange desire to fan myself. I liked a guy who respected girls. Maybe I'd been coddled growing up, but I came from a world where men opened doors for women and held out their chairs at restaurants.

I tried to ignore my erratic heartbeat and rolled my eyes at the smiling boy who thought way too highly of himself. "I think I'll pass."

"Smart girl." Blake dropped his elbows on the table, his voice annoyed. "Besides, nobody wants to hear about an eighth grader sucking down a liter of Dr. Pepper and then spewing it all over Kasey Moore's white shirt."

"It was cream, not white, and I had to do three days in detention for it. I also bought her a new shirt." Chugger winked at me. "I'm nice like that."

I had to admit he did have some charm. The kind that would have my dad locking the doors and taking away my phone. But charm all the same. I fought down a giggle and dared to look at Cody again. He was not amused. Nor had he said a word, and I found myself longing to hear him speak.

"No nickname for you?"

Blake answered for him. "Not to his face. But behind his back, he's known as Saint James. The guy has no idea how to have a good time. He's the most dedicated wrestler at Madison. Our state champion." Blake squeezed Cody's shoulder, but I didn't see the camaraderie. It felt more like disdain or even jealousy. But Blake was supposedly the king of the school, so I must have missed an inside joke.

Ms. Yarnell called for attention and wrote "Revolutionary War" in script on the whiteboard. I turned around, but the hair on my neck prickled as if someone watched me. Someone with powerful brown eyes. His presence heightened my senses, made me aware of every small noise from the shuffling of paper to the scraping of chairs.

I never before questioned what I looked like from behind, until now. I obsessed about my shirt tag. Was it sticking out, flailing around like a lost cause? Was my hair a mane of beautiful waves or the bird's nest that greeted me each morning? Was Cody even looking or had I imagined his interest? Yikes. I was turning into one of those girls Ricky made fun of. Not that the band's lead guitarist could judge. He'd been married three times.

Blake saved me from my internal freak out. "Ms. Yarnell puts twerking and tweeting in the same offensive category, so don't even touch your phone in this class."

Laugher imploded in the back of my throat. Blake chuckled along with me, and tears tickled the corner of my eyes. I could see why the students loved him. Blake's personality reminded me of my father's—charismatic and confident. The qualities people get addicted to.

My laughter died. Remembering my dad at his prime brought the familiar ache back to my chest. The chemo yesterday had taken its toll, and we spent the night curled up on the couch watching old movies. He slept through most of them, but I didn't mind. It was enough to have him near. We'd beat the sickness. I chanted it again and again in my head until my shoulders relaxed.

"Skylar?" Blake's voice showed a hint of concern.

My mind catapulted to the present. Ms. Yarnell was busy passing out the worksheets, yet I had been staring blankly at the board. I turned around. "Sorry. Zoned out for a second."

Our eager teacher slid the paper in front of us. "These boys can explain the drill to you, Skylar. This is your opportunity to discuss, to reason, and to have a viewpoint that isn't given to you on some YouTube video. And boys, don't think you're getting away with ditching. There will be makeup work. I just haven't decided how hard to make it yet."

Her passion was admirable. Even if it was met with snickering from most of the class.

As soon as she took her seat, Blake passed the paper and book over to Cody, who pulled out his pen and began filling in the sheet without bothering to read the questions out loud.

"Shouldn't we be helping him?" I asked.

"Nah. It's his turn today. I'd rather hear more about you." Blake was the type to make eye contact the whole time he spoke. It was unnerving, in a way, to have so much energy focused on me.

"Not much to tell. My parents traveled a lot, so I've been homeschooled my whole life. We recently settled here, though, so I thought, why not see how the other half lives?"

That seemed to pull Chugger into the conversation. "Homeschooled? I thought you all wore Little-House-on-the-Prairie clothes and raised goats or something."

I resisted smacking his arm. "Last I checked, there were no goats in my yard. Although I do keep my prairie clothes available for smart-mouthed wrestlers."

Chugger caught my humor and came back with feigned shock. "Why, Skylar, are you saying I lack a filter?"

Cody's snort was the only sign he'd heard our conversation.

Chugger punched him in the arm. "Nobody asked you."

Cody glanced up, those soulful eyes doing crazy things to my insides before they returned to the writing assignment. He smiled. It was faint and barely recognizable, but I wanted more.

By the end of first period, I'd learned that Blake had an older brother who held the school record for touchdown passes. Chugger was the youngest of three. His two older sisters were mother hen types, so he was spoiled rotten with no remorse on the issue. I also learned that they'd been friends since grade school. Cody was the odd man out. Joining their crew only a year ago.

"So, how bad was it yesterday?" Blake's words came out amused.

I shrugged. "Quiet. Boring. But at least no one saw how lost I was. Well, except Henry, but he was very helpful."

Chugger choked out a cough. "Henry Watkins? The four eyes with high waters?"

My mouth tightened. "You do need a filter. Henry is a nice guy and could have said mean things about any one of you, but didn't. Maybe you could offer him the same courtesy." My hearted pounded by the time I finished, and my hands trembled.

I stared at the boys, but only Blake made eye contact with me, and his expression was blank. I couldn't tell if I annoyed him or if he respected my gumption. And why did I feel like I needed his approval? That bothered me almost as much as Chugger's words.

"Apologize." The demand came from Blake. It was cool and effortlessly powerful.

"You're right," Chugger said. "Sorry I said anything."

An awkward silence hung around the table. Cody stopped writing and, although he wasn't looking at me, I sensed something in his shoulders. They were tight. His neck strained as if waiting for an explosion.

"Personally, I love a good set of glasses." Blake smiled like a man who knew he would look good in anything. "What do you think, Skylar? Would I look good in glasses?"

"Of course, but it would be a shame to hide those eyes." My answer was meant to be cute and truthful—Blake had remarkably blue eyes—but I realized too late it sounded flirtatious.

Cody's head lifted and he tossed his pen. "Done."

My nerves prickled under his stare. Why did I feel like it was now my turn to apologize?

"Dude, that took you almost the whole period," Chugger said.

Cody fell back in the chair. "Ms. Yarnell must have been all kinds of ticked when she wrote up this worksheet." He flexed his fingers like they cramped and passed the sheet to Blake. We each signed our name and passed it back to him.

He glanced at mine and stared at me with bewildered shock. "Da Lange?"

My cheeks flushed hot red. He knew the name? No eighteen-year-old boy should know who my mom is. Fear rattled my otherwise steady tone. "Um, yeah. It's Irish."

The bell rang before he could probe further.

I darted to my feet and Blake followed, grabbing my bag off the floor. "I'll walk with you."

Cody glanced from me to the paper and back up again. He was going to figure it out. I could see the recognition in his eyes. Maybe that's why he made me unsteady. Maybe it had been there all along.

"Sure. Let's go." My ears were on fire. I wasn't even going to get a full day of "real" high school before everyone knew I was Donnie Wyld's daughter.

CODY

I WATCHED SKYLAR run out the door and knew I was right. That's why she looked so familiar. Her dad was a freaking rock star! And not just any superstar. My idol. A man whose music carried me through some of the darkest moments in my life.

I heard the faint mention of Skylar's name.

"What?"

Chugger brow creased. "Blake. He has a thing for her. Sucks, you know. It's like he has first dibs on all the hottest girls in school. First, Lindsay. Now, Skylar."

"Yeah." I couldn't think about that now. I had to confirm what I already knew to be true. Donnie Wyld married Brianna Da Lange two decades ago, and they had a daughter. I pulled out my phone the minute we cleared Ms. Yarnell's "no cell phone" cave and typed "Donnie Wyld's daughter" into the search engine. The pictures were old, probably seven or eight years, but Skylar's face was too special to duplicate.

The warning bell rang, but I didn't care. Never before had I used my popularity to get something, but nothing could derail me now. For a moment, Skylar made me want more than my calculated existence. But it wasn't her. It was the music. The heartbeat of Donnie Wyld that pulled me in like a drug.

I pushed though the glass doors to the main office, leaned

my forearms on the counter, and began my best Blake impression.

"Hey, Steph."

"C-Cody, um, hi." Stephanie Moore looked like a modern day Snow White, and making her cheeks flush bright pink was as easy as pulling an A in Life Skills.

"That haircut looks great."

She looked down at the desk and doodled on a sticky note. "Um, thanks. I-I really didn't think it was noticeable." It wasn't, but most girls cut their hair often enough that the compliment always worked.

"So, I've been designated our group leader, and I need Skylar Da Lange's phone number to set up a study group. She'd give it to me herself, but I won't see her until after school. I really need to get this knocked out." My mouth tilted and I winked. "Can you hook me up?"

Steph quickly glanced to her left and leaned back in her chair like she was trying to see into another room. "I'm not supposed to," she whispered, but she still moved the mouse and clicked. "But since it's you."

It was odd to see the way she bit her lip and fumbled with the keyboard. Two years ago, she wouldn't have known my first name.

"Blake was right about you. You are a sweetheart," I said hoping she wouldn't change her mind.

Her cheek color deepened. Steph spied the area around her one more time and quickly wrote down a number. "A-are you, um, nervous about, um, your first match?"

Yes. Terrified. "Nah. It's all good. Are you coming to watch us?"

She lifted a shoulder and handed me the pink note. "Maybe."

"You should." I scanned the numbers and stuffed the paper in my pocket. "Thanks. I owe you one."

She watched me with a dazzled stare. "S-sure Cody. Just don't tell anyone."

"You got it." I left the office a victor, but felt like I needed a shower. Manipulating her was way too easy, and definitely another situation Matt wouldn't approve of. I reminded myself I wouldn't be this person forever. That one day I'd be free from the memories that still drifted through these halls.

SKYLAR

BY THE END of second period so many people had talked to me I couldn't remember all their names. Amber, Kara, Erin, and someone with blue hair streaks and a nose ring. I desperately wanted to bond with other girls, but all they seemed to care about was Blake inviting me into the group during first period.

What did he say? What did he do? Were you totally shocked?

I leaned my head against my locker and closed my eyes. At least Cody hadn't blown my secret. Maybe I'd misread him after all.

"Careful. It's dangerous to sleep standing up."

My eyes popped open as my locker neighbor shoved a notebook into her locker. Her face was covered by the open door, but she peeked around it. "I'm Zoe. You must be the new girl."

"That obvious?"

She grinned. "Um, yeah. Don't worry; I'm totally harmless. Not like the rest of these chicas."

Wow, a whole sentence without Blake. I returned her smile. "Skylar. And I'm really glad." Really, really glad.

Zoe shut her locker door, and I was able to see her in full length. Long dark hair hung to her waist; so black it appeared to have a blueish tint. Her oval-shaped eyes were dark as well. "I just moved here last year, so I totally get why this school has you freaked out." She smiled and her eyes tilted up. "Where you headed to now?"

"AP English."

Zoe brushed a long strand of hair off her shoulder. She was really pretty, but not in a conventional way. She looked ethnic, maybe Polynesian, but her style and makeup were *Cosmo Teen* all the way. "Ugh. I'm not taking any AP classes. Too much work. Everyone here is obsessed with dual credit and getting college hours, but I don't see the rush, ya know? Why not spend five years in college? It's supposed to be the best time of our lives, right?"

With each question, she looked up, waited for my nod and then continued. It fascinated me, the number of words she could string together in one sentence. The boys I knew never talked this much. I'd get a grunt and a nod if I was lucky.

"I don't know what I want to do yet, anyway. My dad says I need to focus on math and science, but please, do I look like a math girl? My mom is a health nut, so she wants me to be a nutritionist, but again, do I look like I don't eat cheeseburgers?"

"I think you look great." The words tumbled out after I'd caught up with her speech, but I meant them. I was built like my mother, tall and rail thin, where as Zoe's hips and chest curved like a 1950s pin-up model.

"What about you? Do you know what you want to major in?" She paused and waited. It was like the battery died in her vocal chords. The silence was strangely unnerving.

"Fashion design."

A big smile cut across her face. "Sweet. Well, Ms. Skylar, runway extraordinaire, I'm gone. Look for me at lunch, okay?" She took off down the hall and talked to several more people she passed.

I pressed my hand to my cheeks and resisted jumping up and squealing. A girl. A friend. A teenager. Why did I wait so long to do this? Public school was exactly where I needed to be.

CODY

I SPOTTED SKYLAR the minute she walked into the cafeteria. You'd never know from her stance she was the new girl. Head high, posture straight, she moved through the crowded tables like a queen among subjects. And from the number of heads that turned, most of the guys in the room would gladly bow down at her snake-skinned boots. Only they knew better because Blake had staked his claim with one push of an empty chair.

Something bounced off my forehead. "You're staring."

I looked down at the mangled fry on my tray and tossed it back to Chugger. "So what?"

"So, if Blake sees you he's going to have a coronary. Just be less obvious." Chugger glanced where my eyes had been moments ago. "Who's she sitting with?"

"I don't know, but I think I had Poli Sci with the dark-haired girl last year. Zoe or something like that. She talked constantly."

Chugger spat out food when he laughed, reminding me why he'd kept his nickname all these years. "Oh, yeah. I had her in my Biology II class. I'm pretty sure she wanted some of this." He pointed to his chest and bounced his eyebrows. "But Karrisa was also in our group and, wow, that girl gave the best private study sessions. Speaking of which, I need to call her again."

My gaze traveled back to Skylar's table. "You're disgusting."

"And proud of it."

As if Skylar sensed me watching, she turned. Our eyes locked for one, two, three counts before I forced my attention back to my food.

Chugger leaned in and spoke in a hushed whisper. "Did you hear about Henry?"

My heart stuttered, but I kept my face relaxed. "Nah. What happened?"

"A couple of guys jumped him after second period. He was in the nurse's office when I went by to get some Tylenol for the massive cramps in my legs. Stupid practice. But, yeah, he was in bad shape."

"He say who did it?"

"No, of course not. His mouth is what got him into this mess to begin with. If you ask me, it's all a test to see if he's learned his lesson."

Bile burned the back of my mouth as *Fatty James* floated across my ear like a whisper. "That's sick."

"Hey, I don't make the rules. I just follow them. Henry should have too." He jammed his fries in the ketchup and stuffed them in his mouth.

My appetite was gone. Shoved down with the words I couldn't let out. I pushed away my tray desperately wishing Chugger would shut up.

"I bet Principal Rayburn schedules another one of those bullying rallies. What's he had, like six of them in the last year? Dude needs to give it up. Nobody's gonna talk about the list."

"The list?" I shouldn't ask. Every time I learned a new ritual, I was expected to participate. The last one left me half-naked and puking in the bathroom. My first and last Tequila morning.

Chugger shook his head and went back to talking with his mouth full. "I forget how out of the loop you are sometimes. It's nothing. Besides, in this case, it's probably good you can claim ignorance."

"Why's that?" I stiffened and searched between the lines of his words. "Do you know who attacked Henry?"

He leveled a stare. "I told you. I don't know anything. Just like you."

I sat back, but my nerves felt raw. I rubbed at my neck, trying to take the growing tension out of it. Skylar's laughter floated across the loud space, and Chugger and I looked over at the same time.

Blake. Hand on her shoulder. Smile on his face. One of the girls shifted over, and he sat next to Skylar like they'd already had a first date.

"I'm out," I said and stood to leave.

Chugger stood too and grabbed his tray. "Whatever you gotta do. Just get that girl out of your head before you do something stupid." His warning lingered while he strolled over to Skylar's table and sat opposite Blake. The way Zoe played with her hair and giggled confirmed Chugger wasn't too far off base about her admiration.

I slammed my tray on the edge of the trash bin to empty it feeling restless and slightly wild.

It felt like a hundred years had passed by the time I pushed through the lunchroom doors. I needed to calm down. Needed to let this thing go and focus on what mattered. Winning state, getting a scholarship, and getting out of this four-year prison.

Yet, I wandered the halls in a daze. Memories drove me to

places I hadn't visited in years. Places where the ghost of Fatty James haunted me.

Skylar had only been here a few hours and already she had altered my world. And why? Because her dad sang about freedom and justice, and she defended Henry at our table?

Tom Baker's face tore through my mind and ripped through the last of my calm. I fell back into the wall, sweat beading on my forehead. For two years I endured their wrath, praying it would stop, begging God, but it only escalated. That day in the locker room was the breaking point.

Tom's girlfriend had been crying and sitting alone. I touched her back and offered her a tissue. She accepted it and then smiled. The kind of smile that came with tears and heartbreak.

That was it.

One moment of kindness. One moment of not being on guard. One moment that would change the rest of my life.

I wiped my forehead and searched for my center the way Matt had shown me. That nightmare needed to stay locked behind its see-through wall. The one that forced me to remember and stay on guard, but kept the pain at a distance. I wouldn't go back to the past. Not now. Not ever.

When my eyes opened, I spotted Lindsay at her locker. The pull was strong, even from across the hall. In so many ways, we were the same. Weak. Maybe that's why I'd always liked her more than the others. She always seemed to be pretending, too.

"Hey," she said, approaching.

I pushed off the wall and met her halfway. "Hey."

"I wanted to thank you for this morning. You know, in the parking lot."

"It's no big deal."

"Yes, it is. No one else would have dared to interrupt him."

She rubbed the spot on her arm where he had been gripping her. "I guess you heard, huh?" She rolled her eyes. "Of course you have, the whole school's heard."

I felt like any answer would be the wrong one. "I'm sorry."

She shrugged, but it was sad and not very convincing. "It's fine. I chose this. I pushed him away. It's just that sometimes things in theory are easier than things in reality."

"He still loves you." I knew that much was true, even if Skylar momentarily distracted him.

Lindsay gripped her notebook to her chest and tears pooled in her eyes. "Love isn't always what it appears to be." She ducked her head and turned, her pale hair swinging across her back as she rushed down the hall.

A part of me envied her choice—to walk away from Blake and all that he represented. I wondered how long she'd last before going back to him. Four years at this school, and I'd never seen anyone successfully take a stand.

SKYLAR

ZOE AND I had fifth period together. She was a gift. Like a Tiffany's box with blue wrapping paper and a big white bow. We talked fashion and movies and made plans for a slumber party. She was beyond what I had hoped for.

"So, are we going to talk about the big glaring elephant between us or what?" Zoe's whispered question sent my pulse into hyper speed. Did she recognize me? It'd only been five hours. I didn't even get a whole day.

"What elephant?" I choked out, wishing our teacher would start talking, and I could avoid this conversation.

"You and Blake." She furrowed her brow. "Why? What did you think I was talking about?"

My relief was so huge it came with muffled laughter. "No. I-I knew you meant Blake. Of course. I mean, it's *Blake*." Sheesh. I was the world's worst liar.

Her head tilt and inquisitive stare said she didn't believe me.

"He, um, asked me out for this Saturday." I hadn't planned to say anything, but desperately wanted her to stop examining me. It worked.

She sat straight, muffled a shrill, "Details, details, details!"

"Calm down. There's nothing to tell. I told him I couldn't go."

A bird could have nested in her open mouth. "You said

NO? To Blake Mason?" She leaned over and rested her palm against my forehead.

I slapped it away. "Stop." She didn't get it. Bringing a guy home to meet my dad was out of the question.

"Do have any idea how lucky you are? You were invited to the head table during your first class. It took me two months before I made any real friends." Her eyes flickered to a girl at the front of the class, and I wondered if there was more to the story.

I suddenly felt like I should apologize. "I'm not trying to sound ungrateful. It's just that I can't."

"Can't? Can't what?"

"Date, okay?" I put my head in my hands, embarrassed. Normal girls dated. Normal girls brought boys over for dinner and family barbeques. Normal girls didn't have to worry about some hyped-up guy selling her story to TMZ.

Zoe tapped her finger to her lips. "Super strict parents. Should have guessed with the homeschool thing."

"Something like that."

Ms. Harrell flipped off the lights by the Smart Board and started to write an equation.

"Don't worry," Zoe whispered and winked. "I've got it all figured out. I don't know Blake very well, but Chugger and I were in the same biology group last year."

I shrank into my chair as she pulled out her phone and started furiously texting. Whatever was happening under Zoe's fingertips scared me almost as much as cheap polyester. The lies were piling up. One after one, they multiplied. My father always said no lie was small or white or insignificant. And yet, to be normal, truth had suddenly become my enemy.

I LEANED AGAINST the doorframe of my final class and stared at all the missing students from yesterday. One more class. One more chair to find. One more group of girls asking me about Blake Mason.

Three seats remained empty. One in the front and two in the back of the room. I chose solitude and scurried past the curious glances. For once, I understood why Daddy opted to just rent out a restaurant instead of trying to go in disguise. People were much too nosy.

My purse vibrated and I froze. Nobody had that number but my dad, Aunt Josephine and Principal Rayburn. I jerked my bag up, fumbling to make sure something wasn't wrong.

> **Unknown:** *You have Ms. Bakerfield for sixth period? Poor thing.*

I checked the room. A blond girl had her phone in her lap, and another guy had ear buds hidden under his long hair. I slouched in my desk, hiding the phone on my lap, and punched in a response.

> **Me:** *Who is this?*
>
> **Unknown:** *The guy who did all the work in first period.*
>
> **Me:** *Cody?*

He dropped into the seat next to me, cell phone clutched in his hand. Our eyes met and he smiled. Not Chugger's cocky smile or the confident swagger that surrounded Blake. A sweet smile, like we were old friends.

> **Cody:** *You look surprised.*

Me: *I am. You haven't said more than two words to me all day.*

Cody: *Maybe I'm shy.*

The guy could practically have a conversation with just one look. Quiet, deliberate, fascinating, yes, but nothing about his squared shoulders and searching gaze said, "shy."

Me: *I'm not buying that for a second.*

Cody: *Ok. Maybe I'm intrigued.*

My insides fluttered and I peeked at him. He sat back, eyes locked to the front like Ms. Bakerfield was the most interesting person ever. She wasn't, but Cody might be.

Me: *How did you get my phone number?*

Cody: *I'm resourceful.*

Me: *You must be. It's unlisted.*

Cody: *I'm also a pro at Google, Ms. Rock Star Princess.*

My phone suddenly felt like a boulder.

Me: *Does anyone else know?*

I looked up after typing, my stare icy. I shouldn't blame him, but I did. He shook his head with an answer that allowed me to take a full breath.

Cody: *Don't worry. I won't say anything.*

Maybe it was the way worry crinkled his brow or the way his shoulders fell forward, but I believed him.

Me: *You'd really keep my secret?*

Cody: *Secret keeping is what I do best.*

I inhaled deeply and tried to calm the nerves assaulting my stomach. Even if Cody did keep my secret, the truth was bound to slip out at some point. Not just that Donnie Wyld's daughter was attending high school in North Carolina, but that the reason was because he was sick. Pictures of my dad would be plastered on every paper in every supermarket with some cheesy headline like, "Rock Star's Days Are Numbered."

Me: *I actually thought no one would recognize me.*

Cody: *They probably won't. I'm a rock junkie. Totally on another level.*

I looked sideways at Cody. He had eased back in his seat, one notch above a slouch, and studied me with fascination. He flashed his rare smile and somehow it pushed the storm clouds away.

Me: *That's a bold statement. Especially to someone who knows music as well as I do.*

Cody: *Test me.*

I bit my lip and racked my brain for something that would stump him.

Me: *Colitas?*

Cody: *Hotel California. First verse. Means marijuana in Mexican slang.*

Me: *I'm impressed.*

Cody: *Your turn. Dec 9th, 1967. Jim Morrison.*

Me: *Arrested on stage for causing a riot.*

Cody: *You might just be my soul mate.*

My burst of laughter earned a stern frown from Ms. Bakerfield. I slipped my phone into my bag, unwilling to lose it like she promised would happen my first day. But even without Cody's words on my fingertips, my body flushed with an unfamiliar simmer. I tried to focus on the lecture. But the part of my brain in charge of analyzing and processing data was turned off. Blocked out by the brown-eyed boy who just made me regret accepting a group date with Blake.

CODY

THE HIGH FROM texting with Skylar dissipated the minute I stepped into the gym—mats waiting, coaches ready with whistles dangling from their lips, the air heavy with anticipation.

Wrestling drills.

Any other day I'd be stoked, ready to show off my skill and power. But today, my throbbing skin ached and stung like a thousand wasps had attacked me. I'd slathered on three rounds of aloe, but lifting my arms still hurt.

Blake, on the other hand, sported a nice tan and an out-for-blood expression.

Standing opposite me, he hopped, and then crisscrossed his arms for a lengthy stretch. "Joey said you and Skylar were awfully cozy in sixth period today."

His spies were merciless. "We may have sent a few texts."

He cracked his neck, twisting it side to side, but kept his eyes locked on mine. "I heard it was more than a few."

"So?" I knew that look in his eyes. Possession, ownership. Like a kid with a shiny new toy in his greedy little fist.

His eyes flashed. "So, you know I'm into her." The king's authority rolled off his tongue.

"What about Lindsay?"

"Lindsay and I are on a break." His shoulders tensed, his hands clenched before releasing. "I'm not going to be a monk in the meantime."

Irritation inched up my spine. He wasn't even serious about Skylar. "So what? I can't even talk to her?"

"You can talk to her all you want." He stretched his arm across his chest. "As long as I'm standing right there."

Coach Taylor approached, glancing between the two of us before lifting his whistle. The excitement on his face meant he noticed our intense exchange.

Blake scanned me, sized me up, and seemed unimpressed. "This is going to be a great year."

The whistle blew and we attacked, slamming into each other like two bears going after the same fish. Arms locked, bodies pressed together, muscles strained as we fought for control.

Blake's hands shifted and his fingers pressed into my enflamed skin like a branding iron. I faltered for only a second, trying to block out the pain. But a second was all he needed. I was trapped; his weight pushed me onto my back despite fighting against him with all my strength.

My second shoulder hit.

Match over.

It didn't matter that I was taller and stronger and more skilled than Blake. Or that my sunburn gave him a significant advantage. All that mattered was timing, and Blake just proved himself the Alpha.

"Nice job, Blake. Cody, get your head in the game. You're worse now than you were at the start of the school year!" Coach Taylor turned to watch the next group of boys go at it.

I pushed Blake off me. He stood and offered a hand I wanted to slap away, but I accepted the help back to my feet.

He grinned as if we'd been playing Xbox and not vying for dominance. "Skylar's parents are all kinds of strict, so we set up a group date on Saturday. And, don't worry, I've already picked out your girl." He slapped my shoulder and took off toward the circuit loop we needed to run through between drills.

A fire that had nothing to do with my sunburn engulfed me as I stared at his retreating form. Blake had always been an arrogant jerk, but being king had multiplied it by a thousand.

It wasn't enough that he had a date with Skylar. He was going to make me watch every second of it.

SKYLAR

HENRY RETURNED TO school on Friday after missing two days. He walked by after second period with a hoodie pulled low on his face like he wanted to remain invisible.

"Hey," I said, leaning against the locker next to his. "Where have you been?"

He shut his locker and looked at me.

I flinched. He had a green and black bruise below his right eye. His lip had scabbed down the center. "Oh, my gosh, Henry! What happened?"

"Car accident." His answer sounded dull and rehearsed. "No airbag."

I wanted to reach out and touch him, soothe the pain I saw in his eyes. "Does it still hurt?"

"A little, but the doc says I'm healing up nicely." He pointed to his side. "Only one broken rib."

"I guess you're tougher than you look."

An arm draped around my shoulders. "Henry, my man." Blake put out a fist to Henry who bumped it with cautious eyes. "I heard you took out a very innocent tree."

"Yeah. Good thing I had a seatbelt on. From what I understand, it could have been a lot worse." Henry kept his eyes locked on Blake's.

"Not anymore. I'm going to take care of it."

Take care of it? My mind whirled with a million questions.

Henry shuffled back a step, his mouth open. "Really?"

Blake nodded and a genuine smile crossed Henry's face. A smile that radiated relief, joy, and surprise all wrapped into one shiny package. There may have even been tears. "I won't mess up again."

Blake pulled me closer, although I was too absorbed in Henry for it to matter. "I know. We're all good."

Henry walked backwards two steps before turning. His posture was now straight. His shoulders no longer slumped.

Blake slid his hand down my back. "Everything's all set for tomorrow night. We'll meet you at Mass Theater 12 at seven. Play some pool. Watch a chick flick if you want."

I was still staring after Henry, hardly listening to Blake's words. "What was that all about?"

Blake tugged on my hair, and I turned. His mouth and eyes pulled down like he felt the same pity I did for Henry.

"There was a big cheating scandal last year. Caused an uproar throughout the school."

"Henry cheated?"

"No. He was the narc. Got a lot of students in trouble. Kids who were just trying to stay above the tide. It's not easy to maintain Madison standards."

His words landed like a cement block on my chest. Right or wrong, Henry had broken the unspoken code among teenagers—never tell.

"Is that why nobody talks to him?"

"People take loyalty very seriously here. But I can't condone violence."

My mouth dropped. "Wait, Henry just said he was in a car accident."

"Henry's learned how to lie. Truth is, some guys jumped

him for showing up at school during senior skip day. They wanted to make sure he wasn't going to rat them out again."

My head ached. Henry hadn't exaggerated when he said he was an outcast. But to hurt him that badly? "How could they—"

"I'll stop it." Our eyes connected, and there was a fleck of something dark in his. Like he shared my outrage. "There are some perks to being the king of Madison. This is one of them."

I felt a hint of something I couldn't define. It wasn't Blake's fault that Henry was jumped; yet, something in me wanted to put distance between the two of us. Maybe it was the casual way he said "king," like he was proud to hold puppet strings over the entire school. Or maybe I was just looking for any excuse to justify my growing fascination with his quiet friend.

CODY DIDN'T SIT next to me in sixth period. He took a chair three rows up. The same one he sat in yesterday when he didn't text me.

He'd kept his promise not to tell my secret, and that should have been enough. But it wasn't. He said I might be his soul mate and then completely stopped talking to me. Who did that?

I reached down and slid my phone into my lap.

Me: *Any advice on a movie choice for tomorrow?*

His motions were so slow I barely caught them. But he reached back, pulled a phone from his pocket.

Cody: *I've been scolded for texting you in class*

Me: *What? By who?*

Cody: *Doesn't matter*

Me: *What if I want you to text me?*

Cody: *Then I'm flattered. Big plans tonight?*

Me: *Date night with my dad. It's our Friday ritual.*

Cody: *Movie premier or rock concert?*

I smothered a laugh. I guess my life was a little fairytale-like. Daddy made Fridays an event. One time, he'd left a trail of presents to the movie theater we had in our California home, the final one being a visit from Kelly Clarkson, who was just as cool in person as she was on stage.

Me: *I think it's just Monopoly tonight. :)*

A dark-headed guy leaned over and whispered something to Cody before looking back at me. I didn't recognize him, but his stare said he knew exactly who I was. I didn't like it.

Cody: *Gotta go. Don't spend too much time in jail.*

Me: *You either.*

I eased my phone back into my bag, a weird creepiness taking root in my gut. Who would tell Cody not to text? And why would he listen?

CODY

I WAS THE first to show up at the movie theater on Saturday. It wasn't intentional. In fact, if given the choice I wouldn't be there at all. I needed a Skylar cleanse. I'd known her less than a week and already felt addicted.

She kept my stomach in a constant state of unease. The way she chewed her pen in class or touched my shoulder when she sat at our lunch table yesterday. The way she watched me with those transparent eyes that said she wanted to know all my secrets.

A flash from headlights pulled my attention to the parking lot and the sweet black Mustang that Skylar drove. Her hair was the first to emerge—red and curly with all the sass and fire I'd expect from the daughter of Donnie Wyld. What I didn't expect was her genuinely kind nature or how comfortable she was in her own skin. I didn't expect the confidence she carried that lacked any conceit.

"Hey!" Her bright smile had me pushing off the wall. It took a monumental amount of self-control, but I resisted pulling her into a hug. "Are we the first ones here?"

"Yep. Seems that way."

She looked around at the movie posters lining the outside walls then back at me. Her fingers tugged on the locket around her neck. "Wow, I'm never the early one. I guess I'm nervous."

I wanted to take her hand in mine. Calm her nerves. But if

I started touching her, I wouldn't stop. With Blake coming in minutes, that was equal to starting a war I couldn't possibly win.

I cleared my throat. "So, who won last night?"

"My dad! I couldn't believe it. He never wins." Her face lit up when she talked about her father. It made her eyes sparkle like blown glass. "I blame you. You jinxed me with all that jail talk." She lightly hit my arm, sending heat to my middle. I should've run five miles before coming to the movies instead of three.

I pulled out my phone to check the time. They were late. A blessing or a curse, I wasn't sure.

"Can I see your playlist?" Skylar asked.

"Is that supposed to be a pick up line?"

Her cheeks suddenly matched her hair. "No. I just want to see if you're really the great music guru you claim to be."

I smirked, feeling completely sure in my music selection. "Don't start a battle you can't win." I pulled up my iTunes before handing her my phone. She tapped and studied the screen. I moved closer to see what she found so fascinating. Big mistake. She smelled like springtime after a rain, when the sun has just popped through dark clouds.

Her finger paused. " 'Redemption Road' is your most played? It didn't even get air time on the radio."

I slowly took the device from her. She couldn't possibly understand what her father's music meant to me. How that song kept me sane when my life was darkness and despair. "Yeah. It's your dad's best one."

"I think so, too." She slid back into her carefree tone. "Your others aren't bad either. Hendrix, Rolling Stones, Nirvana. It's passable."

I flinched. "Passable?" I claimed to be good at two things—wrestling and music. No way I was going down without a fight. "Okay, rock star princess, let's see what you listen to."

She put her phone into my waiting hand and allowed me to invade her iTunes. I think I fell in love with her right then. The girl knew music. Half the songs on her playlist had never even broken the top 100. Except one. The one I chose to focus on in hopes it would make my heart stop pounding.

"You listen to One Direction? Really?"

Her brows scrunched in a deliciously cute way and she leaned in, giggling. "I forgot that was on there."

"My image is ruined. The daughter of Donnie Wyld listening to pop music." I "tsked, tsked" and passed the phone back.

"Hey. The rest are stellar choices." She gripped my shirt playfully and looked up. We were so close that if I leaned in a few inches, I could end my suffering and kiss those beautiful lips. "And, besides, Harry was really sweet to put that on there for me."

I rested a palm on the cool brick wall behind her. It closed the gap buzzing between us. Skylar was shorter than me by several inches, but I loved how she didn't back away. "I'm going to forget you just said that."

She studied the curve of my bicep then refocused on my face. I'd been around women enough to sense attraction, and her eyes said I wasn't the only one wondering what it would be like to make contact.

A double honk had us both jumping. I took two giant steps backward. They weren't far enough. My hand still trembled, and my pulse was creeping into manic speed.

"Skylar!" Zoe waved from her open car door and slammed it shut. The passenger side opened a second later and my nightmare evening was confirmed. Jill Spencer—Blake's little present—and she looked ready to pounce.

"Hey, sorry we're late," Zoe said when she reached us. She hugged Skylar, and then she threw me a scowl that made me wonder if I offended her in a former life.

Jill didn't bother to say anything. She sauntered right up to me, gripped my face and pushed her lips on mine so hard my mouth hurt. It took a second for the shock to wear off, but she was already letting go by the time I processed what happened.

"Hey, baby." Jill smirked and wiped her red lipstick off my open mouth. She slid her arm around my waist. "Hey, Skylar. Blake is just behind us. Zoe was so sweet to pick me up at the last minute."

Zoe rolled her eyes. "It's not like you gave me much choice."

Jill blew her a snide kiss and latched on to my arm. The wide sidewalk outside the theater suddenly felt very narrow. I dared to look at Skylar for the first time since Jill's display. She wouldn't meet my eyes and instead gave Blake the hug I wanted for myself.

"I'm a jerk. I'm so sorry we're late." Blake stared at me from over her shoulder and there was no doubt he'd seen something he didn't like.

Chugger bounced onto the sidewalk and lifted his hands. "My fault, Skylar."

Our circle had become a square with Jill and I banished to the outskirts. Blake released his hug and slid his hand into Skylar's. I wanted to rip it right out.

"It's fine. Really. Cody was already here." She fingered the locket again and met my stare for only a millisecond before glancing away.

"I bet he was," Blake said with an affection as fake as Jill's nails. "So, you ready for some pool?"

She smiled, but it wasn't the same one she had on earlier. It looked unsure and forced. "Sure. But I must warn you. I'm really good."

"Oh, no, we have a fighter," Chugger teased and belted out four air punches as if to demonstrate.

The foursome walked toward the double glass doors on the arcade side of the theater. Zoe giggled like Chugger was the king of her universe. Stupid girl. At least I understood the whole group date thing now. Zoe wanted to be Chugger's next castaway.

Jill held me back from following. When they disappeared inside, she dropped her arm and spun around to face me. "Do you have a death wish?"

I started walking. The last thing I wanted was Jill's advice.

She gripped my bicep and tugged. "Cody."

I blew out a frustrated breath and turned to listen.

"This won't end good. You know that."

Yeah, I knew it. But when Skylar was near, I forgot to care.

SKYLAR

"EARTH TO SKYLAR."

Zoe waved a hand in front of my face blocking my view of Cody at his locker. His jeans hung just slightly lower than his hips and each time he lifted a book, I could see a strip of tan skin. Tight, muscled tan skin.

I closed my eyes and sucked in air. "Sorry." The guy was driving me crazy. Cody…the gorgeous, emotionally shut off, made my heart swoon, most fascinating person at Madison… hadn't looked at me all week. I'd even texted him two awesome songs that he never acknowledged.

"Who were you staring at?" She leaned around me to catch a peek, but it only led to another warning glare. She had sent at least twenty of those my way on Saturday. "Chugger's having a party on Friday. Will you come with me?"

"I can't. Every Friday is a no-go, remember? Dad time."

"You can't get out of it?" she growled.

"I don't want to get out of it." The chemo hit my dad hard this week. Vomiting, more pain, sleeping five to six hour stretches in the afternoons. But it was like that last time, too. A sure sign we were fighting back.

She sagged against her locker. "Fine. I guess I'll skip it too. My other friends won't go, and no way I'm getting stuck with Jill again."

Her name scratched at my skin. "What's the deal with her

and Cody, anyway?"

"Who cares?"

Odd. Zoe usually loved to gossip.

She picked at a fraying paper from her binder. "They're both terrible people."

"What? Why do you think that?"

Lockers jerked open and clanged shut. Chatter filled the hall, and I watched Cody head up the stairs without a look in my direction. Or anyone's direction for that matter.

Zoe's voice lowered. "Do you remember I told you that some girls were really mean when I first got here?"

"Yeah."

"Well, Jill was the ringleader. They acted all nice to my face and then slammed me behind my back. I even ate lunch at their table for like two weeks before I found out." Her lip quivered, and it took her a second to continue. "And Cody's not a whole lot better. He doesn't do the commitment thing or the whole date in public thing, so he just uses Jill when he needs...you know."

Her "you know" made me wish I could have rewound time and never asked.

Zoe shook my arm. "Forget Cody. You have Blake Mason, the perfect boyfriend."

Perfect was subjective, and Zoe and I had a very different definition. Yes, he was cute, but he also knew it. Yes, he'd invited Henry to join us at lunch yesterday when I asked him to, but Blake didn't speak to him. Yes, he was a perfect gentleman, kissing me on the cheek when he walked me to my car. But his touch didn't make my skin burn, and his love for rap music was sacrilege.

Plus, I was pretty positive Blake's interest in me was less

about me, and more about his ex-girlfriend. When he saw her, he would either shift closer or longingly stare at her until she disappeared.

"Hey, what do you know about Lindsay?"

"Only that she's as much of a skank as Jill. Why? Are you worried they'll get back together?"

More like wishing for a solution. "Just curious. Everyone talks like she and Blake were on the marriage track."

The warning bell rang, and Zoe and I became engulfed in a mob of seniors heading toward fifth period. We followed the crowd, but Zoe remained close enough to give me the scoop on the school's favorite jock.

"From what I've heard, Blake and Lindsay began dating freshman year but broke up this summer. Last year they were like the 'it' couple. Did everything together. I swear Blake worshiped her." Zoe grimaced. "Oh, gosh, Skylar. That sounded bad. I'm sure he'll feel the same for you eventually."

"It's fine, really." She didn't understand her words were more a relief than a slam. From the beginning, I sensed something missing with Blake. Now, at least, I knew what it was. We both wanted someone else. "Why did they break up?"

We entered class and took our usual seats by the back window. Zoe leaned in. "She cheated on him this summer. No one knows who with. Blake found out about it or maybe Lindsay told him, I don't know. But he broke it off. I've seen her crying in the bathroom more than once." She shrugged and pulled out her book. "It's poetic justice if you ask me."

I nodded because it seemed like the right response. But nothing felt right. Not Blake or Cody or Jill or Lindsay. It all felt like the real story hid behind a thousand shadows. And I was so sick of complications. Just once, I wanted something in my life to be easy.

CODY

BLAKE STROLLED INTO my room, looking cocky as ever in his jeans and tight Trojan wrestling shirt. "Come on, man. I've got a hundred people at Chugger's just waiting for us to get there. I've been calling you for the last hour."

Yeah, and I've been avoiding you for the last hour.

He closed my calculus book. "You can finish this weekend."

I set my pencil down and leaned back, the leather chair squeaking in protest. "No can do. I'm on lockdown tonight. Parentals say I've been out too much lately." It was a total lie and Blake's "yeah right" expression said as much.

"Since when? Your parents are usually kicking you out of here."

As if on cue, my mom walked in the room and set a laundry basket on my bed.

Hands on her hips, she sent me a reprimanding stare. "I want this done now, and fill it up with your dirty clothes when it's empty." She'd asked me to put away my clothes at least five times. Now I wished I'd just done it.

She turned a smile to Blake. "How's school going this year?"

"Wonderful, Mrs. J. I was just trying to talk Cody here into hangin' at Chugger's house tonight. You know, going through some strategy for our first match."

Mom quickly glanced in my direction but ignored my pleading eyes. "Well, if you can get him to put his clothes away, he's all yours." She turned back to me, her pleased expression reminding me how happy she was that I now had a social life. "If it gets late, stay there and come home tomorrow."

Great. She just ruined my excuse not to drink.

My mom patted Blake on the shoulder, told him it was nice to see him and exited the room leaving a whole lot more than laundry in her wake.

Blake smiled smugly. "Get your undies put up so we can go."

I sucked in a frustrated growl and grabbed a pile from the basket. Blake picked up a picture of me on the podium at state and examined it while I stuffed shirts and socks in my drawers.

"Skylar coming tonight?" The question burned in my mouth and made my phone feel heavy in my pocket. I hadn't sent her a text all week, despite the numerous drafts I'd started.

"Nah. She does some kind of date thing with her dad on Fridays. Why do you care?"

"I don't."

"Good." Blake set the frame down and watched me finish emptying the basket. "'Cause I get the sense you're holding out on me."

I didn't like his tone. It was calm, like the eye of a storm. Blake had never been one to yell. He didn't need volume. He had all the power.

"Nope." I tried to repress thoughts of Skylar: the way her forehead wrinkled when she concentrated or the fact that I'd played her two songs on repeat for days now. "Just trying to focus on the season. More pressure this year." This, at least, was a partial truth. I still hadn't been back to the gym, unwilling to grovel after Matt had thrown me out.

"You sure that's it? You've been a walking bad mood for days now. Ever since Saturday at the movies."

The temperature spiked and sweat beaded around my collar. "Nah. Just need to relax."

"I agree. We'll have to make sure that happens tonight." Blake pulled his keys from his pocket and strolled toward my door.

Grabbing my own set, I told myself this was the last time I'd let him dictate my weekends. "I'll follow you."

"Whatever you want. It's not like you'll make it home tonight, anyway."

SKYLAR

"DAD, I BROUGHT food," I yelled through the quiet house as I hauled Italian take-out to the kitchen. The aroma of garlic and red sauce made my stomach growl, and I felt sorry my dad was stuck with the gluten-free, whole-grain, vegan whatever pasta he had to eat. "Sorry I'm late. Zoe sucked me into a marathon trip to the mall and then we found this fabric store—"

I froze. Aunt Josephine was in our kitchen, rummaging through the cabinets with a shopping list in her hand. The first item likely a reminder to make my life miserable.

I dropped my bags on the counter. "What are you doing here?" My tone sharpened to an edge that could slice through our invisible wall of hate. "Where's Dad?"

She turned her beady, judgmental eyes on me and glanced at my shoes. "You spent three hours shopping in those?"

I compared my three-inch, peep-toe boots to her drab, black flats. "You're seriously giving me fashion advice?" I cringed at my own words. My dad would have a fit if he heard me being so disrespectful.

Aunt Josephine barely flinched, as if she expected my snotty reply, and continued taking inventory. "Your father is resting at my house. The cleaning crew was here, and I didn't want a cover story on tomorrow's *Enquirer*."

Like she'd know anything about that. I was the one who

had spent seventeen years dodging the media, not her. "Well, they're gone now, so why don't you go on home? I can take care of Daddy the rest of the night."

She turned and straightened in her stiff black blazer. She was a lawyer at a prestigious law firm in Asheville. A major partner, my dad had said, and she looked every bit the part. Hair too tight, posture too straight, heart too cold.

She folded her arms as if I were on the witness stand. "Skylar, this chemo is vicious. It's time you start adjusting your expectations."

"Because you're now the cancer expert? You've only been around for two months. I'm the one who nursed him through his last round of treatment." Me and the guys from the band. I still couldn't figure out why Daddy hadn't just us let stay in Germany where we belonged.

She pushed back an invisible lock of hair. "Things are different this time. It's far more advanced. I know you don't want to hear this, but you need to start preparing yourself for the possibility that he might not—"

"Just bring him home." I fought back the tears, refusing to give her the satisfaction. "And for once, keep your opinions to yourself."

I spun around and ran to my room. Daddy would be fine. I knew it. He knew it. We had faith. We prayed.

God would spare my father. He had to.

CODY

CHUGGER'S HOUSE WAS jammed with kids from school. His parents traveled a lot and let him do whatever, as long as no one ended up in jail.

The bump of music rattled my chest the minute I stepped from my truck. Blake parked a few spots over. I was losing his trust, which meant my loyalty would soon have to be proven. Madison was like the Mafia. You were in or you were targeted. There was no middle ground.

Groups huddled in the front yard, most hanging out on the back of truck beds. Since Chugger lived on ten acres of land outside the city limits, the scene mirrored a tailgate party, complete with two kegs and a portable shelter.

Blake walked beside me as we headed to a mob of football players and their groupies. "Time to mingle." He loved these parties. The music, the energy, the unending attention. Two girls pushed toward him, offered hugs that implied they heard he was now single. They were both juniors and wore hip hugging jeans and halter-tops low enough to be lingerie. I recognized the blond from the lake. She'd been sitting on Chugger's lap last time I saw her.

Blake slipped an arm around each of their waists and pulled them close. He took turns nudging their necks with his nose while they giggled. Someone tossed him a beer, which he caught to the disappointment of the brunette who lost his embrace.

"Cody?"

I knew it wasn't really a question. "Sure."

A cold can slid into my hand, and I took my obligatory first swig. It tasted bitter and cheap like most of the alcohol brought to these parties. Someone laughed at a punch line I didn't hear, and I faked a response.

After two more beers for Blake while we talked about sports, we made our way into the house. I tossed my nearly full can in the trash by the door and followed Blake to the living room. Chugger sat fixated on the TV, engaged in his latest video game saga. The crowd was much lighter inside; only a few couples scattered throughout watching the sixty-inch screen.

Everyone knew the house rules. Alcohol stayed outside. Food stayed in kitchen. Back bedrooms were off limits, unless you were on the wrestling team, of course.

"Hey, you made it! Dang Blake, how'd you get Cody to crawl out of his hole?" Chugger asked, turning from his game long enough to notice.

Blake wrapped an arm around my shoulder, pushed my head forward and knuckle-rubbed my scalp. "Had to sweet talk his Mommy." His voice was ripe with sarcasm.

I detangled myself from Blake's arm and pushed him back.

Through the large windows, I saw various couples dancing, some grinding as if the back bedrooms had been moved to the patio. Jill Spencer was front and center, her hands moving down the length of her body when she caught me looking. She hooked her index finger back and forth and pointed a come-and-get-me smile right at me. I turned away.

"Looks like we found your way to relax." Blake's eyes were

riveted even though he'd never been one for random hookups. Well, until this year anyway.

"Not interested."

A loud whoop from the surrounding chairs started a round of smack talk and challenges. Blake took a seat next to Chugger and stole a drink from his red Dixie cup that I doubted was alcohol-free. The two wrestled for the controller while I found an empty spot against the wall. I'd been to this house dozens of times, but tonight even the air made my skin crawl.

I spotted my sixth period nemesis moving through the crowd like a medieval messenger. He wore fancy jeans and a watch that cost more than my car and had spent most of the summer kissing up to Blake. Joey was too weak for the wrestling team, which is why he'd always be just shy of the prize.

He crouched down, whispered something in Blake's ear that made him bolt out of his chair. "Where? She bring someone?"

The fury in his voice had Joey's face twisting. "I-I don't know. I saw her and came to tell you."

Blake pushed Joey forward until they disappeared from the room. I banged my head against the wall, my heart thumping with an adrenaline I couldn't hide.

"Cody, come play." Chugger lifted a controller without taking his eyes off the screen. I forced my legs to move toward the couch, even while my heart demanded to know if my rock star princess had come.

I sat and haphazardly moved the levers.

"I remember the first time you walked into the gym last year," Chugger said, eerily absent of his usual humor. "All wide-eyed and eager. Nervous. I couldn't believe it was Fatty James."

The name made my chest burn while my knuckles around the controller faded to white. No one had uttered that name in years. Not since I pinned Blake in tryouts.

I stood slowly. I should have known Blake would use Chugger to do his dirty work. "Your point?"

Chugger lifted the controller, tapped wildly until a tank exploded. "I just find it amazing how far you've come. Captain, girls like Jill begging to get into your pants, planning senior skip day, jumping Henry. It's been quite a year, and the season hasn't even started. Would hate to see all that hard work wasted."

His threat rang loud and clear: stay away from Skylar or we'll nail you for all our crimes. Blake could get the whole school to confess I was a monster, and Henry wouldn't dare speak up and tell the truth now that he was at the head table.

Gunfire snapped from the TV while Chugger's fingers moved seamlessly over the controls. An enemy in black fell dead. He'd managed to kill us both simultaneously.

"So, we're on the same page here?" His eyes locked on the soldiers blasting their targets.

"Your message is crystal clear."

Ignoring the simmering fury in my stare, Chugger turned his head and offered an innocent smile. "Perfect. Now, get a drink and relax."

The blinds vibrated when I slammed the back door. Past the dancing drunks, a large trampoline and a swimming pool was a path to the line of parked cars. I pushed through the groups clustered around a keg, including Jill who was too drunk to even speak coherently.

Madison's rules were simple. I knew them. Hell, I'd memorized them. I fisted the keys in my pocket. Blake wanted me here to deliver a message. I got it. Now I was leaving.

But since my luck was up there with lottery losers and stranded drivers, the "she" who had Blake in a fury stood between my escape and me. I tried to slip by, but Lindsay's soft hello caught me mid-stride.

"Hey, Cody." She wiped her face, her hands trembling. On closer inspection, her entire body trembled, and her eyes were red.

Crap. I was so screwed. "Are you okay?"

"I'm fine." She wore a pair of tight jeans, boots that went up past her knees and a long sleeved green sweater that she pulled at endlessly.

She wasn't fine. Not even close. Even her voice was raspy. "Lindsay, you're shaking."

"I just needed some air. You know me." She waved it off and swayed. "An emotional breakdown waiting to happen."

Her self-deprecating laugh didn't make me feel any better. I reached out, feeling the need to steady her, but she flinched when my hand made contact. Okay. She didn't want to be touched. Fine by me.

Self-preservation said to walk away, but a voice inside my head screamed to do something. It was Matt demanding I be more than some puppet on a string. I followed her line of sight and moved in front of it, forcing eye contact. "Did someone hurt you?"

"It doesn't matter." There was a hitch in her breath and those hands would not stop tugging and tugging at her sleeves.

"Well, isn't this sweet."

The slur cut across the yard before I could answer.

Fear flashed in Lindsay's eyes, and I spun around to see Blake a couple of feet from us, his fists clenched.

I approached Blake slowly and watched his shoulders in case he decided to use that closed hand on my face. "I was just walking by."

The fire in his eyes could have set off a massive explosion. He pushed me aside and turned his accusing gaze to Lindsay. "I told you to leave. You gave up your right to come here the minute you asked for space." The hatred in his tone drained all the color from Lindsay's face. "You don't look at my friends. You don't talk to them. You wanted out. You're out."

She wrapped her arms around her torso as if she could shield herself from the world. She didn't turn away or respond. It was as if invisible chains held her stationary. Chains that only Blake seemed to hold the keys to.

"Let's just go." I grabbed his arm and attempted to pull him away from her.

His anger swung from Lindsay to me. He grabbed my shirt, and the smell of alcohol stung my nostrils. "You better stop trying to take everything that's mine."

I pushed at his iron grip. "You're crazy."

"Am I? You're supposed to be my teammate. My friend."

My insides boiled, while my face stayed a mask of steel, refusing to justify Blake's jealous tirade with a reaction. People around us whispered, their stares darts of accusation. Blake's performance was Oscar worthy.

He dropped his hands, and I backed away. With a quick look to my right, I saw that Lindsay had left. Now, I could too. "You're drunk, Blake. I'll talk to you when you can walk a straight line."

"Don't you walk away from me!" he hissed, but I did, pushing through the sea of bodies surrounding us. "I made you! You hear me? You're nothing without me!"

My feet sped up. I needed to escape before I did or said something stupid. *He didn't make me. I made me. I buried Fatty James!*

My truck was sandwiched between an Acadia and a two-ton Ford, so I didn't see Lindsay leaning against my driver's side door until I rounded the corner. The urge to punch the side panel and scream, "Why me?" was consuming.

"I'm so sorry, Cody. I didn't mean to put you in that situation. No wonder everyone hates me now." Her voice was a mixture of exhaustion and sadness.

"Stop apologizing. I'm not mad at you." I was mad at the world. I was mad that my easy senior year was turning into a nightmare. I'd been here before. Tom's ex. That day in the locker room. It all happened because I couldn't walk away.

"Do you have a ride?" Even as I asked the question, I knew it meant trouble. This wasn't allowed, being alone with Blake's girl—former or not.

"I came with Jill."

Jill wasn't getting anywhere near a car. "Come on, I'll drive you home." I could almost see the rope being tied for my inevitable hanging.

She eyed the crowd watching our conversation like people staring at the scene of an accident. They wouldn't be too far off base. "That's probably not a good idea."

"No, it's not, but I'm doing it anyway."

I opened the truck door for her and slammed it hard after she was seated. Looking back at the house once more, I slid into the driver's seat. I wouldn't allow myself to consider tomorrow. At least not until I could fully breathe.

Rounding the final curve out of Chugger's yard, I turned on the radio, hoping it would drown out the heavy roar of unanswered questions. My truck blazed a good fifteen miles above the speed limit with the glow of the full moon the only light besides my brights. I needed the speed, and cops wouldn't be a factor until I hit the highway back into town.

"I'm not a slut," Lindsay said out of nowhere. "I know that's what people are saying, but I'm not. Blake's the only one I've ever been with."

"You don't have to explain it to me." *Please don't explain it to me.*

"I shouldn't have come. I knew it was a mistake and did it anyway. I just thought, with Skylar and him dating…" She squeezed her eyes closed and clenched her teeth like she was delivering a punishment to herself. "He's been telling people I cheated on him. I didn't."

"Okay." I prayed she'd end the conversation there. The hole I stumbled into was already twelve feet deep, and each word heaped another bucketful of dirt on top of me.

"You probably think I'm a coward for not saying anything. For not standing up for myself."

I felt her waiting gaze even though my eyes were locked on the road ahead. I had no intention of ridiculing her for doing the same thing I was doing. "I'm not here to judge. I just want to get you home."

"This summer we had a scare." Her voice cracked. "I was two weeks late."

"Lindsay, you don't have to tell me this."

She continued as if I hadn't said a word. "All I could think of was that I was trapped. And the idea of being with him for the rest of my life scared me more than walking away. When the test was negative, I knew I had to separate myself from him somehow."

She exhaled slowly. "The scare affected him too, so he was okay when I said I needed some time to myself. After a week of distance, I grew stronger. Soon a week turned into a month, and I thought for a few glorious days, I might really be free."

"And that's what you want isn't it?"

"It doesn't matter what I want. He still watches me. Calls me. Demands to know where I am and who I'm with." She hung her head and whispered, "He still controls me." With those words, she finally quit talking and stared out the window.

Her two-story brick house came into view, and I pulled into her driveway before the silence grew any more awkward. She opened the door and slipped out. "Thanks for listening, Cody. I know I dumped the world on you. I guess I just needed a friend tonight."

I dipped my chin, and seconds later she was safely inside, but the chaos inside lingered.

He still controls me.

The streets were quiet as I drove home, but the song Skylar sent me blared through my speakers. I pictured Lindsay standing in the field, refusing to fight Blake's words.

He still controls me.

I'd played the game for years. Was willing to sacrifice my reputation, my pride and my conviction just to stay in line. To stand there like Lindsay while Blake called all the shots. But maybe freedom was possible. Maybe I just needed to be smarter than the king of Madison.

He still controls me.

I hit repeat on the song.

Not anymore.

SKYLAR

I WOKE UP to my cell phone ringing with a number I'd added only a week ago.

"Blake?" My voice was hoarse with sleep and surprise. "It's two in the morning."

"I know. Sooo sorry. I just...I just needed to talk."

I recognized the slur in his soft murmur. Ricky would come to our house sounding just like that after a long night of drinking. My father would make him coffee and listen to all his sad stories. I'd listen, too, through my cracked bedroom door. The stories always seemed to revolve around a woman.

"Is something wrong?" I sat up and rubbed the sleep from my eyes.

"Yes. I feeeel...lost." He sounded barely coherent. "You go...sleep. Bad to call."

"No, it's fine. Really." I switched on the side lamp and let my vision adjust to the light. "Did something happen?"

"You're sooooo pretty. Especially your lips. I like your lips." A long silence followed. "But I don't like Cody looking at them."

His name brought a familiar twisting in my stomach. I swallowed.

Blake muttered a curse. "He takes everything."

I was about to ask for more details when he cut me off, his voice suddenly deep and thoughtful. "Nobody really cares about me. They just want to use me. They take…take…take."

His words tugged at a buried memory. To my tenth birthday when a girl from my neighborhood secretly took pictures of me hugging the band's drummer, Raif, after I opened my present. He was in the middle of a custody battle, and when those pictures showed up in the *Enquirer* looking provocative, his ex-wife used to them to imply he was a danger to children. It took six months to get his rights back. The girl made $5000 on that picture.

"Maybe you can't see the way people admire you here, but I can see it. You have some really great friends." And in my world those weren't easy to come by.

"Not my dad. It's just never enough for him." His voice trailed off.

My dad always referred to Ricky's crying spells as "drunk honesty." And right now, Blake was swimming in that kind of raw honesty.

"I love her." He mumbled, sounding half asleep. "Cody won't take her too."

"Take who?" He had to be talking about Lindsay. But why would Cody want Lindsay? I squeezed a pillow to my chest. Why couldn't anyone just tell me what was going on? "Blake?"

But only steady breathing answered.

My screen flashed back to the menu like the call never happened. And I wished it hadn't. A million questions buzzed in my head, and every one of them had to do with Cody.

CODY

THE SMELL OF rubber and sweat greeted me the moment I walked into The Storm on Monday morning. This place had been my home for almost two years and yet marching to the gallows would be less terrifying. Two weeks had passed since Matt threw me out, and part of me wondered if he'd calmed down yet. Or if my absence made him regret ever taking a chance on me.

I spotted him watching two guys grappling inside the farthest ring. Hand on his chin, his eyes were locked on the match, no doubt analyzing their moves and strengths. Matt was always calculating strategy and gauging improvement. It's why he was the best. Why every time I wrestled him, I left a stronger fighter.

He ignored me when I invaded the space to his right. I deserved the silence, but it still stung. I assessed the guys in the ring: their height, their weight, their focus. The larger one was black as midnight and towered over his quick-footed opponent. But he was struggling and soon was stuck using sheer strength to stay off the rubber.

"He dropped his left shoulder too soon," I said. Only a raised eyebrow from Matt, but finally, an acknowledgement. "His foot placement was also sloppy. He used way more energy than necessary just to balance."

When the corner of Matt's mouth lifted, pride swelled in

my chest like air filling a balloon. "Very good. How's your sunburn?"

I raked a hand through my hair and gripped the back of my neck, wishing I could erase my stupidity. "It's all healed."

"Should be after two weeks." His words were edged in disappointment and judgment. Both of which I'd earned.

My pulse raced in my wrist, my fingers moving in and out of a fist to settle the slight tremble. "I wanna come back and train."

Matt slid his arms across his chest, a motion that had his forearm flexing. His face was a mask of indifference. Watching. Analyzing. Just like with the guys in the ring. "I thought you said you were just coasting the rest of the year."

I did say that. And he had every right to kick me out.

"I'm sorry," I said, but he didn't respond. I planted my feet. I didn't care if I had to stand there all day. I wouldn't let one careless morning overshadow how hard I'd worked. "Sorry for my attitude and for my mouth. I had no right to speak to you so disrespectfully. I let the pressure get to me."

We stared at each other for what seemed like a century. Matt held his body like a stone carving. "And who are you training for?"

"Me. Just me. I want to prove my worth as captain and win." Win state and my freedom.

He stepped forward. "The coach didn't choose you for captain because you won a bunch of trophies last year. He chose you because he saw something in here that mattered to the team." A stiff finger poked at my chest. "Character."

He was wrong. I'd spent the last year compromising everything about myself. But maybe one day he would be right.

"Are you still hanging out with those friends of yours? The

ones who like to skip school and break the law?"

I stared at the fighters taping their fingers. The answer was yes, but I wanted it to be no. I just needed time.

Matt sighed and moved toward the ring.

"It will be different this time," I promised in a rush. "I'll make sure it's different."

The cold expression slid off Matt's face and his tone softened. "Cody, you can't have your feet in two different houses. If you try, it's going to rip you in half." He stepped past me but didn't walk away. "Get in the ring and start stretching. I've had weeks to come up with new ways to torture you, and today's gonna hurt."

Relief unraveled the knots in my stomach. He was giving me a second chance.

SKYLAR

BLAKE WAITED BY my locker on Monday and covered his face when I approached. "Please tell me the five minute conversation I noticed on my phone this morning was me talking to your answering machine." He peeked through spread fingers.

I bit my lip and shook my head.

His hands dropped. "How embarrassed should I feel?"

"You shouldn't. It really was fine." I concentrated on turning the dial instead of glimpsing around Blake to watch Jill in her short denim skirt hanging all over Cody. Her brown hair was combed into a side braid, and I was sure she used a half pint of foundation on her face. I'd spent all weekend telling myself to forget him. That he was every bit the player Zoe said he was.

Blake rested his forearm on the locker and leaned in. "I'd like to make it up to you. Dinner? Maybe just the two of us this time?"

I manufactured a smile, but my stomach soured. "I told you, my parents would never let me." I'd started saying parents instead of dad. It made kids at school think I had two of them, and I liked how it sounded.

Blake's arm slowly dropped, but his face pinched into a scowl. "Do you always tell your folks everything?"

"I don't want to lie to them, if that's what you're implying." Despite the calm in my voice, there was a chill. "Especially when I know I'm the rebound girl."

He shifted his weight. "So, I guess I did screw things up with that phone call."

"No. I appreciated your honesty. But I think we both know you're not over Lindsay."

"But I want to be." His words came out so forcefully they had me backing away. "She walked away from us."

I rested my hand on his forearm. The muscle was tight and warm. "I didn't mean to upset you."

"No, it's not you." His shoulders relaxed, and his finger touched the ends of my hair. "You're perfect. And, if it's at all possible, I'd like another chance. Friends who might become more?"

The look on his face was hard to refuse: the unguarded vulnerability, the cringing embarrassment, the sudden apprehension of a possible rejection. I spotted Henry talking with two seniors in the hallway. Something Blake made possible. Maybe I was passing judgment too quickly. "Okay. Friends."

"But maybe more?"

Blake did puppy dog eyes really well and I caved. "Okay, maybe more."

"Thank you. So listen, I have to take care of something. Tell Ms. Yarnell I'm in the office."

"Okay."

He took off in a fast walk, leaving me a clear view of Cody at his locker. Jill was gone, thankfully, but the questions lingered.

Cody spotted me, and the corners of his mouth lifted. I didn't want his smile. It made my stomach flutter and my cheeks warm. He moved casually, crossing the space that separated us in three easy strides. "Two outstanding songs. You are redeemed."

His casualness bothered me, like he'd done nothing wrong. "I sent you those days ago." *Before I heard about Lindsay.*

"Yes. And I had to give them each proper air time before I made my decision." He motioned for us to move.

He was acting differently. Not holding back. And he met my eyes every time we spoke. We weren't touching, but the electricity between us could have zapped innocent bystanders. Stupid chemistry. I'd always hated that subject.

"I have one for you, too," He shifted closer, and the heat of his body wrapped around mine. He smelled like hot, delicious cinnamon. Ugh. He was intoxicating. "I'll text it later."

"Why not now?" There was a challenge in my words. A demand to know what was going on between us. Because I wasn't blind, and I wasn't crazy.

His voice lowered to a whisper that sent chills down my spine. "Wouldn't want the Madison spies to know my secrets." There was nothing light about the way he said it. In fact, his tone hummed a warning.

"What secret do you have that's bigger than mine?"

My words hung in the air a second before Cody's eyes aligned with mine. "Listen to my song. It's all right there."

Heads turned when we walked into class together, and Chugger lasered a stone-cold stare at Cody all the way to our seats. Something had definitely happened this weekend.

The SMART board lit up with a map of Eastern Europe. I turned around to listen to Ms. Yarnell, but the whispers between Chugger and Cody behind me had my ears straining to hear them instead.

"You brought her home? Are you insane?" Chugger hissed.

"I did him a favor."

"How?"

Cody didn't answer, but the hair on my neck stood up as if both guys were both watching me.

Blake strolled into class minutes later with an apology and a pass from the office. He squeezed my shoulder and sat down.

By the time Ms. Yarnell began passing around the usual sheets, the tension at our table was suffocating. Blake glared at Cody, who refused to engage in a staring contest. I was grateful it was my turn to write. I wanted this horrible moment to disappear, but I also wanted to know what Cody was doing with Lindsay.

Time ticked on. They didn't speak. They barely moved in their seats while I was as restless as a two-year-old in church. I tried to focus on writing four reasons why Communism failed, but could hardly think past the aggression bouncing around our silent table.

"Boys, are you helping Skylar with the work? This is a group effort." Ms. Yarnell's question stilled me. The fact she noticed, said it all. Only one of us ever did the work.

The guys huffed and moaned, but eventually leaned on the table.

"What's the next question?" Cody asked, obviously preferring to help than to engage in conversation with Blake.

"I've got a question." The hate in Blake's voice froze my hand above the half-completed paper.

"And what's that?" Cody's exasperated words flew across the table, wrapped around Blake's fierce expression and settled like a stone in the pit of my stomach.

"How does a guy stab his friend in the back and not feel remorse? Doesn't even call the next day to apologize?"

Cody ignored the stab-in-the-back comment. "I just took her home. I knew she was bothering you, and you didn't want her there."

Cody and Blake had an entire conversation with their eyes, and the already stifling temperature rose again. With a squeak of his chair, Blake was suddenly next to me.

"Whatcha got left?" Blake leaned in until our cheeks practically touched.

Cody's hand clenched, but he quickly slid it into his lap. "We've only got ten more minutes."

A tickle from Blake pierced my side and I flinched.

"Number four is Bulgaria," he said before adding, "and you smell like sunshine." His hand slowly came off my waist and hung over the back of my chair.

I took a deep breath and tried not to wish that Blake and Cody would trade places.

Epic fail.

CODY

A BOILING PRESSURE usually only reserved for wrestling matches knocked inside my stomach. He touched her, often, and each time with more familiarity.

Blake and I crossed gazes, and that cocky grin appeared on his face. Like he knew how I felt, but didn't see me as a contender. And that was good. He couldn't prepare for a battle he didn't know was coming.

The bell rang and Blake grabbed Skylar's bag. She hesitated, and it was all the hope I needed. Maybe she could see it—the corruption and the lies. I wanted to end the pretense right then, but it wasn't the time yet. I had to be smart and cunning, just like the guy at her side.

I focused on the pain across my pecs from the two hundred pushups Matt made me do in the gym and stood to leave.

Chugger slammed his books on the table, his eyes pierced mine. "Meet us out back before lunch. You know where."

"Fine."

Blake had shown me the hidden cove two weeks after we won against Clearview High our junior year. The entire team was there except the freshmen, each with a Dixie cup of vodka. I remembered feeling special, like I was a part of something grand. I sucked down the shot without blinking, and that was the start of my acceptance.

I didn't know at the time that shot meant giving up my

soul.

Life Skills didn't require books, so I skipped watching Blake fawn over Skylar at her locker. I had to find a way to be alone with her. To gauge if she was everything my mind imagined or if the draw was deeper. Her father. The music.

A loud crash forced my head to whip around. Lindsay stood frozen in the hallway, her books and pens scattered in a halo around her.

"Oops, sorry," the girl said sweetly, coughing the word 'slut' at the end of her fake apology. Her giggle as she stepped over the papers and books was enough to make my ears burn.

Lindsay began picking up her stuff, but a few passing students kicked them out of her reach.

I grabbed the shirt of the guy who'd just sent her algebra book sailing. "Go back and pick it up."

His eyes widened in fear. "Okay, Cody, I was just kidding around."

"Well, it's not funny." I released his shirt with a murderous glare, shoving him toward the book. I knelt next to Lindsay as she gathered the scattered materials. No one else messed with her. Instead, they made their way down the hall with haughty glances, sidestepping the mess. Students' loud voices became judgmental whispers as Lindsay and I worked to gather her supplies.

"This is Blake's doing," she whispered while blinking back tears. "He called four times yesterday, and I didn't pick up the phone."

This girl had a bad habit of giving me information I didn't want. Information that made holding my tongue nearly impossible. I looked at the cold linoleum under my knees and pulled us both upright. The warning bell rang seconds ago and staying here with Lindsay would get me more than just a tardy slip.

"You good?" I felt guilty for not offering more.

She steadied her shoulders, a pretense of confidence that didn't match the pale, gloomy shadow across her face. "I'll be fine. Thanks. You keep coming to my rescue." She looked up and her eyes were like shards of sapphires: crystal clear but tormented in an alarming way. They held more secrets I didn't want to know.

BLAKE AND CHUGGER waited for me at my locker before lunch, a clear sign they didn't trust I'd show on my own. I'd crossed Blake, and now it was time to take the punishment. Like Lindsay.

"Let's go." Blake's voice was a harsh, low, grinding buzz against my skin.

I followed, like the well-trained dog I wanted him to believe I still was.

We continued past the old theater, the grass and shrubs manicured to Madison's pristine expectations, and rounded the corner to the most secluded part of the building. The part with loud air conditioning units and two large dumpsters. The place hidden in the shadows, so no one could see its ugliness. Or the ugliness that happened here on a regular basis.

Blake cracked his knuckles and stretched his neck. I wondered if this was going to be his version of a woodshed beating until he locked his arms tightly across his chest.

"Obviously, we need to establish ground rules when it comes to Lindsay."

I didn't say a word, which seemed perfectly fine to him.

"I don't want you talking to her or defending her." His eyes locked on mine. "Or giving her rides home. You understand?"

My hands itched, my nerves burned along my arms. "I understand."

"Chugger says you thought you were doing me a favor. Explain."

I wanted to punch that smirk off his face. I didn't. "I was just thinking of how all of that would look to Skylar. You yelling and carrying on about your ex-girlfriend." Even then, the word "ex" made his jaw clench. "I had your back, man." I couldn't tell if he believed me or not, but I kept my face steady, a mask of respect.

Blake stepped closer and spoke through his teeth. "What did she say about me when you took her home?"

"Nothing. We didn't talk."

Blake kept his eyes locked on mine. There was no trust in them. "It's time for you to pick a side, Cody. You're either in the circle or you're out. Something's up with you this year, and I'm done putting up with your hormo—."

I cut him off. "I'm in." *Until I take you down.*

Blake glanced at Chugger and curved his lips into a victorious grin. "Then you won't mind proving it."

Every inch of my skin went taunt. "What do you want me to do?"

"I'll let you know when the time is right."

I pushed out the suffocating wind and tried not to recoil from Blake's friendly slap. I'd play his little game and document every word from his lying, wicked mouth.

SKYLAR

HENRY AND ZOE waited by my locker after third period, Zoe talking a mile a minute. Henry listened to her animated chatter, interjecting a few nods or "uh-huhs" whenever she stopped talking long enough to wait for his response. He seemed different. Relaxed, happy, and almost stylish. The jeans were looser and the right length. The shirt was still a short-sleeved button up, but at least the pens were gone from the pocket.

"Ready for lunch?" he asked me in a lighthearted tone that was becoming common.

I halted in front of them. "Sure."

Zoe trembled with excitement and latched onto my arm. We'd only seen each other in passing today, and her bugged-out eyes screamed she was bursting to tell me something. "You and I need to use the ladies room. Right now."

I heard the side doors click, and suddenly Blake and Chugger were walking toward our little group. No Cody.

"We'd better move if we're going to eat anything," Blake said.

"We'll meet you in there." Zoe tugged on my arm and practically dragged me to the closest restroom.

"What is going on with you?" I asked.

She did a quick check under the stalls and, once satisfied there were no listeners, took a preparatory breath. "Lindsay went to that party on Friday night and threw herself at Blake. He pushed her off, said he only wanted you." Her eyes went doughy. "Isn't that so sweet? Of course, Cody tries to be the hero. Consoles her. Brings her home. He acts like it's okay that she cheated on Blake. I don't know. Part of me wonders if there's something going on between the two of them. Cody's a risk taker, but he's not that stupid. Or maybe he is."

The stab-in-the-back comment from first period. Blake's jumbled words on the phone about Cody taking everything, and Cody's casual reference of spies knowing his secrets. A sharp pain of some distant emotion hit me in the heart. "How do you know all this? I thought you weren't going."

"I didn't have to be there. It was only topic discussed in first and second periods. Not really, but seriously, there's hardly anyone who *doesn't* know about it."

I closed my eyes against the stinging pressure in my sinuses.

"Skylar, honey, you're upset. Why?" Zoe rushed over and wrapped her arms around me and hugged me. "Blake is over Lindsay. You should be happy."

"Can I tell you something?" I whispered, a slight plea in my voice because I was desperate to tell someone.

She released me and stepped back. "Sure."

"I think I like Cody. Not Blake." The words gave me freedom from my cage. The one nugget of truth in the sea of lies at this school. But Zoe's mortification clipped my wings.

"You cannot like Cody." Her tone was a combination of disappointment and scolding, but not surprise.

I walked over to the mirror and pretended to check my makeup. "I know you're not a fan, but he makes me…" *Burn from the inside out. Takes me up and down with just one smile.* "Feel different. Special."

Zoe stood next to me and leaned against the sink. "That's how he makes all the girls feel. Why do you think Vicky Donner cried over him all last year? And why do you think Jill Spencer, who can have any guy at this school, is okay with only being a bed warmer? He's that tortured, disconnected, hot guy. Every girl thinks she's going to be the one he falls for."

"What if it's just his image?" I thought of my dad. "What if he's playing a part on stage?"

"Well, Skylar, then he deserves a Tony award because I've seen Cody in action, and he cannot be trusted."

My chin fell. I studied the droplets of water left in the sink basin.

Zoe wrapped an arm around my shoulders and squeezed. "You and Blake are right for each other."

For all the bad blood between Zoe and that crowd, she seemed to worship Blake and Chugger. It didn't make sense. "Why do you hate the rest of them and not Blake? He's like their ringleader."

She shrugged. "I don't know. I guess I feel like Blake got betrayed by Lindsay and deserves a happy ending. And Chugger's nice to everyone. I've never heard either of them bash people behind their backs. I guess I respect them. And I think you're fabulous, so, of course, I'd want the two of you together."

This conversation wasn't going anywhere. Zoe and I had two different views of the same people, and I wasn't about to let that damage the only real friendship I'd ever had. "Okay. Just forget I said anything."

She gave a smile of approval, and we walked toward the door right as Lindsay stumbled in. She froze when she saw us.

It was the first time I'd seen her up close. Dainty features surrounded by silky, blond hair. Stunning. She studied us, but her eyes remained lifeless. Two blue pools that locked away any story I might have gained from them.

She extended her hand to me. "I'm Lindsay Clark. I've seen you around but didn't have the chance to introduce myself yet." Her hand was warm and her grip light.

"Skylar."

"I know. I've heard." Her tone didn't imply meanness, but Zoe stiffened next to me.

"We have to go. *Blake* is waiting for her at *our* table." It was odd to hear the malice in Zoe's voice. "In the meantime, try to stay out of the backseat of cars."

I was too shocked for manners. Zoe pushed me out into the hallway, and my wits came slamming back the minute the bathroom door shut. "Zoe! That was unbelievably cruel." I was tempted to walk back in an apologize to Lindsay, even though a part of me hated her for being so pretty and for riding in Cody's truck.

"Trust me. She's the enemy."

"She's still a person."

"A person who pretended to be my friend, and then laughed when Jill called me a social climbing heifer just because I sat at their table. Come on, Skylar, you know girls like her. They parade under fake smiles but will turn on you in an instant. She's the mean girl, not me." Zoe's voice trembled as a year's worth of pain spilled from her mouth.

I pulled her into a hug. She was only trying to protect me. "I'm sorry they hurt you."

Zoe offered a weak smile. "It doesn't matter now. Everything has changed this year. A toast to karma."

I doubted karma had anything to do with it. "Let's just go

to lunch. I'm sure we've missed some grand story from Chugger."

Zoe's face burst with life and color. She'd never admitted to her crush on Blake's best friend, but I knew if he ever asked, she'd say yes in a millisecond.

I thought back to Cody. I would probably do the same. I guess that made me just like all the other poor girls who pined over the one they couldn't have. Maybe normal was closer than I thought.

CODY

JOEY'S GAZE FOLLOWED me as I took my seat in the back of Ms. Bakerfield's class, the seat I'd abandoned last week. He was spying on me again. Ready to report back to Blake if I so much as raised my phone to text Skylar in class. Like I'd be that stupid after this weekend.

But I needed something. A look. A smile. An accidental touch.

Jill's hand slid across my arm right before she took the empty chair next to mine. "Hey, handsome." I bit my tongue. It wasn't a coincidence that Jill decided to switch seats. Of that, I was positive.

Skylar walked through the door, and my temperature spiked. Everything about her was beautiful to me, but her profile could be immortalized in art. The slope of her neck, the slight lift in her dainty nose, how her green eyes popped against her fair skin.

She didn't look my way and, instead, took a seat next to Stoner. That wasn't his name, but long, scraggly hair and the leather jacket he wore, even in a hundred degree weather, earned him that title. His reclusiveness and the headphones permanently jammed into his ears didn't help the image.

Skylar introduced herself, and they spoke for a few seconds. He offered her one of his ear buds, a gesture I'd never seen him make before. She accepted and then rocked her head back and forth.

What was with that girl? She was like a magnet for misfits and outcasts. Or maybe she was just a magnet for everyone. It made sense. Her father had captivated an entire generation, and she was now captivating every person at Madison High.

Ms. Bakerfield came in and slammed the door.

Skylar returned the earpiece to its owner, but not without a smile that could melt the polar ice caps. My stomach burned. I didn't want to be the one on the outside watching. I wanted inside in her head. I wanted to figure out how she could so easily fit in a world where labels and status dictated happiness and security.

Jill leaned over. "Still pining, I see."

Yes. "Not at all."

She pulled back and whispered, "Yeah, right."

I SAT ON a bench in Veteran's Park, staring at the empty play set. Two of the four streetlights were out, casting shadows along the pebbled area. They matched the shadows in my mind. I hadn't been here in two years. Not since I walked from the locker room in a daze, pants dripping with toilet water, lip split open and ribs bruised.

Blake had given me the loyalty assignment during wrestling practice. It wasn't big. I just had to "accidentally" spill chocolate milk on a snotty sophomore girl who called one of our teammates "brain deficient" in class. Never mind that Toby was a walking imbecile and probably deserved her comment. Rules were rules, and no one badmouthed the wrestling team. The spill was to happen in two weeks. On picture day. Biggest impact, and enough time so that it didn't look like retaliation.

Another brilliant set up by the king of the school.

I continued to watch the swings sway in the breeze and wished for the same clarity that came after I stood from the locker room floor. The clarity that said no matter what, I would no longer be a victim. I wondered what that naïve kid would think if he knew he'd one day become the bully.

Pounding a fist on the empty space next to me, I contemplated how I would get out of this mess. I needed Blake to screw up just once. To give me one piece of evidence I could use to buy my freedom.

I pressed my back against the bench's hard wood, stretched my legs out in front of me, and texted the one person keeping me sane.

Me: *What were you listening to in class?*

There was no response, but I sensed she was reading.

Me: *From the head banging, I would guess Steel Panther.*

Me: *Or maybe Fall Out Boy? Come on, I need a new song.*

A bubble finally appeared.

Skylar: *I'm still trying to figure out the one you sent me.*

I'd been telling myself I didn't care that she hadn't responded after I sent a song that bared my soul. But right then, I knew it was a lie. I wanted her to know me. Wanted her to see past the music.

Me: *You're in the stillness.*

Skylar: *That doesn't help.*

Me: *It's all you're getting. Keep listening. I lost sleep picking out that song for you.*

Skylar: *Really?*

Oh, if she only knew how much time she'd already consumed. How much time I spent thinking about her, wanting her, hating myself for letting Blake have her.

Me: *At least an hour. :)*

Skylar: *So why weren't you at lunch?*

Because I can't see Blake touch you without wanting to slam his head into the table.

Me: *Last minute homework*

Skylar: *Slacker*

Me: *I know. So, my song?*

Skylar: *You'll have to earn it.*

Me: *How?*

Skylar: *Eat with us tomorrow.*

The girl had no idea what she did to me. No idea how hard it was to hide my feelings when she simply bit her lip or twirled a lock of hair.

Me: *What about Blake?*

Skylar: *What about Lindsay and Jill?*

Me: *Not interested*

Skylar: *Me either*

And with those words, the shadows suddenly became a burst of color.

Me: *I'll be there, then.*

I was walking into a landmine, and I didn't even care.

SKYLAR

MY DAD WAS lounging on the couch when I came down for breakfast. His cheeks were sunken, and his shoulder blades protruded through his t-shirt. He was still losing weight, despite my aunt's attempts to keep us supplied with gluten-free food that would supposedly not upset his stomach.

"Hey, you're up early." I'd gone from seeing my dad all day to spurts of time in-between naps.

"I wanted to see you before school. Sorry I conked out so early yesterday."

I slid next to him. "Don't apologize for being tired, Daddy. Your body is fighting, so give it whatever it needs."

He glanced at the ceiling, and the weight of the world seemed to be resting on his face. "Maybe it's time to stop." Defeat was the only sound out of his mouth.

My heart beat against my rib cage. "No. You can't quit. You can't." Tears stung my eyes, and my dad wrapped me up in a tight, bony hug.

"Don't cry, Princess. I'm sorry I said anything."

"No. I want you to talk to me, but I don't want you to give up. Is Aunt Josephine trying to convince you to stop? Because I will happily take over. I'll quit school right now. I mean it."

"Nobody's quitting. Me or you. It was just a stupid statement in a dark moment."

"You promise?"

He kissed my forehead as an answer, but it didn't bring me any relief.

"Speaking of school. How is it going?"

"It's fine." I didn't want to talk about school. I wanted him to allow me to help him. I wanted my father to trust me like he used to before North Carolina and my stupid aunt.

"That tells me absolutely nothing."

Sucks doesn't it.

"Skylar, please. Give me something."

Fine. No matter how frustrated I was with my father's refusal to let me help, I wouldn't add to his stress. "I'm really happy there. Zoe is awesome, and I'm a part of a 'group,' believe it or not."

My dad adjusted his fuzzy blanket. "So, when am I going to meet this Zoe?"

I studied the lines in my palms. "We talked about this."

"You said you didn't want to tell anyone before you had a chance to let them get to know you." He lifted my chin, his brows pinched. "I want to be a part of your life. Even this new one."

And I want to be a part of yours. But time had shown me we don't always get what we want. If we did, there would no dead mom or no dad with cancer. No "can we meet the band?" or stories sold to the highest magazine bidder.

I understood that he was protecting me. I was protecting him too. "Let's get you better first. Then we'll see who can be invited into our little world."

My dad caressed my hair like he did when I was little and scared of the boogeyman. "Not everyone will betray you. At some point, you have to start trusting outsiders again."

"Yeah, like Ricky did with his girlfriend who photoshopped

you with a stripper? Think about it. One word to the media, and your cancer will be the hottest news on TV. Not to mention Facebook and Twitter."

My dad cringed. "I miss the days before the Internet."

I wouldn't know. The Internet had been the enemy my entire life.

CODY

IF SKYLAR'S IDEA of earning my song meant torture and agony, then she succeeded. Somehow lunch had become three of us, with me being the third wheel.

"Where's Chugger?" I asked.

"He needed tutoring this afternoon." Blake reached up and moved Skylar's hair off her shoulder. She startled, and he quickly added, "It was getting in your food."

I forced my eyes off his hands, reminding myself to play the game. "Since when does Chugger need tutoring? He's a boy genius."

Blake shrugged. "I'm not his keeper. Maybe he's with Henry. They do have Western Lit together." He reached out, his hand hovering over my fries. "You done?"

I pushed the tray over with more force than intended. Something was off. Chugger hanging with Henry? Not in this lifetime.

"And Zoe? Doesn't she usually eat with you guys?" Not that I liked her. At all. But this situation felt way too constructed.

Skylar picked small pieces from her sandwich. "She wasn't feeling good. Went home after second period."

"Did you hear Clearview is ranked number two this year? Some talk that they could beat us." Blake mashed the stolen fries in his ketchup.

"Not a chance." My tension eased slightly. I could talk wrestling. Wresting was safe.

Blake snorted. "That's what I said." He turned to Skylar, offered one of his smiles that often resulted in rosy cheeks and giggles. "What about you, beautiful? You gonna come watch us sweep the state this year?"

Sure enough, her skin flushed, marred the softness in her face. She glanced my way; a motion Blake didn't miss. "I don't know. Maybe."

The silence became strained, edgy. I stood, my momentum so abrupt, the chair screeched against the tile and wobbled. I couldn't sit there and not look into those eyes. And if I looked into those eyes, Blake would know I wasn't playing by the rules.

"You're leaving?" Skylar scanned the empty seats around us. The hurt and confusion on her face were even worse than this morning when I ignored her during first period.

"Yeah. There's something I've got to do."

"See ya around, man," Blake said. I sensed his approval, as if I'd just realized this was all some grand scheme to get Skylar alone. Knowing Blake, that was exactly what it was.

I pushed through the cafeteria doors with frustration. Nowhere to go and twenty minutes left for lunch. Without thinking, I stomped toward the gym. Weights, pain, sweat. Those were all things I could control.

A soft sob echoed on the other side of the basketball court, and I froze. It was a girl's cry, but Fatty James still burst from the crevices of my mind. His wails were always the loudest.

I moved toward the sound of whimpering.

Lindsay sat crumpled in the corner outside the girl's locker room, her face buried in her knees.

Run, run, run. I crouched and gentled my voice. "Something happen?"

"I'm on the Torments List. I hadn't looked at it in so long that I never realized..." She wiped at tears that wouldn't stop. "I've probably been on there for weeks."

Chugger's comment popped in my mind. *The List.* The one he said I was better off not knowing about. "What's the Torments List?"

She took out her phone and started tapping. She zoomed in, put in a password and handed it to me.

I'd never seen the website, but it was clearly for Madison. Our crest was on the banner with the title. Five discussion threads were available, each with someone's name on it. I recognized Lindsay's, and the sophomore girl who bashed Toby, but not the other three.

A suffocating pressure built in my chest with each comment I read. They were cruel and disgusting. Lily, the sophomore, had twenty comments about the chocolate milk plan. Date, time, what to say after it happened. How long to moo at her when she walked down the hall. All planned. All calculated viciousness that would hurt her for years.

I looked up, my throat so tight I couldn't swallow. "How did you know about this?"

"I've known since we started high school." Her face fell as if a judge declared her guilty. "You were on the Torments List for a long time. Up until you made the wrestling team." She turned away. "They posted pictures of what happened to you."

The pressure was now constricting my airway. I pushed a palm hard against my sternum to ease the gripping pain. All those years I'd suffered. All those nights I'd lay in bed and wondered why people hated me so much. All those times I hated myself. All because of a stupid list. Some teenage joke taken too far.

"Whose site is this?" I choked out the words, tried to push away the memories.

Her shoulders rose and fell. "No one knows. It's been around forever. If you're chosen, a password is texted to you from the site, anonymously. Anyone can post within the threads, but it's a mystery who adds or deletes the names."

I continued to read through the filth until Lindsay put her hand on my arm and squeezed. Her light touch and anxious eyes showed the sacrifice. I'd never seen her touch anyone but Blake. "I'm sorry, Cody. If I ever made you feel…like this."

"It's okay," I whispered. But nothing felt okay. Everything felt like pounding misery. I handed back the phone. "I'm telling Principal Rayburn. He'd never let this continue."

Her voice lowered, hushed and serious. "You can't. It's been turned in before. They simply take down the site, and then it pops up again on another domain with new passwords. The last guy who turned it in ended up withdrawing from school." She shook her head. "It's not worth it."

"We have to do something."

She leaned against the wall and closed her eyes, defeat showing in the set of her shoulders. "What can we do? It's the Internet."

SKYLAR

I PARKED MY Mustang in one of the three spots left in the school parking lot and tried to focus on the positives: Friday. Date night.

Because the negatives were piling up.

Daddy hadn't come out of his room last night or this morning. Cody hadn't sent me a text in two days or even talked to me with more than a few grunts. And Zoe was pushing me to go on another group date with Blake, her and Chugger.

I grabbed my backpack, did a quick makeup check and barely slid into my seat before the first period bell rang.

Ms. Yarnell gave me "the look" and defeat ripped through my shoulders.

Great.

I blew a piece hair out of my face and faced the three boys at my table.

The sight of Cody's disheveled brown hair made my heart ache. The guy was strikingly handsome and didn't even know it. A tight gray t-shirt pulled against his chest under an unzipped hoodie. His clothing choices were simple, a complete contrast to the complexity of his personality. Cody had become my obsession, my fascination and my misery all at the same time.

"Hey," I said with a longing I couldn't hide.

Cody studied some non-existent spot on the table. "Morning."

His flat, aloof tone worsened my foul mood.

Blake scooted his chair closer to mine. "Blue is definitely your color. You sure I can't talk you into coming with me tonight?" He, too, was beautiful, but the appeal ended there. And even with our new "friends" talk, I didn't want to be alone with him.

"Nope. Fridays are off limits. Sorry."

Ms. Yarnell began her lecture and our conversation ceased.

Blake's hot breath brushed my neck. "Saturday, then?" he whispered.

His closeness made me want to cringe, and I wondered if he'd always been this annoying and why I didn't see it before. "Maybe another weekend?"

His hand brushed mine. "I'm going to hold you to that."

Great. As far as blow-off lines go, that was the most ineffective one ever.

When the lecture ended, Cody passed the discussion sheet to Blake. "Your turn."

Blake slid the paper between us. "Why don't you help me with this today since you struggled last time."

Chugger snickered, but didn't say anything.

I looked up at Cody, and the frustration and confusion I'd felt all morning crushed me further. If emptiness could be an expression, Cody had mastered the art.

"Do what you want," he said, avoiding eye contact with me.

Heat inched up my neck and into my cheeks. He was dismissing me…again. And worse, he practically gave Blake a green light to move closer.

The minutes dragged on forever, but finally the bell rang. I bolted. Needing space. Needing my dad. Needing Cody to stop being so frustrating.

Zoe watched as I furiously shoved books into my locker. "What's wrong with you?"

"Nothing." *My world has exploded and no one cares.*

She flinched. "Okay, fine. Sorry I asked." With a slam of her own locker, Zoe walked away.

Remorse seeped in. I was spewing my bad mood over everyone.

I ducked into a corner and pulled out my phone. My father's voicemail answered.

"Hi, Daddy, I just wanted to say good morning. I missed seeing you. I hope you are feeling better. I'll be home around four-thirty, and we can plan our night together. Nothing big. We can just lay around if that's all you're up for." I let my hand fall to my side and refused to consider a life without him. He'd win. He had to.

The empty halls matched the hollowness in my heart, bringing tears past my dam of denial. I ran down the hall to the bathroom, locked myself in a stall, and buried my head in my knees.

I kept it there until I could breathe.

I STOOD OUTSIDE my father's bedroom and knocked lightly. "Daddy? I'm home."

A loud bang like something was dropped and hushed voices were the only response. I knocked again, harder this time. "Daddy, are you okay?" I checked the knob. Locked. I smacked the wood with both hands. "Daddy. Let me in! Let me in!" I screamed as panic clawed up my spine.

The door opened, and I stepped back. Aunt Josephine. She slowly closed the door behind her and stood there like a guard at Buckingham Palace. "Skylar, your father is very sick. He's not going to be up for anything tonight."

Adrenaline pumped though my bloodstream. I wanted to hurt her, which should have made me feel guilty, but didn't. "You're always doing this. You're always trying to keep us apart." I pushed forward, but she gripped my shoulders, halting me.

"I'm not doing this. The cancer is. And you have to accept that things will not be what they used to be."

I detangled myself from her hold. "You don't think I know that? My entire life is different! I just want to make sure he's okay." I was so angry her face faded out and then came back into focus. My breath was broken and loud like a bull released from its pen.

She must have noticed because for a moment, she hesitated. I thought she might move and let me see my father. But instead her voice turned firmer. "I'm sorry, Skylar, but he doesn't want you to see him like this."

I flexed my hands, then squeezed them, hiding the way they trembled. He wanted her. Not me. Trusted her. Not me. And I knew my aunt well enough to know she'd fall dead before letting me pass. I darted back to my room and slammed the door. Throwing myself on the bed, I let all the rage come out, with loud, ugly sobs. Shoulders shaking, I curled into a ball. I tried to pray, tried to understand the cruelty of this test God was putting me through. I found no clarity. No relief.

Tears soon gave way to exhaustion, and I fell asleep only to be startled awake two hours later by a new text.

Cody: *You okay? You seemed upset all day.*

Me: *I'm surprised you noticed, with ignoring me and all.*

My snootiness should have made me feel better, but it didn't. I set down the phone and walked into the bathroom to clean up. The skin around my eyes was red and puffy. The only mascara not smudged on my pillow was smeared across my face. I splashed cold water until my skin was clear and then returned to my phone. I was too tired to play games tonight.

Cody: *I'm sorry. It wasn't you. My head's a mess right now.*

Me: *Yeah. Mine too.*

Cody: *Maybe this will help.*

Seconds later, a new song appeared in our conversation. I played it, letting the electric guitar and powerful lyrics offer an escape.

Cody: *Forgive me?*

I wanted to stay mad at Cody, but I just didn't have the energy for it, especially when he sent me songs that tore into my heart like a bulldozer. The air began to thin, the heavy burden getting lighter. I'd grown up around music. It was part of my culture, as essential as water. My father had instilled in me a love for the classics and a respect for any artist who could make a guitar sing. Then again, my father was considered one of the greatest guitar players in the world.

Me: *Yes. But only because you know good music.*

Cody: *Years of isolation will do that to you.*

Me: *You? I doubt that.*

Cody: *So, what are you and your dad doing tonight?*

Me: *Change of plans. No date.*

I didn't say how much typing those words hurt. How betrayed I felt by my father's unwillingness to let me be a part of his suffering.

Cody: *I can stand in for your dad. Meet me at Veteran's Park? It's two blocks from school.*

Me: *I've seen it. I'm not in a great mood, though.*

Cody: *I'll bring food…*

A heartbeat of hope. A night alone with Cody. A chance to see the real him. To understand him. I already knew my answer.

Me: *Are you trying to bribe me? Do you think I'm really that easily swayed?*

Yes. Yes, I am.

Cody: *They are seriously great burgers.*

Me: *Well, in that case, how can I refuse? But, no onions. I draw the line there.*

Cody: *Why? Expecting a good night kiss?*

A parade of butterflies hit my stomach; my fingers froze over the keys.

Cody: *j/k. See you in ten.*

Me: *ok.*

The screen on my phone went dark.

I was really doing this.

I slipped on jeans and grabbed my favorite t-shirt from the closet. My hands twitched with nervous energy while I quickly touched-up my face.

The hall was silent now. Hollow.

My fist hovered at my father's bedroom door. I wanted to knock, but my hand dropped along with my heart, and I settled for scribbling him a note in the kitchen.

Part of me knew I shouldn't be leaving. Not only was it totally against his rules, but also what if Guardzilla went home and he needed me?

But something equally strong pulled me to the front door. To a possibility that in the midst of madness, normalcy did exist.

Glancing up toward his room one more time, I whispered, "I miss you, Daddy," and shut the door behind me.

CODY

MEETING SKYLAR COULD threaten all my plans, but I didn't care. I'd been obsessively watching the List, writing down login IDs and trying to pair them up with the actions they took at school. So far, I had ten confirmed names, but not any from the inner circle. I needed Blake to do something. But none of the comments or actions were his. Just those made by his stupid minions.

Skylar's Mustang was already there when I pulled up to Veteran's Park. It was dusk, but I still didn't like her out there by herself. I parked my truck and jumped out with the sack of food, nearly dropping the bag when she stood from the picnic table. Her smile could have lit up the streets of New York.

A rush of heat fell over me. She looked great. Better than great. Gorgeous. The near-tears defeat she wore all day had disappeared, and a huge part of me hoped I had something to do with the change.

"Sorry I'm late. The burger joint took longer than usual."

"No worries. It's beautiful out here." She sat back down and stretched out her legs. "Thanks for this. I needed it tonight." Eyes closed, she tilted her face toward the sky. A soft breeze blew a few strands of hair around her cheeks.

My gaze moved lower. Her ripped jeans perfectly fit her hips, and a Skylar Wyld t-shirt molded her figure, yet it didn't flaunt her body like some shirts other girls at school wore. She was sexy without trying, and it only added to the appeal.

She opened one eye. "Are you going to sit?"

"Oh. Yeah." I wanted to slam a palm to my head. She'd just caught me checking her out. I cleared my throat. "Um. I like your shirt. I've never seen that style."

She bit her lip, no doubt resisting the urge to laugh at my not so subtle ogling. "They didn't release it to the public, only the band. My dad has about a million if you want one."

"Sure. Thanks." I offered her the burger, and an electric current passed when my hand grazed hers. Everything felt elevated tonight. We were alone. Just the two us, and I now had no idea what to say.

Skylar took dainty bites of her burger while silence covered us like a blanket.

"This is goo…" she said the same time I blurted, "Do you like…"

"I'm sorry. Go ahead." I wanted to punch myself in the face for not having more game.

"Um, nothing. I was just going to say that these are good. I'll mark them on my take-out list."

Our eyes met and heat inched up my neck.

She giggled. "This is so awkward."

"I told you I was shy." I ran a hand through my hair.

"I thought you were kidding."

I focused on the setting sun, silently cursing Fatty James for surfacing at the worst time. My phone vibrated in my pocket.

Skylar: *Is this better?*

Her back was to me.

"Very funny. Turn around."

She did, her green eyes sparkling like jewels in moonlight.

"Just checking. It seems the minute we're face to face, you pull back. I won't bite, I promise." As if to kill the last ounce of self-control I had, she bit down into her food, keeping her eyes locked on mine. I'd never been so jealous of a cheeseburger in my life.

She wiped her mouth with a napkin. "Have you always been a fan of my father's band? Or were your parents groupies?"

"My parents?" The idea was ludicrous. "No, they're more the classical music type. Very serious, very intellectual."

"Do you guys get along?"

"Yeah, they're cool. They work too much, but they still try to attend my matches when they can." It was hard to explain my relationship with my parents. Close, but still detached. "We've always kind of done our own thing, you know?"

"So, you're an only child, too?"

"Yep. Just me."

She wrapped up the rest of her burger and tossed it into the trash bin nearby. "Wanna swing?" She ran over to a swing set that looked one ride away from the metal graveyard.

"Um, sure." I ate the last piece of my burger and followed. The chains screeched in protest when my large body dropped onto the faded strap of plastic next to her.

She pumped her feet, throwing her head back as she glided through the air. Long red hair flew in the breeze and almost touched her lower back. Two flip-flops suddenly went flying. "I bet I can go higher than you," she called out as her swing rushed past mine.

"No way. I've got least seventy pounds on you." And those extra pounds could not seem to get moving on this thing.

"Which makes me lighter, like a bird."

She made me feel like a bird. Light. Pressure-free. Invincible. I pumped my legs harder to keep up with her. Right when I'd stretched just a little further, she jumped and my stomach followed.

Skylar hit the ground with so much force, her body fell over from the momentum, tumbling a couple feet before she stopped.

I was at her side in an instant. "Are you okay? Did you hurt yourself?"

Laughter stole her voice, but other than that, she was totally fine. I dropped down on the sand, willing my heart to stop racing.

She shook my shoulder. "Cody, you are waayyy too serious. Lighten up."

"You jumped like twelve feet."

"I had to win." She shrugged as if flinging herself off high objects was a daily routine. Maybe it was.

Skylar found her flip-flops and slipped them back on. She offered me her hand, tugging until I stood too. Her cheeks were flushed with pink, and her hair encircled her face like the glow around the sun.

I was hypnotized. She was my fire goddess again, ready to destroy and restore all of me. The heat and energy pulled me closer, and my hands found her waist. Her chest rose and fell, while our eyes stayed locked. My fingertips brushed her cheek, its softness a dream. A few more inches were all I needed.

But the goddess had other ideas. She backed away and jogged over to the merry-go-round. Grasping the metal, she ran in a circle and jumped on for the ride.

I took a deep breath, working to regain the control I'd almost lost. I needed to be careful. Needed to be sure I could go back to my old life after a night like this. Because right then, with Skylar, it felt like my world was shattering into a million unfixable pieces.

She lay on her back staring up at the sky, now red and orange and stunning. I walked over to the merry-go-round and hopped on, holding tight while it still spun around. I lay next to her, our shoulders separated by a metal pole.

"Do you know I've only been to a public park one other time."

I stared at her beautiful profile. "How old were you?"

"Ten." A gloom settled over her features. "I didn't know it, but the police had come to tell my father about my mother's accident, and Ricky took me out for ice cream and then to a secluded park. Ricky's the craziest person I know, so you can imagine how much fun we had."

"I read about your mother. I'm sorry." The website had shown a picture of Skylar and her dad dressed in black as they ducked into their car at the funeral. The site said her mother was involved in a deadly accident on the German Autobahn. I couldn't imagine having such an intimate moment plastered all over the Internet.

"It was a long time ago." Her voice was a whisper of acceptance.

"I'm still sorry."

"Death is a funny thing, you know. I think about it a lot. Dying. I wonder what heaven is like and if my mom is happy up there."

My eyes flicked over to hers. "I'm sure she is. Who wouldn't be?"

"Yeah, I guess so. I suppose it's pretty selfish to be angry when people die."

"I don't think so. I'd be angry too if I lost either one of my parents."

She shifted to her side, allowing me to see a rare vulnerability. "You know who I am. And you seem to understand me. But I don't get you at all."

I mimicked her position, and the two of us faced each other. We made a "V" with our bodies. Our faces were dangerously close, our chests separated only by the bar between us. Both our feet dangled off the side. "I've told you all about me. Haven't you been listening to my songs?" In every verse, I exposed pieces of my soul.

"Obscure lyrics aren't enough." She licked her lips. "Tell me what you're thinking right now."

The merry-go-round stopped spinning, and suddenly the air felt charged between us. The ache in my chest was new and glorious. I could lean in, even with the bar, and cross an impossible line. A line that separated action from inaction. Freedom from bondage.

I swallowed, fighting against every instinct. "I'm thinking how lucky I am to be here with you, and how I want to know everything about you."

She fidgeted with her necklace. "Because I'm Donnie Wyld's daughter."

I sensed the hurt. She'd been used by others before.

I stole her hand away; let my caress linger before setting it down. She seemed to touch the locket when she was anxious. I never wanted her to feel that way around me. "No. It's because you have "Revolver" on your iTunes, and you know who The Velvet Underground is. It's also because you're kind and thoughtful and quite possibly the prettiest girl I've ever seen."

Her responding smile invited me in. "What do you want to

know?"

"We'll start easy. Why did your dad name you after the band?"

She scraped at a fraying line of paint with her fingernail. "It was my great-grandmother's family name. She'd given my dad his first guitar, and then fronted all the money for their first demo. When my parents found out I was a girl, my dad said he knew I should be her namesake. He loved that it also represented the band."

"You were smart to go by a different name at school. Skylar Wyld would have been a dead giveaway. But why your mom's? You're lucky no one else made the connection."

She opened her locket and showed me matching pictures. They looked very similar except Skylar had a softer face, while her mom was all sharp lines and high cheekbones.

"You look a lot like her," I offered. Skylar was prettier, but I kept that to myself.

Those stunning green eyes met mine. "Brianna Da Lange was remarkable. Fearless. I guess I just wanted to channel some of that energy when I stepped through those doors."

"You didn't seem nervous at all."

"Oh, but I was. Homeschooled, remember?"

"I remember." Heck, I remembered every word out of her mouth. My hand slid over, taking hers slowly, one finger at a time. I needed the contact. Needed her to know I was more than a fleeting presence. "Your turn for a question."

She studied our joined hands. "Do you like wrestling?"

"Sometimes. When I wrestle with my trainer, Matt, I love it. The rush, the accomplishment. But the team? The expectations? I don't know."

I was sure she could see right through me. See all the doubt and fear behind the façade. But she didn't press for information I wasn't ready to share. Instead she pulled her hand free and stood. "Show me."

"Show you what?"

Skylar jumped off the platform and kicked off her shoes again. A wicked grin curved her beautiful mouth. "Your moves."

I eyed her willowy form, unsure if I could hold her without a physical reaction. "You're too delicate. I'd snap you in half."

She crossed her arms. "I'm almost 5'7" and strong. Show me."

Unable to resist, I walked up behind her, and wrapped her in a bear hug, trapping her arms straight down. *Dang it, she smells good.*

"How do you think you get out of this?" I kept my grip light, still concerned about her slight frame.

She pushed against me and tried to slide down, but my grip tightened, keeping her immobile.

"Nope, you just gave me a tighter hold."

She grunted and pushed against my locked arms, slamming her head back against my chest. I easily blocked her lame attempt at a head butt and tightened my grasp again.

"Geez, you're strong," she conceded, slacking against my hold.

My male pride satisfied, I leaned toward her ear, allowed a puff of air to come with my words. "No way you could break my hold with your own strength."

She shivered.

At least I wasn't the only one affected by our closeness. "Do exactly what I say. Turn and step back with your right leg so your knee is directly behind mine."

Her body shifted, following my directions.

"Now, grab my right leg with your right hand, and push your knee into the back of mine."

She did, and my knee buckled, taking us both to the ground, my arms still locked around hers. I eyed my now vulnerable position. "Do you see where your elbow is?"

Her mischievous giggle had me quickly releasing my hold and closing my legs. I wasn't taking any chances. She was completely unpredictable.

Scrambling to her feet, she looked ready for battle. "That was awesome. Show me another one."

I led her through three more defensive techniques. By the time we finished, the sun had set, and our conversation was light and easy. She had somehow managed to diffuse all my defenses.

She ran to the slide and started climbing. "Come on, Cody!"

Her hair whipped around and although Blake's face filled my mind, I pushed it aside, refusing to consider my next move. Suddenly, taking down the elite wasn't nearly as appealing as the free-spirited girl sliding with her hands high above her head.

SKYLAR

MY FEELINGS FOR Cody grew with each second we spent together. I'd managed to pull him out of his shell and even had him laughing and joking. This version of him matched the texts he'd sent, a complete contrast to the stoic guy who walked the halls of Madison High.

His hands strong against my back, he pushed me on the swing set with a silence that was not only comfortable but also soothing.

The cry of an electric guitar filled the air. My dad's ringtone.

"Is that your phone?" Cody gripped the chains, stopping the swing.

I jumped off and ran to where it sat on the table. "Hey," I said, trying to catch my breath.

"It's past eleven. Where are you?" His voice was weak, but still strong enough to create a pit in my stomach.

Was it really that late?

"I left you a note. I'm sorry. I didn't notice the time. Are you feeling better?"

"A note, Skylar, really? When has that ever been acceptable? Come home. Now."

"Yes, sir." I pressed end on the phone and turned to tell Cody, but he was already walking toward me, keys in hand. "I'm sorry. I have to go."

"No problem." His gentle smile sent a flush of heat into my cheeks, a reaction I'd had to him all night. Cody had been my obsession, the fantasy guy who took my emotions on a roller coaster. But tonight he showed me the man behind his façade of indifference. His soft spirit and touching compassion. Tonight, he stole my heart.

We walked to my Mustang, side by side, and though we didn't touch, I felt him over every inch of my body. I didn't want the night to end. Didn't want to go back to school where the real Cody might disappear.

We stopped at my car door, staring at each other, the weird will-he-kiss-me-or-not moment vibrating between us. Electric tingles created a duet with the drumbeat in my chest. My lips parted, sending him a clear signal I wouldn't flee this time.

Cody dropped his head, not making eye contact. "If I'm standoffish at school on Monday…" He paused, kicking the dirt, and then looked back up. "Just know it's not you."

Irritation, like ice water, doused my fantasy of a leg-popping moonlight kiss. "Why would you be different at school?"

His eyes pleaded with mine. "It's complicated."

Embarrassment, disappointment and irritation battled inside me. Zoe was right. The guy sucked you in and then refused to acknowledge anything. I shook my head and jerked open my door. "No, Cody, it's not."

He reached out and lightly gripped my arm, pulling me back to him.

My breath hitched, the combination of anger and anticipation turning our growing heat into a scorching fire. Heart pounding, I looked up, glanced at his mouth before staring into his tortured eyes.

"Blake and I are teammates. There's a code for these situations. If we go public, you have no idea what will happen at school."

"But I don't like Blake. And he's not even over Lindsay."

Though he seemed relieved by those words, it didn't take the sadness out of his eyes.

"It doesn't matter. Blake expects absolute loyalty."

I was beginning to hate that word. It had been corrupted into something dark. An excuse to control others. "Then why are we here if you had no intention of taking it further?"

He brushed a piece of hair off my face. "You were so sad today. I just wanted to make you smile again."

And yet, all he'd done was hurt me more.

He dropped his hand and stepped back, a dark emptiness replacing his strong arms. "I like you a lot, but I need more time to figure out all the moving pieces."

Rejection and rage warred within me. "You still don't trust me." Cody was pushing me away just like my father had. When were they going to realize I was strong enough to share their burdens?

His head recoiled as if I'd smashed it with a baseball bat. I kinda wish I had.

"This isn't about trust. It's about me protecting you."

"From what?"

"Madison preys on the weak, and if certain people saw how much I care about you, they would try to destroy us."

My spine went rigid. "They don't need to. You already have."

I was halfway inside my car when strong arms tugged me back and spun me around. Hot lips pressed to mine. Everything came alive, my cheeks, my hands, my stomach that wouldn't stop swirling. I touched his back, gripped his t-shirt. I wanted him everywhere. Wanted the moment to go on for eternity.

When his lips no longer warmed my own, he put his forehead to mine, his voice husky and uneven. "Don't walk away from me."

I pulled him closer, laid my head against his solid chest. His heart had a strong, steady rhythm, and I inhaled the scent I wanted on my pillow at night. "Then don't play with my heart. I'm not like Jill or other girls who do this for fun."

"Rumors, Skylar. All rumors. I made one mistake last year, and I've hated myself for it. But there has been no one else since."

"My whole life is a secret, Cody. I don't want this to be." I felt the weight of his sigh. The tightness coiling through each muscle.

"Then it won't be. I'll talk to Blake. I'll tell him how I feel, and then no one will blame for you for any of it. Just give me the weekend to figure it all out."

Hope rose in my chest. "Thank you."

He cupped my cheek, and I could sense something in him changed. His eyes darkened into shadows, and his words felt like promises too heavy to grasp. "Know this. Whatever happens on Monday, you're worth it."

I SET MY purse on the counter, the flicker of the TV in the living room telling me my father was waiting.

He paused the show as soon as I came in the room and turned to face me. "Skylar Anne, giving you a car was not granting you permission to trek around Asheville without a curfew."

My eyes drifted over him wrapped up in a blanket and weak with fatigue. The deep crevices under his eyes made me wonder how bad his night had really been.

I sat next to him, careful not to pull off his coverings. "I'm sorry. I just lost track of time." I hated that I'd worried him.

He leaned over and picked up the note I left, scanning it with his eyes. "This 'friend.' Was it a guy or a girl?"

I bit my lip nervously. Casting down my eyes, I slowly replied, "A guy."

My father's head hit the top of the couch, and he looked like he was saying a silent prayer. Then he turned his pointed gaze to me. Seeing the disappointment there, I felt tears sting my eyes.

"Sweetheart, I know tonight was a letdown. I'm so sorry we weren't able to hang out. But, under no circumstances are you to go out with a boy I have never met." He took my hand, giving me a second to acknowledge his reprimand.

When I nodded, he continued, "This is a lot to get used to, us being here now, not having so many people around all the time. I'm sure it's lonely. But, you still have boundaries very much in place."

"I'm not lonely, Dad." He was the only person I missed, but it wasn't fair to say so. He couldn't control what was happening any more than I could.

He pulled me in for a hug, and I snuggled up to his side, relishing the calming smell of the man who was my rock and my hero.

"What's his name?"

I sat back up, allowing a sheepish smile. "Cody. He's the captain of the wrestling team."

"Did he keep his hands where they belonged?"

My mouth dropped open, my face flushing from embarrassment. "Dad!"

"What? It's a fair question. I don't want your first kiss to be from some meathead in a public park. Sue me."

I glared at my father like he'd lost his mind. "I'm seventeen years old. I've already had my first kiss."

He furrowed his brow. "Who have you kissed?"

"Whatever, Dad. Just play the movie." I reached for the remote, but he grabbed it instead.

"No ma'am. Who have you kissed? And why didn't you tell me?" There was an edge to the words, even while his tone seemed playful. He wasn't going to let this one go.

"Fine. I was fifteen. Tyler and I were curious." I shrugged my shoulders. "No big deal."

"No big deal?" My father's voice went up an octave. "You kissed Ricky's nephew? The kid is a menace, Skylar, a felony waiting to happen. Ugh. And here I thought you had taste."

I lightly pushed his arm and giggled. "Stop. It was just one time in a closet. Honestly, it felt like kissing a brother or something. No fireworks."

He shook his head, still looking stunned. "I'm a terrible father. My only daughter gets her first kiss in a closet from…" He scrunched his face. "Tyler Prescott."

Rolling my eyes, I reached for the remote again. He was starting to make me feel embarrassed, and I didn't like it.

Still holding the darn thing out of reach, he gripped my chin and pulled it around to face him. "Now listen to me. A man who's worth your time, energy and affections won't want to kiss you in secret. He'll want to kiss you in front of the world so everyone knows you are his. Don't you dare settle for less."

I flung myself into his arms, forgetting for a second he was so fragile and squeezed him tightly. "I won't, Daddy."

"I know I haven't always been the best father. I drank too much. Partied too much. I took you and your mom for granted."

The ache in his voice tore at my heart. He must have been looking at old pictures. This was always the story he told when he missed her most. "You changed. I don't even remember that person."

"That's because Brianna took you away from me. Your mother forced me to face my demons and if she hadn't..." He pulled me tighter, held on like he'd lose me if he didn't. "I'm so sorry I let you down tonight."

I held his sad face in my hands. "You didn't let me down."

The depression seemed to ease a little, but I still sensed he was trying to hold our crumbling world steady. He took my hands in his. "Will you do something for me?"

"Sure, anything."

"Will you go to church tomorrow with Josie?"

How could I say no when he looked so pathetic? "Why?"

"Because I feel like I've left you stranded. I don't know what's going to happen in the future, but I do know when tragedy strikes, it's the people in your church family who surround you and lift you up. When your mother died, I wouldn't have made it without their support."

"Stop saying that. You're going to be just fine."

His pause highlighted his struggle to believe. "I hope you're right, sweetheart."

"I am right. God wouldn't be that cruel. I know it."

"God is never cruel, Skylar. We may not understand His

ways, but it doesn't change who He is."

I stretched out on the couch, laying my head across my father's lap. His hands found my hair and began long rhythmic strokes as if he were strumming chords on his guitar. Soft music filled my head, and my body relaxed with its harmony.

"Skylar, I need you to do this for me. For my peace of mind. Can you? Please?"

There was only one answer, even though I felt certain her church would be exactly like her—snobby and judgmental. "Okay, I'll go. But no more talk of death and support." I took his hand and tucked it close to my heart. "It's you and me, Daddy. It always has been, and we're going to beat this cancer."

SUNDAY MORNING DIDN'T hold its usual appeal. Instead of curling up next to my dad, I had ten minutes until my obligatory field trip with Aunt Josephine. She was probably already here, tapping her fingernails on the counter while she glared at the cuckoo clock in the hallway.

The woman was frustratingly punctual, and I wondered for the millionth time how she and my dad came from the same parents. He and I both suffered from chronic tardiness.

As expected, she sat by my father at the bar, waiting, when I walked into the kitchen. She fussed over him, checking his temperature and then stood to pull his meds out of the cabinet.

My heart softened a little. She did love my father. That much was impossible to deny.

Daddy hugged me and whispered a warning in my ear about holding my tongue, which I agreed to do.

I followed Aunt Josephine out to her glossy, white Lexus in the driveway—even the rain wouldn't dare leave a smudge—

and resigned myself to two hours of torture.

She droned on about something from the minute we left the driveway. I tuned her out. Sure, I agreed to go with her. I'd even be polite for my dad's sake, but I wasn't going to be her new BFF.

When it was obvious I wasn't listening, she stopped her chatter and turned on the stereo. The sounds of Bach filled the car.

Ten minutes later, we pulled into a crowded parking lot, not a vacant space to be found anywhere near the front doors.

Six brick columns shot up to the sky and the dome on top of the building imitated the European Renaissance architecture Ms. Stapler forced me to study. The building reminded me of home. It took me back to a time when our family could actually attend church and worship together. Familiarity swept over me, and my icy heart began to thaw. Images of my mom and dad played like a movie in my mind, bringing me back to a time when life seemed like a fairytale.

My eyes burned, unshed tears threatening to undo my carefully applied makeup.

"This church is almost a hundred years old. Beautiful, isn't it?" She stared at the historic structure. "The design is based on the cathedral and dome of Santa Maria del Fiore in Florence. Your father told me you've been there."

I nodded as a new wave of grief stole my voice.

She must have sensed my feeble composure and turned off the car, ending our short conversation.

My dad would say we shared a moment, that for one second Aunt Josephine and I were on the same team. But we weren't. I was on team life, believing with all my heart God would spare my father. She was on team death believing each day might be his last.

CODY

WHEN I WALKED into the gym Monday morning, Matt was waiting for me in the ring. He'd arranged two chairs facing each other and was sitting in one of them.

I set down my bag, confused and slightly annoyed he wasn't ready to work out. "What's this?"

"This is what you call a mental break. Come sit down."

I did as he asked, but I fidgeted with the drawstring on my shorts. The space felt electric, as if any minute another guy would appear to play good cop, bad cop.

Matt laced his fingers together and then set his elbows on his knees. "You're in the best shape of your life. You're stronger than last year. More skilled than last year. Yet, if you went to state tomorrow, you'd lose. Why is that?"

"I don't know." My answer probably sounded as lame to him as it did to me. I could see it in the set of his jaw, but I had nothing else to give him.

"You're holding back. You're fighting against yourself, and I want you to tell me why."

Forceful and agitated, his voice cut through layers of my skin. "I'm trying. I feel like I'm giving everything."

"Why are you holding back?"

I swallowed twice, hoping to somehow moisten the desert that had become my throat. "I don't know."

He didn't move, but grew louder, more demanding. "Why

are you holding back?"

Because there's too much pressure. Because every day I have to pretend to be someone I'm not. Because in one hour I'm going to defy Blake and lose everything I've worked for. Because I don't even know if Skylar will want the man who's left behind when the smoke clears.

"I don't know."

Matt jumped up from his chair. "That's a crap answer, Cody. Look inside yourself. Find that fire you used to have and tell me what you want."

"I want to stop being afraid, okay? I want everything that's jumbled around in my mind to stop tormenting me."

Matt calmly sat back down. The gym was eerily quiet like he'd closed it just for this conversation.

I put my head in my hands. "Why can't I be like you? You never hold back. You never waiver."

Matt's tone softened and his hand squeezed my shoulder. "You can't be me, and I don't want you to be. We all have a purpose that's unique. You need to figure out who *you* are. What *you* stand for. Until you do that, nothing in your life is going to make sense."

He left me there to think about his words.

What *did* I stand for? I had no idea. I knew I wanted Skylar. But I also wanted to take down Blake and the Madison elite. I wanted to destroy the Torments List and free every person who ever felt like Fatty James. But I was out of time. The minute I told Blake that Skylar and I were together, it would be me against the world.

I pulled out my phone, clicking my way to the Torments List for the hundredth time since I found out about the horrible website. How was I supposed to fight a legacy?

A new thread had appeared under Lindsay's name, and my insides went wild. When was it ever going to be enough? They'd raided her Facebook, created a hate account on Twitter; she couldn't even walk down the hall without hearing, "slut" every time she passed someone.

I clicked the new tab and my heart stopped.

No. No. No.

I grabbed my keys and bag and sprinted to my car. I had to get to Madison before anyone saw them.

I STILL COULDN'T believe the naked picture in front of me wasn't photoshopped. Lindsay had posed for this picture. Eyes wide, smile bright, a woman obviously in love with the man behind the camera. A man who would betray her without remorse.

Blake. His name was a fist around my raspy throat.

I'd seen the website. I'd seen the threads that planned their vicious attack, and I knew photocopies of Lindsay would line the halls this morning.

Ripping down the tenth one, I followed the trail into the boys' locker room. Every bathroom stall, every shower, every locker displayed Lindsay's mistake.

The stack under my arm was getting thicker as I pushed into the gym. The bleachers showcased more photos. Our Trojan mascot held two of his own.

I checked my watch, panic pushing my feet faster. In minutes, the school would be filled. Minutes were all I had before Lindsay's world crumbled into the shreds of these eight by ten images.

The gym now clear, I snatched each picture leading to the

secluded music hall, sick from knowing how carefully they picked their locations, ensuring teachers wouldn't get a clue until it was too late. My insides quaked, my hands cut from the sharp edges of the papers as I ripped them down from the wall.

And then I saw him—MCH25—the one who said he had fifty copies ready to hang. The guy was only ten feet from me, rounding the corner to finish his handiwork.

A chill started at my core and worked through every limb. I needed to move, needed to stop him from destroying what was left of Lindsay's fragile resolve, but seeing Blake's new lackey made me numb.

Henry Walkins III.

I watched him tape up the last picture in his hand, and then walk away, leaving behind a mess that was mine to clean up. Only now I had his name and his login ID. And this time they weren't going to get away with it.

SKYLAR

BLAKE WAS THE only one at our group table when I took my seat Monday morning.

"She lives. I was beginning to wonder." His usual swagger was noticeably absent. "Busy weekend?"

He'd called twice. I let the call go to voicemail.

I touched my mom's locket and scooted closer to the table. "Very. You?" I watched the door for my missing friend, boyfriend, whatever he was. Had Cody talked to him yet?

"More enlightening than busy." His unblinking blue eyes sent chill bumps down my arms. "What'd you do?"

I rubbed a hand across my skin and wished I were a better liar. "Just the typical family stuff. Shopping, cleaning, watching movies." Listening to my dad throw up at least six times.

Blake sat there, cataloguing my every word, monitoring my every expression, and heat filled my cheeks. A commotion by the door finally stole his interest and I exhaled, my heart beating faster than it should.

Chugger hurriedly took his seat right as the tardy bell rang.

"Everything cool?" Easing back in his chair, Blake appeared casual, yet his question felt weighted.

"From what I understand," Chugger answered.

I straightened. "What's cool?" And where was Cody?

"We've got the outing of a lifetime planned for this Saturday," Chugger said.

Blake's elbows landed on the table, his eyes targeting mine like a dare. "And you, Beautiful, have to come. We made sure it wasn't on a Friday, and all of your girlfriends will be there too. No excuses this time." He angled his head. "Unless you already have plans with someone."

I swallowed my unease. Blake was looking at me like I'd ripped his heart out. "Is something wrong? You're acting weird."

"Am I?' Blake rolled his pencil to the right and then back to the left.

"Yes."

He slammed his hand over the wood and finally looked up. "I guess I don't like being lied to." There was no humor, no playful banter, and for the first time, I actually understood why Cody was careful around him.

My breath hitched. Maybe the guys did talk this morning. "What do you mean?"

"Let's just say the other weekend wasn't the first time Cody and Lindsay have been alone in his truck. Turns out St. James isn't so innocent after all. He and Lindsay have been sleeping together for months."

It took work to keep from gasping. "It's not true." I wouldn't believe it. People fabricated stories all the time. Even when my mom was alive, lies circulated that my dad had multiple affairs.

"Really?" Blake practically spit out the word. "'Cause I have proof."

CODY

I WAITED IN the front office for twenty minutes before Principal Rayburn would see me. The list of names I'd acquired was not as extensive as I wanted, but I wasn't going to waste this opportunity.

"Mr. James," Principal Rayburn's baritone invite boomed through his cracked door. He wasn't an impressive man to look at, but his voice could rival Darth Vader's.

I stood, clenched my phone, the sheet of paper with the login IDs, and the only copy of Lindsay's picture that I didn't destroy.

He didn't stand when I walked in, but pointed to a lone chair in front of his massive oak desk. The wood surface was freakishly clean, with only one sheet of paper in front of him, an extra-wide computer monitor, and an Oktoberfest mug with supplies inside.

"What can I do for you?" He held a pen in his hand and hovered it over the lone paper on his desk. I could tell by his body language and the set of his jaw that he wasn't my biggest fan. I'd been labeled a troublemaker this year thanks to Blake's skipping fiasco.

I slipped into the cold, wooden chair that I'm sure was put there to intimidate and began typing in the url for the Torments List into my phone. "A month ago, you had an assembly on bullying. Said if we were aware of it or were victims of it, we should come talk to you. So, I'm here."

Principal Rayburn relaxed in his chair, and his smirk practically accused me of pulling a prank. "Are you here to tell me you're being bullied, Cody?"

"No, Sir." Not any more. Losing sixty pounds and learning how to fight took care of that one. "I have something to show you."

A circle continued to spin in front of the Madison webpage. I stopped it and pressed refresh. But this time, I didn't see the banner or the password screen, just a blank page and a "Safari can't find the server" error message. My pulse shot up and I tried again, then again, then one more time. "It's gone."

He sat up and tossed the pen he'd been holding onto his desk, his earlier amusement replaced by irritation. "Bullying is a serious crime, and this school is a cesspool. I won't have you and your little entourage making a mockery of something so serious." He steepled his hands, his lips pressed in a tight line. "I've heard your name more than once this year, Cody. And if your coach hadn't promised me he'd take care of it, I would have already suspended you for planning senior skip day."

I was so screwed. Guilt by association.

His lecture continued. "I know you were part of that group that jumped Mr. Watkins, too. And the minute I can prove it, you boys are going down." His threat came with angry brown eyes. The man's future at this school was questionable. He knew it. We all knew it. And his glare said he'd make a statement on his way out.

Words stayed lodged in my throat. I'd saved one photocopy from the shredder, but without access to the Torments List, the naked photo now wrinkled in my fist would only incriminate me. "I'm sorry. I didn't mean to waste your time." I stood, my legs shaky.

"I'm not sure what you thought would happen with this little visit, but next time you decide to skip first period. Do it with someone who can't give you detention." The pink slip he handed me was my dismissal.

I walked to my locker, too stunned and defeated to go to Ms. Yarnell's class. The dial twisted under my fingertips until I heard the familiar click. I raised the handle and pulled, trying to steady my trembling hands. A paper flew out, glided through the air like a feather and slid two feet away from me. It was a photo, an original on glossy paper.

My legs felt ready to collapse as I walked toward the letters in red print on the back.

My sweet Cody:

Think of me often.

With love, Lindsay

I didn't have to turn the photo around to know what it was. I'd taken down fifty copies of this picture.

All this time, I thought I was one step ahead. That I'd beaten them at their own game. Yet, somehow they figured out I was using Lindsay's login. They figured out my loyalty was no longer to the king of the school.

It was all a set up. Even if I hadn't seen the threads, the impact would have been the same.

Destroy her and frame me all at the same time.

SKYLAR

THE SCHOOL WAS ablaze with whispers, the atmosphere heavy as if a natural disaster was on its way to level the building. Students moved too quickly, gripped their books too tightly, watched those around them too carefully.

Cody never showed. I'd checked my phone at least a hundred times waiting for some kind of explanation, but nothing came.

"Skylar, wait up."

I turned to see Blake jogging toward me before sixth period.

"Can I talk to you?"

I hesitated. "Okay." He'd been cryptic and weird in first period, and I wasn't looking for a repeat.

"Can we go somewhere alone?"

"I have class." I eyed the room filling with students, none of them the one I wanted to see.

"I'll get you a pass. Come on, Ms. Bakerfield takes all her test questions from the footnotes anyway. Please? I want to explain."

He took my hand and pulled before I could protest. He led me into a large storage room with two big copy machines and rolls of colored paper, and shut the door.

"Blake?"

He paced like a tiger in a cage. "I wanted you to tell me the truth. That's why I acted like I did this morning. I was upset." He ran a hand through his pale hair and stopped to meet my eyes. "I saw you and him at the park."

I touched my locket, hoping for some wisdom. Wondering at the same time why Cody hadn't saved me from this confrontation.

"I wasn't going to say anything, but then all this stuff blew up about Lindsay, and I realized I was less hurt by her and more by you." He stepped closer, inches away from contact. "My feelings are real, Skylar. You're not the rebound girl or my way to pass the time."

The tension those words brought caused me to shift away from him. I'd never been in this position before. Never had to let a guy down easy or explain I just wasn't attracted to him. Maybe I should have told my dad more details. Gotten some advice. But what would he know about rejection? The man's had women throwing themselves at him most of his life.

Blake watched me intently. Too intently. I fidgeted with my hands. "Cody was going to talk to you this morning."

"I should have seen it coming. It's a pattern with him." Blake fell against the only wall not blocked by machinery and banged the back of his head twice.

My back stiffened. He'd basically just implied I was a pawn Cody used to hurt him. "None of this was planned. It just kind of happened. It was never about you."

"Yet, I'm the one left looking like an idiot. First, Lindsay. Now you."

My cheeks warmed, guilt nibbling at my insides. "I'm sorry."

He banged his head again. "No. Don't be sorry. It's not you I'm mad at. I'm mad that Cody went after you the minute

I showed interest." Blake looked up, pain visible in his crystal blue eyes. "And this thing with Lindsay...it makes it all seem premeditated. She was my girlfriend for three years, and he was my best friend. He knew how much I cared about her. Everyone's saying they've been carrying on since he won state."

On the inside, jealousy shook my confidence. "You can't really believe that. They're just rumors."

"Honestly, Skylar, my head's not in the best place right now. I've got people telling me they saw them kissing in the parking lot. He's always hovering around her, and I know she put a naked picture in his locker."

I'd heard that one too, from more than one person. I glanced down at my phone; the screen was empty. *Why hadn't he called?*

Blake shoved his hands into his pockets. "You've come to mean a lot to me, and while I don't think Cody and I will be on speaking terms ever again, I don't want you to feel awkward around me."

"I don't want that either." And I didn't. Our groups had merged after that first group date. And Zoe loved being at the head table.

Relief showed in the tilt of his smile. He stretched out a hand. "Friends still? With no possibility of more this time?"

I was glad he could joke about it. Glad we could maybe find a way back to normal. I placed my hand in his. "Friends."

CODY

MY FALL FROM the inner circle had been swift and full of well-coordinated attacks: Ms. Sandival confiscated my phone in second period when Stacey Morgan asked very loudly who I was texting, Coach found out I had detention and demanded I serve it during lunch so I wouldn't miss practice, and Zoe pulled Skylar into the bathroom the one time I saw her between classes.

And now, fifteen minutes had passed in sixth period, and Skylar was a no-show.

I raised my hand.

"Yes, Mr. James?" Ms. Bakerfield didn't even glance my direction. A skill we still hadn't figured out.

"I'm not feeling well. Can I go see the nurse?"

"Nice try. I've already heard about your skipping today." She went back to her boring, monotone lecture, and I sank deeper in my desk.

Another five minutes passed, and finally I saw her, my fire goddess. Only the look she sent me could have withered roses in spring. She handed our teacher a note and walked down the aisle to the back of the room.

The pain in my chest eased a little when she slid into the desk next to mine. I pulled out a sheet of paper and scribbled the words I'd wanted to say to her all day. *Rumors aren't true.* I carefully slid the note on her desk.

She stared at them. I silently pleaded for her to believe me, but the hope drifted away when she slid the paper back.

Did you have a naked picture of Lindsay in your locker?

Ms. Bakerfield narrowed in on my note and shook her head in warning. At least she had the courtesy not to call me out. I folded the paper and slipped it in my bag. I needed more than a one-liner to explain what happened this morning.

SKYLAR STAYED MOTIONLESS long after the final bell finished ringing.

I scooted closer and took her hand. "Do you remember when I said no matter what happened today, you were worth it?"

She finally made eye contact. "Yes."

"Well, this is what I've been talking about."

Skylar sighed. "So, the naked picture is just a lie."

Why did I feel like honesty was going to get me in trouble? "No. There was a naked picture of Lindsay in my locker this morning, but she didn't put it there. And the rumors about us this summer are absolutely untrue."

I could see the wheels spinning in her head, weighing what she'd heard all day with the words I now offered her. "Why didn't you text me?"

"Because my phone was confiscated in second period."

Sounds from the hallway filtered into the almost empty classroom. A hand tapped the door frame. Drew, our newest sophomore wrestler. "Coach said you better get to practice. I won't quote him exactly because there's a lady present, but it had something to do with detention and suicide sprints and whole lot of pukin'."

"Fine. I'm coming." I waved him off and touched a lock of hair on her shoulder. "Can I stop by tonight? We can talk about everything?"

"I don't know." Skylar scratched at a nail, her hands tucked delicately in her lap. Her leg crossed over the other and began to swing. Boots that could impale a person rocked back and forth.

Tension cramped my neck and I popped it to the left. *How did everything slip away from me so fast?* "Please, Skylar."

She stood. "Okay. But I don't want any half-truths like at the park. I don't want any more surprises."

I followed her out to the hall and braced for her to walk away, but she wrapped her arms around me. I slid a hand through her hair, gripped her neck and held on like she might disappear. Without another word, Skylar pulled herself away from me and walked toward her locker.

The gym was in the other direction, and I sprinted the entire way there. No one said a word when I pushed through the locker room doors. A few of my teammates stood and shook their heads. Others mumbled under their breaths. It was as if someone had died, and I was the one responsible for putting him six feet under.

Blake was already on the mat when I stepped in the gym. He watched his opponent, circling, just waiting for a moment to strike. When it came, he pinned the guy in less than a minute.

I was seeing him for the first time without blinders. He had trimmed down over the summer, but still had enough girth to be in the 182-pound weight class. The weight loss created a quickness and agility he never had before. Blake had been power and strength, limited only by his ability to strike quickly enough. Once he caught a limb, opponents rarely ever escaped.

When coach blew the whistle and gushed about Blake's progress, a twinge of jealousy hit. Coach hadn't even cracked a smile in my direction this season.

Blake walked over, his eyes focused and confrontational. "You ready for a round—Captain?" His voice, sarcastic and sharp, made my body temperature spike. If Blake thought I'd be an easy pin, he was dead wrong.

"Always." I leveled my eyes at him, refusing to be intimidated. I strapped on my headgear and took my position opposite him.

"You're not the only one who learned a few tricks this summer." Blake's mouth curved into an arrogant smile. He said something else, but I tuned him out, instead getting my mind ready for the coming battle.

The whistle blew, and we lunged forward, gripping each other's necks. His strong arms attempted to push me down, but I kept my body locked, twisting to get a better hold on his frame. We dropped to our knees, still latched onto one another. I pushed down hard, and Blake's head dropped to the ground. Coach blew the whistle, giving me a point for the take down.

We released and stood again. Blake's intense stare matched mine, and immediately we were locked in a hold once more. He attempted a leg grab and dropped his shoulder. My counter move was faster, leaving us locked again. The time ran out before either of us could get the upper hand.

"Wow, you boys look good today," Coach Taylor beamed, thrilled to see his two strongest athletes at their best. "Cody, you take the bottom position for round two."

I got down on all fours with Blake positioned over me. The whistle blew, and immediately Blake tried to force me on my back. He trapped my head to the floor, but I quickly pulled the switch move Matt had shown me and took control, forcing Blake on all fours. I went for the cradle and had almost pinned him, when Blake reached up and jammed three fingers against my throat.

The move was dirty and illegal, but he was so subtle with the motion that Coach didn't notice. I struggled for breath while I pushed against his body.

"You picked the wrong side," he hissed in my ear, never letting go of the chokehold on my neck.

The room went gray as dizziness stole my focus. Blake overpowered me, flipping us over until he had me pinned.

The whistle blew as I gasped for air. Rage exploded inside my chest.

The second Blake stood, I tackled him, sending us both sailing across the floor. My fist made contact with his face twice. The loud pop in my ear told me that Blake had gotten in a punch as well, but I felt nothing, just blissful numbness.

In the distance, shouts and whistles screeched as two strong arms latched onto me and pulled me back. Eyes locked on Blake, I surged forward, driven by the need to retaliate.

"Cody, enough!" Coach Taylor screamed in my ear, bringing my focus back to the gym, to the other wrestlers watching wide-eyed, and the shocked expression on the other coach's face.

The salty taste of blood reminded me I'd taken a hit. But I doubted I looked as bad as Blake whose cut lip and swollen eye told me the punches I'd landed were solid ones.

Coach dragged me into his office and slammed the door. Without a word, he pushed me down into the chair and threw me a towel for the bloody sweat trailing down the side of my face.

"What am I supposed to do with you, Cody? You're the captain!" He paced the room, his temper as elevated as mine. "You want to tell me what in the world is going through your head?"

"No sir." I could tell him about Blake's dirty move, but it wouldn't matter. Actions have consequences and despite the fallout, I didn't regret hitting him. Or standing up for myself.

He pointed an accusing finger at me. "You boys better settle your stuff and I mean now, or so help me, I will kick you both off the team and call this year a wash." He got in my face, his eyes blazing. "You got me?"

I met his infuriated stare. "Yes, Coach."

"Now, go home! I've already seen you way too much today."

I stormed toward the locker room keeping my eyes straight ahead. I was too on edge to deal with anybody mouthing off to me. The gym was back in full swing, the echo of wrestlers vying for dominance bounced off the wood floors. The assistant coaches monitored matches with keen focus, and no one intercepted me.

His eye already starting to bruise, Blake stood by his locker when I entered. Turning, he slammed it shut and stared at me long and hard. I stared right back.

He broke our silence. "Next time you decide to take what's mine, you might want to do it in a less public place."

I forced myself not to flinch. He knew about Skylar. He freaking knew and that's why he set me up. "Good. Saves me the trouble of telling you." My dismissal made him falter, and I watched him trying to rein in his anger.

"You and me. We're done. You hear me? Done."

"We were done weeks ago. The minute Skylar walked into the classroom." My gaze flickered from the red split in his lower lip to the phone in his hand. "I suppose my name's already back on the Torments List." I scanned his face for any proof that he was responsible but was met with only a calculated smile.

He stepped forward, our faces barely a foot apart. "I don't need some silly list that doesn't even exist. I brought you to glory, and I will bring you down, one notch at a time."

His eyes showed he believed his words. Believed he had the power to control. What he didn't realize was that I was no longer willing to be his whipping boy. "If you hurt Skylar to get to me, I will hunt you down, and there will be no one there to pull me off next time."

He backed away, still looking much too smug and self-assured. "You don't get it, Cody. Skylar isn't the weapon. She's the prize. And I don't lose."

Then he was gone.

Nausea assaulted my stomach, and I ran for the sink. Gripping it tightly, I concentrated on breathing in and out. I was in this locker room when my life changed. I gave up that day. Chose survival over fighting.

I looked up to see a different man in the mirror. This man wasn't a victim. This man was set apart. And this man was done following orders.

Whatever the backlash, taking a stand was worth it.

I was finally free.

SKYLAR

THE MOST BEAUTIFUL sound I'd heard in weeks greeted me as I walked into my house. My father lightly strummed his guitar and sang a soft melody. Setting my backpack down as quietly as I could, I tiptoed to the living room. He rested comfortably on the couch, his bare feet propped up. His hair was still shaggy from sleep, but his coloring was the best I'd seen it in days. I was grateful the chemo didn't attack his hair this time. Seeing him like this almost made me forget he was so sick. Almost.

Easing my way to the other end of the couch, I sat and smiled at him. Immediately, the strumming stopped.

"No, please, keep playing." I needed the music, especially after all the drama at school.

He started again and I snuggled in, resting my head on the armrest while tucking my feet under his thigh. Eyes closed, I let the melody wash over me. I knew all the words, but I wouldn't dare tarnish his voice with my tone-deficient one.

After letting the song fade to an end, he set his guitar on the coffee table and let out a satisfied sigh.

"You seem good today." I sat up, crossing my feet under me.

"Yeah, princess, today is good." He turned with a grin that went all the way to his eyes. I almost cheered at the picture it made. I hadn't seen this version of my dad in a long time.

"Speaking of good," he continued. "I have some great news."

"What's that?"

"Ricky and the boys are coming for Thanksgiving. We may even try and lay down the rest of the album we started." My father always referred to the band as Ricky and the boys. Mostly because he and Ricky were the first members, and they picked up Raif and Stinger later. They were my family, so the news lightened the heaviness in my heart.

"Really? That's awesome. We haven't had Thanksgiving together in years." I pushed aside the nagging thought that this might be our last one and chose to focus on the positive. Daddy looked good. Surely, the chemo was working.

"Also, Josie is coming by tonight, and we are going to have a nice family dinner. Sound good?"

My smile dissolved. "Why can't it just be you and me? We haven't had any time together, and you're actually feeling good tonight."

The whine in my voice made my father sigh in exasperation. "Sweetheart, Josie's been by my side through all the really bad days. It's only fair that she gets to be here on the good days."

"I could be there for you too, if you'd let me." The words came out in a mumble, but he heard me.

My father reached out and ran his hand over my hair. I leaned in, enjoying the comfort of his touch. "You're my daughter. I'm supposed to be your hero. Your rock. It would hurt me to be so weak in front of you. Can you understand that?"

I nodded. My dad asked very little of me, but this seemed to matter to him a great deal.

He clapped his hands together and picked up his guitar again. "Any requests?"

Smiling, I leaned back and closed my eyes again. "Yes. 'My Little Heart.' " My father had written the song when I was born but never recorded it. I loved having a piece of him the world had never heard.

The music floated around us, his voice as crisp and perfect as a nightingale in song. But he didn't even make it to the second verse before the front door shut and shoes padded across the marble floors. Only one other person would just walk in. Aunt Josephine.

Irritation shot through me like a blade. She was an intruder, ending the best moment I'd had with my dad in months. Wasn't it enough that he'd chosen to share his hurts with her? Did she have to take the little time that was left for me?

The music stopped, and I heard my father set down his guitar and stand.

I was sure he was hugging her, but I feigned sleep. They whispered quietly and left the room. The silence felt deafening after the beauty that had been there seconds before. I reached for my phone, wondering if Cody was out of practice yet.

Zoe's name popped up.

Zoe: *Cody attacked Blake during wrestling practice.*

I pressed my temples. Normal felt further away than ever. More surprises. More rumors. Was it ever going to stop?

Me: *How did you hear this?*

Zoe: *Ashley told me. She saw them all in the parking lot. Blake had a black eye and split lip.*

Me: *How's Cody?*

Zoe: *Fine, I guess. She said he walked straight to Lindsay's* *car. They sat together for like ten minutes before he finally went to his truck. I guess the rumors really are true.*

I was too stunned to know what to type back.

Zoe: *Hey, do you want to go to the mall?*

Me: *Can't. Dinner with the family. I'll see you tomorrow.*

I bolted to my room and picked up the Pop's Burger napkin I'd saved from Friday night. My mind immediately recalled every moment of that night. Cody's laugh. His strong arms around me, his lips. The way he looked into my eyes.

I had to calm down. I had to think rationally. I had to make a choice.

Trust Cody or ends things before he broke my heart.

CODY

IT ONLY TOOK fifteen minutes to discover who Blake's weapon would be.

Lindsay sat in her car, head down, crying. I tapped on the passenger side window and pulled open the door.

"I'm sorry. I'm so, so sorry," she said between sobs. "It's all my fault."

I slid into the seat but kept the door open. "What are you talking about? This is between Blake and me. You had nothing to do with it."

She wiped at her cheeks. "But I did. I told him I gave you my password. I told him you knew about the Torments List." Her fist hit the steering wheel. "I'm the worst person ever."

I shook my head trying to make sense of her broken sentences. "Wait. When?"

"He came over Saturday when my parents were out. I wasn't going to let him in, but he was so spastic and angry that, I don't know, I thought he might break down the door or something. He accused us of sleeping together. Can you believe that? And when I tried to deny it, he said my hanging all over you was why the school thought I was a slut." She shifted in her seat to face me. "Cody, I snapped. I yelled at him. I've *never* yelled at him." She dipped her head. "He interrogated me until I finally just told him whatever he wanted to know."

I had a bad feeling that Blake's "interrogation" was more

than verbal. Not that I'd had any luck in getting her to admit it.

We sat in silence. There was so much I wanted to say, but trying to convince her that Blake was responsible for his own actions was like trying to convince a vegan to eat meat. She'd been programmed to take the blame for years.

"Oh, look at this. Two love birds," A voice crooned, and I whipped around to see Jill standing in the space between my leg and the open door.

Arm perched on top of the window frame, Jill leaned over and sent a lethal smile to Lindsay. "I knew you were easy, but seriously, servicing Cody in the school parking lot is a little much."

Lindsay's face went sheet white.

"Shut up, Jill," I hissed.

She backed away when I stood. "What is it about her that's so freaking fantastic, huh? How is she any different than me?"

It had taken me a long time to truly grasp Matt's words about being set apart. About using my influence to make a difference in someone's life outside of my own. I'd let people down in the past. Turned away when I should have intervened. But I knew what I stood for now.

Lindsay was my redemption. My way to vindicate Fatty James.

"She isn't, Jill, which should terrify you more than anything. Because one wrong move and this is you. That is what our silence has done."

Her eyes widened, a hint of fear breaking past her stony stare. "She did this to herself."

Very carefully, I shot back words she would know well, "Sure Jill, keep telling yourself that."

A TWO-DOOR GUARDHOUSE and security personnel with clipboards protected the entry in to Skylar's neighborhood. I slowed to a stop and rolled down my window.

"Cody James. I'm here to see Skylar Wyld."

The balding man scrunched his eyebrows and examined his sheet. Once satisfied, he lifted the barrier arm, and I drove forward.

Following the directions she texted, I wound my way past mansions three times the size of my house with acres of land between them. At the end of its very own street, Skylar's house glowed against the setting sun. The two-story structure resembled a Spanish castle with terracotta shingles and cream stucco. My family wasn't poor by any means, but this level of wealth brought an immediate reminder that I was dating a rock star's daughter. Well, hopefully I was still dating her. Her texts had been too short to give me any sense of security.

I parked the car and gave myself a final pep talk before trudging up the three marble steps to the arched entryway. I had an hour before I needed to be at the radio station. I prayed it was enough time to fix everything today had broken. At least I had my topic for tonight—lies and heartbreak.

The door opened before my hand ever made contact and Skylar slipped out. Her long hair was pulled into a messy bun on the top of her head, and her dress and boots were replaced with jeans and a t-shirt. I preferred this look—natural, beautiful. I stepped back, giving her room to come onto the porch. She shut the door behind her.

"I'm not ready for you to meet my dad yet." Her arms crossed, shielding herself from me. Women aren't easy to read, but everything in her stance screamed trouble.

"Sure. That's fine. Do you want go somewhere?"

She shook her head, her mouth formed into a small pout.

When I reached out to touch her, she took one step back.

"I thought we were going to talk?"

"That was before you punched Blake and hung out with Lindsay in the parking lot. You said no more surprises, but that's all it's ever been with you. Since we've met you've been hot and cold. Sending me mixed signals. Giving me one half of a story. It's not enough."

It was unbelievable how fast Blake's minions worked. I pointed to the steps. "Can we at least sit?"

Begrudgingly, she sat keeping several feet between us. I ached to close the gap. "I'm sorry I didn't call sooner. I should have."

"So, what exactly happened?"

This was my chance. My opportunity to explain the Torments List and why I needed to protect Lindsay. But even as the words rolled around on my tongue, I couldn't say them. If she knew about Fatty James, she'd see me differently. I'd see me differently. I'd be the weak boy on that locker room floor, not the man who'd fought to become the very opposite.

No. I'd have to find a way to give her the truth without digging up my past. "Sometime between getting to school and the middle of first period, someone put that picture in my locker. It wasn't Lindsay and it wasn't me. I don't know who has my combination, but I would bet money it's Blake."

She shook her head. "He was with me the whole time in Ms. Yarnell's class. It couldn't have been him."

"Skylar, he had one of his many followers do it for him. That's how he works." I was one breath from mentioning

Henry's name, but if I ratted him out, he'd surely turn around and lie about me jumping him.

Her bare feet tapped on the stone steps in no set pattern. "I thought you were going to talk to him," she said, looking down. "He pulled me aside before sixth period. He was really messed up about us and the rumors."

Hair prickled on the back of my neck. "You need to stay away from Blake. He's a master manipulator and he's not safe."

She flinched at the sharpness in every word. "Is that why you punched him? Because he spoke to me? For the record, I'm not into the whole alpha male, possessive thing."

"This isn't me marking my territory, Skylar. He's a liar, and he still wants you."

Skylar bit her lip and suddenly the last thing I wanted to do was talk about Blake. I ached to kiss her.

"Cody, I wanted normal for the first time in my life. I don't want to be stuck between some power struggle with you and Blake. All my friends are his friends."

Because he knew inviting Zoe and her friends to the head table would make it impossible for Skylar to walk away. I ran my hands down my face. "I don't want that for you either. We'll find a way to make it all work, I promise." I didn't usually make promises I couldn't keep, but something in her eyes made me wish it were true. That I could make this nightmare I'd dragged her into vanish with a snap of my fingers.

Her head dropped, her voice much too quiet. "I try not to let things get to me like this. I know people misrepresent the truth. It's just when Zoe told me about you and Lindsay together, I felt jealous. Which is a stupid emotion and one I wouldn't feel if things between us were more clear."

"Then I'll make it clear." I inched even closer, allowing my thigh to graze hers. "You're the only one I think about. The only one I want to do this with." My hand reached up and touched the delicate skin on her face. I leaned in, my goal nothing less than to find out what flavor lip-gloss she was wearing.

"I can guarantee my father is watching us on the security camera."

Lightning shot through me, sending me sprawling to the farthest side of the stairs.

She burst into giggles at my stricken face.

"That's not funny." I searched for the camera that had been monitoring my every move.

"No, it's pretty funny. You looked like you were going to have a heart attack."

"I almost did. All I could picture was Donnie Wyld coming at me with a guitar in one hand and a .45 in the other."

"You're crazy. My dad would use a shotgun." The stress was gone from her features, replaced by the smile I'd come to rely on.

She stood and offered her hand. I let her tug me until we were inches apart. My heart beat irregularly, but not from panic like earlier. From her closeness, from the heat searing the small space between us.

I swallowed. "Are we good?" I had to remind myself that kissing her was out of the question.

"For now." She walked me back to my car. "So, what happens tomorrow?" Her hesitant question made me curse myself for ever making her doubt my feelings.

"We let the whole school know you're my girlfriend."

"Really?" Her lips tilted playfully. "The infamous Cody James who never does relationships is ready to put a label on us? I'm shocked."

I wrapped an arm around her slim waist and pulled her close. "I've wanted to stake my claim since you walked into Madison High." My fingertips brushed her perfect, fresh skin. "Do the cameras reach this far?"

Her hands inched up my chest, and she shook her head.

I moved slowly, wanting to savor every second. My lips touched her forehead and trailed down the side of her face. Her skin was smooth and tasted sweet, like a garden breeze. Skylar's breath caught, and I continued my exploration until I reached my goal. Her mouth was as warm as I remembered, soft and open. I pulled her body flush with mine connecting every part of her with every part of me. Her fingers explored paths through my hair causing a jolt that traveled down to my toes. Never before had I felt this kind of sensation, this need to hold on like my world would end if I dared to let go.

Being with her made me feel invincible, as if I could do anything and be anything. When I kissed her, I didn't dread tomorrow.

NO ONE SPOKE to me at school. Not a word. Not an echo. I tried not to care. Tried to focus on what mattered as I waited at Skylar's locker. Ten minutes later, she rushed in, looking as if she just came from a teen magazine photo shoot.

She stopped short when our eyes met. A sweet smile replaced the stressful concentration that had been there moments ago.

A tingle raced through my limbs. "Morning," I said as she fiddled with her combination lock. "We've got like two minutes to get to class."

She glanced at me sideways. "Yet, you still waited. I'm flattered."

"You should be. I hate being late."

She slammed her locker and placed a hand on her hip. "Well, here's a fair warning, I'm never on time."

"Maybe together, we can work on that." I reached out and captured that same hand in mine and motioned for us to walk. Her light touch made me forget I was officially back in exile.

Blake and Chugger were already at our table when we entered class and neither acknowledged our laced fingers. It'd be an hour of awkward silence, but I didn't care. I held victory in my hand.

My books barely hit the table when Ms. Yarnell called me to her desk. She was shuffling papers when I approached, the stench of herbal tea drifting from her "Teachers Rock" coffee mug.

"Cody, it's come to my attention that you and Mr. Mason are unable to remain in the same group." My pulsed jumped. "Blake volunteered to move to another group. Unfortunately, the only one that isn't full declined working with him. Some bad history, I guess." Then she muttered something about teenage drama.

I spotted the table with only three students. I knew them all. Two were Jill's besties and the third was Gary Lawson from the football team. Didn't get along with Blake? What a joke. They worshiped him.

"Anyway, I have no choice but to move you instead. You'll be working there for the rest of the year." Her curt tone and dismissive wave made it clear that arguing would be futile.

I grabbed my books in a daze. Blake's smug expression made me itch to add more bruises to his already discolored face.

"Where are you going?" Skylar's hushed voice only added to my frustration.

"It seems the games have begun. Isn't that right, Blake?"

Skylar glared at Blake like she was waiting for an explanation.

He raised his hands. "I offered to move. Ms. Yarnell felt Cody leaving was best. I tried to argue, but she was pretty firm. I'm sorry, Skylar, but I can't be around a guy who betrayed me."

My jaw ached from how hard my teeth clamped down. His ability to lie without so much as a flicker of guilt rivaled notorious sociopaths.

I kept my focus on Skylar, afraid of what I'd do if I had to see Blake's satisfied grin one more time. "I'll see you after class."

The minute I slumped down in my new chair, Karina stopped picking at her split ends to sneer at me.

"The fall from grace is a painful one, huh Cody? Hope slut Barbie was worth it."

I didn't bother responding. She was obviously in the camp that believed Lindsay and I betrayed Blake, and no denial from me would change her mind.

Across the room, Chugger chatted away, showing no remorse for my banishment. Blake's responding laughter drifted past the tables and settled like a chain at the bottom of my stomach.

He'd just declared war.

SKYLAR

THE MINUTE I stepped out of my third period class, Zoe pulled me into the bathroom. "Okay, spill, because my head is about to explode." Her hands made a boom motion before she continued. "You're with Cody now? How in the world did this happen?" Her fists dropped to her hips like a scolding grandma, and all she needed to complete the picture was a bandana and rolling pin in her hand.

I fumbled with the buttons on my shirt, uncomfortable under her I-think-you've-lost-your-mind stare. "I told you I liked Cody. Turns out he likes me too. It's not really a big deal."

"It is a big deal. Especially when he still walks Lindsay to class. Call me cynical, but this move feels very calculated."

"The only thing calculated is the way everyone is treating him. Even Ms. Yarnell moved him from our group. Cody didn't do anything wrong. I don't know who started the rumors, but they're not true."

Zoe stepped closer, took my arms in her hands to make sure I was paying close attention. "I'll be the first to admit I don't trust anything when it comes to Lindsay, but I also don't want to see you hurt." Her sigh implied she didn't want to fight with me, either. "I'm sorry. I'm just disappointed I guess." She walked over to the mirror and patted down a few stray strands of hair. Two girls walked in and disappeared into the stalls. She waited until their doors were shut. "Chugger finally asked me out."

My mouth dropped as our eyes met through the mirror. She bit her lip and then burst into a huge smile. I felt like a terrible friend. I'd been so caught up in my drama, I missed the biggest detail in Zoe's life.

"Zoe, that's awesome."

She spun around and clapped her hands. "I know." Her voice turned dreamy, and she closed her eyes.

"When did it happen?"

Her lids popped back open, exposing two dark, infatuated eyes. "This past weekend. And we've talked every night since."

I embraced her and let go. "I'm really happy for you."

Her chest deflated. "Me too. I just wish…" Toilets flushed in the background. Zoe shook her head. "Never mind."

She pulled on the heavy bathroom door and the sound of footsteps and voices replaced the sudden strain between us. Neither said what I knew we were both thinking—how different this conversation would be if I'd picked Blake. How, now, there would be no double dates or group outings. Our boyfriends were enemies.

We turned the corner, and my moment of sadness flew away like chaff. Cody stood by my locker, waiting. He stared at his boots, his hands deep in his pockets. The droop in his shoulders said the morning had been hard on him. I walked faster, moving two strides ahead of Zoe and headed straight for my target.

He glanced up, and I was quickly encircled in broad strong arms. Cody held on like I was his energy source. His nose brushed the side of my face and dipped into the curve of my neck. "You are so who I needed to see." His lips touched my skin and an electric charge exploded between us that made me wish we were back at the park, naïve to the chaos our relationship would bring.

Zoe's exaggerated, "Excuse me," made me realize we were blocking her locker. Cody glanced around for teachers trolling the hall and seconds later, my back was against a different locker, and his lips against mine. He was asking permission without words and I pressed in, craving reassurance.

Zoe cleared her throat, loud and drawn out. "You're gonna get detention if you keep that up."

Cody pulled back, but his grin lingered over my flushed skin. "So worth it."

I straightened, my mind clearing of the smoke and heat. I'd kiss Cody all day if it didn't mean an hour serving time in detention.

He held my book while I opened my locker, and I didn't miss the dejected look on Zoe's face as she waited. I wanted to reach out and assure her somehow that our friendship would sustain this challenge.

"Are you eating with us?" she asked in a tone that implied she already knew my answer would be no.

But I didn't want to say no. I wanted to go to our table and joke and laugh. But I also wanted Cody with me. I peeked his way. He waited too, his jaw tight. I knew he'd never ask me to choose.

"I will tomorrow," I said, hoping that would ease the worry in Zoe's eyes.

"Okay." Her shoulders fell as she slowly walked down the hall toward the lunchroom. Cody slid my book into my open locker and wrapped his arms tightly around my waist. His chin rested on my shoulder.

"It'll get easier," he whispered.

I choked on a humorless laugh. "I feel like I'm going to lose her as my friend." I knew that sounded selfish, but Zoe was important to me. And now, her dating Chugger made everything more complicated.

"You won't." Irritation leaked into his voice. "I'll eat alone a couple days a week so you can hang out with her at lunch."

I turned in his arms, surprised. "You would do that?"

His thumbs pressed a comforting circle into my back, and I wanted to drown in his soft brown eyes. "I never wanted to stick you in the middle."

A low buzz of conversation was around us. A few loners, their backs against the lockers, sat on the floor eating. A group of girls to our left eyed our embrace.

We walked toward the exit, hand in hand, and I lay my head against his shoulder, allowed his warmth to calm the anxiety brewing inside me. "Will the rumors ever stop?"

"Probably not."

I shouldn't have asked. Knowing the rest of the year was going to be spent defending lies and whispers reminded me too much of the fame. I never wanted my dad's world to collide with this one, and now, it was all a blur of lines. "Why is everyone so obsessed with you and Lindsay? I mean, what is the big deal?"

Cody opened the door and held it until I stepped through. "It's not often that people defy the king of the school. Two of us within months of each other started to rock the ground this school is built on."

"So, this is about Blake?"

"No, it's about control. Madison thrives on rules and hierarchy. This school has been around a hundred years. Traditions don't die easy."

"What do we do?"

He kissed my fingers. "We trust each other."

The parking lot was nearly empty, minus a few nicotine addicts getting a hit in their cars. He pulled me between his truck and a red sedan and tucked me in front of him. Tenderly, his lips touched mine. My fingers curled into his t-shirt, my heart pounded from his touch and the adrenaline of possibly being caught. Strong arms wrapped around my waist and the kiss shifted deeper, desperate. The closer I moved, the closer Cody pressed in until there was no beginning or end.

A car door slammed in the distance and we reluctantly parted. "You keep kissing me like that and no one will even mention Lindsay's name," I said like I was waking from a dream.

The muscles in his shoulders flexed and the smile that had been there seconds earlier faded. "That was irresponsible of me. I'm sorry, Skylar."

Talk about a cold splash of water. "Sorry? Why?" My dad had said a man who cares would never hide me in the shadows. I loved that Cody was so openly affectionate.

"Because shoving our relationship in Blake's face will do nothing but bring new rumors. Ones that could be about you, and that's unacceptable." He put more distance between us. "It's one thing to be together. It's another thing to give them ammunition."

I felt a wave of disappointment, but seeing the almost explosion between Blake and Cody in first period, I knew he was right.

"But I have an idea to pass the lonely days." His hand slid into mine, and he pulled me toward the sidewalk leading to the outside picnic area. "Tell me something about you no one knows. Something that's just mine."

I smiled because I desperately wanted to be inside his head. "Okay, but tomorrow is your turn."

"Sure thing, Rock Star Princess, but my life is sadly vanilla compared to yours."

Maybe it was the slight hesitation in his voice, but somehow, I knew that wasn't true.

CODY

I TOOK A deep breath and pushed the weights off their holder. Matt's fingers hovered just under the bar in case I needed a spot. I didn't. Adrenaline alone would have lifted it.

The Storm was alive with fighters, even at six a.m. on a Monday morning. I fed off the energy, the sweat and testosterone pulsing in the air and knocked out ten reps.

The bar clattered into its holder.

"Nice," Matt said, pulling off the weight lock so he could add another twenty pounds. "You ready for the Super 32?"

"More than ready." The biggest individual wresting tournament was a week from Sunday, and it had become my obsession outside of Skylar.

Blake and I were the only ones representing Madison, and the school had taken on an eerie calm like students were waiting to see who would rise up the victor. There was no picture day chocolate milk scandal, and even the commentary on Lindsay had settled into hushed whispers.

But my guard was up. A hurricane was brewing, and I no longer had access to the Torments List to see what it was.

"You're quiet today." Matt's words didn't judge. He understood the need for silence.

I lay back on the bench and wrapped my hands around the heavier bar. "Lots to think about." With a push, the weights were high above my chest. The extra twenty pounds made my biceps burn and stretch, but I did all ten reps without help, reveling in the pain. It kept me steady. Focused. Controlled.

Two weeks had passed since I punched Blake and took back my life. I should have felt free, but with every secret Skylar and I confessed to each other, the one that I refused to share taunted me. Yesterday, Skylar told me how a girl used her birthday party to sell a story to the tabloids. The time before, she told me how once a fan broke into their house, and she woke up to him stroking her hair. Her father moved them permanently to Germany the next week.

She had no emotional boundaries, gave herself freely to me with only one expectation. That I did the same. I tried. I told her I was overweight in junior high. I told her all about Matt and how he turned me into a fighter. I just left out the parts of me that sat shattered in the back of my brain.

The bar fell back into place, and I sat up to rest my muscles.

"Grab a drink and meet me on the incline for dumbbell flys. I want to go heavy chest today, so we can ease off before your competition." Matt's hands rested on the weights before he twisted the lock free.

I noticed the watch on his wrist. It wasn't gold or fancy, but the thing looked indestructible and very expensive. "New jewelry?" It wasn't often I teased Matt, but he'd shifted when he saw me looking at it.

"Present from my father-in-law."

"He rob a bank?"

"Something like that." His sharp tone had me chuckling. I knew his wife came from money. She oozed class and wealth even while working at an underprivileged children's center. But Matt was a street guy and kept that world and his carefully separated.

I stood up and stretched, feeling slightly proud I'd rattled his chain a little.

"I caught your radio show last week," he said after dropping the last weight to the ground. "It was pretty good."

"Yeah? I'm taking Skylar there tonight. You should listen in. She's got an incredible ear for music."

He pointed to the bench a few feet away and scowled. "Go. And get that goofy grin off your face." I laughed and he sighed. "I don't know what's worse. You with a chip on your shoulder or the constant daydreaming about your new girlfriend."

"I prefer the girlfriend."

He shoved me forward in his odd way of showing affection. "Yeah. I bet you do."

SKYLAR

CODY WANTED TO pick me up, but I met him at the radio station instead. In one night, I'd lied to the two men I cared about most. My father thought I was with Zoe, and Cody had no idea that being here with him was outright defiance. My dad's latest ultimatum was clear—no contact outside of school until he met the guy who had me too infatuated to eat.

But I wasn't ready. Daddy's chemo was the one secret I locked away. He'd lost another twenty pounds, and his face seemed permanently pale, the kind that screamed terminal disease. When Cody met him, he would know my dad wasn't well. And if he started acting like Aunt Josephine, expecting my father to die, I couldn't take it. Hope was all I had left.

Cody pulled open my car door and lifted me right into his arms. His broad shoulders dwarfed mine, and I swore the guy had biceps made of steel. My stomach began its tiny flip routine when he kissed me without a word. My hands landed just above his belt, and the heat of his body flowed up my arms and right into my cheeks.

"I've wanted to do that all day," he said.

"Me too." Cody had been strict about the kissing at school. I knew it was respectful and gentlemanly, but mostly it made me crazy.

"I'm so glad your dad eased up. Did you tell him you'd be

my cohost?"

"No. Not this time." I'd forgotten how differently Cody acted outside of Madison. Guarded indifference became smiles and banter. Careful grazes became full on hugs and stolen kisses. I wanted more of that person.

With his left hand laced in mine, Cody pushed open the door with his right one and ushered me through. "It's just us, Joe and the station manager here, so I don't think you have to worry about being recognized. Joe's a metal head, so your dad's music is a little too soft for him. My manager wouldn't know rock from rap, but he's good at the business side and lets us play whatever we want, as long as the ratings stay up."

I watched his eyes light up as he pointed out each room and who did what during the day. "You really enjoy this, don't you?"

He stopped, pulled me close. "Yes. And you are the only person I've ever shared it with. I think that's worth a week of secrets."

I kissed his mouth and smiled. "Nice try, Radio Boy, but a deal's a deal." His turns had become my lifeline. For every moment my dad kept hidden from me, Cody gave me one of his. He'd chosen me. Trusted me. It filled an emptiness I didn't even know was there.

We entered the sound booth, and Joe waved from the shared glass. When he thought I wasn't looking, I saw him flash Cody a ten with his hands and bounce his eyebrows. Laughter bubbled in my chest. Joe had long salt and pepper hair braided down his back and glasses thick enough to make his eyes appear twice their normal size. He probably couldn't even see the color of my hair let alone rate my prettiness.

"Everything is digital," Cody explained, pulling up the

playlist and the songs the station had rights to. "I have fifteen minutes of commercials to disperse throughout the hour and then another ten I usually take for phone calls. The rest is music, and tonight, it's all you."

He slid his chair back and pointed to the library of singles waiting for my selection.

"The theme is Ladies' Night, so I won't question any of your choices."

"Really? So if Taylor Swift ends up on my list tonight, you won't care?"

His brow crinkled, but he kept his face a mask. "Nope. Your choice."

"And what about Demi Lovato? I heard her new single is number three on the pop charts." I was baiting him, and even though red inched up his neck, he continued to pretend he didn't care.

He swallowed twice. "I trust you."

His words sank deep into my heart, and I put him out of his misery. "My first choice is Janis Joplin, then we'll hit some Alanis Morissette and then PJ Harvey." With each name, his shoulders relaxed.

"Sounds like the perfect mix of sass and depth. I'm sensing a kinship." The glint in his eyes reflected his double meaning, but he caught my hand before I could smack him. Strong arms pulled me onto his lap. "Will you go to the Super 32 next weekend?" He must have sensed me tensing because his voice turned to a plea. "I know it's far away, and you'll have to beg your dad. But maybe tonight is the start of him letting go a little."

And this is why lying is stupid. It always led to more and more deceit. "I don't think so."

Sadness replaced the earlier cheer. "You don't know what it's like to have a team that wants you to fail, to know that everyone is against you."

I brushed my hand though his hair. "I'd go if I could."

"I know."

"I'll be cheering for you in spirit. I promise."

Though I sensed his growing frustration, Cody never pushed to meet my dad. He accepted my wariness even when it meant our time was limited to school hours and a few stolen moments in the park.

With a pat to my thigh, Cody lifted me off and back into my chair. "You better hurry and pick. We go on in ten minutes."

And with that Cody was back to his radio alter ego, CJ. But part of me recognized I'd missed out. Because for all the secrets he had shared, that was first time he'd let me see any real vulnerability.

CODY SAT WITH his back against the picnic table while I lay across the bench seat with my head in his lap. His fingers danced through my hair like air through wind chimes.

"When do you guys leave?" I asked with my eyes closed. It was a beautiful November day, mid sixties, cloudless skies, mild breeze.

"Friday evening. Coach wants to make sure we get plenty of sleep."

The Super 32 was only a few days away, and Cody's mood had become darker and more withdrawn as it approached. It was like the radio show had been a turning point, only taking us backward instead of forward. His secrets were hardly even noteworthy this week. A fall from his bike at four gave him the scar on his right arm. He always ordered a cheeseburger, but took off the cheese because he only liked a hint of the flavor.

Nothing significant. Nothing to ease the pain of the newest rumor that had settled over the school. Last week, Cody started eating with Lindsay in the library on the days I ate with Zoe. I couldn't exactly complain. Zoe wanted to be with Chugger, which meant we sat at Blake's table. But the move had fueled a new wave of whispers and accusations.

"You're pouting," he said, running his thumb along the line of my lips.

"I'm sorry. I guess Jill's comment about you and Lindsay bothered me. Quickly, tell me your secret so I can focus on that next time I hear how you guys hooked up behind the N-P aisle. Or was it the W-Z section?"

Soft lips lingered on my forehead. "You're welcome in there anytime."

"I know. I just thought things would die down by now." But I'd been known to live in my own fairytale world. Or at least that's what Aunt Josephine had said when I yelled at her for replacing dad's bed with a hospital grade one. She said the new bed would be more efficient and comfortable for him. I said she needed to stop turning our house into a nursing home. We hadn't spoken since.

"I threw up before my first match."

"What?" My eyes popped open, and I shielded the sun to watch Cody's face.

"My secret today. Last year at our first match, I saw Matt in the stands, and I ran to the bathroom and hugged the toilet for like five minutes. Coach had to send someone after me. Strange thing is, I think I'm more nervous about Saturday than

I was then."

I sat up and spun until I straddled the bench next to him. He'd lowered his defenses, given me another chance to put him first. And this time I would. "Come over to dinner tomorrow night. I want you to meet my dad so I can see you kill it in Greensboro."

He didn't even pause before pulling me close to him and dropping his mouth to mine.

We separated, and his eyes sparkled with a happiness I hadn't seen since our first night at the park. "Thank you." He cupped my face. "I don't think you realize how much I needed you there. How much you matter to me."

"You matter to me, too." The alarm on my phone dinged, telling us our twenty minutes were up. My dad would start asking questions if I showed up later than five.

I pulled his hand until we both stood and shook off the gnawing unease about what I'd just agreed to do. There was no going back now. Tomorrow night, Cody would learn the only secret powerful enough to destroy me.

CODY

MY PALMS WERE like double-sided tape on my steering wheel as I parked in Skylar's driveway. I prayed the four layers of deodorant I put on would actually work. I was about to meet my girlfriend's dad. My girlfriend's highly protective dad. My girlfriend's top-50-greatest-artist-of-all-time dad.

Gripping the wheel, I forced the air in and out of my lungs until my heart rate settled to a manageable flurry. Her front door swung open and soon the reason for all my anxiety walked out on the porch. It baffled me that she could evoke such conflicting physical responses. Tingly, hot fire and relaxing peace, all with one smile.

I opened my door, stepping out to meet her as she crossed the grass to me. Now close, I could see worry in the set of her brow. Her hands twitched, touching her locket, then her hair, then her locket again. She was nervous.

"Hey." I reached out, her skin the only cure for the drum line in my chest.

She stopped without folding into my arms—our usual greeting.

"You okay?"

She fiddled with her hair again, moving it into a ponytail and then releasing it down her back. "Yeah, I just need to talk to you before you go in there."

Lacing our fingers, I lifted her hand up for a light kiss, pulling her closer in the process. "What's up?" She waited, watching me, deciding, I guess, what to say. I didn't like it. "Skylar, what's going on?"

"My dad won't look like you expect. He's sick. He's been sick for a while. That's my secret. It's why I've waited so long for you to meet him." Her gaze dropped to the ground, and she tried unsuccessfully to pull her hand from mine.

Instead, I tugged her closer and lifted her chin to look at me. "How sick?"

Tears flooded those crystal clear eyes. "Nothing we can't handle, but sick enough that you'll see a difference." The last word no more than a breath.

My heart ached, a twisting pain that settled to a dull throb. I knew what this meant for her. I wrapped my arms around her rigid body and enclosed her in the warmth of my embrace. An embrace meant to show that she could lean on me, rely on me, let go with me.

"I wish you had told me sooner. I could have been there for you all this time." I ran my hand down the back of her head, her crimson curls soft under my fingers.

"I wanted to. But telling you makes it more…real. And I don't want to talk about his illness or focus on it. I just want you to come in and act like everything is normal."

Skylar's favorite word and one I'd come to loathe. Giving Skylar "normal" was like taking a crowbar to my head over and over. It meant backing off when I wanted to smother. It meant letting her sit with Blake two days a week so she could hang out with Zoe. And now, when I wanted to hold her and help her through her pain, it meant pretending it wasn't there.

"So, should I be worried about coming out of this in one piece? I mean, is your dad going to strangle me with his guitar cords?" I asked, reluctantly following her tugging.

She stopped, her hand resting on the door that would carry me into her world. "I have no idea. I haven't brought anyone home in seven years. Not even girlfriends."

"I'm honored then."

Her head tilted, that playful look I loved magnified by a perfectly arched eyebrow. "You should be."

She swung the door open, and we stepped into what I guess could be called a foyer. High ceilings, huge chandelier, marble floors. Every inch was immaculate. My mom could probably rattle off the names of every item, but my mind summed it up into one cold reality—I was about to meet Donnie Wyld.

My hand tightened in hers.

"Don't be nervous," she whispered.

I leveled a stare. "Are you kidding me?"

She giggled, and we walked into a living room. The large leather couches and huge T.V. were almost enough to make the room seem ordinary, except for the black and silver guitar placed on its stand in the corner. The red "W" with one edge an eagle's wing meant this was Donnie Wyld's signature piece. That guitar posed in every picture, went on every tour, and now I was within two feet of touching the iconic instrument. My hands itched, the fan in me fighting every instinct to reach out.

I looked at Skylar, trying to see the fun girl at the park or the girlfriend I'd kissed dozens of times. But all I could see was Donnie Wyld's daughter.

"Skylar?" A voice called from the distance.

"In here, Dad."

I dropped her hand and put at least three feet between us while my eyes watched the door in terrified anticipation. Then he appeared and sucked all the air out of the room.

I scanned the man who filled the doorway, the surrounding halo of light a perfect fit for the introduction of a rock legend. Skylar was right. He was thin, his face slightly more pale than I expected. But nothing about this man in front of me seemed weak.

My pulse raced faster than the band's Grammy winner, "Road to Oblivion."

He glanced between us before putting out a hand. I stared at it. That hand could do things on a guitar that weren't human. I'd been reduced to a blubbering fan, my own hand trembling as it met his firm shake.

"Donnie Wyld. Nice to meet you, Cody." His tone matched the hard set of his eyes.

I willed my mind to work. "Yes, sir," I croaked. "I'm your biggest fan. I have all your music. Your guitar riff in "Sanctuary" was so insane, I wanted to cry." *Did I really just say that?* "I mean, if I was the type to cry that is."

He stared at my hand, still gripped in his, and I released, mentally kicking myself for sounding like a teenage girl at a Taylor Swift concert.

"Thank you. I heard you're quite a fan of my daughter's, too."

I suddenly remembered Skylar, my head jerking in her direction. Her shoulders were shaking, her teeth practically biting a hole in her bottom lip as she tried to hold back her laughter. I shot her a desperate look, but she didn't come to my rescue. She seemed to be enjoying this moment.

"Yes, sir." What else was I supposed to say? Tell him I thought she was the most beautiful woman I'd ever seen? That when I kissed her, my body exploded in a way I only thought possible in movies? That her smile not only lit up the room, but changed my entire outlook on the day? Yeah, that would go over like a brick wall.

Donnie leaned in and whispered something in her ear that made the laugh she was holding come out with a snort. Her hand flew to her mouth as her cheeks flushed, and she pushed her dad away with a warning look.

I could only imagine what he said to her in that moment, but I was sure it wasn't flattering to me. Jamming my hands into my pockets, I tried to think of anything to say that wasn't idiotic.

Suddenly Skylar's arm was around my waist and, by instinct, I pulled her in, leaning over to smell her herbal shampoo that she had told me was called Jasmine. Whatever the name, I didn't care. As if on cue, my heartbeat slowed, my unease spun away like a musical note in a windstorm.

"Cody's one of the few people at my school who still appreciates quality music. He's like Wikipedia. Give him a title, and he can name the album and the band." Her proud, affectionate words came with a squeeze.

Donnie crossed his arms. "Good to know. We're working on a new cut. It would be nice to get an opinion from someone your age. Especially if you have an ear for music."

My mouth dropped open as if a genie had just granted me one wish. "I'd be honored, sir. Really, wow. That would be…wow."

Skylar nudged me, a clear sign I was sounding star-struck again. "We should go eat," she said.

Pulling myself together, I let her lead me to the food. We passed a grand dining room that could easily seat an army, but ended up at a small round kitchen table.

The smell of roasted chicken and potatoes filled the air as Skylar poured each of us a glass of lemonade. If I wasn't so nervous, I'd be starving, but the rocks that lined my stomach like a retaining wall pretty much killed my appetite.

"So, Skylar tells me you're the captain of the wrestling team." The statement was an invitation to tell him about myself. He took a bite of his chicken, carefully chewing as he waited for a response.

I rubbed my sweating hands on my jeans. "Yes, sir."

"Cody won state last year," Skylar volunteered, sending me a proud look.

Her dad raised an impressed brow. "Really. You must be pretty good then. Have you been doing it for a long time?"

"No, sir. Just a couple of years. During the spring of my sophomore year, I started training with Matt Holloway. He's a genius in the ring. I walked on last year just hoping to make the team. I had no idea we'd go to state."

He finished chewing and took a drink. "How is this year going? Will there be a repeat?"

Immediately, my shoulders fell, my mood following them. "Not sure yet. We're not the same team we were last year." That was the understatement of the century. My position as captain was a joke. The team had turned on me, making practices strained and unproductive. Even Coach was losing faith in me.

I glanced at Skylar, my lone cheerleader. "My first competition is this weekend. It's in Greensboro. I'd really like Skylar to come if that's okay with you."

He took a bite, continuing to chew slowly and watched me like a man preparing for a western showdown.

"I'd be with my coach, so we wouldn't be alone." Nor

would I disrespect him like that. "She could ride with Zoe, so she didn't have to take the trip by herself. A lot of kids from school reserve a hotel room together."

His muscles tensed, his eyes darting to his daughter who watched in anticipation.

I went in for the final push. "This tournament is critical if I want to wrestle in college. It would really mean a lot if she could be there to support me. You have my word, I won't do anything to disrespect her or you."

He paused. I held my breath. And the moment of anticipation that followed stretched on like a road to nowhere.

SKYLAR

"I'LL HAVE TO think about it."

My heart leapt into my throat. I knew that tone. Daddy would let me go, but not until we'd had an eight-hour lecture on the subject. I tried to hide the huge grin that threatened to spread. My dad was playing tough guy, and I was enjoying seeing Cody squirm.

"Skylar tells me that you're the only one at school who has recognized her. Why do you think that is?"

I kicked my father's foot and gave him the don't-go-there stare. He ignored me. My father had expressed his concern about Cody's intentions, despite my reassurances.

Cody swallowed his food and took a drink, his Adam's apple moving slowly as he processed the question. "I don't know, sir. I thought she looked familiar but didn't put two and two together until I saw she used your wife's maiden name. Most kids our age don't get past downloading a song to iTunes, so they wouldn't make the connection. But I love the history and the people behind a song as much as the music."

My father pursed his lips and I smirked. Score one for Cody.

"And next year? What are your plans?"

Now my father was just being cliché.

"I'm looking at a few wrestling programs. I'd like to stay close to this area, but I'm open to seeing what happens." Cody sent me a smile that made my heart flutter.

"Really? That's good. Skylar's got big plans too. She just applied to fashion school in Paris. ESMOD has a great program and she's a shoo-in."

My dad slid his foot away before I could kick it again, but the damage was done.

Cody set his fork down and focused all his attention my way. "You're moving to Paris?" His voice didn't sound right. It was too grainy, too high-pitched.

I opened my mouth to say something, to justify my actions in some way. It wasn't a serious application. My father made me send in my portfolio. Insisted that I shouldn't let his illness stop my dreams.

When I didn't deny it, Cody slowly turned back to my dad. "That's um...great."

My father continued his battery of questions for another twenty minutes. No subject was left untouched—school, home life, faith. Cody answered every one, but his posture had shifted and his smile was no longer natural.

When my dad finally decided his interrogation was finished, he stood to clear the table. Cody gathered his plate and silverware and offered to help. I noticed he had eaten very little since my dad dropped the ESMOD bomb.

"It's a school night," my dad reminded him. "Best you get on home."

"Oh, okay. Yes, sir." Cody's voice cracked and his ears reddened.

My dad stood between the kitchen and our exit, shoulders square, legs spread, arms crossed. His attempt at intimidation made me want to burst into laughter. I couldn't believe it was working on Cody, but the constant hands in and out of his pockets spoke volumes.

"Cody. It was good talking to you." My father's hand shot out, clasping Cody's again. "You understand that Skylar is my life. You hurt her and I will personally end yours."

"Dad!"

Cody's eyes practically overtook his face as my father squeezed his hand harder. They were close to the same height, my dad having only an inch on Cody, but in that moment, my dad resembled the gun-toting robot from *The Terminator*.

"I understand, sir. Skylar is an amazing girl, and I would feel exactly the same way if I were her father."

That seemed to appease my dad and made me want to smother Cody with kisses. With his hand free, Cody nodded toward the foyer. I nudged my dad, getting him to let us pass and then walked Cody to the door.

"When were you going to tell me about Paris?" he whispered, barely touching me.

"I wasn't. I can't see past next week let alone next year."

"Is that how you feel about me, too?"

"What? No. Of course not." I reached out, put my hand on his arm. The muscles were tense, the bump of a vein hard against my fingertips. I'd never seen Cody so upset. He was generally the epitome of calm and controlled.

"You sure?"

"Yes," I lengthened the word, wanting to say more, but not in range of my dad's prying ears.

The tension fell from Cody's shoulders. "Okay. Let me know what your dad says about Greensboro." With a platonic squeeze to my arm, he disappeared behind the door.

I spun around to glare at my father. "Was that necessary?"

He walked toward me, concern etched in the lines that

spread from his eyes. "Yes. And after seeing the way you two look at each other, this next conversation is necessary too." He pointed to the formal couch in the great room, the one with claw legs and hard cushions that he knew I hated. "Sit."

I rolled my eyes but did as he commanded. He took a seat on the coffee table in front of me, studying my face with disappointment. "How serious is this?"

My finger moved to my mouth, my teeth gnawing my recently polished nail. "What do you mean?"

"I mean he practically spit out his food when I said Paris. This kid thinks you two have a future together."

When he eyed my half-chewed nail, I quickly dropped my hand. "Maybe we do. I like him. A lot."

He took a deep breath and clasped his hands. "Okaaay." He said the word as if he was already thinking about his next statement. "In that case, it's time we have the sex talk."

The blood drained from my face.

"I know your tutor discussed the mechanics with you, so we won't do that, but I doubt you understood hormones or desires at that point."

I wanted to die. I wanted to curl into a ball and hide under the table my father sat on.

"Teenage boys think about sex a lot."

"Daddy, please stop." My mortification was met with equal discomfort.

"Do you think this is easy for me, Skylar? You don't think I wish your mother was here to have this chat? But she isn't, so I'm what you've got."

I put my head in my hands, shaking it back and forth in hopes of removing the sound of my father's words as he continued to discuss a boy's hormonal mind.

"The point is, Skylar, if a boy thinks he can get sex, he will more than likely try to. Especially if he likes a girl as much as Cody obviously likes you. So, it's important you let him know right away that you have boundaries and what they are. A good guy will respect them, and a guy who doesn't needs to be dropped."

"Okay, I got it. Can I go now?"

He went on as if I never spoke. "I know your generation takes sex lightly, thinks the idea of waiting for marriage is archaic. God doesn't give commands to torture us. He gives them to protect us."

My father removed my hands from my face, replacing them with his, so he could look into my eyes.

"This is important. I saw the way you touched, the familiarity that's there. As your closeness grows, you will continue to move forward physically. You need to understand that when sex enters a relationship, the relationship changes, and you can't take it back."

Despite my absolute loathing of the conversation, I took pity on father. "I understand. And I do plan to wait 'til I'm married."

He sighed with relief, looking as if he aged ten years during that conversation. "Good." One hand fell away. The other stroked my cheek. "You've grown into a smart and beautiful woman. You're almost eighteen, and the truth is, if you wanted to take the next step, there is little I can do or say to stop you. But I do hope you wait."

"I will. Now can we *please* stop talking about this?"

He chuckled. "Okay."

I stood, ready to leave the room.

"Skylar?"

I froze, wincing at what else my father could possibly say to me.

"If you want to go this weekend, you can. Just, please, promise me you won't put yourself in a situation where you're alone with no accountability. Hormones tend to trump good intentions."

I kissed him on the cheek. "Thank you! And I promise. No compromising situations."

I practically danced up the stairs while I texted.

Me: *Get ready to kick some butt. I'm going to Greensboro!*

CODY

"YOU'RE AWFUL CHIPPER this morning," Lindsay said as she turned the knob on her combination lock. She wore all black again, covering every possible inch of skin, and it bugged me. She used to wear bright colors and dresses.

"I met Skylar's dad last night."

"Yeah? How'd that go?"

I shuddered, remembering. "Terrifying, but he did say Skylar could go to the Super 32, so the threats were worth it."

Her lips tipped up a centimeter, which is more than they'd done in a week. I counted it a positive. "Getting serious, I see. Way to go."

She was my biggest cheerleader when it came to Skylar. It seemed to make her feel better, being able to focus on someone's life besides her own.

I leaned back against the lockers. "I'm way past serious."

A flash of green caught my eye as at least a hundred fake one-dollar bills fell out of Lindsay's locker. I picked one up. Both sides were marred with blood red marker that read, "WHORE."

My muscles tightened like ropes stretched to their breaking point. "This has to stop. You have to say something." I glanced toward her locker and saw a metal stick made to look like a stripper's pole wedged in there as well.

"It's fine." She pulled out the offending piece and tossed it into the nearest trash can. "I'd rather this than the phone calls."

"What phone calls?"

"At least ten a day. I swear I've blocked a million numbers." She didn't elaborate, but I could only imagine.

Squatting down, she frantically scooped up the bills lining the floor in front of her locker.

I crouched next to her and stopped her manic cleanup. "Lindsay, who has your locker combination?"

Her movement stilled and teary eyes met mine. "I don't know. Who had yours? Don't you see? It's never going to stop."

"It will if you would just tell someone." The chill in my voice was a small reflection of the anger coursing through me. I wanted to scream, punch and kick the locker, do anything to stop her being a target of this hatred.

"What? Like you did sophomore year?"

I hated that she knew. That she had been a part of the Torments List's exclusive group and had seen the pictures. "That was different."

"How?"

I was suddenly in that dark locker room again, the cold floor hard against my naked back. Helpless. Hopeless. Pain gripped my chest, and I willed the image away. I never told a soul. Never turned in the guy who terrorized me for years. "Because I won't let it happen again. I won't cower to another bully."

Lindsay touched my arm. "Please, Cody. Don't say anything. It will just get worse."

Obnoxious laughter came from above, and some kid I didn't recognize stood over us, his arms crossed. "I heard this is where we come for lap dances. I guess I'll have to get in line."

Lindsay disappeared in my furious haze. So did the fluorescent lights that flickered and the squeak of shoes pounding down the halls. Only his laughter remained. Laughter that matched the echoes in the locker room. Laughter that stopped the minute my fist struck his jaw.

The world returned in a flash of sound. Screams from the students, yells from teachers, but I kept pounding, pounding, pounding. The memory of that laughter banging around in my head like a wrecking ball.

Strong arms trapped mine, pulling me off the bloody kid who was now writhing in pain. My eyes began to focus, first landing on Lindsay's terrified, tear-streaked face. Then on Blake who appeared out of nowhere. His smirk was subtle, victorious. The quiet, the calm. It'd been a trap. He slid to the right, pushing through a crowd until he found his goal.

Skylar.

She watched with horror, glancing from me to the bloody boy, then from me to Lindsay.

I lunged when Blake whispered something in her ear and pulled her out of the crowd. *No, no, no. This wasn't happening.*

"That's enough!" Principal Rayburn hissed before pushing me toward his office. "I told you I'd make an example of you if you pulled another stunt. Well, congratulations, Mr. James, you officially have my attention."

"They put a stripper pole in her locker." He pushed me through the hall with more strength than I expected. "They called her a whore."

We went right past the receptionist and into his office. He shoved me into the blasted wooden chair I hated.

"When are you kids going to realize you aren't the authority in this school? Violence isn't the answer."

"Then what is?" I balled my fist, ready to fight for my life. "Because nothing you have done has stopped it."

The heat from his stare could have dried the sweat beading on my forehead. There was no trust in his eyes, just accusation like I was responsible for the whole scenario. "You're suspended. Three days. No Super 32 and you're off the team for good if I catch you fighting again."

"Sir..." It was too much. A penalty far greater than the crime.

"My decision is final. I'm done with you boys thinking you run this school."

I let my head fall into my shaking hands while Principal Rayburn called my parents. I wasn't trying to run the school. I was fighting for my life, for Lindsay's life. And failing miserably.

SKYLAR

MADISON HIGH FELT tarnished. The echo of footsteps a rumbling sound in my ears. The chatter of students a constant reminder of Cody's brutality. He was a madman, punching and punching even after the guy had stilled.

A locker slammed next to my head.

"He was suspended three days. Chugger just texted me. Coach is sending him in Cody's place this weekend." Zoe's need to dive right into gossip made me want to storm off. Instead, I stayed frozen. My back pressed against the locker, and my arms folded around my economics book.

"Skylar?"

Disgust weaved into my voice. "I don't want to talk about it, okay?"

Her face paled. "I was just trying to tell you what's going on. I'm sorry. I should have known this would upset you."

Yes, she should have known. Because my boyfriend wasn't just suspended for fighting. He'd become someone I didn't recognize. Someone who made me question sharing my deepest secrets. Someone I never would have taken to meet my dad.

My phone dinged, and my stupid heart stuttered because I hoped it was Cody. The one person I wanted to slap, yet comfort.

Zoe eyed my purse. "That's probably him."

The phone dinged again, and I pulled it out.

Cody: *Meet me at Veteran's Park*

A demand. No, "Please." No, "I'm sorry." Just an expectation that I'd skip school to talk to him. And sadly, I knew I would.

Zoe saw the text and frowned. "Go talk to him. I'll cover for you."

"You will?" My anger faltered, replaced by gratitude that Zoe would put aside her feelings for mine even though she still believed Cody betrayed Blake.

She spun her pinky ring round and round. "I don't like it, and I still think he's bad for you. But if I were in your shoes, I'd want to know what happened."

"I won't be gone long." I hugged her quickly and took off toward the parking lot. Hoping. Wishing. Praying Cody's sudden violence would make sense.

CODY

MY CUT AND bruised knuckles throbbed almost as much as my chest. I'd texted Skylar ten minutes ago, and she never responded. Blake pulled her away, and Coach wouldn't even look at me when Principal Rayburn told him what happened. Could the day get any worse?

A flash of black caught my eye, and I walked toward Skylar's Mustang the minute she parked, willing myself to be calm and ignore the crashing anxiety brewing inside. She came, so maybe I hadn't lost everything.

Skylar emerged from the car, her face encased in hurt. There was no smile. No greeting. She barely made eye contact.

My hand itched to reach for her. "Talk to me."

She slammed her door. "Why did you have to punch him?"

The explanation choked me. I'd lost control, reverted to a time that wouldn't stop haunting me. "He was harassing Lindsay."

"So? There wasn't a better way to handle it?" She pulled at her locket in jerky motions. "You could have turned him in."

A muscle in my jaw jumped. "And then what? They investigate and the entire senior class lies and says they don't know who did it? Stuff like this has been happening since school started. It's happening outside of school, too. Social media. Prank calls. I had to send a message."

Her teeth gnawed on her lower lip. "You didn't stop. Even

after he quit fighting back."

Her words tore at the fabric of my resolve. "You're right, and I regret losing control. But I've done the easy stuff. I've walked her to class, sat with her at lunch. I've called people out when they act like she's trash." I squeezed my eyes, trying to get my swirling emotions under control. "No one should ever be made to feel like that, Skylar. I had to do something."

"Well, you did, and that something got you suspended, took away your chance to compete, and will probably make my dad even stricter when I tell him. I'm not trying to be selfish, Cody, but when is Lindsay going do something for herself?"

I cupped her cheek, willed those green eyes to stop looking at me like I'd let her down. She leaned into my touch, and I felt my pulse at every pressure point. My free hand found her waist, and I pulled her close. "Lindsay's scared. She's never been the outcast. She's always had the security of Blake and his friends. Eventually, I know she'll find the inner strength to get through this. She just needs support in the meantime." Matt had been mine, and I would be hers. He had saved me. I would pay it forward.

She tapped her forehead against my chest. "I'm just so disappointed about this weekend."

"Me, too."

Skylar rubbed her hands up and down my spine. "How bad is it going to be for you?"

I exhaled like I'd been holding my breath for an hour. "I'll probably be grounded for the rest of my life." I pulled her closer, played with the strands of hair that fell down her back. Lunch was almost over, and she'd have to leave soon.

"Are you still going to Greensboro?" I asked even though the question brought another round of disappointment. I still hadn't accepted that my only chance to win Super 32 was gone.

"I have to. Zoe's parents only let her go because I was going. And now that Chugger is competing, she'd kill me if I backed out."

I was glad she talked to my chest because she couldn't see the way those words ripped at my gut. Chugger took my place in the competition. Blake wanted my place in Skylar's life.

He was doing exactly what he threatened—taking everything from me one piece at a time.

SKYLAR

I'D NEVER CONSIDERED myself a mean person or a vengeful person or even a jealous person, but when Lindsay cornered me in the crowded hall after school, I felt a little of all three.

People gave us a wide berth as they walked past but slowed down and strained their necks to listen. In their minds, Cody's girlfriend and his mistress were about to have a cat fight. Maybe we were.

"What do you want?" I wasn't in the mood to talk or to be nice. Zoe called Lindsay a drama queen, a liar, and a threat to my relationship with Cody. I was beginning to believe her.

Lindsay swung her hair to the side, used it as a shield to those on our left. "I just wanted you to know that it wasn't Cody's fault. He was defending me."

Duh. I was his girlfriend for crying out loud. "I know. Cody tells me everything." Okay, maybe that last part was unnecessary, but, seriously, did her eyes have to be so dang blue and innocent looking? No wonder Cody wanted to save her. "Damsel in distress" was in her DNA.

"Yeah, of course he does. Good. I was worried you'd be upset and with everything that happened sophomore year with Tom Baker and the pictures, he's just really sensitive about things."

I flinched but kept myself still. "Right. Sophomore year."

"But he was so excited about meeting your dad; he really

was."

For a moment I could only panic. "What did he say about my dad?"

Her eyes widened. "Just that he was really scary. And he asked a bunch of questions about wrestling and the future."

My mouth dropped and my emotions moved from mildly irritated to fully ticked off. He was talking to her about me? About my dad?

Her voice became rushed, and I wondered if she could see the damage she was doing with this little contrived apology. "I'm saying all the wrong things. I'm sorry. I just wanted you to know how much he cares about you. And after all his struggles, and after all he's been through, I want him to be happy."

"Yeah. Me, too." Zoe was right. The girl oozed sweetness and cyanide at the same time. "Listen, I gotta go."

I walked to my car in a daze. He told her things about us. Things about him I didn't know. All our secrets we shared. Had he shared them with her too?

THE ELECTRICITY IN the Greensboro Coliseum was a living, breathing thing. It bounced off the walls, swirled through the stands and settled on the wrestlers sparring in different areas. It zapped me, too, my heart pounding in anticipation.

It was nine in the morning on Saturday, and after a sleepless night in a lumpy hotel bed and four unreturned calls to Cody, I fed off the energy. Ten circle mats lined the floor with teams surrounding them. Stadium seating ran the length of the mats and, while mostly full, Zoe and I found an entire row to ourselves.

"I'm so nervous for him," Zoe said, squeezing my hand. Chugger was stretching and getting ready for his first match. "He doesn't think he has a shot, but I know he really wants at least one win."

The guys walked toward the circle with puffed chests and killer expressions.

I bit back a laugh. Wrestling uniforms were ridiculous. It was like Speedos and overalls collided to produce a fashion disaster. I wondered what Cody would look like wearing one. His body was muscle and sharpness. The lines in his arms carved like stone. Every inch of his broad chest would be on display, his tight six-pack etched in the black spandex.

Zoe poked my side. "Why are you blushing?"

"What?" My cheeks burned. "I'm not."

"Oh, yes, you are." Her mouth hung open. "Skylar Da Lange, what were you just thinking about?"

"Nothing." Cody. "I was thinking how ridiculous their uniforms are." And how hot Cody would look wearing his. "Stop staring at me like that."

The whistle blew the same time my phone dinged.

Cody: *I finally got my phone back. Are you at the match?*

Zoe hit my arm and pointed to the arena floor. Chugger struggled against his opponent, the two spinning as they hung on to one another. Blake catalogued every move from the sidelines, cheering on his friend. I wondered if Cody would do the same thing. If he'd find joy just from being here and watching the sport he loved.

Me: *Can you FaceTime?*

The noise level was manageable. Most people were either

engrossed in a match or waiting for one while they played on their phones.

Cody: *Yes. Hold on.*

Seconds later, the face I hadn't seen in twenty-four hours hit my screen.

"Hi," he said with a grin as wide as mine. "Gotta love technology."

"Were you in a lot of trouble?"

"Yes and no. Yes, because of how I handled it. No, because I was defending someone. Only grounded for a week." He lay back on his bed, and I noticed he had a dark blue pillowcase with stripes on the edge.

I wanted to see more. Know what his world was like when he wasn't in school. Know what happened his sophomore year. "Show me your room."

"No way. It's messy."

"Ah, come on. I want to see what posters you have on the walls."

Panic flashed in Cody's eyes, and I burst out laughing. My dad. Hundred bucks said my dad was on his wall. "You have his…"

"Don't judge."

Zoe nudged me. "You're missing it. They're about to start round three."

Cody sat up. "Is Blake wrestling?"

"No, Chugger. It's his first match. Wanna see?"

There was a twinge of pain in his eyes, but he said, "Yes.'

I walked down the steps, holding the rail for stability. When I hit the fourth row, I held up my phone, so Cody could watch the match over the spectators' heads. "Can you see?" I asked into the speaker.

"Down just a little. Okay. Yeah. Hold there."

I stood at the rail through Chugger's last round. He beat his opponent, I think, because Blake hollered, and I heard a faint "yes" through the phone. Chugger ran back to his coach and got a slap on the back. I turned the phone back around.

"Good?"

Cody heaved a big sigh. "Yeah. That was cool. Thank you."

I sat on the closest empty seat. Whistles reverberated off the walls, and two men with huge drinks stepped past me to get to the aisle. I ached to ask him what Lindsay meant about Tom Baker and the pictures but wouldn't do it over the phone. "I miss you. I really wish you were here."

Cody brow dipped. "I know. I wish I was there, too. What are your plans?"

I groaned. "I think we'll be here forever. And I'm already kinda done." It wasn't that I wasn't having fun, but wrestling was pretty boring to watch, and without Cody, everything felt empty. My first real independent outing, and all I wanted was to be home. Sad. Very sad. "What about you?"

He tapped his lips. "Hmmmm. Well, I'm grounded from TV. Grounded from the Internet. I finished all my homework an hour ago. So, I guess I'll sit and mope." His smile said he was teasing, but he fell silent. The kind of silent that told me he was sorting though a million thoughts.

A knock had Cody dropping the phone. My screen was suddenly a close up of his comforter, but the voices remained clear.

A woman's voice, whose tone definitely implied authority, spoke. "You have a friend here. Five minutes."

"Who?"

"She said her name was Lindsay. Was she the one?"

The curiosity and innuendo in her words made my heart pound against my ribcage. I sucked in a breath to calm myself and licked my suddenly dry lips. I heard a faint, "I'll be there in one second," and then a door closing.

Cody's face appeared back on the phone. "I have to run just real quick. Can I call you back?"

I forced a smile. "Sure."

The rumors swirled in my head. The ones I chose not to believe. The ones that said Cody and Lindsay had been intimate on more than one occasion. Had she been in his room? Did she know how his bed felt? Had she seen my dad on his wall?

A painful pulse started beneath my skull as I trudged up the steps to Zoe.

She beamed like sunshine against my darkness. "He won. Did you see?" She practically bounced in her chair until she noticed my scowl. "What's wrong?"

I clenched my phone. "Nothing."

Everything.

CODY

THE TINY BLOND I defended waited for me on the porch.

"Are you okay?" I pulled the front door shut and away from my parents' eavesdropping.

Lindsay fiddled with the hem of her shirt. "I came to check on you."

"I'm fine."

A strangled beat of silence.

Finally, her eyes met mine, her teeth mashing her bottom lip. "Principal Rayburn asked me what happened."

"Did you tell him?" Maybe one good thing would come from this mess.

"Yes. Not that it made a difference. You're still suspended because of me. And we both know his supposed investigation will turn up nothing."

"Maybe so, but you told the truth, which means they'll lay low for a while." I reached out and gently took her arm. "I should have handled the situation better, but I don't regret putting him in his place. No one should ever speak to you like that."

"I've cost you too much. Super 32. Skylar. I tried talking to her, but I swear I only made things worse." Her shaky voice told me tears would be coming soon. I'd never known Lindsay to be so fragile; but every day they attacked her, I saw her shrink further and further into herself.

"Don't worry about Skylar. We're good." I dropped my hand when Lindsay nodded.

She glanced toward her car then stepped in that direction. "Well, I'm going to go. I just wanted to say thank you. You left school afterwards."

"They kind of make you do that when they suspend you."

She recoiled from my words, apologizing again.

"Lindsay, stop. It's not your fault."

"You keep saying that, but it doesn't feel like it's not."

I couldn't help it. She just looked so broken and lost standing there. I pulled her into a hug, and she melted into me, clinging as if I offered her some kind of lifeline. She needed me, and I needed to see this thing through. Needed to vindicate all the Fatty Jameses in the world who suffered this kind of abuse.

She pulled away, but I kept my hands on her arms, urging her to look at me. "You good? Done apologizing for other people's stupidity?"

"Yes."

It was a weak, "Yes." Weak because she didn't believe me. Weak because she still hadn't accepted that the things happening to her were not her fault.

She hugged herself. "So, when will you be back in school?"

"Wednesday. Thankfully, they counted Friday as day one."

She started down the steps. "I'll see you Wednesday, then."

"Hey, Lindsay." Her head turned. "Will do you something for me?"

"Sure. Anything."

"Will you change your number? Today?"

"I'll try." With a wave, she walked slowly back to her car.

I suddenly felt like her father, keeping her in my line of

sight until she was safely pulling away from the curb. She was changing. The sweet, easy-going girl I'd known for years was barely a shell of her former self. A bitter taste coated my tongue.

I would never understand how people could be so cruel.

SKYLAR

BLAKE MADE IT to the quarterfinals, but didn't make it past round two. I was glad. Nothing since my phone call had been fun. Not the arcade or the laser tag or the movie. Cody called me three times, and I made an excuse not to talk all three times. Lindsay knew his secrets. She went to his house. He talked about my dad. Until I could sort through what that meant, I couldn't pretend everything was okay.

"Dad, I'm home," I called into our house on Sunday. There was no answer, and I wondered if he was sleeping again.

I forced my heavy feet to the stairs and dropped my bag at the bottom. I was too tired to climb. Too tired to sort through the cascade of emotions.

Our back door slammed, and I jumped.

"Skylar?" Dad rounded the corner and swept me into a bear hug. He was sweaty and grimy soil smudged his cheeks and forearms.

"Were you outside?" I squeezed him despite my shock. My dad hadn't been outdoors in weeks. Something about the sun hurting his eyes and draining his already fragile energy. But this man was vibrant and full of life. I pulled back and studied him. "Are you feeling okay?"

"I feel great. Better than great." He squeezed me again, leaving an arm around my shoulders. "Come on. I finally cleared out that weed bed that's been bugging me. You can help me plant some flowers."

I was too stunned to speak. I walked on, trying to make sense of his dramatic change.

"Princess, I missed you like crazy." He leaned down and kissed the top of my head. "I know you're all about independence and stuff, but I'm thinking no more overnighters until you're off at fashion school."

Tears fell from my eyes. I tried to stop them, but that only led to more sobs.

"Hey," My father voice grew very serious, very fast. "Who do I need to kill? Cody? Did he try something?"

I cried harder because he wasn't even there to try something. He was with Lindsay. "No," I said through sobs. "He got suspended. He didn't go."

My father pursed his lips. I hadn't told him about Cody's fight or about Lindsay or Blake. I'd tried so hard to keep my two worlds separate. To be the strong one for my dad while he fought for his life.

"It sounds like you and I need to have a long conversation." He pulled some tissue from the box on our end table and waited for me to blow my nose and wipe away the tears. He opened the back door, and we sat next to each other on the swing. "You've been keeping things from me."

"You've been so sick. I didn't want to burden you." I messed with my fingernails, picking off the color Zoe and I put on just hours ago.

"Sweetheart, you are not a burden. Ever."

I lay my head on his shoulder. I knew that. I did. Maybe part of me was pulling away before he could leave me. "How did you know you could trust Mom? You were already famous when you met her."

Dad's arm settled around my back, and he brushed my hair with his fingers, our bodies rocking back and forth on the wooden seat. "Well, your mother was a pretty successful model, but, yeah, I guess there was some risk that she wanted more fame or money."

"So, how did you know?"

"It's hard to explain, Skylar. Love is trust. It's risk. They hurt you. You hurt them. Your mom had to do a lot of forgiving, and so did I. There are no fairytale relationships. Every one takes effort and work."

I sighed. "I thought Cody and I had something special. Something just between the two of us, and now I'm not so sure."

A weighted silence built between us like my father was choosing his next words carefully. "I think you will meet a lot of boys in your lifetime, Skylar. They will come and go, and you will learn with each relationship. You have a big future ahead of you. Paris. Fashion. Your dreams."

In other words, Cody wasn't forever.

CODY

FOUR DAYS DIDN'T sound like a lot of time, but any number was too long when the girl I'd fallen for stopped calling me back. Any number was too long when I wondered if she still cared about me or if she'd been sucked into the vortex of Madison.

My suspension lifted today and, yet, the hour between waking and getting ready felt like a walk to the guillotine.

"I'm ending your punishment." Mom said when I came downstairs. She tapped her nails on the counter, and though her words meant my weeklong sentence had been reduced, her tone did not imply absolution.

"I know I screwed up." It was the same sentence I'd spoken all weekend. And I meant it. Matt had warned me that once I became a fighter, control trumped all. Anger and rage made you stupid and sloppy and guaranteed regret. Boy, did I live that lesson.

My mom stepped forward, her mouth pinched while her eyes searched mine for the truth. We'd never been super close, she and I, but I knew she loved me and wanted only my happiness.

She put my confiscated truck keys in my hand. "Cody, you're eighteen. If that boy had pressed charges, you would have been arrested. I thought…" She paused. "I don't want you going backwards. Before Matt started training you, things were bad. Your depression, your isolation. I don't want that for you again."

I pocketed my keys while Mom fidgeted with her pearl necklace. This conversation made us both uncomfortable. I had fallen into a dark place after Tom's attack, one that scared my parents enough to pay for Matt's training.

"I'm fine. I'm not depressed. I just got angry with a guy who was being disrespectful to a friend of mine. I know I shouldn't have hit him. Don't read into this."

She backed away with an I-want-to-believe-you-but-I-don't expression haunting her face. "It's been weeks since I've seen Blake come by or Chugger. You talk about a girlfriend, but we've never met her."

My pulse jumped. "You will. I'll have her come over for Thanksgiving." I hoped my voice didn't give away my uncertainty.

Her cold, soft hands palmed my face. "Promise me you'll tell me if something is going on. You are not alone."

The problem was I felt alone. And helpless. And like I was one second from losing everything that mattered to me.

"Okay," I said and hoped my mom didn't notice that I couldn't look her in the eyes.

SKYLAR

MY HEART DID a skip, squeeze, and beat twice combination the moment I spotted Cody next to my locker. I knew he'd be back at school, and I intentionally ran ten minutes behind my normal tardiness in hopes he'd go on to class. No such luck.

He didn't give me a chance to speak, just grabbed my hand and pulled me right back through the metal doors and out to the parking lot.

"Cody, I—"

He kissed me, pulled me so tight against his chest that I crumbled like a wall of sand into his arms.

"Whatever I did, I'm sorry," he said, his lips hovering centimeters from mine.

How do you explain to someone that you're mad he shut you out? You're mad that he didn't trust you with his deepest hurts when you had trusted him with yours?

"It's what you're not doing. I need you to open up to me," I said.

"I have."

The frustration in his voice had my insides writhing. "Really? So there wasn't anything deeper that drove you to punch that kid?" *Just tell me, Cody. Tell me about sophomore year.*

He recoiled. Actually recoiled from me. "Are you still mad about the Super 32? Don't you think I've paid for my mistake a million times over?" He said the words like I was a spoiled, uncaring brat, and I wanted to slap him.

"No. I'm not still mad you got suspended."

"Then why, Skylar? Why are you avoiding me? We're supposed to be stronger than this."

But we weren't. He was doing just what my dad was. Letting me in on the good days and shutting me out when the bad stuff hit. Only this time it was Lindsay who was chosen to carry his burdens instead of me.

"I'm not avoiding you." *I'm heartbroken.* "The band is coming for Thanksgiving, so we've been working in the yard. I got caught up in the upcoming holidays."

He took my head in his hands. "You're sure?"

No. I wasn't sure about anything anymore. "Yeah. Everything's fine."

CODY

MY EDGINESS HAD no limit. Neither did my jealous insecurity. Blake was talking to Skylar again and too close. Much too close. Like it wasn't bad enough he'd had her all weekend, while I was stuck in my house waiting for her to call me back.

I joined them at her locker, wrapped a possessive arm around her. She'd been pulling away from me, physically and emotionally. She'd shift slightly when I touched her, and she didn't return any of my affection. All through lunch she watched me like she wanted to say something but wouldn't. A thousand emotions played with my head until one horrifying thought slammed into my chest—she was going to leave me. No. I couldn't even think about it.

"Blake." My terse greeting was met with challenging eyes. Ones I held with the same disdain.

"You missed a great weekend." His expression softened as he turned to Skylar making the knot in my gut tighten. "Ms. Skylar is quite the laser tag queen."

Skylar's cheeks flushed under his stare. "My dad's trained me well."

"Chugger has a huge piece of land. I bet you you'd be killer at paint ball." His smile deepened and was the final end to my wavering patience.

"Like she wants to be surrounded by a bunch of drunks

with weapons." My harsh sarcasm didn't deter him but made Skylar tense under my arm.

"Skylar's a big girl. She doesn't need you making choices for her." His voice was so calm; it masked the storm that would come from his next words. "Besides. I don't recall you minding so much when Lindsay played with us. But, then again, that was before your long, dark, ride home this summer, wasn't it?"

Adrenaline pumped into my bloodstream. With only two feet between us, I took a step forward, every muscle ready. "Don't say another word."

Blake didn't flinch. He closed the gap, and we stood nose to nose. The air was saturated with violence. I longed to hit him. He was itching to hit me.

But, instead of contact, he backed away with his arms in the air like a man surrendering. "You better check that temper of yours, St. James. People will start to think you're a bully." He winked at Skylar and my hand curled. "Whenever you're up for some fun, you just let me know."

He walked away, but the fury wouldn't leave with him. I had to hit something, do something now. I felt the rage spread, just like it had after they left me weeping on the bathroom floor, and after I saw the dollar bills fall out of Lindsay's locker.

I raked a hand through my hair and paced, but the pounding fury wouldn't stop.

"Cody?" Skylar's simple touch seared my skin.

I was going to lose it and right in front of her. I held my breath, fought for some kind of control. "You should get to class. Don't you have a test?" I wanted her to leave, but she didn't. She just stood there, waiting for me to fall apart. "Skylar, I need some space. Please." I focused on sucking air and blowing it out.

"What is happening to you?" Her plea was my undoing.

My body was pure anger. It beat at my lungs, pulsed in my throat and my target became the one person I swore I'd never hurt. "I am so sick of everyone thinking Blake's a god, okay? I'm sick of you eating with him and acting like he isn't scum. I'm sick that you spent the weekend with him and didn't return my calls. You want to know what's bothering me? Fine. You are. I've given everything up for you! And you can't even give me the courtesy of leaving me alone when I ask you to."

I slammed my palms on the locker, bent over and blew out a breath with the last of my rage. As soon as it had its release, I wanted to pull back every word, lock them away and beg her forgiveness.

"I'm sorry." Her words sliced me open because they were shaky and so wrapped in hurt that a thousand apologies wouldn't make a dent.

I stepped forward and she backed away, her hand raised in a warning to stay back.

"Skylar, wait. I didn't mean any of that."

She kept walking backwards.

"Skylar."

Nothing.

I stared until she disappeared, moving only when Henry walked up to me. I'd barely recognized him at first. Long gone were the glasses, and he must have bought out The Buckle. His life was on the fast track, while mine was spiraling out of control. But that was Blake's game—making others rise to glory or tumble off the pedestal. He was the puppet master.

Eyebrows pinched, the hard line of Henry's mouth said I was about to get an earful. "Are you trying to hurt her?"

I eyed his expensive clothes and the highlighted tips in his hair. Thought about how he set me up with Lindsay's naked picture. "Don't lecture me. You sold out."

He crossed his arms. "Yeah? Like you last year? Like when you lied to Principal Rayburn about Blake cheating? When you let me take the fall so Blake could compete at state?"

Shame mixed with my already unsteady emotions. He must have seen it because he took an aggressive step forward.

"Where was all this conviction then? Or am I not blond enough for you?"

Once again, fury blinded me and, before I could register my actions, I had his shirt in my fist and his back against the locker.

Henry was inches shorter than I was and weighed as much as a feather, but his eyes carried the fierceness of a warrior. "What are you going to do? Beat me up like you did that poor sucker last week?"

His words stunned me out of my combative haze. I released him, backed away and tried to still my shaking hands.

He pulled his shirt straight and picked up the books he'd dropped in our shuffle. "I saw an opportunity and took it. Just like you. And a hundred Lindsays won't change the fact that you sold out too."

I WAS FINISHING my warm-up mile when Coach called my name. "Cody. My office, now." The team snickered as I jogged off the track.

My neck muscles were wound so tight I could barely move them. Skylar, Blake, Henry. I was a sizzling pot of aggressive energy with nowhere to release.

I shut the door to Coach's office and stood opposite his

desk with my hands laced behind my back.

"I'm going to give captain to Blake today. I just wanted to let you know."

No, no, no! Fire pounded in my ears and burned down my cheeks and back. "Please, Coach, give me another chance."

"How many chances do you think you get? First, you skip school, then you attack Blake during practice. Next, you're suspended for fighting and miss the biggest individual event of the season." His fist pounded the desk. "You could have won."

I flinched at his words. At my own regret. I'd lost the respect of the team, the school and my coaches. I was losing Skylar, too.

"I heard this was about a girl, Blake's ex." He shook his head. "It's bad form to date a teammate's ex, Cody, and this is why. Combine teenage hormones with jealousy, and they become a raging inferno that ruins any chances for victory."

My head dropped. Would the lies ever stop? "Sir, I promise, this isn't about a girl. It's about me freeing myself from Blake's control."

He placed his elbows on the desk and leaned forward. "If that's the case, then why are you the one going around punching everyone and getting suspended?"

Because I'm an idiot who played right into Blake's manipulative hands.

"It won't happen again, sir. You have my word."

"Your word doesn't mean a whole lot right now."

The weight of his comment ripped through my heart, sliding down to take root among my growing list of failures. How did I even respond to that?

Forcing myself to stand straight, I met his eyes. "I will respect your decision even if I don't agree with it." Even if it tore apart my last shred of hope.

Coach paused, watching me with skepticism. His fingers stroked his chin, but he didn't respond, simply pointed to the door to excuse me.

I won every match that afternoon, and at the end when Coach pulled us in for our dismissal, I braced myself for the announcement he warned was coming. Only it never came. Instead, we were released to the lockers with a reminder that Saturday's match would be our hardest this season, and he expected every one of us in this gym to be giving one hundred percent the rest of the week.

I hung back while the others jogged to the locker room, my eyes searching Coach's for an explanation.

"Don't make me regret this decision," was all he said before walking off.

I sucked in air, closed my eyes and exhaled a current of relief and gratitude.

Finally, a victory.

SKYLAR

THE PARKING LOT outside Madison's gym was packed along with the overflow parking on the side of the school. I wedged my small car into a spot between two huge trucks and prayed I'd still have a paint job when this match was over.

Cody had been relentless with the calls, texts, and songs about heartbreak. He knew music was my weakness, and the last YouTube link he sent thirty minutes ago, along with his plea that I come watch the finals, had me caving.

Heavy, sweaty air assaulted my nose when I pushed open the gym door. The bleachers were full, whistles blew from every direction and the echoing noise was enough to cause my eardrums to ache. Greensboro had nothing on the sizzling tension that pulsed throughout the gym.

I only made it three more feet before Cody appeared.

"You came!" He immediately pulled me in for a tight hug. "You have no idea how happy I am you're here. My bracket is done. I'm just waiting to see who I wrestle in the finals."

I hugged him briefly, refusing to get lost in the feel of his arms around me. They were too strong. They made me feel safe when he wasn't. Secure when I knew I had to let go.

Cody's hands gently touched my cheeks. "I know things are rocky, but you being here…" For a split second I saw a flash of hope, one that made me want to forget my hurt.

"It means everything," he said.

I was back in his arms, overwhelmed by the scent of him and the feeling that maybe we could make it.

He pulled me to the corner, kissed me like we hadn't kissed since before his suspension because, for the first time in days, I returned his affection.

"This week has killed me," he admitted, pushing my hair from my face, watching me with eyes that seemed more vulnerable than those of a fierce champion defending his title.

"I know. Me, too." I looked around, searching for my friends among the mass of students. "Have you seen Zoe?"

He squeezed his eyes shut and opened them. "Just for today, will you sit with people cheering for me?"

I couldn't say no, not after he'd made me feel like my being here was the difference between him winning and losing. "Okay, sure."

He took my hand and pulled me along until we were in the middle bleachers about six rows up. Stopping at the end of a row, Cody waved at a guy with short, dark hair and tattoos. He'd be handsome if he weren't so scary. The guy waved back and started his trek through multiple sets of legs to reach us.

When I squeezed his hand, Cody laughed and wrapped an arm around me. "That's Matt, my trainer. He's here with his wife."

The pride on Cody's face said it all. Matt's opinion mattered to him. Which meant Matt's opinion of me mattered to him. Suddenly, I was nervous, feeling a little of Cody's pain when he met my dad.

Matt finally made it to the end of the row and stood next to Cody, slapping him on the back. I didn't know if it was his height or his size or the hardness of his face, but I immediately took a step back, completely overwhelmed.

Cody's arm tightened, pulling me forward. "Matt, this is my girlfriend, Skylar."

Matt stuck out his hand and grinned, his expression softening a little. "Nice to meet you. Cody's told me a lot about you."

I shook his hand lightly and tucked closer into Cody's side.

"You ready?" he asked Cody. "Got your head where it needs to be?"

A silent conversation happened between them and Cody stiffened, his face getting the same ready-to-fight expression that seemed to be permanent on Matt. "I'm winning this thing."

Matt squeezed Cody's shoulder. "No holding back."

"No holding back," Cody repeated.

I felt like I was in the middle of a *Rocky* movie, and any minute "The Eye of the Tiger" would start playing.

Cody finally remembered my presence and kissed the top of my head. "Wait for me after the match, okay?"

I nodded, and he took off down the stairs leaving me with a man who made my palms sweat.

Matt stretched out his arm, indicating I should start my journey to our seats. "After you."

MY STOMACH WAS an array of flips and tingles and just a slight bit of nausea. Blake had swept the other bracket, which meant he'd be Cody's opponent. The guys stood opposite each other, their faces a mix of hatred and competitiveness.

I peeked over at Matt. His face looked exactly the same, and it sent a shiver through my spine.

"You'll have to excuse my husband," Grace said with a

dimpled smile. "He gets emotionally involved." Affection hung off every word while she gently stroked his flexed arm.

For a moment, the vicious fighter was gone. Matt turned and kissed her temple, glancing at her like she was his sun and moon and stars. It's what I wanted. What I thought we had.

Pushing down the envy, I turned my attention back to the two boys in the center. Nothing good could come from this match. Cody and Blake were already at war, and I had a bad feeling the winner today would secure a whole lot more than a trophy.

The whistle blew and the boys grabbed at each other like animals vying for dominance. You'd think the Super 32 taught me something, but I still had no idea what was happening, only that Matt seemed excited about the moves Cody used. The whistles blew again, and Matt clapped and cheered.

A point was given to Cody.

Time continued, but I was in a daze. To me, there wasn't much going on, just both boys gripping and thrashing and moving, but neither ended up on his back. Grace tried to explain what moves got points—takedowns, reversals, escapes, near falls, and the list went on.

I stopped listening after the first four points, knowing I'd never remember what she said anyway. My mind didn't process numbers. They floated in my head, jumbled around and then disappeared, quickly replaced with a new design for my sketchbook.

"This is it. Third and final round."

The excitement in Matt's voice had my pulse jumping. Was Cody winning? The points showed Blake having six. Cody with five.

Matt must have seen my confusion. "Blake's tired. Look at the way his arms are shaking. Cody's going to pin him in the first minute."

My throat tightened. I wanted him to be right. I wanted Cody to have that moment. That victory. Everything in me wanted us to make it. I wanted prom and graduation. I wanted late nights picking out our college together. I wanted Cody to be my future.

The round started with Blake on all fours and Cody leaning over him. The whistle blew, and the boys began their locked and strained position again.

Suddenly, there was chaos. Blake had Cody flipped around, struggling to keep his upper back from touching the mat. Matt was screaming about dirty moves and that the ref was blind.

The crowd roared.

Then it was over.

Matt sat down and shook his head ferociously. "So, the punk wants a street fight." He turned a determined stare to Cody who had his head in his hands, but Matt didn't say another word. Grace rubbed her husband's back in a gesture that was obviously meant to calm him. It seemed to work.

I glanced around the gym. Faces everywhere glowed with victory, Blake's being the brightest of all. But my heart hurt for the man bent over as if second place branded him a loser. I kept my eyes locked on his face hoping he would look up and see that I was there to support him. That I believed in him. That I was strong enough to share in his pain.

He said my being here meant everything, and I wanted him to know he was right. This loss wasn't the end. We had everything to look forward to.

But his eyes didn't find me in the seat he had picked out. They flashed toward the front of the gym instead. I turned to follow his gaze and caught a view of Lindsay's shiny blond hair right before she slipped through the wide gym doors.

CODY

THE MEDAL HUNG around my neck like a weighted chain. The metallic silver was one I would have been proud of just a year ago. But today, it only meant failure.

Matt and Grace stood next to Skylar, waiting, but I didn't want to talk to anyone. I needed a shower. Needed to wash away the sweat and pain of yet another loss.

I approached them, trying to hide the explosion going on inside. Matt would expect me to be in control. To push through the desire to find Blake in a dark alley and beat him until the word "illegal move" was wiped away from my memory.

"We'll resume after Thanksgiving," was all Matt said, but his eyes showed so much more. "Take a break until then."

I felt myself crack. "I'm sorry."

"No. But Blake will be." Matt gripped my shoulder in a gesture normally meant to encourage and empower. It did neither. He and Grace said their goodbyes to Skylar and left the gym.

I didn't want to look at Skylar. She'd already seen me fall short, and I couldn't take seeing disappointment in her eyes.

"Congrats on second place." Her voice was light, but I could sense an edge to it. A fakeness that was rare with her.

I finally looked up and saw all I needed to in a glance. Her tight-lipped smile was paired with an unnatural stiffness in her shoulders.

"Thanks." The word came out as bitter as it felt on my tongue.

One, two, three beats of silence followed and began choking what was left of my airway.

Her eyes misted and blinked, her face turning toward the gym doors as if they held a much-needed escape. "I should probably go. My dad wanted me back."

A fist beat on my heart. "Wait," I whispered, taking her hand and pulling her toward me. Maybe she wished she'd chosen differently. Maybe she wanted to be standing next to Blake as the team high-fived and cheered. But I didn't care. I had to hold her. Had to believe for one moment that my life wasn't unraveling.

I buried my face in her mass of red curls. Even her scent soothed me, made me believe in happy endings.

"I could stay. If you need me." Her voice was a whisper in my ear. A promise to be there for me.

"Cody," Coach hollered from inside the circle of my teammates. His face beamed. He couldn't care less who took first place as long as it was a Madison student. "Get over here."

"I'm coming," I yelled back but kept a hand on my girlfriend. "It'll only be a few minutes. Then we can go out and forget everything that happened today."

Her face fell. "Actually, I forgot I told Zoe I would come over. I'll just see you after the holidays."

"Wait. What about Thanksgiving? My parents want to meet you."

"Yeah, we'll see. I'm going to be swamped with company." She spun around and practically jogged to the exit.

"Cody! Now." Coach's voice was a warning I couldn't ignore.

I made the defeated trek back to the team trying my best not to look disappointed in winning a medal some of these guys would kill for. I passed Blake, refusing to look at the smug, arrogant expression I knew would be there and found a place on the opposite side of Coach Taylor.

We whooped and hollered and shouted victory chants that dated back to the days when Madison dominated the prep leagues. But, in my soul, I felt no power. No victory.

Only one word echoed in my brain—Defeat.

SKYLAR

I'D NEVER BEEN so excited for the Thanksgiving holidays. Raif and Striker were already at my house, and in minutes Ricky would be walking through the door.

My father ruffled my hair. "You know Ricky is never on time."

The clock showed he had exactly two minutes to prove Daddy wrong. And I knew because I hadn't stopped inspecting the second hand.

Raif walked in from the kitchen holding a steaming cup of coffee. He'd resemble a preppy Englishman about to sit for a spot of tea except for the white-blond spikes of hair so gelled and stiff, they shimmered in the light. "I don't recall getting a Skylar welcome party." His face scrunched, a fake pout directed at me.

"Skylar's always loved Ricky more than us. I accepted her poor taste a long time ago," Striker said, joining us in the fancy parlor no one used.

Striker and Raif stood together like a yin yang symbol. Striker was as black as Raif was white. Only Striker's hair hung down his back in long dreadlocks. He also had three earrings in each ear and more fashion sense than Vera Wang.

Truth was, I loved them all. They were my family and, more than anything, I just wanted Ricky to get here so we could all be together.

"Speak for yourself, mate," Raif said. I scooted over, giving him a place to sit. He delicately set down his coffee mug and pulled out a small box from his pocket. The baby blue color had my heart fluttering. "Some of us know the way to a woman's heart." He handed me the Tiffany's box and winked. "Happy Birthday, Kiddo."

My birthday. Eighteen. It was only a couple of weeks away, but I'd hardly thought about it.

"Thank you." I pulled the delicate white ribbon and opened the box. My throat thickened. It was my name, Skylar Wyld, in platinum with small stones lining both *y's*. The first was lined with my father's, mother's and my birthstones. The second was lined with the birthstones from the rest of the band. I knew because I'd been obsessed with birthstones at fifteen and made them all suffer through my phase with gaudy Christmas presents.

His voice caught. "It's a one of a kind, like you."

I hugged him tight. "It's perfect. Thank you so much"

"What's this? We're apart four months, and now I don't even get a hug?"

I sprang off the couch and into Ricky's arms. "You're here!"

He smelled like home. Stiff leather, Boss cologne and spearmint. Ricky was the heartthrob of the band. Tall, tan, shaggy brown hair and a chiseled jaw that still turned heads, even at forty-eight years old. He'd been my first, second and third crush until I was finally mature enough to realize he was an old man. A fact I liked reminding him of often.

"That's more like it." He pushed me back, keeping a grip on my upper arms and studied my face. "My goodness, Skylar, you're the spitting image of your mother." His eyes flicked to my father's. "Better get your shotgun ready."

"I'm one step ahead of you." My dad pulled Ricky in for a man hug, and I didn't miss the way Ricky's face flinched when he squeezed my father's disappearing frame.

The harsh reality of the situation poured off Ricky like steam from a latte. I could ignore it with the others. Ignore that Raif and Striker had left their families at home to fly halfway across the world and spend this time with my father. But with Ricky, I knew there would be no pretending. They all were coming to say good-bye.

The others hugged and greeted while I stayed rooted in place, my chest burning as I tried again and again to push away the sudden weight of sadness.

"Once again, you stole my moment," Raif complained. "I give a woman jewelry, even get a hug out of her, and with one word she's flying across the room. Shameful."

"Skylar's my girl, what can I say?" Ricky slung an arm around my shoulders and kissed the top of my head.

I nestled in, reveled in the reassuring security of my dad's best friend. Reaching out, I took my father's hand and focused on the faces of the men I'd known my whole life. A sea of tears streaked down my face.

My father did a double take at my sudden emotional shift. "What's wrong, Princess?"

Three pairs of eyes followed his, and the room became eerily still, like the tiniest movement would send me over the cliff. But the silence only pushed me forward. Laughter bubbled in my chest and then came out in a hysterical laugh/cry where snot mixed with tears and words became a slur of sobs.

Ricky snapped his head toward my father. "What the heck, Donnie! What'd you do to our stable, happy girl?"

My father threw up his hands. "Don't blame me. She's the

one who up and got a boyfriend."

They all gasped, and I doubled over. Maybe from the laughter or the pain or from how unbelievably tired I felt trying to stay hopeful. Hands rubbed at my back, soothed my hair and held mine as the four men who raised me tried their hardest to make all my sorrow go away.

TUCKED IN A chair with a blanket up to my chin, I fought off the autumn chill in our backyard. It had taken numerous jokes, a box of tissues, and a hot bath to finally calm me down, the flood of repressed emotion so overwhelming that hiccups followed my burst of tears.

My hair, still wet, left splotches of water on my t-shirt, but I was past caring. I just felt empty.

Wood from our new fire pit crackled and offered a tiny bit of extra heat, but mostly it was there for ambiance. Dad had turned our backyard into an outside oasis, yet I was the only one seated on the wicker sectional. Proof that my hysterics had scared them all away.

Four unlit Tiki torches with citronella marked the corners of the patio. We'd planted a rose bush near the back door, and I stared at it wondering if my dad would ever see it bloom.

"Finally calm?" Ricky hesitated, waving a steaming cup of tea like a peace offering. "I've been kicked out of the kitchen, and I need a place to land."

I patted the space next to me and tucked my bare feet further under the blanket.

"So, where's this so called boyfriend? Aren't y'all supposed to be meeting parents, stuffing your faces with too much turkey and trying to sneak away for stolen kisses?"

I pushed his arm. "It's not like that. We've only been dating a little while." And we're heading right into breakup territory. Cody had left me four messages. None of which I returned.

"That's not how your father explains it. 'Gooey eyes' he said."

"My father exaggerates."

"This wouldn't have anything to do with Donnie saying Cody is our 'biggest fan'?" The air quotes were as annoying as the tilt of his lips.

"No."

"Then why isn't he here?"

"Because I don't want him here. I-I just want it to be us, like it used to be." The answer flew through my mouth without a filter.

Ricky gave me his you-can't-live-in-a-bubble scowl. And I gave him my just-watch-me one right back.

At a stalemate, we settled for staring at the woodchips in silence until Ricky's voice sliced through the calm. "I just bought myself a nice little bachelor pad in Southern Cal. Ten thousand square feet, a pool, tennis courts. It even has a sauna. You can come stay with me any time you need to."

Around my neck lay my mom's locket and Raif's gift. I touched them both.

"You're leaving Germany?" Another change. Another tear in the fabric that once was our life.

"I only went there for the band. And now, well, things are different." He tipped my chin. "You can talk to me about it, you know."

"About what?"

Ricky kneaded his eyes with his fists like my question

caused him stress. "You may look like your mother, but you and your dad share one unmistakable curse—you both won't stop pretending."

My heart pumped hot lava. He was siding with Aunt Josephine. Traitor. "There's nothing wrong with being hopeful. Dad's healthier than he's been in months. He has color back in his face. He isn't reacting to the chemo anymore, and I know he feels better because he's playing every day and writing again."

"That's good, Skylar. I'm glad." But his sad eyes and drooping shoulders told me he was placating me. Just like he did when I was twelve and begged Sheila and him to save their marriage. I begged them not to divorce. Insisted they could work through their problems. Six months later he signed the final papers and last year signed another set, ending his third failed attempt.

"So..." I could tell he was fishing for something to talk about. "You're graduating this year. What fashion schools have you applied to?"

I poked the chips with a fire rod, already hating this new subject. "Dad made me apply to ESMOD in Paris, but I'm not going."

"Why not? That school is all you've talked about for years."

I exhaled a frustrated stream of air. "You know why."

"Yes, because you father is sick. He's dying—"

"Don't say that!"

Ricky's voice lowered to a soft purr. "Honey, we have to make plans."

I closed my eyes and pushed away the creeping panic. "If you came out here to discuss caskets and wills and where I plan to go if my father dies, you can just go back inside and braid

Striker's hair or something."

A loud laugh rolled out of his mouth and fell over me like at iron vest. This wasn't funny.

"Yep. Just like your dad."

I twisted the blanket in my fists until warm hands pulled them free.

"Being prepared doesn't mean you're giving up. Allowing yourself to hurt, to grieve, to share your feelings doesn't mean you've lost hope."

He didn't get it. I was the only one willing to share. Dad had cut me out. Cody had cut me out. They'd put their trust in someone else and left me stranded in the process.

"You need—"

I put a finger to his mouth and pleaded with eyes that had gotten me my way so many times I'd lost count. "It's Thanksgiving, Ricky. Let's just enjoy our day."

Ricky pursed his lips and leaned back against our shared cushion. After a long drink from his mug, he chuckled.

"What's so funny?" I almost didn't want to know.

"Nothing. Just that your dad said the same thing to me not ten minutes ago."

CODY

SKYLAR NEVER CAME to Thanksgiving, and now my parents were sure I was spiraling downward. Maybe I was. I'd gone back to listening to music for hours. Only now, I pictured Skylar's face in every song.

The crappy weekend and fitful sleep culminated in pure edginess when I walked into the gym on Monday morning. Matt stood ringside, talking with a man whose biceps were easily the size of my thighs. The giant glanced my way, his face as dark as midnight, and soon a white row of teeth appeared.

"You the kid who needs some street sense?"

I froze, my skin crawling with fear as his dark eyes challenged mine.

Matt let out a deep, resonating laugh. "You're supposed to help the kid, not terrify him." He waved me over. "Come on, Cody. This is Devon. He's going to spar with us today."

My feet stayed planted. Get in the ring with *him*? Matt must have lost his mind.

It was Devon's turn to laugh at me. "I see whach'a mean. Kid's 'bout to wet his pants."

I stepped forward, a burst of adrenaline pushing away the fear. "The name is Cody."

He took my outstretched hand and appeared to be impressed by my boldness. "You may just do okay, featherweight." His tight grip and insulting words said otherwise.

Matt threw me my headgear. "Half those referees have never even wrestled, so Blake's gonna push the limits every time he's tired. You hesitated, waited for a whistle that never came and you got pinned."

I knew he was right. Blake won the mental game, and it cost me.

Matt and Devon stepped through the ropes, and Devon pinned me with a stare. "When we're through with you, ain't no one gonna take you down."

And they weren't kidding. By the time our hour was up, sweat poured from my scalp and into my face, and my arms felt as if they were made of Laffy Taffy. But it worked. I'd gotten out of a move that would have easily disqualified Blake from a match.

"If you can handle that one," Matt said huffing, "no way Blake's going to take you off guard again."

Devon left fifteen minutes ago, missing my great victory. Part of me was disappointed. The other part, relieved. That guy would make hardened criminals tremble.

I sucked down more water and continued to catch my breath. "I wish girls were as easy to learn as wrestling moves."

Matt's eyebrows shot up at my abrupt change in subject. "Wanna talk about it?"

I hadn't meant to start a conversation about Skylar, but she had my head and heart in a constant spin cycle, and I was too tired to think before I spoke. "Nah." Of course, I did, but I felt stupid.

"How's school going?" He sat on the floor next to me.

"It's been better."

"Kids bothering you again?"

I'd never told Matt the details, but he knew the general facts—that I'd been bullied, that I had needed to learn to fight, and that I had been teetering on the edge of a cliff. A cliff he'd managed to pull me back from after only a few months of training.

"Not me. But there's this girl." I stopped, feeling as if I was betraying Lindsay in some way by talking about her. "It's bad. And she won't tell."

"She have anything to do with your missing the Super 32?"

I shrugged, neither confirming nor denying his question.

"You know you can't save her, right?"

He met my eyes, his expression as vulnerable as I'd ever seen it. There was an understanding. A kinship that had my heart pounding. "At some point, she's going to have to fight for herself, too."

MATT'S ADVICE ON Lindsay haunted me all the way to school. *You can't save her.* That was exactly what I'd been trying to do. Save her because in some way it was like saving the fat kid on the locker room floor. Her helplessness had become mine all over again. But that kid fought back. Skylar and Matt were right. It was time for Lindsay to do the same.

Lindsay's car was already in the parking lot, and I wasn't surprised. When she did attend school, she came early and hid in the library until the last possible second. Avoiding people had become her new pastime.

I had twenty minutes before Skylar arrived and planned to get this out of the way, so I could spend the rest of the day winning back my girlfriend.

I spotted Lindsay's pale hair the minute I pushed through

the library doors. "We need to talk."

My words startled her, and she jumped back.

"Cody, don't sneak up on me." She was as jumpy as a five-year-old on a sugar high. Hands shaking, she chewed on the edge of her pen. "What's going on?"

She looked paler than usual, and dark circles marred the skin beneath her dreary eyes. "I'm sorry, Lindsay. I'm so sorry you are going through all of this. But it's time to fight back."

She lowered her head. "Some fights cannot be won. The dollar bill incident was weeks ago, and not one person has been punished. You need to move on with your life, and let me deal with this on my own. I can't stand the guilt of what I'm putting you through."

I dropped into the chair next to her and scooted it closer. "Tell your parents."

Tears spilled over and down her cheeks. "I can't tell," she whispered between sobs. "If my father read some of those comments, I'd die. What if he believed what people are saying? He'd never look at me the same."

I thought of my mom after the suspension, and her unconditional love even in the face of disappointment. I pulled Lindsay's hands away from her face, so she could look at me. "Your parents love you. They would never want you to go through this on your own. They would support you, Lindsay. I'm sure of it."

She wiped away her tears. "You've never even met my parents."

"I don't have to. They're your parents. End of story." I leaned in, took her hand in mine. "I need you to do this for me. I need you to tell your parents."

She stared at our hands and then squeezed. "Okay. I'll tell

them. Tonight—"

A commotion in the hall stopped her midsentence, and the library became a whirlwind of whispers. Cell phones were going crazy. I reached for mine right as I heard a gasp from the girl who ran over to the window.

"Reporters are everywhere," she said.

Then another shriek. "OMG! Skylar is Donnie's Wyld's daughter."

SKYLAR

HOW IS IT possible that I'm late again?

I'd even rushed this morning, wanting to get a few minutes alone with Cody. Four days with the band had filled me with optimism. They sang, worked, laughed and finished the record I thought was a lost cause only four months ago. It was my father's best work, and I already had the sketch of my dress for next year's Grammy awards.

The parking lot was packed, several cars even double parked like they had during Cody's match. Had I missed an announcement? Was there some event going on at school this morning?

I shut my door, clicked the lock and only made it four steps before chaos erupted. Doors slammed, photos flashed and two girls with '80s hair and long red fingernails shoved microphones into my face.

"Skylar, how long has your father been sick?"

"Did you know he was dying?"

"Why did he stop treatment?"

"Is he trying holistic medicines?"

"Where will he be buried?"

The words jumbled around in my head, no more coherent than the splotches of light now obscuring my vision. I tried to move, but they'd pressed up against me, body odor and perfume singeing my nose as they continued to ram me with questions I had no answers for.

I covered my face, ready to sink into the pit that suddenly formed at my feet, but two strong arms stopped my collapse. I was cocooned, pressed against a solid chest as he pushed our way through the crowd. I focused on our feet moving forward, past the sidewalk, up two steps.

"It's okay, Skylar. I've got you." He smelled like citrus and clean linens waving in the breeze.

I clutched him tighter, basking in the safety of his arms, although they held no familiarity. These weren't the arms of the boy I'd dreamed about last night. It wasn't his smell that pushed away the noise and stench of my life falling apart. It was Blake.

He pushed us through double doors where, thankfully, their lies and spiteful commentary didn't follow. I was in a dream. I had to be. Reporters couldn't be here; they couldn't do this. There were laws.

Blake pulled me into an empty room and forced me to look at him. "Hey, you need to calm down. Breathe, okay? Like this."

His mouth opened as he filled his lungs with air and then blew out. He did it three more times until I found myself copying the motion.

My breath returned, but their lies wouldn't stop assaulting me.

Stop treatment, holistic medicine, buried.

"Skylar?" Blake's voice brought me back to the present. We were in Ms. Stacey's art class. Jars of paint were scattered on the tables and six easels stood ready by the back wall.

Two male teachers rushed past the open classroom door speaking into walkie-talkies. Moments later, threatening yells filtered through the air as they shouted at the reporters.

My eyes flashed to Blake's. "Does everyone know?"

"Yeah. He's trending on Twitter."

All of the pretense, all of the extra work. All the time put into protecting our secret was for nothing. They knew. My heart caved and my feet would have followed without Blake reaching out to steady me. He cradled me in his arms again, but all I could think of was finding a way to fix this. There had to be a way.

With shaky hands I pulled out my phone, detangling myself from Blake's hug. My dad's manager was on speed dial, but I'd never had to call him before. He picked up in one ring.

"I've got a security detail coming now, kiddo," Carl said without even a hello. "What they did was illegal, and we are absolutely pressing charges."

"How? How did they find out?" Anger was starting to replace the shock, and I could stand straighter, my feet getting firmer under me.

"We think an aid at the hospital. We're investigating it now." He sounded rushed like he was running while trying to talk.

"Tell me it's not true. Tell me he didn't stop the treatments."

Silence. Not the silence of a person thinking. The silence of a person not wanting to be the one to tell me the truth. My chest constricted. I reached for the wall, trying to steady myself, and felt flesh instead. I gripped Blake tightly while the searing heat of disbelief filled my lungs. "Carl…please. Tell me it's not true."

"The team will be there in minutes. We'll discuss everything tonight." His voice was soft, but nothing about it soothed me.

The world became a mass of lights and colors all blended into a blob with Blake's face at the center. I swayed. Blinked twice.

"What do you need me to do?" Blake's typical bravado was replaced by panic.

I dropped my phone into my purse and forced my eyes to focus. I needed to get control before the other students discovered us and recorded some video of me falling apart. I pulled calm from the depths of soul and brushed the hair out of my face.

"I'm good. Thank you. They took me off guard."

Blake exhaled and dragged his hand through his hair. "Geez. I thought you were going to pass out."

Outside the door, noise, bodies and chaos filled the hallway. Teachers were shouting to get to class, and I knew any minute this room would be filled with gawkers.

"Don't worry. Ms. Stacey doesn't have a first period. We're fine in here." Blake shook his head, scratched it and looked at me again. "So, you're Donnie Wyld's daughter. Like really his daughter?"

This was exactly why I didn't want people to know. I was back to being this strange apparition. A celebrity, but not really. I squared my shoulders and tried to prepare myself for the change.

"Does Cody know?" he asked.

Cody. I couldn't think of him right now. It was all too much. "Yeah. He knows."

Over the loud speaker, Principal Rayburn called my name to the office. I stepped toward the exit, telling myself I could do it. I could walk these halls without breaking down.

Blake stopped me. “Do you want me to go with you? I can keep the vultures away.”

I nodded because I knew he could. If there was one thing Blake did well, it was control the student body.

CODY

I'D LOOKED FOR Skylar everywhere. Her locker, the bathroom, Ms. Yarnell's class. Now I stood hiding by the stairs near the front office waiting to see if she'd answer Principal Rayburn's summons.

Blake rounded the corner first, his arm wrapped around Skylar's shoulder, his face masked in an expression I'd seen too often across the wrestling mat. I pushed off the wall and stalked toward them, but kept my eyes glued to Blake's. There was a pulsating in my blood that begged for a fight, but it dissolved the minute I focused on my girlfriend. Skylar was ghostly pale and trembling.

I pulled her to me. Relieved to finally have her in my arms. "I've been looking for you everywhere." I slid my hand in hers and tugged, forcing another several inches between her and my enemy.

Skylar's fingers shook against my skin. "Everyone knows."

"I know. It's going to be okay."

Blake's harrumph was followed by a snarled, "How convenient you show up, now that she's fine." He faced Skylar. "You deserve better than this idiot."

"Shut up. You will not manipulate this situation," I said through clenched teeth.

"You're unbelievable. I pulled up not two seconds behind Skylar, watched her get mauled in the parking lot and helped her. *Your* girlfriend, in case you've forgotten. Not mine." He pushed between us.

Two steps and he turned, obviously not finished with his rant. "But, then again, if she was mine, you probably would have been there." He slammed his palm against the cinder block wall and stormed off toward the office.

Crap. He was going to tell Principal Rayburn where to find her. I pulled Skylar into the alcove by the stairs, slid my thumb against her skin and kissed her forehead.

She sagged into me. "He lied to me. He promised he wouldn't quit."

"I'm sure he was trying to protect you."

Skylar flinched like I'd slapped her. "I don't need protection. I need the truth." She was raw, completely unguarded and way too angry. "When are you going to see that I'm not some little china doll that breaks the minute hard times hit? I'm strong. I can handle the bad stuff too."

"Wait? When did this become about me?"

"You're just like him. You shut me out. You let someone else help you at your darkest."

"I shut you out? You've barely spoken to me in two weeks."

"Because you hurt me!"

"How?" I hissed, and then reminded myself to rein it in. She was in shock. The news had ambushed her. Nothing she said was going to make sense.

Her voice turned icy. "Why don't you ask *Lindsay*? She seems to be who you love to run to with all your secrets and some of mine, too."

My girl had officially turned crazy. "I didn't tell Lindsay anything."

"Yet she knew about you meeting my dad. She knows

something happened to you sophomore year. Something I know nothing about. Why didn't you tell me?"

The muscles in my body jerked. Even from the grave, Fatty James wouldn't stop tormenting me. I rubbed my hands down my face. "You can't have it both ways, Skylar. You can't beg me for normal and then get mad when I pretend everything is fine."

"So, it's my fault? I suppose it's also my fault that my dad quit chemo. That I'm such a diva I have to be coddled every second."

"That's not what I said."

She angled away from me. "Just leave me alone."

"Skylar." I moved closer, tried to wrap her in my arms, to take the frustration we both had down a notch, but she pushed me off. I pulled at her again, forcing her to look at me. "You're angry and you're hurting. I get that. But don't push me away."

She stubbornly lifted my hand off her arm. "I told you about my dad being sick. I brought you to my house. I've done nothing but let you in. And I'm finished being the only one who's trying."

"You're not the only one. I'll tell you whatever you want to know. Just don't give up on us."

"You really don't get it?" Her expression was dead. "I don't care anymore. I don't care about sophomore year or the suspension or Lindsay. None of it matters now. My dad is dying. His face is going to be plastered on every magazine from here to Timbuktu. And, once again, I trusted the wrong person."

Principal Rayburn appeared in front of us, flanked by two men I didn't recognize. "Ms. Da Lange, it's time to go."

I hung back, knowing from the principal's glare that he

wasn't too pleased to find me with her in the corner.

The tallest man, wearing a pinstriped suit, wrapped her in a hug. She clung to his jacket while they disappeared from sight.

Principal Rayburn pointed down the hall, and I knew my options were gone. "Go to class, Mr. James, or it's two hours in detention."

SKYLAR

I STORMED IN the house and immediately found my father and Aunt Josephine at the kitchen table.

"Is it true?" My chest hurt and my pulse pounded in my ears.

Aunt Josephine watched my father. She knew the truth. Everyone knew the truth. Everyone but me.

My dad stood slowly. "Sweetheart, you need to calm down. You've had a terrible morning, and we all need to sit and talk about what happens next."

His calm and rational tone infuriated me more. "Calm down? Do you have any idea what just happened to me at school?" I turned accusing eyes to my aunt. "This was your idea. Wasn't it? You convinced him to quit."

"Skylar. That's enough." My dad's warning didn't stop me.

I continued to stare at the object of my blame. "My mom was right. You're just a spinster, a cold-hearted woman who doesn't give a damn about anyone but yourself!"

"Skylar Anne!" The sheer volume of my father's voice stopped my malicious attack.

But I wanted to say more. The rage inside bubbled and pulsed through every limb and organ. I wanted to throw my father's glass of lemonade across the room. Wanted to take my aunt's hair and rip it out of her meticulous French twist.

I stomped out of the room, my hands shaking, my lips

trembling, my throat burning from choking back my cries. I slammed my door, but it didn't give me enough satisfaction, so I slammed it again and again.

The fourth time was met with resistance as my father pushed through the opening. "Young lady, what is wrong with you?"

I shook my hands, jumping on the balls of my feet like a boxer getting ready for a match. Suddenly, I understood the appeal to fight. I wanted to hit something, too. Break anything, the way my heart was breaking.

"Why did you do it? Why did you give up?" I let out a huge breath to stop the onset of tears. I didn't want to cry. I wanted the truth.

He ran a hand through his hair, and I noticed how loose his shirt was today. How had I not seen it earlier? How had I been so blind?

"The test showed no progress, and the chemo was killing me. I don't know how much time I have with you, but I refuse to spend it puking my guts out, missing the last few moments we may have together." There was no hesitation in his voice. No wavering. He'd made his decision without me.

I stared at the ceiling and blinked, praying the tears would stay back. Praying the adrenaline would continue, so I didn't have to feel the pain ripping at my insides.

"I'm just so angry." The words came as the first tear dropped. A flood that seemed endless started down my face.

"I know, sweetheart."

"No, you don't! You can't possibly understand." I met his eyes through the blurry lenses of my own. "I want to curse God. I want to scream at him and demand why. I want to erase every note of music on Cody's iPod. I want to pull out Lindsay's perfectly straight blond hair and slap her tiny, innocent face. I want to take a key and scratch the heck out of Aunt Josephine's car, and I want to smash your guitar into tiny little pieces. That's how mad I am!"

My father stared at me like I'd lost my mind. A beat of silence and then, "Who's Lindsay?"

The confusion in his voice combined with the lost expression on his face brought a giggle so huge and loud my stomach clenched when it came out. Sob-filled laughter overwhelmed me. I dropped on the bed, hunching my shoulders and covering my face, all while trying to control my conflicting emotions.

I heard my father cross the room. Then music filled the air. It wasn't a symphony or even a guitar. No, it was the tinging tick of my music box. The music box my mother had given me on my ninth birthday. The music box that played in my room every night, calming me into peaceful sleep. Beethoven's "Für Elise" floated like a leaf twirling in the wind and began to heal the sting of my scorching heart.

The bed dipped, my father's arm reached around my shoulder and pulled me into his solid embrace.

The tears fell heavier.

"I know this is hard. I wish so much I could take away all your pain." The crack in his voice made me wonder if he was crying too.

I looked up, moved a matted piece of hair from my face and saw his tears matched my own. "I don't want to be alone." My whispered cry tore the last of my heart in two. My rock, my mountain, my strength was withering away in front of me. Soon, I'd only have a song or a memory. It was too much.

"You will mourn. You will cry. And I know you will hurt.

But Skylar, I promise you, you will never be alone. God will be your father, your best friend and your comforter. He will heal your heart again."

My sobs came louder, drowning out the slowing music until the knob turned its last click. My father cradled me and replaced the music box with the soft, raspy song he'd written just for me.

And I grieved.

For the first time since hearing the word "Cancer," I accepted my father was going to die.

CODY

SKYLAR'S PHONE DIDN'T even ring twice before her voicemail picked up. She had either turned it off or was screening her calls. Either way, her message was clear.

Like the other ten times I heard the beep that meant I wouldn't talk to her, I ended the call and shoved my phone into my gym locker. Two hours of practice, then I could leave this miserable school. Figure out how to fix this mess.

The media was relentless. Tributes to her father, along with speculation on his condition, headlined on every news channel and social media site. The worst image, though, was the video of Blake holding Skylar as he pushed their way into school this morning. That one stayed on repeat in my mind. A minute-by-minute reminder that I'd failed her.

Blake sauntered over to my locker in his gym clothes, a smug smile on his face. "So, you're bangin' a rock star's daughter. My, my, you never stop climbing that ladder do you?"

I clenched my hand but stopped there. I wouldn't do it. One more fight, and I was off the team. My stupidity lost me the Super 32 and Skylar. I wouldn't let it take away my chance to get her back.

I kept my gaze fixed on the locker in front of me, my voice calm and controlled. "Talk about Skylar like that again, and I'll call the cops on Chugger's next kegger." Not an idle threat and he knew it.

His mild laugh twisted everything inside me, but I still didn't move. "Face it. You lost. The team thinks you're a joke. Lindsay's a walking zombie, and Skylar dumped you. And after Zoe calls and comforts her and sings all my wonderful praises, she'll come to me. Beg me to give her another chance. And I'll be ready and waiting."

Over my dead, rotting body. I met Blake's soulless eyes. "Keep dreaming. Skylar sees right through you. She has since day one."

"That so?" He stepped away, pulled out his phone, and pressed a number on speed dial. A second later, his face lit up. "Hey, beautiful. Just wanted to see if you got home safely." He walked backward toward the gym, smiling like he did after winning a match. "Of course. I'm more concerned…" His voice disappeared behind the locker room door.

I grabbed my keys out my bag. They slipped through my fingers and landed on the floor. I cursed. My hands shook as I snatched the keys back off the tile. I cursed again when my vision went blurry.

Screw practice. I'd storm the gate if I had to. She was going to talk to me.

THE LINE OF cars that stretched to Skylar's gated neighborhood was literally a quarter-mile long. I'd been inching up for forty-five minutes, wondering, hoping they'd let me in. The media, perched like vultures, surrounded her neighborhood. Fans lined the strips of grass along the fence, laying flowers and get-well signs as a tribute to their idol. If they really wanted to honor Donnie Wyld, they would back off and let his family deal with his illness.

Another round of anxiety rolled through my stomach. She wanted honesty. I was about to drown her in it.

There was only one car in front of me now, arguing with the guard who checked his list and shook his head. The car lunged forward and squealed around the U-turn. My hopes plummeted. There was no way Skylar marked me as an approved visitor.

Inching my truck to the guard, I noted he looked stressed, tired, agitated and was probably thinking he didn't get paid enough to deal with the circus surrounding the gatehouse.

"Cody James. I'm here to see Skylar Wyld."

He recognized me. He'd worked here the night I met her father. Even gave me a pep talk when I rambled on about it.

"Go ahead," he said without even consulting his clipboard.

I wanted to get out and hug him but focused on getting to the girl I knew was hurting.

The driveway held two black Town cars, a shiny Lexus and her Mustang, which was parked haphazardly at an angle. A sure sign she'd barely made it in before storming the house. The last memory I had of her face flashed before me. The unshed tears, the tight lips, the shredded way her eyes bore into me.

The edgy, disheartened feeling escalated as I knocked on Skylar's front door. I should be cold, freezing even, since it was forty degrees, and I was in workout clothes, but my body was a furnace.

The door swung open to a father's scowl.

I stood straighter. "Hi, Mr. Wyld. I wanted to see if I could talk to Skylar."

Donnie Wyld laid his forearm against the doorframe and assessed me from head to toe, much like he did the night I came to dinner. "I've got a pretty upset little girl in there. You here to make it better or worse?"

"Better." I hoped.

He raked a hand though his hair, his face etched with stress and frustration. "I'll give you ten minutes because I'm desperate." He stepped out of my path. "But if I get a hint that you're upsetting her more, you're done."

"Yes, sir." I stepped into the grand foyer and immediately heard the buzz of news from a television in the other room. He gestured for me to follow and I did, keeping my eyes peeled for red hair.

The two security men from school were in the kitchen, and a tall skinny guy was standing in the living room watching the headlines scroll across the flat screen on the wall. He turned when we walked in.

"This is bad, Donnie. She told them just enough to give them a story, but not enough to press charges. Speculation alone is going to kill you. I think it's time to make a statement."

Donnie stared at the ceiling for two beats, ignoring the advice. "Cody, why don't you wait out back? I'll get Skylar." He pointed around the corner and left without an introduction.

The skinny guy turned back to the TV.

The tension in the house was so suffocating it was like pushing through thick, wet sludge as I made my way to the backyard. I felt Skylar's loss. The ease that was there before had been completely sucked away.

I thought about sitting, but the pulse in my veins was too intense, so I walked. The mulch around the shrubs was bright red with a lingering smell of fertilizer. I touched a leaf, hoping in some way it would connect me to the girl who painstakingly planted it.

"What are you doing here?"

Skylar's voice made the hair on my neck stand straight. It was still harsh and distant. I turned around to see her standing just outside the door. Her arms wrapped around her torso and her eyes red and puffy.

I approached slowly. "I came to check on you."

"I'm fine. You can leave now."

"Okay, I came to talk to you."

"There's nothing left to talk about." Her expression was blank except for the creases at the corners of her eyes, as if looking at me was painful.

It certainly hurt to look at her. "There's everything to talk about." I hoped the desperation wasn't as obvious to her as it was to me. "I want to explain."

She faltered for only a second before her stare went back to its indifference. "I told you, I don't care anymore."

"Yes, you do." I reached for her hand, but she pulled it away. Frustrated, I gripped the back of my neck. Wished the sickness in my stomach would stop for just one moment. "I need you to understand why. Why Lindsay's fight became mine."

She stared down at her hands, turning them over as if to check for scratches or bruises. Seeing her cold expression was bad, but not seeing it was worse. I'd have to do this blind. Confess my worst nightmare without knowing if she was even listening.

"I used to be fat and shy and socially awkward. It didn't make much difference in junior high. Kids just ignored me. But at Madison, it changed." I shoved both hands into my pockets and kicked at some stray rocks. "Freshman year was bad. Teasing, some roughing up behind the school, papers missing. But nothing like sophomore year. Tom Baker had it out for me."

"Tom Baker?"

I closed my eyes. She was listening, even if she still wouldn't look at me. "The king of Madison two years ago."

"What did he do?"

My chest burned with pressure and every breath felt like a victory. "Fatty James. That's what he used to call me. Every day. Every time he passed me in the halls." Finally, she met my eyes. There was recognition.

Heat engulfed me. "You heard this before?"

"No. Lindsay said something about Tom Baker and pictures."

Sweat trickled along my forehead and stung my eyes. I prayed for calm. I had to do this if we had any chance. "Tom's girlfriend was like Lindsay. Shy, timid, kind. But he was cruel to her on a regular basis. I saw her crying outside and gave her a tissue. We didn't even speak, but that one act of mercy sealed my fate."

"What happened?" Her voice was soft, barely over a whisper. I clung to it, immersed in the fact that the bitterness was gone.

I rubbed my palms across my eyes, feeling sucked back into my horror. The bullied kid, the outcast, the crushed boy who fought to forget. "He broke me."

Seconds passed. I'd spent years pushing away the memory, fighting to forget the agony of that day and yet keeping it a secret. One that rotted inside me like a decaying body. Telling her was like opening an infected wound and pouring alcohol on it.

Skylar would know the ugliness. The broken parts of me that couldn't be fixed.

"One day in the boys' locker room, Tom and five other guys stripped me down, beat me, drew on me and then took pictures. Those pictures were posted on a private webpage usually seen by juniors and seniors. Lindsay knew about the pictures because Blake had access our sophomore year. I didn't even know the website existed until Lindsay showed me."

Her eyes shimmered.

"I didn't choose Lindsay over you. She already knew."

I dared to move forward. To touch her cheek. She didn't turn away. "You said I didn't trust you. You're wrong. I didn't trust myself. I'm broken. They broke me. And I've spent two years putting together the pieces, doing everything I could to make sure they never shattered again. I've made terrible mistakes. Compromised my values. Tried to heal by fitting in with the very group that laughed at me.

"But never once have I felt whole since that day. And I didn't really even notice it until I met you. Then suddenly I was aware of every crack and splinter. Protecting Lindsay made me feel like I was fixing it. Made me believe that I could be happy again. Made me think I could be a man worthy of someone like you. When I see them attack her, it's like I'm getting punched all over again."

She didn't say anything and I waited, giving us both time to process everything I'd just admitted to her.

"Thank you for telling me." Skylar didn't look me in the eye when she said it, and her words were so quiet I almost missed them.

I placed my hands on her shoulders. "I should have told you sooner. I just didn't want you to ever see me as weak."

Her eyes shifted to mine. "My mother left my father when I was three years old. He was touring in Europe, and she brought me home to the States. My father told me it took him one week before he completely fell apart, canceled the tour and came to find us. My mom didn't take him back for six more months. Do you know why?"

I shook my head.

"Because he was messed up, Cody. And he had to fix himself before he could ever be the kind of father and husband he needed to be."

I pointed to her house. "But he changed. He became that man." I could, too, if she'd just give me more time.

"He did." She touched her locket while a tear slid down her cheek. "But not because my mom took him back."

She was going to rip my heart out. Right here on her back porch. I took her face in my palms and begged. "Don't do this. Please, Skylar, it's not the same."

"It is." Her voice cracked. She pulled my hands down and squeezed them. "It doesn't matter if you take care of Lindsay or if you help me through this mess with the media. Or if you beat Blake in a round of wrestling or even win state. Until you face what happened to you. Until you move past it, you will never stop fighting."

I spread my arms, frustration exploding inside every vein and muscle. "I'm fighting for us! I'm trying to be a better man. That's all I've done since I met you."

"But who's fighting for Fatty James? You can't erase him, Cody. He's a part of who you are."

I couldn't look at her. "Don't say that name."

"Why not?" Skylar pulled me back, angled me until I met her eyes.

"Because he died on that locker room floor."

"No, he didn't."

Skylar's voice lowered as if calming a wild animal. Maybe she was. Maybe I'd finally lost it.

"That scared kid is just as alive as Lindsay is. And sooner or later you are going to have to face him. Just like I had to face the fact that no matter how much I wanted normal, I can't have it. My mother is dead. My father has cancer. I will forever be a rock star's daughter. There are things in life you cannot change, no matter how much you want to."

I shook my head as if doing so would make her words not true. For the first time since I met Skylar, I didn't want to be near her. Didn't want to get lost in her eyes or buried in her smile. She didn't understand. "You're wrong."

"I'm not." There was a heaviness in her tone that twisted my gut into a tighter pretzel. "I know you care about me. I know you want to be there for me. But you can't. Not until you deal with the ghost inside you." She hovered by the door, gripping the handle while I stood frozen.

"What about you? Us?"

"My father's dying, Cody. That's the only 'us' I can worry about right now."

And with those words, she walked away.

SKYLAR

CODY LEFT TWO hours ago, but my heart still felt like it'd been crushed into microscopic pieces. Did I make the biggest mistake of my life by letting him go? My father had told me that story a million times. And every time he said they wouldn't have made it if my mom had let him stay.

In the end, that decision saved my father. I could only hope the same for Cody.

My phone buzzed for the fiftieth time. Zoe again. I pushed the phone away, watched it glow against the ceiling. When people found out about my dad, they changed. I didn't want to know if my only girlfriend would join the list of many disappointments. More buzzing.

Zoe: *School is not the same without you.*

Zoe: *I cried when I realized you had been dealing with this all alone.*

Zoe: *I'm your friend. Please don't think your being famous changes that. I listen to pop music anyway.*

A laugh bubbled in my chest. Zoe had the absolute worst taste in music. She was also a gossip and too easily enticed by popularity. And my being Donnie's Wyld's daughter was certainly something Madison would feast on. But as I sorted through our conversations, our gut-shaking laughter, how much she cared, even when we didn't agree, I knew our friendship was worth the risk.

I picked up the phone and dialed.

"Hey," Zoe said, lengthening the word like she exhaled at the same time. "I've been so worried about you. The news and your dad, and gosh, Skylar, I'm so sorry he's sick. I can't believe you were going through this on your own. That must have been so hard."

And with those words, I broke down for the second time that day.

"Oh, Skylar, I'm sorry. I didn't mean. Don't cry. I won't talk about it any more." She sounded helpless, and it made me smile through the tears. She thought she'd said the wrong thing, but it was just the opposite. In Zoe's long breathless sentence, she never once mentioned the band or the fame. I was simply her friend.

"It's okay, really," I said in a hoarse, cracked voice. "What are they saying at school?"

"Everyone is talking about it, but I didn't tell them anything. Not that I knew anything." She paused. "It's brought out the worst in some people, though. I've seen a side of Blake that isn't so pretty."

I was shocked. If Zoe was anyone's fangirl, she was his. "What did he do?"

"He's just acting like y'all were best friends. And that he knew all about your little secret, which I know he didn't because Blake would have told the whole school by now." She inhaled a deep breath. "Did Cody know?"

I rubbed at my temples. "Yeah, he knew. He's known since the first day. He recognized me."

There was silence on the other line. From Zoe, it was a bit unnerving.

"He's a good guy, Skylar. I'm sorry I ever said he wasn't." Her tone dripped with a mixture of remorse and sadness. "He could have totally capitalized on this. Been a super star by just knowing you. But he hasn't said a word. Not one."

Misery weaved through every one of my ribs. He was a great guy. And I let him go. "Thanks for telling me."

As if she sensed my sorrow, she switched her tone to light and chatty. "So, I bought December's *Cosmo* and, oh, Skylar, you could totally make this dress that's in here."

I closed my eyes and told myself to just say it. "Do you want to come over?" I rushed the words, so I didn't have time to take them back. "My dad's been wanting to meet you, anyway, since I talk so much about you."

She responded with a squeal. "Yes! I'm dying to see your house and your room. And OMG, try on your clothes, not that they'll go past my hips, but still."

She stopped long enough for me to tell her that I'd send a car for her. She squealed again and proceeded to tell me about a scene from her favorite movie where two girls hung out of the top of the limo. I ended the call with the first smile I'd worn all day.

But, it didn't last long. The resulting silence weighed on me. Heavy and unmoving.

My hand trembled as I played the first song Cody ever sent me. He had told me to look inside the music. And now that I knew the truth, I understood every heartbreaking word.

The song talked of being a prisoner in his own mind. Of walls tearing down only to rise again. Of scraping and clawing until every finger bled.

The agony of the melody grew bolder and louder as the drums pounded and pounded and then there was a crashing quiet before sweet softness of hope poured through an a capella brilliance. Cody's text after the song hadn't made sense at the time, ***Cody:*** *You're in the stillness.*

I'd brushed it off. Thought it more of the same confusion.

I slid to floor, gripped the phone to my chest and prayed Cody would find that stillness in himself.

CODY

EVERYONE IN THE hall stopped and stared when I walked through the double doors. They no longer saw the wrestler, the guy who'd been unceremoniously tossed from the inner circle. I'd been given a new label—the guy who dated Donnie Wyld's daughter.

I strode down the hall, head high, shoulders straight. No one approached me, but the whispered questions floated through the air.

"Do you think he met her dad?"

"I heard he got to play Donnie's guitar."

That one almost made me smile. I was pretty sure Skylar's dad would gladly remove my appendage if I touched his precious Fender.

The whispers stopped, and I looked up to see why. Lindsay was at her locker, a rare sight, pulling out textbooks. She had enough in her arms to avoid coming back there the rest of the day.

I closed the distance before she could run away. "Did you tell them?"

The sigh from her was deafening. She wasn't shaking or crying. She didn't even look rattled. Her movements were robotic, her shoulders slumped. She was a girl who'd given up.

Lindsay shut her locker. "Yes. I told them."

"And what did they say?"

"They argued." She looked up at me with empty eyes. "My mom said I needed to toughen up. That I was being too sensitive and that it couldn't be that bad. Then she accused my father of babying me. Said it was his fault I didn't have a stronger backbone. It's what they do, Cody, fight, and all I did was give them more ammunition."

Stunned silence engulfed me. She had to have been cryptic when she told. "Did you tell them everything? Did you show them the Twitter feed?"

She jutted her chin, her lips trembled. "No. I didn't show them that I've been labeled 'slut Barbie,' nor that fourteen guys talked about what my body looks like naked while they supposedly had sex with me. No, Cody, I didn't tell them everything."

I lowered my voice. "What did you tell them?"

Lindsay's eyes darted around, never making contact too long with the people who tortured her. "Just that some kids were saying mean things about me and spreading lies. I told them that Blake had been cruel, and how I've gotten a few prank calls." She coughed out a sad, defeated laugh. "My mom actually asked me what I did to make him hate me. Told me to try and get him back."

A second bell rang, and I clutched her arm to keep her from bolting. "Lindsay…" It was a plea and an apology in one.

Then the dam burst. She was a mess. A puddle of sobs so broken and gut wrenching, I wanted to burn my own soul for pushing too hard.

"I'm sorry," I whispered, cradling her to my chest. "We'll tell someone else."

"No." She pushed away, and her face returned to that terrible mask of coldness, her eyes holding as much emotion as a corpse. "I'm done. I'm done with all of this. I'm sorry." She walked away before I could find a response significant enough to change her mind.

I stood there, frustrated and helpless, and wished for once, I could catch a break.

Skylar's abandoned locker stood out like a beacon of light. Maybe she was right. Maybe all of this was to force me to do the impossible.

If Lindsay wouldn't tell her story, maybe it was time to tell mine.

I SAT AT an empty picnic table and furiously wrote out the fifth page of my confession. Only ten minutes left until lunch ended, and I was determined to cleanse my system of every horrific deed. I'd written the details of the two years I was bullied, including my nightmare on the locker room floor. I was too humiliated to give specifics, but recounted enough to hopefully put protection in place for others. I recorded every aggression I'd witnessed against Lindsay and what I knew about the Torments List.

The last page hurt almost more than the others. It disclosed all the pranks I'd participated in last year and this year. There was enough information on these sheets of wide-ruled paper to ruin me. But somehow, nothing seemed to matter more than telling the truth.

An overpowering scent of peaches and honey stopped my scribbling. Jill was at my side, seated, her back against the table I was using. I flipped the pages over.

"I'm busy," I said, sliding away. She hadn't even left an inch between our hips when she sat.

"I can see that." She relaxed against the table and extended her long legs, crossing them at her ankles. "But I have something to say to you."

Of course she did. And it probably included some slam about Skylar.

"You know, Blake has envied you since the beginning of junior year. I'd go so far to say he's afraid of you."

That got my attention. "You think Blake's afraid of me?" I snorted. Nothing in our history together implied fear.

Jill faced me, propped her elbow up on the table and nervously played with her hair. "I do. That's why you've always been kind of on the fringe. An outsider within the inner circle. He knew one day you'd break free. He knew you were the only one strong enough to do it."

I shook my head, feeling the weight of my failure in every word I'd written. "A lot of good it's done."

Her eyes burned a hole through me. "That's where you're wrong. It takes people a while, but eventually they recognize a true leader. Even when his words hurt."

She reached in her pocket and pulled out a folded piece of blue paper. "I should have stopped Tom that day. And I should have been a better friend to Lindsay." With that, the paper was in my hand, and Jill stood to leave. "Consider this my apology."

The blue note crinkled in my fist while I watched her walk away. In that moment, I actually felt a twinge of respect. Maybe even forgiveness.

Slowly, I opened Jill's apology and a rush of adrenaline pulsed through me. She'd just handed me the key: Her login and password along with the new URL for the Torments List. Two seconds later, I was past the firewall and staring at my name in bold black. A strange power engulfed me. I felt no compulsion to read the comments because, for the first time in my life, their opinion didn't matter.

I packed up and walked, no, ran to the front office. I wouldn't wait this time. I wouldn't give Blake one second to figure it out.

Our school secretary, Mrs. Johnson, stepped around her oak desk to meet me at the counter. "Cody, you're making a habit of being in here. What is it this time?"

"I'd like to see Principal Rayburn. It's critical."

She lifted a receiver hidden behind the counter and touched some buttons. "Cody James is here. Do you have minute to meet with him?" She eyed me chewing my nail, and I dropped my hand. "Seems important."

Mrs. Johnson placed the receiver down and tilted her head toward the office.

I took off so fast, I was halfway to the back before I muttered a thank you.

"Come on in, Mr. James." Principal Rayburn said through his open door.

I walked directly to his desk and slammed down the five pages I had written, the login ID sheet, and Jill's note. "It's all here. Everything you need."

He slid over his half-empty Tupperware and spread out the pages, his eyes darting back and forth as he quickly read through them.

I took a breath. "There's a website called the Torments List." With that, I handed him my phone already set to the page.

He zoomed and clicked; his brow furrowed and released several times. He met my eyes, and I saw something in there that confirmed I'd done the right thing. Respect. "I've been trying to get my hands on this website for six years."

I dropped into the chair, stunned. "You already knew about it?"

He pulled my sheet of login IDs from the bottom of the stack. "Rumors. Confessions from punished students, but none were ever able to back it up." He tapped the page. "Nothing like this."

"That's because the Madison elite probably sent them a painful message right after they moved the URL and reset the passwords."

He stared at me and I stared back. Neither of us said it, but somehow I think he knew I wanted to tell the truth months ago.

"Thank you." His words were so sincere I had to swallow and find something else to look at.

He handed back my phone. "A lot of this will end up being your word against theirs. But it will enable to me to put some fear into the offenders. Fear is a very powerful tool."

Didn't I know it. I'd spent years cowering in fear. I leaned my elbows on my knees. "What happens to me?"

He rubbed his chin. "I could kick you off the wrestling team for this stuff."

I hung my head. "I know."

"But I won't."

My eyes lifted to his, my heart pounding against my chest. This was the same man who was determined to show me his authority just weeks ago.

"I'm sorry about the Super 32. I think that punishment will suffice."

A two hundred pound weight lifted off my shoulders. For

the first time in months, it felt like I wasn't fighting the battle alone.

BY FRIDAY, SIX of the ten people on my login list had been suspended. The other four, including Henry, were given in-school suspension for this being their first offense. The Torments List held all the proof Principal Rayburn needed, and even though it disappeared after the first suspension, there was a measurable change at Madison.

A stillness settled in the halls. A recognition that, for once, Blake didn't have all the power.

SKYLAR

MY FATHER BOWED, decked out in a new tux that actually fit his too thin frame. Hair styled and eyes bright, he made me forget the two weeks of media frenzy.

He'd outdone himself on our Friday date night, down to the dress I found in a big box this morning. The floor length chiffon gown was midnight blue with an elegant beaded bodice and was stunning enough for a princess at a royal ball.

It wasn't a ball, though, just my eighteenth birthday, but Daddy couldn't be convinced otherwise. He'd rented out a fancy Italian restaurant and a limousine for the occasion. My future prom date was going to have a lot to live up to.

I stepped past him and through the doors being held by our waiters. Candlelight lit the empty restaurant and soft music drifted effortlessly from a woman at the grand piano.

"Happy Birthday, Princess," My father said, placing gentle hands on my shoulders.

My gaze drifted over the room. A large chandelier hung from the ceiling, reflecting light off mirrored panels in the walls. Our table was round and centered in front of a small dance floor. A man in a suit stood waiting by my chair.

My father offered me his arm, and I gladly wrapped my hand around his elbow. Forgetting about the sorrow that pulsed below my tumbling resolve, I determined I would enjoy every second of this night with him.

His movements were stiff, sweat beading from the pain I knew he was experiencing. But he kept smiling at me. Made sure every minute was the fairytale night he wanted to give me.

The waiter pulled out our chairs and we sat, facing each other. Blue and white china gleamed in the light while our champagne glasses bubbled with sparkling grape juice.

My father lifted his glass. "To Skylar, the most talented, beautiful, strong-willed and kind woman I know. I am truly honored to be your father."

"Figures you'd throw the strong-willed part in there."

He grinned, still holding up the glass. "I can't lie, my dear."

Tears burned my eyes, but I lifted my own glass and matched his grin. "To my father, the most talented, caring, *strong-willed* and self-sacrificing man I know."

He bellowed out a laugh. Our glasses clinked, and we swallowed the sparkling liquid.

My father clapped his hands and rubbed them together. "I'm starved. Let's see what they have for us. A little birdy told me you might like this meal."

I knew he was pretending. Knew he barely kept any food down anymore. But the five-course meal began nonetheless. I made sure to savor each bite, my father taking his enjoyment from watching me.

We teased and talked, but not about the next week or the next year. We talked about the past, about my mom, about his life on tour. He told me stories that made his face light up and stories that had me bursting out with laugher so consuming, I once knocked over my champagne glass. Thankfully, it was empty.

When our meal was over, I wished time could stop. That we could walk through the glass door again and relive every moment over and over.

One of Daddy's songs filled the room, the pianist obviously given a signal that we were finished eating.

My father stood, gallant and strong, despite needing to steady himself with the table. "May I have this dance?" he asked in a voice that would rival the training of Prince William.

"Why, of course." I placed my hand in his and let him lead me onto small dance floor.

Pulling me close, my father swayed to the music and hummed the song along with the piano chords.

I could no longer hold them back. Tears trailed down my face, and I squeezed my father, wanting to hold on forever. To beg and plead with God to change the fate I knew was coming.

He sensed my break and ran a hand down my hair, comforting me. "I want you to know something, Skylar. I leave this life with no regrets. I married the love of my life, followed my passion for music with three men I'd die for, held the most precious baby girl in my arms and watched her grow into an amazing young woman. And I served God while experiencing more joy than should be allowed in a lifetime."

I sucked in the sobs that kept any response at bay and squeezed him tighter.

"When God takes me home, you remember one thing, okay?"

I nodded, still unable to move through my grief.

"You turned wailing into dancing. You clothed me with joy. My heart will sing your praises and not be silent."

The words came from Psalm 30 and were the lyrics in one of his new songs. The first release that would really showcase my father's faith. The world knew, of course. He'd always been bold about his beliefs, but his music had been abstract. Subtle messages of hope. This last record, his masterpiece, was a tribute to everyone he loved.

"I'm not ready to let you go." I sobbed into his jacket.

"Oh, Sweetie, you don't have to let me go. I'm a part of you. Your eternal cheerleader. Know without a doubt that just because my body is gone, my love for you is not. Tuck it inside your heart, next to your mom's and you'll always have us there."

I looked up at him through the blur of tears. "When you see Mom, will you tell her I love her?"

His eyes glazed, his smile broadening like a man waiting to see his bride on their wedding day. "Of course, I will."

Despite my grief, despite his pain, I knew my father couldn't wait to be with my mother again.

The song ended, and we made our way back to the table. My father's movements were even more strained. That dance had taken its toll. His last sacrifice for me.

Another present soon appeared in front of me. A thin, square box.

I tugged at the ribbon and lifted the lid, tears already flowing again before I even saw the present. I would have gasped, but couldn't get enough air through my constricted lungs.

My song.

I stared at the CD untouched in the box.

My father reached across the table and took my hand. "Ricky and I finished it over Thanksgiving. It's nothing fancy, just me and my guitar, but I had a feeling you would want it that way."

I couldn't take the heartache and buried my face in my cloth napkin.

"Skylar." My father's words displayed his own sorrow.

"Please, don't cry."

"I'm sorry," I choked out. "I love this. I do. It's the most precious thing you've ever given me."

I dug deep and found a smile that brought joy back into my father's eyes. No more tears. This night was ours. It was about celebrating life, not anticipating death.

My father nodded toward our waiter and soon a cake appeared, full of eighteen candles. Smoke billowed from the two-layer chocolate monstrosity while my father sang "Happy Birthday" to me in perfect pitch.

I blew out every candle in one breath, making a wish I prayed would come true.

My father clapped and cheered. Then went on to tell me about how I'd smashed my entire cake into my face when I turned a year old.

In those four hours, my father gave me his greatest gifts.

His memories. His life through his eyes.

His successes and failures, and most importantly, the clear proof that his love for me held no boundary.

CODY

SWEAT DRIPPED FROM my scalp and down my back as the referee declared me the winner. Two more matches, and the victory would be mine. I could taste it, sense it in every muscle strain and heartbeat.

The smell of burnt popcorn and scorched chili from the concession stand lingered in the stuffy gym causing my empty stomach to clench. Or maybe it was watching Blake take down his opponent, guaranteeing once again that he and I would be battling it out.

But not for first place this time.

Our brackets had collided, so whoever won the next match would be in the finals. The loser would wrestle for third. I wasn't going to be the loser. Not this time.

My gaze drifted to the packed bleachers. Matt and Devon sat in the middle, watching and discussing every move. A halo of empty seats around them suggested I wasn't the only one intimidated by their bulk and street-thug appearance.

My parents sat two rows lower, looking uncomfortable in their business attire. They had only arrived thirty minutes ago, and Blake had made a point to hug my mom and act like we were still best buds. My mom had even wished him good luck, which made me want to vomit.

I scanned the bleachers again, looking for the two scouts rumored to be here. North Carolina State and Georgia Tech.

Both Division I schools. Each an opportunity I couldn't miss. It wasn't even about the money as much as it was about knowing I was talented enough to compete at that level.

"Looks like it's me and you again," Blake said, taking the seat next to mine in our team's designated area. "Must be hard to lose so many times." He reached down for his Gatorade and took a long swig from the bottle.

I wouldn't play his game. Not today.

Looking for a distraction, I ruffled through my gym bag and found my phone. The missed text sent tingles through my fingers. Three words, but they were enough to light a fire inside my gut.

Skylar: *Good luck today.*

Skylar hadn't returned to school, but we'd been slowly texting again. Little updates. New songs when we found them. Nothing too deep. But it felt like a fresh beginning. One that had no secrets.

Me: *Thanks. Made the semi-finals. My match is in a few minutes.*

Skylar: *You'll kill it.*

Me: *Everything okay with you? Your dad?*

Skylar: *I guess. It's lonely here. He's been sleeping a long time. Haven't seen him yet today.*

Me: *I'll come over right after the match.*

Skylar: *It's ok. You don't have to.*

Me: *I want to. I miss you. I miss your voice. I miss seeing your face. I miss your smile.*

Skylar: *You tell me that every day.*

Me: *It's still true.*

The wait for her answer stretched on to eternity. I held the phone close, as if my grip could make her reply come faster.

Skylar: *Maybe we can start slow. A phone call?*

Me: *I'll take it. Should be done in an hour or so.*

Skylar: *I'll be rooting for you.*

Me: *That's all I need.*

I turned to Blake and smiled, feeling more empowered and eager than I did ten minutes ago.

He narrowed his gaze, then squeezed my shoulder in fake camaraderie when coach stood in front of us issuing last minute pointers.

Pointers I didn't need. Because I knew something neither of them did. That while Blake sat basking in his stolen victory, I was learning how to fight him.

The ref called us out, and we each took our stance opposite each other within the inner circle of the mat.

The cheers were deafening. Most of them were for Blake, but my section had grown too. Another reminder that a shift was happening.

I lunged at the shrill of the whistle, capturing Blake by the neck. He pushed me off, countered and then we were both locked on. We spun in a bid for dominance. Knees knocked. Elbows slammed. Blake twisted, but I locked onto his thigh and pushed him out of the circle.

Two points.

They were the first of many, and I was the clear favorite to win when we stood ready for round three. The gleam in Blake's eye warned me he'd do something illegal. Something to throw me off my game. But I was ready this time.

I started the round on my knees, Blake braced over me. But

in one swift move, we were both standing, and I received another point for the escape. This match was mine.

Blake lunged, I countered. He grabbed. I escaped. I was one step ahead, one second faster, every time.

Then I saw it. His mistake. Three seconds later, he was locked on the ground, his back flat against the rubber and victory rang in my ears louder than Matt's and Devon's cheers.

I DUCKED MY head, received the first place medal and walked to stand at the top of the small wooden podium a few feet away. Blake was to my right, on the floor, wearing a third place ribbon. I bit back a smile at the sight of his face. No arrogance. No smug satisfaction. That was all mine today.

Flashes blinded me as parents, friends and coaches took our pictures. My mom's face held a proud grin behind her iPhone. I smiled back. For all the times my parents disappointed me, there were moments like these. When they showed up, the other days faded into the background.

Our moment was over. I stepped down and into my mother's strong embrace.

"We're so proud of you, Cody!"

"Thanks." I felt proud of myself, too. Not just for the win, but also for everything I'd become through the journey.

My dad's firm handshake came next. "Good job, son." His face beamed with pride although we both knew my dad had no interest in sports or anything that caused perspiration. I think he owned one pair of sneakers. The ones he wore to his company's mandatory picnic each year.

He pulled me in for a quick hug and then released me.

"Thanks, Dad."

They offered dinner out, but I declined, wanting a shower and a long conversation with Skylar. I wanted to tell her about my victories. All of them. At school and at the match.

Blake was suddenly next to me with his hand outstretched. "Great match, Cody. That last move was wicked."

Matching his performance, I quickly shook his hand and then jammed my fists into my warm-ups.

"The team's heading to dinner. You should come."

My mom's smile broadened at Blake's invitation. She still worried that the reclusive, depressed kid I used to be would appear again. The kid who had no friends, no invitations and certainly no gold medals around his neck.

"Thanks, but I'm not hungry." It was a lie. My stomach was a hollow pit of hunger, but I wouldn't subject myself to an unnecessary hour of Blake's company.

"Oh, Cody, go. It will be fun," my mom said, getting that look I remembered too well. Worry. Misplaced concern.

Blake wrapped an arm around my shoulder and squeezed tighter than necessary. "Yeah, come on."

Pushing him off, I agreed. For my parent's sake, though Blake and I both knew I wasn't going.

My parents said their goodbyes and left the gym.

I spotted Matt, waiting. Watching Blake and me with arms crossed and keen eyes.

"What do you want?" I growled, facing off with Blake, his innocent expression long gone.

He took a step closer.

So did Matt.

"You lost, Blake. And not just today's match. Lindsay's done with you. I'm done with you. You're losing your power at school, and soon you'll just be some has-been jock who used to be popular."

Blake didn't move. Not his body or his expression. "You have no idea what I'm capable of."

Maybe I was high from my win or maybe having Matt there gave me a confidence I shouldn't have, but I smiled. The kind of smile that provoked. "You're right, but I no longer care. You're insignificant."

The last word hung in the air. Two things powered bullies. Our fear and our insecurity. I had just deprived him of both.

The hostility in our stance must have driven Matt forward, because he was suddenly next to us, his words careful and slow. "It's time you boys take a step back."

I obeyed, but Blake made a point to meet Matt's eye, then dropped his gaze down the length of Matt's body.

A beat later, he stepped back too. At least the boy wasn't completely brainless. He snatched his gym bag. "Later." Not a goodbye, but a promise.

Matt kept his focus on Blake until he was through the double doors of the gym, and then faced me. "Nice match." I was expecting a reprimand for the face-off, but there was nothing but pride in Matt's eyes.

"Yeah, it was."

We walked out to our cars. Several kids from school congratulated me. The same kids who just weeks ago had mumbled "loser" under their breaths. Unreal.

"I've got a new move I want to show you. It's a tough one, but I think you're ready."

"Okay. Sounds good." I wanted to focus on what Matt was saying, but my head was no longer at the match or even on wrestling at all.

As if Matt could sense my distraction, he let me be. Told

me to enjoy my moment and he'd see me in the gym next week.

"Hey Matt," I called after him.

He turned, waited.

"Thanks for coming today. It meant a lot."

A rare grin split his face. "You're welcome. Now go talk to that girl of yours. I can tell she's all you've got on the brain anyway."

I laughed, set my bag on the hood of my truck and rummaged for my phone. A missed text from Lindsay was on the screen. I slid the lock and everything stopped with her words.

Lindsay: *The news just said Donnie Wyld is dead.*

SKYLAR

MY FATHER DIED on Saturday, and I expected the world to stop. Expected the sun not to shine and the moon to disappear.

But the exact opposite happened.

Instead of time standing still, it took off in a haze. All of us rushing around like Pac-Man, devouring items off a never-ending to-do list, while skillfully avoiding the grief that chased us.

Grief that finally exploded in my chest when his coffin was lowered into the ground.

Grief when Ricky gripped my hand as if he needed my strength to get through saying goodbye to his lifelong friend.

Grief when I thought of all the milestones my father would miss. My prom, my graduation, my wedding, my first child.

I now understood why people stay busy after a loved one dies. It's so the grief doesn't smother you, doesn't rip your heart out with the knowledge that life will never again be the same.

CODY

SECURITY HAD BECOME my nemesis. It kept me from the hospital, from the funeral and almost out of Skylar's neighborhood. Thankfully, I convinced the snotty new guard to call the house and confirm I was welcome.

Her street was a mass of cars. I had to park down the block behind a shiny black Bentley. I glanced down at my standard church attire. Khaki slacks and a blue button-up shirt. I should have worn a suit.

Stupid. Stupid. Stupid.

I closed my eyes, took two deep breaths and began walking toward the door. I didn't blame Skylar for ignoring my calls and texts. She was in pain and, so often with her, I'd failed to rise to the occasion. Failed to put her needs before my demons. Not today. Today, I would be the hero she needed.

The door swung open after two knocks, and bad-boy Ricky Night stood in front of me in a three-piece suit.

For a moment, I couldn't breath. Couldn't speak. Then, as if a frog had jumped on my vocal cords, I finally croaked out, "I'm here to see Skylar."

He eyed me suspiciously, sweeping his gaze over my less than impressive attire. "You the boyfriend I just let through the gate?"

Sweat beaded on my forehead. "Y-Yes sir."

"It's about time." He moved out of the doorway so I could

come in. "She's been in her room since the funeral. I can't get her to come down." Irritation and sadness colored his voice.

He watched me stand there, unsure what to do or say next. "Well, go on, kid."

"Um. Yes sir. Um. Where is her room?" I glanced around the massive house and spotted Raif Hilliard picking up abandoned plates in the living room. How was it possible that this was her normal?

Ricky's laughter brought me out of my star-struck haze. "That's right. Donnie was a strict old cat. Upstairs. Second door on the left. Clothes better stay on." His laser-focused stare could have split an apple in two.

I bolted, taking the stairs two at a time. My heart pounded louder than my footsteps.

Her door was shut. I knocked. No answer.

Turning the knob, I gave the door a little push until a small crack allowed me to see her curled up on her bed, still dressed in black. Music played in the background. A song I'd never heard before, but the voice was unmistakable. Her father's.

"Skylar?" I pushed the door open further, my words just louder than a whisper. I felt like an intruder, but I couldn't pull away from the broken girl in front of me. The girl who'd pushed me to face my fears, who'd given me strength and courage when I needed it most.

She didn't move except to tighten around a small stuffed animal clutched to her chest.

I shut the door behind me and moved to sit on the small patch of space between her knees and the edge of the bed.

She blinked. "Cody?"

I moved closer and pulled away the chunk of hair that covered her eye. "Hey." I let my hand linger where my fingers had brushed her cheek.

"Will you lay here with me?" Her voice was weak with heartache. She scooted back, giving me space to join her.

I kicked off my shoes.

Her pillow was soft, and her bed like a mass of feathers. We faced each other, side by side. I didn't know what she wanted. What boundaries to cross or stand behind.

I stretched out my arm, offering.

She slid over, buried her head in my chest and cried. I cried too.

For her pain. For her loss. For the fact that I couldn't do anything to take it away.

Tucking her tightly against me, I prayed for God to heal her broken heart. I caressed the soft hair by her temple. "I'm so sorry about your dad. I'd give anything to bring him back to you."

"All I could think about was black sand. During the funeral and the burial. I just kept picturing black sand running though my fingers."

I rested my cheek against her, inhaled. "Why black sand?"

"It was our last family trip. To a set of islands off Portugal. Volcanoes formed them, so they all had this strange black sand. It's funny the things you remember. I remember the way the sand felt rough between my toes, how it didn't stick and form like the sand in Florida." Her breath caught as if the memory caused her physical pain. "But I can't remember my mom's laugh anymore. Can't remember if it was high or low. If it came out in giggles or was one continuous sound. I've tried for days to remember, but all I think about is black sand." She squeezed my arm, choked on a sob. Then, with the last of her strength, she whispered, "I don't want to forget him."

I cradled her face in my hand, littered light kisses on her trail of tears. "I'll help you remember. Tell me all about them. Every moment, and I'll make sure you don't forget."

Minutes passed without out a word. Then suddenly Skylar let out a soft chuckle. "My dad didn't think you were good enough for me."

"Your dad was right. I wasn't. But I will be." My hand trailed down her back. We were already locked together, but I needed more. I needed her to understand the depth of my feelings. "I'm sorry. I'm so sorry I hurt you."

Skylar picked invisible lint off my shirt, then smoothed out the material before starting the process again. "I'm sorry too. I wanted you to make life normal and perfect, to chase away the doom I felt every day. That wasn't really fair."

I slid my hand into her nervous one, laced our fingers. "I should have told you about my past months ago. Should have turned in what was happening to Lindsay instead of trying to be Superman. There're so many things I wish I could do over."

Silence filled the room, but it wasn't awkward or strained. Just a moment where two people ponder how different things might have been under other circumstances.

"So, did you win Saturday?" Her head was still pressed against my chest, slightly muffling the sound.

"I did. Got a call from the coach at Georgia Tech, too."

Her head tilted up, those remarkable eyes meeting mine. "Really? Oh Cody, that's wonderful."

"He didn't make any promises, but he said he'd come watch me again after the new year."

"I'm really happy for you."

I leaned in, brushed my lips over the delicate skin on her forehead. "Thank you."

Skylar's door swung open, slamming against the doorstop on the wall. We both jumped, our grip getting tighter when I should have bolted off the bed.

Ricky stood in the entry, hands on his hips. "Darn. I really wanted to use Donnie's shotgun."

I let her go and stood quicker than was probably necessary. I mean, he'd already seen me next to her.

Ricky's voice lowered. "Skylar." She sat up, her almost bare legs still stretched out on the bed. "It's time to come downstairs. There are people here who want to see you. Talk to you. It's not okay for you to hide."

"I know," she said, pulling her feet over the edge. "I'll come down."

Ricky's eyes flashed to mine. "Well, I guess you're not a total waste of space. That's the first word I've gotten from her all day. Next time, don't wait so long." He spun on his heel and walked away.

Skylar shook her head. "Meet dad number two. The annoying one. Three and four are downstairs."

She stood and pushed away the wrinkles in her dress. "I hate this thing. Had to buy it right off the rack." Color infused her cheeks and the dullness in her eyes faded a little.

"So change. You're dad wouldn't want you feeling uncomfortable."

She eyed her closet and a small smile appeared. "You're right. Will you wait for me?"

My heart exploded. She was still the most beautiful thing I'd ever seen.

I stepped closer, and leaned down to kiss the softest lips given to womankind. "Sweetheart, I'm not going anywhere."

SKYLAR

THE HOUSE WAS finally silent.

Ricky and the rest of the band said their goodbyes moments ago and, with one final click, the house went back to its familiar calm. Only it wasn't the same.

My stomach growled with persistence as it had for the last two days. Food wasn't appealing when everything on my tongue felt as bitter as the loss I'd suffered. But now, the leftover smells of the reception drifted up the stairs and rattled my overly empty middle.

I took each step slowly, hoping the dread I felt earlier wouldn't return. Even with Cody by my side, the string of condolences did more to scrape at the wound than heal my heart.

The sound of water running stopped my descent. My Aunt Josephine was washing and loading dishes. She still looked completely put together. Hair in a tight bun, her sleek black jacket buttoned with only a white collar showing.

Glasses clattered as she loaded dish after dish, her rhythm never stopping.

Then a slip.

The tumbler fell from her soapy hands and shattered on the floor.

She didn't move. Didn't flinch or jump out of the way as shards of glass flung across the kitchen tile. Then she did something I never thought possible. She covered her face and began to sob.

It's a strange feeling when you see someone break. Especially someone who always appeared so solid, so unmovable. It was then I saw what my dad had been saying all along. Josie and I shared the same pain, felt the same loss. We just coped differently.

She was do, do, do. And I was hide, hide, hide.

The woman in front of me wasn't my enemy. She was my family, and that list was becoming frighteningly small.

Shuffling into the kitchen as quietly as possible, I felt an odd sense of strength. She needed me.

At the sound of my entry, Aunt Josephine looked up. Her posture suddenly stiffened as she worked to get herself back into the poised professional she was used to being. "Skylar. I'm sorry. I thought you were upstairs." She walked to the pantry, pulled out the broom and began to sweep. "There's a lot of food left if you're hungry."

As much as she tried to sound in control, tears still streamed down her checks onto her collar. She swept furiously, pushing together the glass as if doing so would piece back together our now broken life.

My feet moved before I knew what I was doing, and soon I had Aunt Josephine in my embrace. "I'm sorry," I whispered.

The broom clattered on the floor, and her arms were around me, too. Her head pressed into the curve of my neck. I'd never noticed before, but we were the same height.

We held on, mourning, sharing, comforting until neither of us could shed another tear. She released me and stood straight, smiled through her smeared mascara. "I'm guessing Donnie's giving himself a high-five right now."

She started laughing right after those words, a sound I'd never heard before. Her laugh was his. Low and solid, coming deep from the gut.

"You laugh like him," I said, still reeling from the sound.

She straightened her jacket and took a long draw of breath. "You laugh like your mother."

An ache curled around my heart. "I'm sorry I said those things to you. Mom never called you a spinster."

Josie laughed again. "Oh, I'm sure she did. Your mom and I used to fight like street cats on a bad day. But I loved her. And I loved your dad." She reached out, took my hand. "I love you too."

I squeezed back. "I guess that's good. We're all that's left."

She let go of my hand and picked up the abandoned broom, soon sweeping the rest of the glass into a tight pile.

I leaned over, held the dustpan as she filled it.

"There are lots of papers to be signed. Now that you're eighteen, your father's assets are yours. There's also a trust, music rights and property." She trailed off and I wanted to cringe.

Ten minutes. That's the most she could go without thinking logistics. Oh, well, one moment of bonding was not going to erase her personality.

"Can we discuss it later?" I stood, walked the broken pieces over to the trashcan and dumped them in.

She leaned against the counter, pushed down the stray hairs around her head. "We can. I just need to know one thing. Are you leaving?"

I paused, never considering that not only was I now an adult, but there was no longer anyone here to direct my path.

"Ricky talked to me about you going to stay with him. At

least until college starts in the fall. I can handle the sale of the house. If that's what you want." She hesitated, obviously trying to be careful not to push too hard.

I thought of Cody and knew I didn't want to leave. Didn't want to join Ricky in some bachelor pad in southern California where he'd parade women in and out and tell me what to do. "Can I stay here until I figure out what I want?"

Somehow the idea of Josie being right down the street gave me peace. It was like my father knew when he moved us here that this moment would happen, and I would need her.

Tears filled her eyes, and she blinked them away. "I'd like that very much."

CODY

THE ANTICIPATION OF tonight led to a frenzied dressing session. Sheesh, I was practically primping like a girl. But I wanted our date to be perfect. It would be the first Friday night without her dad and the beginning of our Christmas break together.

Mouthwash, cologne, deodorant, keys. Phone.

I looked around for the last thing I needed before heading out. It sat on my nightstand charging but was lit up with a flood of texts continuing to come in. I slid the lock and stared at the group message that had a response every few seconds.

Scrolling up, there was a one-minute video from an unknown number.

Dread pulsing in my veins, I hit play.

Lindsay. Naked. On a bed. A shadow pressed over her.

I fumbled to stop the sounds and the actions. The man's face was hidden, but I knew who it was. Blake.

You have no idea what I'm capable of.

His words landed on me like a two-ton rock. My hand trembled as I read the comments popping up in real time:

OMG. She's so fat. Did you see that cottage cheese?

Her boobs are totally fake. Like the rest of her.

What a ho. She should just kill herself.

Who's the guy?

Cody James.

The letters in my name blurred and my knees buckled. Blake hadn't just fired a bullet. No. He managed a lethal shot, right between the eyes.

I gripped the phone and dialed Skylar. Her number was unlisted. Maybe…

My hopes were dashed when I heard the catch in her throat. "Cody?"

"It's not me. I swear to you." I sucked in a breath. She had to believe me. She had to.

"I know." The softness in her voice calmed the storm, pushed aside the panic that had all but overtaken me. "Have you checked on Lindsay?"

"No, I called you first." I found control despite the continued banner of text notifications, each escalating in their cruelty. "It's Friday night, Skylar. I don't want you to be alone." Everything changed that day in Skylar's room. I made promises I had no intention of breaking.

"I appreciate that, but you need to check on her. It's the right thing to do. Those comments are…"

"I know." I squeezed my eyes shut, but the images were still branded in my brain. "Are you sure?"

"Yes." There was no pretension in her voice. It was etched with the same concern I had for Lindsay.

"I'll be one hour, tops."

"I'll be waiting. Text me when you know she's okay."

I ended the call and immediately tried Lindsay's new cell. No answer.

Now that I knew Skylar wasn't upset, I had time to process what this final blow would do to my friend. I thought of how many days she'd skipped the past two weeks. I thought of the sadness in her eyes, the hopelessness that showed when her parents didn't validate her confession.

I dialed again, panic and fury growing with each ring. The stairs felt too long, the distance to my car too far.

Voicemail.

"Lindsay, pick up your phone. I need to know you're okay."

Fumbling with buttons while I unlocked my car, I tried to text.

Me: *Call me. Now.*

She didn't call the entire ten-minute drive to her house. Didn't answer the door when I pounded.

"Lindsay," I banged against the wood, trying to peek though the blinds next to the door. The ache in my chest was enough to kill me.

Her car was out front. I knew she was home.

"Lindsay!" I pounded some more, pulled and jerked on the locked front door.

A stinging fear ripped through my heart. And I knew. Somehow, I knew if I didn't get in there, it would be too late.

Hadn't I faced this same decision? Hadn't I even planned it? Found the rope, decided on the date? Wasn't I just as ready to make all the pain go away?

Ringing filled my head as I continue to scream her name. I knew she was in there. Knew she needed me, but I couldn't get to her.

"God, please," I whispered.

Back door.

The thought hit like a punch to the chest.

My heart pounding, I ran around to the rear of the house,

shoving open the gate. The screen door was locked, but I managed to rip out the mesh and flick up the metal latch.

"NO!" I tugged on the knob, desperate. The door was secure, but the lock, flimsy. Like the one at the back of my house, it rattled as I jerked, giving me hope. I pulled out my wallet, dropping it twice before I managed to find my driver's license.

I jammed the card between the lock and frame and pushed with so much adrenaline the wood gave way. I stumbled on the tile, but found my footing and began to search.

"Lindsay!"

The house was painfully silent, my frantic footsteps the only sound echoing off the walls. I took the stairs two at a time. "Lindsay!"

Room after room I hunted until the last corner revealed my worst nightmare.

I froze in the hall. All I could see was the bottle. The empty bottle.

The room seemed to be floating away. I tried to lift my legs, but they resisted, like feet trudging through wet clay.

She wasn't moving; she didn't even flinch when I called her name from the hall. She lay flat on her stomach, one arm draped over the side of the bed. Her blond hair cascaded like a blanket over the white t-shirt she wore. A fallen angel.

My knees hit the ground before I ever realized I'd dropped. The thud cleared my head. The room coming back from its distance in the tunnel. Adrenaline rushed though me like nitro in a drag race.

She can't be dead. She can't!

Instantly I was at her side. "Lindsay." I said her name calmly.

Nothing. Not a groan or a whimper.

I shook her limp body. "Please, Lindsay, answer me." She moved against my hands, but only from the force I exerted. I willed myself to settle down. To react like a man and not a scared little boy.

Two fingers against her neck brought a flood of hope. A pulse barely detectible, but it was there.

Though only seconds, the time it took to dial 911 felt like decades.

"911. What's your emergency?"

"My friend, she took pills." I reached out, gripped the prescription bottle with my free hand. "Z-O-L-P-I-D-E-M. They're for sleeping. 1520 Mayberry." The rush in my voice, the ache of each word made speaking almost impossible.

"Sir, I've dispatched an ambulance. Can you tell me if she's breathing?"

I dropped the pills and pressed my fingers to her mouth. A small brush of air tickled the skin. "Yes. But her pulse is weak, and she's not waking up."

"Can you tell how many pills she took?"

I dropped to the floor, fumbled around for the bottle. "Um. Ten milligrams each. It says there were thirty pills, but I don't know how many she actually swallowed."

The operator clicked on her computer, asked more question about dates and refills. My hand alternated between the bottle and checking Lindsay's dropping pulse.

"How much longer?" I demanded. The breath that was such a relief had all but vanished. I was losing her.

Sirens filled the air in the distance, promise stirring with each sound. I ran down the stairs and opened the front door just as the medics pulled to the curb.

They rushed past, followed my pointed finger and verbal directions. They had Lindsay out the door in minutes, a bag pushing oxygen into her lungs.

I stood at the entry, watching them rush to load her in the back of the ambulance, and fell to my knees. I prayed the prayer Skylar probably had a million times. I prayed for a miracle. I prayed for God to spare her life, even though she chose to end it.

SKYLAR

I'D SPENT TOO many hours in a hospital like this, watching my father fight cancer the first time. The floor was the same. Cold, sterile, unfeeling.

The difference, though, was the boy sitting alone with his head in his hands. The boy who'd taken on someone else's pain and now sat drenched in the agony of it. The boy, who because of that very thing, was the person I was falling in love with.

I gripped the metal arm and lowered myself into an empty chair.

Cody didn't look up, but his hand reached out, took mine and held on as if letting go would end the world.

"What are they saying?" Cody hadn't given details on the phone. Just told me what and where before hanging up.

"Nothing. They asked me a bunch of questions, then said I couldn't see her." There was a catch in his voice, as if he'd swallowed a sea of tears since being here.

"I should have told Principal Rayburn sooner." He hid his face, but his grip tightened. "I tried to fix it. Tried to be enough and I wasn't."

A tear fell on our joined fingers and then another. I scooted closer, laid my head on his shoulder. He was dressed for our date and the stiff dress shirt felt scratchy against my cheek. "What happened to Lindsay isn't your fault."

He shook his head. "Matt told me. He knew somehow."

"Told you what?"

Another drop. "That I couldn't save her."

I pulled away my hand and wrapped my arms around him. He fell into me, gripping my back and smashing me next to his chest. His head buried in the curve of my neck, he mumbled something I couldn't hear.

Caressing his hair, I whispered, "It's going to be okay."

He released me slowly, keeping his head down until he'd wiped his eyes with the sleeve of his shirt. "Let's go. I can't be here any more."

CODY

THE HOSPITAL EXIT felt further away with every step. I gripped Skylar's hand, let her strength pour into me. Her father had died only weeks ago, and yet she was here. I'd never deserve her.

The mechanical doors slid closed behind us, and I immediately spotted Lindsay's parents off to the side. Their whispered accusations bounced off the brick walls and concrete sidewalk.

"They were your pills," her father said. His suit coat was unbuttoned, his tie loose and crooked. He looked tired, weary and ticked off.

"I didn't stuff them down her throat." Her mother's tone was as stiff as her posture.

"You should have listened. She tried to talk to you. To tell you she was hurting." Worry marred her father's face. He touched his temples, pressed and circled.

"I don't recall you jumping in to save her either." The bite in her tone was intended to sting.

His arm lifted in exasperation. "Because you accuse me of babying her every time I do!"

I cleared my throat. They owed Lindsay more than this. They should be at her side, not fighting with each other.

Her mom spun around and suddenly the tough, hostile exterior crumbled. "Hi, Cody. Are you leaving?"

We'd met earlier and I'd given the same report to her that I had to the doctor.

"Yeah." My throat ached to pour out my own string of accusations. *Why didn't you believe her? Why didn't you support her?*

She pulled me toward her like my dad had once when he'd lost me at the mall. "Thank you for finding her." She was little, like her daughter, but her grip threatened the circulation in my arms.

Skylar's hand disappeared.

"How is she?" I eyed her father, who immediately stalked back inside.

That's right, you jerk. Walk away, just like you did before.

My heart hammered against my chest. I couldn't move, and the hypocrisy of being mauled by Lindsay's neglectful mom only fueled my fury.

She finally let go and wiped away black smudges under her eyes. "She's pretty out of it right now but, don't worry, they say she's going to be just fine." With a final squeeze, she left in the same direction as her husband, never once acknowledging that she practically pushed the bottle into Lindsay's hand.

I rested my forehead on the cool brick and the heat from Skylar's hand singed my back.

"I need to get out of here," I said. "I'm too angry. Angry at her. At Blake. At her parents."

"Okay. We'll go back to my house."

I was trembling. Nauseous. Flushed. "No. I have to go…somewhere else." I backed away. "I'll walk you to your car. Follow you home. I just…." The air was choking me. I paced. I had to move. Had to fight, do something. The pain overwhelmed my senses. My vision blurred until two hands held my cheeks.

"Cody, my car is right over there. I can get home just fine."

I sucked in two deep breaths. "You're sure? Absolutely sure? I will not leave you here if you're not."

Her voice was the only sound holding me together. "I'm sure. Go."

I flew through the parking lot, stumbling more than stepping, whipping around cars, pushing myself faster and harder. Hoping the rush would stop the fury that had an iron-tight grip on my insides.

I never had a sibling, but what Lindsay and I shared created a bond as tight as family. I wouldn't let this go unpunished. No matter what I had to do.

A sharp sting assaulted my chest. It wasn't from the running, but the screams of Fatty James that couldn't be silenced this time. The injustice of seeing yet another victim of cruelty and abuse.

Like me, Lindsay would never be the same. Today was the final break. I could see it in the vastness of her surrender.

I put my truck in drive and beat on the steering wheel. I needed the contact. Needed to find Blake and end him. But I couldn't do it like this.

On instinct, I whipped a U-turn at a stoplight, the sound of rubber against asphalt matching my urgency.

The Storm. Apocalypse. A release.

Then I'd find Blake and rip him apart until his body looked as broken as Lindsay's.

THE STORM WAS scarier at night, even with dusk only an hour behind us. The pothole-ridden lot jarred my truck as I sped toward the building. Matt's bike was still there along with an old Camry whose hood didn't match the rest of the car.

My eyes narrowed at the sedan. I wondered if the engine was as jacked as the paint job, or, if like all of us, the outside was only a sad reflection of what fell below the surface. It didn't matter. People saw what they saw. Did what they did. To hell with the collateral damage like Lindsay and me.

I pushed through the glass doors with such force that the handle banged the wall. Matt was in street clothes. No doubt finished for the night and heading home to be with his wife. I didn't care.

"I need Apocalypse. Now." My voice trembled more than my hands.

Matt glanced at the blond guy behind the counter.

"It's open," the kid said, looking between the two of us like Matt would somehow calm the hurricane in my eyes.

I didn't wait for an okay. Just headed straight down the hallway, past the two guys pounding each other in the ring and pushed open the door.

Seconds later, I was the one pounding. My shirt gone, music blaring, I sent fist after fist into the bag. I kept waiting for the violence to make me feel better, for it to take away the pain in my chest and the memories that flooded my mind.

Fatty James. We know you're in here.

I hit harder, faster.

Wow, Fatty, you're a whole lot of man, aren't you?

There wasn't enough volume to drown out the noise in my head. Wasn't enough strength behind my fists to stop the gut-punch I felt with each word. I wasn't fatigued enough to block the hopelessness I swore I'd never feel again.

I faltered, my arms dropping to my sides. The tape across my hands was torn and red from the splotches of blood. I tried to lift them again, ignoring the protest of my bruised and cracked knuckles. Five more punches, five more attempts to forget, and then I swayed.

Reaching out, I gripped the bag for stability, my heart now a dull thud in my chest.

I spotted movement in the doorway.

Matt was there. Arms folded, watching, waiting. His expression was blank, but seeing him made me feel safe. He represented all I had achieved over the past year and a half. He took a step forward and clicked off the screech of heavy-metal rock exploding through the speakers. "You ready to move on from this?"

His words knocked me back. "I thought I already had." I dropped my gaze, studied the way my shoelaces looped though each hole of my sneakers.

He took another step in my direction. His movements were slow and careful, like a man two seconds from wrestling a bear. "You can slam that bag until every inch of skin is gone, but it's not going to help you move forward." He spoke with gentleness and understanding, like he'd been in my shoes before. Like he'd faced the same demons.

"Then how?" I begged more than I demanded.

"You've got to get control of your mind, Cody. Ignoring or blocking out the past may work in the short term, but eventually, the pain always surfaces. Trust me. I know this first hand." He looked at my chest, his gaze following the line of my new definition until it settled on my face. "You've transformed your body. But that won't make any difference until you're ready to transform your mind and your emotions."

I put my forehead to the bag, unwilling to look into eyes that could peel away every shield I'd learned to use. "When I think about it, I hurt. And when I hurt, it makes me angry and bitter." Gruff and barely audible, my words hung in the air.

Matt's hand was on my shoulder, offering me strength and comfort. "I know. And it may always hurt. You may always struggle. But until you let go, you will never struggle in a healthy way. You will never find healing. Or forgiveness."

I hardened to a statue. "I'll never forgive them."

"Then you'll never really be free." Matt's voice stung like acid dripping on my skin.

I gripped the bag tighter, hit my head against the slick leather twice before the first round of sobs descended on me. They sounded a lot like the sobs I'd released on the gym floor two years ago. But today they were different. Today they meant grief. Every tear for the boy who wouldn't stop haunting me. "I'm so tired of being weak."

Matt moved closer. "You have it backwards. Forgiveness is strength, not weakness. Letting go means giving up your rage. It means allowing yourself and the other person to have grace. It means giving up the hate and facing the pain of what you went through. Because only then, will you truly find peace."

I stared at the man I considered my hero. Forgiveness. The word ricocheted within me like a bullet. "Where do I even start?"

"You start by telling the truth. To yourself. To the people you love. You stop thinking you can do this on your own and let others support you. And, most importantly, you rely on the author of strength to overcome your pain. God tells us that in the world, we will have tribulation, but in Him, there is peace, because He overcame the world." Matt pulled me into an embrace that was as crushing as it was liberating.

I held on like a man drowning.

"You're not alone, Cody. You're never, ever alone."

SKYLAR

I STOPPED BY Veteran's Park on the way home from the hospital, no more eager to return to my empty house than I was to face the choices in front of me.

The swing moved and twisted as I kicked at the dirt. So many decisions to be made. So many that Aunt Josephine had two pages of legal-sized notebook paper attached to my fridge. But nothing on that list was as daunting as the thick envelope sitting on my kitchen table.

ESMOD. I'd been accepted. Early admission too, which had my father's scent all over it. Even from the grave, he was telling me to live my dream. Somehow, though, over four short months, my dream had morphed and dissolved. And now I was floundering with no direction and no purpose.

My iPhone vibrated in my back pocket. It was a text from Henry asking me to meet him at his house. Strange. We hadn't really talked much in the last few weeks. He called after the media broke the story and then when my father died, but that was it.

Henry waited on his porch while I pulled in the drive, his hands shoved into the pockets of his designer jeans. His short-sleeved Henley was tight, showing a splash of muscles that hadn't existed before. He was still skinny and wiry, but long gone was the awkward nerd I met on the first day.

I locked my car and approached him. "Hey, what's up?"

He wouldn't make eye contact, and his foot tapped on the wood porch like he was listening to techno music in his head. "Have you heard about Lindsay?"

"Yes. I just came from the hospital."

His head jerked up, fear flashing in his eyes. "Is she going to be okay?"

"She's going to recover." But it would probably take years and lots of counseling before she was truly okay.

He closed his eyes and nodded vigorously. "Good. That's good."

I took a step forward. "Henry, what's going on?"

"I know things. Things I wish I didn't. Things I shouldn't know." He sank into a white, wicker couch and stared at his feet. "It's not Cody in the video."

"I know that." It surprised me how easily I believed Cody when he told me, but I did. We'd overcome the drama of secrets and miscommunication.

He was slow in meeting my eyes. "Did Cody tell you what I did?"

A chill raced down my arm. Maybe we hadn't moved past the secrets. "No. What did you do?"

He fidgeted and tugged on his earlobe. "Nothing. Just…nothing."

"Henry, you're not making any sense, and you're starting to freak me out. Just tell me what's going on." My tolerance level was miniscule. There'd been too much tragedy in a very short period of time.

"Wait here." He sprung up and with two decisive strides disappeared behind the front door. Two minutes later, he emerged with a silver laptop in his hand. He sat. Motioned for me to sit next to him. "Do you remember my accident?"

I lowered myself slowly, taking the open space on the couch. "You mean when a bunch of guys at school jumped you?"

He sighed. "Yeah." His computer showed several open windows with file icons everywhere. "I hacked a certain king's computer that night for proof, but found something far worse. I downloaded the file from his hard drive thinking I could use it to protect myself, but then everything changed at school. Got better, you know. Blake invited me to lunch. I met Cynthia, and she liked my quirkiness."

I patted his leg. At least one person this year had a happy ending. "I'm glad, Henry."

His eyes met mine, and that look was there again. Remorse, guilt, shame. "I should have turned it in. But I liked being at the head table. I liked having places to go on the weekends. I've been a narc before, and the backlash was insane. I knew if I told, it would be my final act of treason."

He pulled up a video, and the arrow hovered over the play button. "Skylar. I won't be the one to turn this in. Not only did I get to it illegally, but I just won't go there again. If you want it, though, I'll give it to you."

My head was swimming. Henry's words made no sense. "Why would I want it?"

He clicked play. "You'll see."

The video was black for few seconds, with only the audio booming snickers and muffled laughter. Then, out of nowhere, Blake's face appeared on the screen.

"Fatty James, Take One." He pretended to be clapping a scene marker like in the movies.

"Hush. He's in there. Jill just told me so."

The camera did a three-sixty until it was facing forward,

Blake's repressed laugher still being the loudest audio indicating he was the videographer.

"Fatty James, We know you came in here."

"Oh, my God." My hands flew to my mouth as the camera zeroed in on a pair of sneakers peeking out between the lockers.

A dark-haired guy in a letterman jacket crouched down, rested his hands on his knees. The camera made a horrifying visual zoom in.

"Now, now, what do we have here? A whale stuck in a hole." He made a "tsk" sound and looked toward the camera. *"Boys, we need to help Fatty James."*

The screen jumped and jumbled, shadows moving in front of the camera. Blake must have backed away and come around from a different angle.

My heart stopped. They had Cody pinned to the ground. He looked so different, it was hard to believe it was the same person, but I knew. Because for the first time, I could see the image that still haunted him.

Cody struggled and kicked until the ringleader slammed a fist into his face.

I jumped up and ran to the rail, sure I was going to puke the contents of my churning stomach. The audio assaulted my ears.

"Wow, Fatty, you're a whole lot of man, aren't you? Let's see what else you're hiding under there."

"Jiggle him around a little. We'll call him White Jell-O Whale to match those tighty whities."

"Dude, check out his hooters!"

"No worries, I got his training bra right here."

Blake's laughter became a howl.

"Turn it off!" I screamed, covering my ears. How could

they be so evil?

The dry heaves hit twice, but nothing came with them. I heard the click of the laptop behind me and then Henry's footsteps.

"I'm sorry," he said, his voice cracking with the word "sorry."

I pressed a hand against my stomach. "Blake was there. He filmed it."

"Blake's manipulative and cruel."

Henry's flat tone sent anger vibrating through my body. "You should have told me. I almost dated him, and you claimed to be my friend. You should have told me!"

"I'm so sorry." Henry backed away. "I just wanted the hazing to stop."

"Did it stop, Henry? Did your silence keep Lindsay from being next?"

"I didn't know she'd try to kill herself. I didn't know she was that depressed."

"He sent two hundred people a clip of her having sex!" I flattened my palms to my thighs even though I wanted to throw a punch. For the first time, I understood Cody's rage. "I want that video."

He reached in his pocket and pulled out a thumb drive, dropped it in my hand. "I'm sorry."

"Tell that to Cody." I spun around and ran to my car. Blake would pay. There had to be a way to make him pay.

I slammed my Mustang into drive and took off for the highway. It was Friday night, but I knew exactly where Aunt Josephine would be. The law offices of Robinson, Fink and Wyld.

*

"I WON'T ACCEPT that nothing can be done." I sat with my arms folded, my shoulders solid with determination.

My aunt laced her fingers together. They rested on her oversized, mahogany desk, each leg of it intricately carved. The impressive furniture didn't match her drab style or the sour expression that now hung on her face.

"I'm not saying that nothing can be done. Just that it's tricky. That video is almost two years old and, even though it took place on campus, if no additional acts of violence have been reported since, I doubt the school will have any recourse."

"This sucks," I spit out, my aunt flinching at the distaste in my voice. I knew she hated my current tone. Probably because it was typically directed at her. But it was the truth in her words I hated, not her.

"Skylar, we do have some options, legally, but they're long shots." She restacked a bunch of papers that were already tidy.

My shoulders straightened. "What options?"

"We can file a civil suit against the six boys in this video. I might even be able to press charges on the one who actually punched him, but criminally, we are looking at probation at the most."

"What about the one holding the camera?" I asked, thinking of Blake and how I'd like to do some punching myself.

"They were both minors. Harassment, maybe, but it's not even worth the time to process the paperwork." Aunt Josephine flattened her lips and smoothed her already pristine bun. I knew that look. It was her "be practical" look. The one she'd give me when I implied my father would survive the cancer. The one that reminded me how naïve I had been.

I dropped my head to my hands, the images on that video flashing through my mind again and again. "He can't just get away with it."

My aunt rose from her leather executive chair and walked around the desk. With my head lowered, I could see the shine of her shoes as she stepped in front of me and leaned back against her desk.

"Why don't you tell me exactly what you want to happen, and then I'll do my best to come up with a plan."

It wasn't much, but at least it sounded a little like an olive branch. I looked up. Her fingers were laced again, tucked elegantly next to her pressed suit pants.

"I want Blake punished. I want him to lose everything that's important to him. Wrestling, being king at Madison. I want him to suffer the way Cody did in that video. The way Lindsay is now." Tears stung my eyes and I wondered if she noticed because the corner of her eyes turned down. "I just want something in my life to be fair."

My aunt stood straight and unbuttoned her suit coat. It was a rare move on her part. Like removing the covering meant exposure. A silk blouse peeked out. It was pink and unexpectedly feminine. And for some reason, I couldn't pull my eyes away. Even when she neatly folded her coat across the top of a chair and sat to face me.

"Did you ever play poker with your dad?" A slight smile cut her face and widened when my brows furrowed. "He taught me, you know. I was twelve and he was nine, but the boy was such a pro he'd collected twenty bucks from bets at school."

I gasped. "Dad gambled? At nine?"

Her laughter flew through the air, once again reminding me of my father's. I closed my eyes, wanting to capture and save every note in a bottle.

"My brother was the ultimate card shark. And the most important lesson he taught me, the one that has helped me win seemingly impossible cases, is the power of a bluff." Her dark eyes shined like she was holding a royal flush. She'd given my father this look numerous times, but never me. I always got the stoic woman, the one who wanted me to plan and focus, not this silk wearing, poker-talking woman. Or maybe that was all I'd ever allowed her to be.

A flutter hit my stomach, and I matched her grin. "I take it you have a plan?"

She crossed her arms. Her mischievous expression replaced by the serious eyes of Asheville's top lawyer. "Boy, do I."

CODY

STANDING ON SKYLAR'S front porch, I wiped my hands down the sides of my jeans and stared at the etched glass embedded in her front door. I'd left The Storm an hour ago to drive and think, but my arms still burned with exhaustion, the rest of my body not much better.

A year ago, I had everything figured out, had a plan and a goal. But I'd been living in denial. I believed that working hard enough could erase the damage done on that locker room floor. It couldn't.

The door swung open, the light from inside bright against the dark sky.

"Hey," she said. "Why didn't you knock?"

"I was just about to."

She gripped the edge of the door with her right hand and seemed to be using it for stability.

"Can I come in?"

The foyer that had seemed so grand and warm only a few months ago now felt lonely. Soft music played in the background, the source coming from upstairs. She was here alone. I'd left her alone, again.

I closed the door behind me and reached out to touch her sorrowful face. "You're missing him, huh?"

She shrugged. "I always miss him."

"I should've come sooner." I let my hand glide down her

arm until it captured her fingers. I led us into the living room where I'd first met her dad. "You shouldn't be here by yourself, especially tonight."

"I haven't been. Not really. I just got home a little while ago. Are you feeling better?"

"I feel exhausted." I fell into the leather sofa and spread my arms, hoping she'd curl into my lap and make me forget all the chaos in my brain. She did follow me, but her movements were stiff and awkward, and she kept at least a foot between us. On the coffee table sat a water bottle and her laptop. It was open, but the screen was black. A fluffy blanket was crumpled at our feet. Skylar picked it up and began folding it.

"Cody, I..." She glanced at the computer and then back at me, made another crease in the cotton material. She carefully laid the blanket over the armrest and turned the computer so I could see the screen better. "I need to show you something."

"What?" I felt more than heard the edginess in my voice. Had Blake sent out more vile videos or pictures of Lindsay?

She slid a finger over the mouse pad, and all the growth I thought I'd achieved in the gym shattered to the ground. The six of us were paused. Me on the ground. Them holding down my arms and legs. I knew that scene like my own reflection.

Skylar resumed the video I had no idea even existed. What had been shadows in my mind were now faces I knew. Guys I'd even trained with my junior year.

Tom Baker kicked my old body, and a voice snickered next to the camera. A voice I'd heard a million times.

It was as if I swallowed razor blades. I fell back on the couch, dazed, and gripped my fingers above my head. Skylar shut the laptop.

"Has everyone seen this?" I whispered. Taking down Lindsay wasn't enough. He'd come after me.

Hands cupped my cheeks, but I still couldn't focus on her face. There'd been too many blows today. Too much devastation to even register this latest betrayal.

"Cody, look at me."

I didn't want to. Didn't want to see her pity. Didn't want to know she had just witnessed the worst day of my life.

Warm lips caressed my cheeks and then my forehead. She wrapped her arms around me in a hug so tight, I had to drop my hands and grip the couch cushion in an attempt to not break down in her arms.

"No one has seen this except me and my aunt. Henry hacked Blake's computer, and Blake doesn't even know we have it." There was hope in her eyes I couldn't share. "We can get him. We have a plan, but you have to be a part of it."

My mind was a jumbled mess of thoughts and emotions. My humiliation was recorded on video. How many times had Blake watched it? Laughed at it?

A muscle in my jaw ticked, and I jumped to my feet, ready to do what I'd planned to before Matt squashed the idea—find Blake and hurt him. "I have to go. I'm sorry."

She caught up to me in the hallway and yanked my arm in a fierce tug. "No. This is what you always do. You get hurt, then angry and then you shut everyone out or do something stupid. I know it's a lot to deal with. But if you walk away and drown in your bitterness, then all this growth has been for nothing."

"You don't understand. All I've ever wanted is to erase that day from my memory. Now, it's recorded and preserved just to torture me." I was yelling, but I couldn't seem to stop myself. "Blake came to my house. He met my parents and pretended for over a year that he had my back. I almost gave you up out of loyalty to him!"

The way only Skylar could do, she stood straighter and pointed those piercing green eyes at me. "Fine. Go be the hero. Beat him up. Feel better. But what have you done for anyone but yourself? He'll go back to school while you sit in jail. He'll continue to win wrestling matches and party with his friends. He'll win, and all that happened to you and to Lindsay will be just a sad memory. But, if you let me help you, let my aunt do what she does best, we can take all of it away from him. We can get justice."

I let out a long sigh and gripped the back of my neck. I was a fighter, and she wanted surrender.

"Please, Cody. Let me share this burden with you."

Her words slipped underneath my skin and my muscles tightened. I stared at her imploring eyes, the soft glow of her skin in the dim hallway light. She was asking me to let go. To put aside the rage and the desperation. To share my pain. The same thing Matt said I had to do if I wanted to move on.

I buried my head into the warmth of her neck, allowed myself to say my deepest fear out loud. "I'm afraid. I don't want you to see me broken."

Her hands swept up my back, her body pressing against mine. A feathery kiss touched my neck and moved up to my ear. "You're not broken."

"I am."

"No, Cody. I know you. I know your heart and your courage. I know the man you've become. I love that you hurt for others. I love that part of you needs me. I love you, and there's nothing in you that's broken that God hasn't already fixed."

The breath slammed out of my body, the chaos in my

mind finally coming to end. I gripped her waist, and all I could see and feel was Skylar. Her fingers slid to my jawline and the warmth of her touch radiated past my skin and into my bloodstream. I dared myself to believe her words. To believe that I could be whole once again.

There was a magnetic pull, bringing our mouths together, our hearts beating in unison. I trailed a line of kisses down her throat and along her collarbone, then paused, staring straight into the eyes of the woman who'd changed my life.

"I think I've loved you since the first moment I saw you," I whispered.

She smiled. The same one that met me at the park. The same one she gave after I'd kissed her for the first time. The same one I earned when I met her dad. The smile reserved for her best moments.

I had a new purpose and a new goal.

To make Skylar smile that way every day of her life.

SKYLAR

IT HAD BEEN two days since Lindsay went home, but I was just now finding the courage to knock on her door. Cody and I made a promise. We'd each share our greatest suffering with someone else. Tonight he was showing his parents the video, and I would give Lindsay a piece of my father.

My knock was answered quickly by her mom who looked nothing like she did at the hospital. Hair in a messy ponytail and in bleach-stained sweats, Mrs. Clark offered a strained, "Can I help you?"

"I'm here to see Lindsay. I'm a friend of hers."

Her gaze trailed over my face as if trying to decide if I was really a friend or enemy of her daughter's. I couldn't blame her.

"You were at the hospital with Cody," she said.

"Yes, ma'am."

She sighed and opened the door wider. "Excuse my appearance. Cleaning makes me, well, it helps."

I didn't know which way to go, so I stood uncomfortably in the foyer while Lindsay's mom shut the door behind me.

"You can go on upstairs. Hers is the last room on the right."

"Thanks." I took the steps slowly, still not sure what I would say to her daughter.

The hall was lined with baby pictures of Lindsay and two boys, the photos showing them growing in age as I approached

Lindsay's room. It was easy to find even without the directions. The door had been removed from its hinges, and Lindsay lay on the bed in a two-piece pajama set.

I rapped on the frame. "Lindsay?"

She didn't turn over. I whispered a prayer for courage. The room was quiet. So quiet that the soft spin of the ceiling fan echoed in it.

I stepped around the bed and sat where I could see her face. I needed to look her in the eyes when I apologized. I never gave her a chance. I'd judged her by other people's terms. The very thing I hated about being a rock star's daughter.

Blue eyes fluttered open. "I'm sorry," she whispered. "I'm sorry I needed Cody so much."

"No. I'm sorry. I should have been bigger than the rumors." And my jealousy.

"Did you see the video?"

The agony in her voice made my heart clench. I wanted to say no, but I wouldn't lie to her. "Yes. I saw it."

"Of course you did. Everyone saw it. Half the guys in our class probably downloaded it and put it on the Internet. I'm a freaking porn star now!" She hiccupped. "I hate him. I hate him so much."

"I know." A heaviness fell over me, and I wished more than anything that I could rewind time.

Lindsay rolled to her back and stared at the ceiling. "It's my fault. I should never have let him record us. I should have said no…to so many things." She hit the bed with her fist. "I'm so stupid."

"Lindsay, look at me." I hadn't been in her situation, but I knew what it felt like to want to give up. I understood grief and loss, and I knew she would never find any peace without God's help.

She turned her head, and her pain was visible enough to slice a hole under my ribcage.

"You have a choice," I said. "You can let this moment break you or you can get up and *choose* to live. I know it's hard, but one day you will see this situation and know how much God held you through it."

"I don't believe in God. Not anymore. Not after this year."

"That's fine, but He still believes in you. He still loves you. Even if you can't see it." I pulled out my phone. It was time. It was why I had come. "My dad wrote a song when I was born. And, until a month ago, it's only been sung in private to me alone. It's my most prized possession and the source of my greatest grief. It's a love song about how much a father loves his child. He's not just talking about himself. He's talking how God feels about every one of us. How He feels about you. I've never shared it with anyone, and I probably never will again, but I know my dad would want you to listen."

I hit play and the familiar sting of sadness came with my father's beautiful voice.

By the second verse, a light touch moved across my hand. I squeezed back and held on. Lindsay was listening.

My father had been right. Pain is never meant to be felt alone. I thought sharing that song would make me lose him somehow. That sharing it meant the words were no longer mine. But it was just the opposite. Sharing the truth with Lindsay made every word come alive.

CODY

IT'S A WEIRD feeling when you're about to unleash chaos.

My parents sat side-by-side on our old gray loveseat and continued to listen. I'd told them about Lindsay and gave them a brief overview of my own torment. But there were no words for what I was about to show them.

My hands were slick with fear and humiliation. No one wants his darkest moment exposed; yet, I knew this was the first step to being free. Strength was not forgetting the past. It was facing it.

"I want to show you what happened my sophomore year." I swallowed the lump growing in my throat. "I didn't know this video existed until two days go."

My dad took my mom's hand as if he was bracing himself.

I pressed play on the computer and turned away. I couldn't watch them or the video without feeling physically sick. But the gasps and sobs from my Mom were close to having the same effect. I closed my eyes and forced breath in and out. In and out. In and out. Until the sounds faded.

I turned around to see statues staring at a blank screen.

My father was the first to move. He stood. Paced. Took a deep breath. Then paced again. Finally, he stopped a foot in front of me. Anger, hurt, compassion. They all seemed to tear at his features. I expected him to ask why. Why I never told them. But he didn't. He pulled me into a fierce hug that was extremely rare for my father.

"I'm sorry." His words were a whisper, but held volumes.

He somehow knew I couldn't talk about it. Somehow, he knew that just telling was enough for today.

SKYLAR

MY AUNT GAVE me my Christmas present early. Two days early, to be exact.

The conference room in her high-rise office looked out over the city. Tall, bare windows, a table that could seat at least twenty people and a piece of paper that could ultimately decide Blake's future.

"Ms. Wyld," the receptionist's voice boomed from the phone speaker. "Mr. Mason and his son are here."

"Send them back," my aunt said. She glanced between me and Cody who sat next to his parents. They remained stoic, and it was obvious neither slept well last night. Their faces were pale with dark circles under their eyes. Cody didn't look a whole lot better.

I slid my hand to his knee, and he gripped it like I might run away. Every muscle in his neck was strained, and his jaw jumped and twitched.

"You ready?" My aunt waited for us both to nod and then stood. She straightened her already starched blazer and walked around the table to let them in.

If time could stand still, it seemed to as she pulled open the door. Every inch took an hour, and with each step, my nerves flashed like lighting strikes.

"Mr. Mason, Blake, please have a seat." My aunt's tone was sharp, authoritative and unemotional. She was so practiced at the art of control; it was questionable if anything could rattle her.

Mr. Mason was an older version of his son. His hair was a little darker, more wrinkles marred the pretty-boy features, but their expressions were identical. Calculated, arrogant, victorious.

Blake smirked at Cody, and even had the audacity to wink in my direction.

Cody shifted.

"He wants to get a rise out of you. Don't let him," I whispered, holding on to his arm to keep him from standing.

My aunt walked around the table until she found her wingback leather chair and sat. "I assume introductions are unnecessary." When no one said a word, she continued. "Mr. Mason, I see you chose not to bring representation. Is that correct?"

Blake's dad casually released the top button of his suit coat and grinned. Not the kind of grin that was amused. The kind that was cunning. "I see no need to waste $1,000 when this meeting is pointless. I've talked with my lawyer and with the school. Principal Rayburn does not have the authority to punish an act that occurred almost two years ago. And the school board feels no need to take such action. Blake understands what he did was wrong and was operating under peer pressure. Taking this conversation past this room is a waste of both our time and resources."

Mr. James's jaw ticked and the man who embodied the word meek stood, enraged. "Your son not only assaulted ours, but videotaped his humiliation!"

Mr. Mason never flinched. "Blake made a poor choice because he was trying to impress some punk. Since then, he has taken Cody under his wing. Has defended him. Protected him. You should be thanking my son, not conjuring up some silly lawsuit."

I thought Cody's dad was going to lunge across the table.

"Mr. James, if you cannot remain calm, I suggest you wait outside," My aunt reprimanded.

Cody's dad dropped back into his chair, but he remained stiff and shaky.

"Can we move this along? I have another meeting this afternoon." Mr. Mason's blasé attitude had me ready to stand and scream myself.

"Of course." I knew from my aunt's tone that things were about to get ugly. She was ticked, but you would never know by the mask of calm on her face. "As I explained in my letter, we plan to move forward with both civil and criminal charges of harassment and assault against your son. What I didn't mention is that we plan to group it into a six person lawsuit against each boy identified in that video."

"My son was a minor, Ms. Wyld. A stupid kid who made a mistake."

"The courts will probably agree with you."

I jerked my head toward her. *What the heck?*

"However," she continued, "I am more interested in the media impact. You own a hardware chain, isn't that correct?" She shuffled some papers. "It just went public on the stock market a few years ago. Congratulations."

Mr. Mason's neck flushed purple. "Are you threatening me?"

"Absolutely not. I'm simply warning you. As you see, my niece here is devastated about what happened and, unfortunately, very eager to share her thoughts and the video on social media." She eyed Blake. "I bet you know a lot about the power of the Internet."

Blake squirmed. Her tone made it clear we knew he was responsible for Lindsay's attacks, even if we couldn't prove it.

Enjoying the shift in power, I shot a big, fake, cheesy grin at Blake and his father. "Daddy's twitter is up to twenty million followers. And they've all been so supportive since his death. They are ready to do anything to help me cope." I pulled out my phone. "Maybe I should get them started."

"Skylar, please." My aunt scowled in my direction. "Mr. Mason, I am personally sick of the media phenomenon that surrounds my brother's band. But, I'm afraid when they find out that Donnie Wyld's daughter is heartbroken over the documented bullying of her boyfriend, the outpouring will be, what's the word..." She tapped her lips with a polished nail and smiled. "Oh yeah...epic."

Blake looked at his dad, and it was the first time he didn't seem smug. "They're just trying to scare us."

"Shut up. You've done enough damage." At his tone, Blake retreated into himself like an abused child.

I refused to feel sorry for him.

Blake's dad let out a defeated sigh. "What's it going to take to settle this? Money?"

Mr. James slammed a hand on the table. "I wouldn't take a cent from you, your slimy b-"

"Mr. James, please." The tension crackled again, leaving a strained silence in the air.

My aunt slid the paper I had been staring at over to Blake's dad. "I've laid out our expectations. First, you will disenroll Blake from Madison High."

Blake lurched forward. "What? NO!"

"I said shut up!" Mr. Mason's angry words rattled the molecules in the air. "I'm finished bailing you out, and I'm certainly not losing my reputation over your stupidity." He studied the paper. "What else?"

"Blake will sign a no contact agreement for a period of one year. The order will include my niece, Mr. James and Lindsay Clark. If he breaks the agreement, the video will go straight to the media."

Blake stood, shaking. His ears were bright red, his eyes like a rabid dog's. "You can't do this! I never touched him!"

Mrs. James spoke up for the first time, her voice calm despite her tears. "You participated and you laughed. You watched that horrific moment and thought it was funny enough to document on film. Then you came to my house and pretended to be his friend. You had my trust and my respect. Now, all I see is that sneering face on the camera. If it were up to me, there would be no settlement. I want you to experience the same humiliation Cody did."

The broken words from Cody's mom shifted the atmosphere. Blake sat slowly and whispered something to his dad who shook his head and pushed him away. Our agreement gripped in his fist, Mr. Mason stood. "I need to run this by my lawyer, and I will get back to you."

My aunt stood as well and put out her hand. "Thank you. You have forty-eight hours until I file."

Mr. Mason shook it begrudgingly and smacked Blake's shoulder, ready to leave.

Blake sat stunned, his mouth open, his stare unfocused. "What about wrestling?"

His father rolled his eyes and nudged his son. "Madison isn't the only school with a wrestling team. Now, get up. I have another meeting to get to."

No one said a word, including Blake, who finally stood, his shoulders drooping as he walked to the door.

I turned to Cody, who never took his eyes from Blake the entire meeting. I saw the sadness in Cody's expression. Justice had been served, but there was still no winner. Signing the piece of paper didn't change Cody's memory of that day. Nor did it change the fact that Lindsay had tried to take her own life.

I brushed a thumb across his cheek. He captured my hand and kissed the skin on my wrist. The familiar pain in his eyes was one I'd wanted to take away a million times.

"This is a victory," I said.

"I know it is. I'm just waiting for it to feel like one."

His words were truth. The hard part was yet to come. Moving forward. Finding the courage to face the past. And, the hardest of all, finding a way to forgive.

CODY

IF SOMEONE HAD said I'd be spending the New Year with the guys from Skylar Wyld and their families, I would have told them they were insane. Yet, here I stood, ready to knock on Skylar's door.

Lindsay fidgeted next to me, wringing her hands and messing with her hair. "Are you sure this is okay?"

It was the fiftieth time she'd asked that question on the way over. "Yes. Skylar wanted you to come. She specifically told me to force you into my truck if I had to."

Lindsay smiled and her face brightened. She'd been doing more of that lately. Blake had signed the no contact agreement and withdrew from school. Although, rumor had it he'd walked on to our rival wrestling team, Clearview, and that Chugger had followed him there.

Lindsay still hadn't decided if she would come back after the holidays or just get her GED, but Skylar and I hoped tonight would encourage her to return. Lindsay had a right to be in school and learn without harassment. She had a right to graduate and to go to college and to live a full and happy life. They had tried to steal that from her.

The door swung open and loud music filtered out to the porch. Ricky placed his hand on the frame and gave me the once over. Decorated in Mardi Gras beads and a New Year's top hat, he looked strangely normal. "Well, I guess you're still around, huh?"

I returned his smirk. "Yep. I'm still here."

"Okay, then, get inside." He made a sweeping gesture with his arm, and Lindsay practically bumped my side as we entered.

She opened her mouth, and I immediately interrupted. "Yes. She wants you here."

Zoe appeared out of nowhere with a top hat as big as her grin. "Cody! Lindsay!" She followed up her squeal with a crushing hug. I guess Skylar wasn't kidding when she said Zoe had come over to our side.

Sliding her arm through Lindsay's, Zoe began her verbal marathon. "Boy, am I happy to see you. I need a wing woman because Ricky's nephew is h-o-t. And since Chugger was just using me so Blake could get to Skylar, I'm in serious need of an ego boost. And from what I understand, you could use some boy attention..."

They walked away with Zoe still muttering about things I had absolutely no interest in. What I was interested in was finding my beautiful girlfriend.

A stack of papers on the formal dining table caught my eye. I stepped forward and picked up the large envelope. ESMOD. The size alone told me she'd been accepted.

The air suddenly felt heavy. I knew it was coming. It was her dream, but I wasn't ready to let her go.

I left the dining room and found Skylar mingling in the kitchen. I slipped my hand in hers and tugged her away from the crowd. The last week had been crazy, and we'd hardly spent more than a few hours together.

I leaned down and whispered in her ear. "Is there a place we can talk?"

She pulled me out the back door and into the silence of the

yard. A small porch lamp lit the area, but the light from the full moon stole the show.

I pulled her close until the heat of her body warmed the unease in my heart. "You've been crying," I said, rubbing my thumbs under her swollen eyes.

She gave ghost of a smile. "Yeah. That grief thing is tricky. Gets you when you least expect it."

I knew words couldn't heal her hurts or minimize the loss of her father, so I just tucked her tight against me. We were the only ones outside, the noise of the party only a murmur through the windows. I pulled out my phone and found the song that played on repeat when I thought I'd lost her.

Piano chords drifted from the device, and I backed away to set it on the table. She cocked her head to the side, her eyebrows pinching with confusion.

I offered a hand. "Dance with me?"

A smile brightened her sad eyes, and soon she was in my arms swaying to the soft rhythm.

I grazed her forehead with my lips and trailed my lips down the side of her face until we were cheek to cheek. "I saw the package from ESMOD. Congratulations." My heart raced with the words, but I refused to be the guy who held her back. Skylar was always meant for something spectacular, and I had been lucky to get even a piece of this amazing woman.

She rested her head against my chest and held me tighter. "Early admission," she said in a sigh. "I think my dad was making his final wishes known."

An ache pulled at my chest, and I had to bite my lip not to flinch from the pain. "When do you leave?" The words felt like vinegar rolling off my tongue. She'd been in my life for such a short period of time but had completely changed my world.

"I'm not."

I froze, sure I had misheard the words. Pulling back so I could see her face, I searched for clues that I was mistaken. "What do you mean you're not?"

She lifted her hand and softly ran her fingertips along my temple. "I'm not going to Paris."

"But your plans? Your dream?"

"Dreams change. Tragedy does that sometimes. And what I want now is to be close to the people I love. Not halfway across the world."

My heart felt like it imploded in my chest. I cupped her face, placed my forehead against hers. I wanted to just breathe in the scent of her until my mind could process what she was saying. "Are you sure?"

Her hands ran down my arms until each held my wrists. "Yes. I love you. The last few months have shown me that it isn't my situation that decides my happiness. It's the people around me. Those I love and who love me back. My family is here. You and Zoe are here. Dreams adjust."

The music faded, as did the rest of the world. Skylar was staying. She had chosen me just like I had chosen her. We'd find somewhere that had both fashion school and wrestling. We'd have our dreams and each other. I'd make sure of it.

I stared into the eyes that saw past all my defenses and mistakes. Her face was illuminated by the moonlight, her skin a soft glow of perfection. I loved that tears glistened against the green of her eyes. I loved her honesty. I loved her selflessness. I loved that she'd found me worthy to love those things about her.

I kissed her softly on the forehead, then nose, then each porcelain cheek. I found her mouth, its warmth enough to brand my soul with her name forever. I could feel her heart beat in rhythm with mine until the flicker of the porch light and a loud bang on the window had me pulling away and looking toward the noise.

Ricky's face was pressed against the glass, and his hand signal made it clear he wanted us to rejoin the party.

Skylar's soft laughter brought my own to the surface.

I pulled open the back door and let Skylar lead us in. In two hours we'd count down to the New Year and to the promise of new beginnings for all of us.

THE END

Bullying is a crime.

If you are a victim or know someone who is, the greatest weapon you have is to TELL.

YOU ARE NOT ALONE!!

For more information on what to do if you, your child, or someone close to you is being bullied, go to this website:
www.stopbullying.gov/get-help-now

To My Wonderful Readers

I hope you enjoyed Cody and Skylar's story. Please take a moment to leave a review on Amazon. Your feedback is critical to us self-published authors.

Wanna know more about Cody's mysterious trainer, Matt Holloway? His story, *Mercy's Fight*, is available now!

Other books by Tammy L. Gray:

Shattered Rose (Permanently FREE on Kindle)

Shackled Lily

Splintered Oak

Mercy's Fight

Waves of Summer (A Just One Summer Novella)

Sign up at tammylgray.com for Tammy's Occasional Newsletter along with:

* Bonus Scenes

* New releases

* Book news

* Cover reveals and sneak peeks

* and even some exclusive giveaways

You can also connect with Tammy at:

Facebook:

facebook.com/tlgraybooks

Twitter:

@tlgraybooks

Instagram:

tlgraybooks

Email:

tlgraybooks@gmail.com

About the Author

Tammy L. Gray is the kindle best selling author of the Winsor series and Mercy's Fight. She writes modern Christian romance and clean YA/NA romance. She believes hope and healing can be found through high quality fiction that inspires and provokes change.

Acknowledgements

There are some books that seep into your soul and change the very fabric of your being. Sell Out is that book for me. It's taken over a year to write, several revisions, lots of tears and even more prayers.

God has shown me through this process that He is sovereign and I am simply a vessel for His glory. What a beautiful place to be.

There are several people who held me up during this journey:

My husband, Todd. Thank you for supporting those long weekends holed away working on this story. For your endless encouragement and sound advice. You are my best cheerleader.

To my writing partner, Nicole Deese. Thank you for the endless advice on story and writing. You challenge me to dig deeper and have truly made me a better writer. I consider you one of God's greatest blessings in my life.

To my fabulous editors, Kristin Avila and Christa Allen. Thank you for helping me mold this story into something great. Your attention to detail, incredible advice and pointed guidance has made Sell Out my best work to date.

To my sister, Angel. Thank you for trudging through my first and worst draft. For helping me find the flaws and challenging me to make the story shine. You're the best big sister a girl could have!

To my cover artist, Sarah Hansen. Thank you for the time and skill you put into my beautiful cover. Your talent is remarkable, as is your ability to make my vision come to life.

To my street team. Thank you for the emails and messages of support and encouragement. You make me want to write and lift me up when I'm down.

And finally, to my readers. Thank you for sharing my stories and for your constant cheerleading. I do this all because of you.

Printed in Poland
by Amazon Fulfillment
Poland Sp. z o.o., Wrocław